To the woman I used to be.
To the woman I am now.
To the woman I am becoming.

PROLOGUE

"You can't leave me, I love you."

Her tears did nothing to him. Nor did the pain in her voice. It was music to his broken soul.

"I love heroin," he replied, yanking his arm out of her poisonous grasp. "Doesn't mean it's good for me. Doesn't mean it won't destroy me. If I let it."

He stepped back and she tried to scuttle forward but he raised his gun to her forehead. She stopped immediately because she might've been crazy, but she knew him well enough to know that he didn't raise his piece unless he planned on using it.

"I'm not lettin' you destroy me," he said.

He was doing a fine job of that himself.

"I won't let you leave me, you can't," she hissed, straightening her spine, the words a meager threat.

He laughed. The sound was empty and cold. "I can and I am. You try to follow me, I'll kill you," he promised. "Just like I did your fucked-up family."

Then he turned on his heel and walked away.

His steps were measured, even, and didn't even pause at the screeches, threats, and pleads hurled at his back.

It might've looked like he was walking away, but he was fucking running.

He didn't run from shit.

Shit ran from *him*.

He made sure of that.

Physically, at least.

If you wanted to get into all that emotional, psychobabble bullshit, then yeah, he ran. From himself. From those fucking demons knocking at his skull, licking at his heels.

They weren't literal, those demons.

Couldn't tear through his flesh like a bullet, break bones like a fist, or nick an artery like a blade.

But they could kill him.

Though only if he stopped running.

So he didn't.

To make up for being a pussy in his own mind, he didn't run from shit in the real world. Or whatever this was where he lived now.

No, he didn't run from a thing. Not danger. Fuck, he chased that shit, craved it like he used to crave the needle. Like he still craved the needle. He wasn't a recovering addict, if you wanted to get technical—he'd just traded one substance for another. Poison in a syringe for death, pain, blood, violence. His cut. His brothers. The ones he'd die for. The ones he'd kill for. And though they didn't know it, the ones who kept him alive—if that's what he was.

But something changed in LA when shit went down.

He did run.

From a fucking *woman*.

Because she was batshit crazy.

Even crazier than him.

He had a code—he didn't kill women, not if he could avoid it, at least. But this one was gunning to kill him if he stayed in LA. So he didn't.

And then he found *her*.

The woman who might just kill him.

Not literally.

No, the woman who would make him stop running, in more ways than one.

And maybe his demons wouldn't catch him.

But they'd catch her.

ONE

Gage

He didn't save damsels.

He was likely to fuck them, then go on his not-so-merry way —if he was feeling like dipping his candle in that particular wick. He usually wasn't. Damsels were innocent, and he didn't do innocence. He fucked woman who were too far gone for redemption so he only damned them further. Made sure he wasn't the reason their soul was tarnished.

He was fucked up. Some might say cold, calculating, and some might even call him a psychopath—and fuck, maybe they were right—but he wasn't about to wreck something that wasn't already broken.

Hence the reason he didn't save damsels.

His brothers did. Though you wouldn't say a lot of those women needed saving. Not if you liked your balls attached to your body. Gage quite liked the location of his balls, so he kept quiet on that score.

Even if they didn't *need* saving, the women his brothers

ended up with—who they happily handed their balls over to—were something special. Some of them were a little broken—he thought of Bex—and some of them were a lot broken, but none of them were beyond redemption.

Gage had made his peace with the fact that he wasn't going to get what those men had a long time ago. Fuck, he didn't *want* it. He'd had it once. A version of it, anyway. The most beauty he'd ever hold in his hands. Then he'd turned himself into... whatever he was now after it broke him. After he broke *her*.

And every single one of his days was tainted, blackened and bloodied because of that.

No fucking way he'd invite any human—any fucking *woman* —into that wasteland.

So he found the ones who'd already experienced a brutal reality of one form or another. Ones who were so jaded that even he couldn't hurt them anymore.

He fucked them. Hard. Brutal. In ways only a certain kind of woman—a broken one—could handle. Then he left before the rubber even hit the trash can.

Not exactly decent of him, but he wasn't decent, so he didn't give a fuck.

So his thoughts on damsels were what crossed his mind the second he saw one stumbling down a deserted road outside of Amber in the middle of the night.

He barely slowed his bike when she squinted at the headlight —not even trying to wave him down—illuminating the blood from her forehead.

It was trouble, saving damsels.

Because that's what got his brothers married and fucked.

And that's what Gage could never have.

So that's why he drove past the bleeding woman walking alone on a highway in the middle of the night. Because whatever had happened to her wouldn't be as bad as whatever would follow if Gage inserted himself into the situation.

But then that face, lit up for a shadow of second, entered his mind. Haunted it though her ghost was mere moments old.

And on that thought, on that fucking *face*, he wrenched the handlebars on his bike and roared back in the direction he had come.

To save the fucking damsel.

Or, more accurately, to damn her.

Lauren

"You should be wearing a helmet."

That's what I said the second the roar of the motorcycle was snatched away into the eerie quiet of the night and the man—who wasn't eerie, just plain *menacing*—hopped off his bike and stared at me.

Didn't rush toward me, catch me in his arms as I stumbled from the pain and slight delirium—plus hefty amount of fear—I was struggling with. Didn't speak. Ask if I was okay. Ask what happened to have me bleeding and stumbling down a deserted road in the middle of the night.

No, he just kicked the stand down, dismounted, leaned against the bike, crossed his arms, and stared.

Stared.

Somehow his stare was more intense than the inky blackness of the night itself. It was darker. And I suspected—no, I *knew* it was a heck of a lot more dangerous.

Because even through the dim light, I could see his leather vest. His leather *cut*. And I knew what the patch would say if there was enough light to see it.

The Sons of Templar MC.

Amber's resident motorcycle club.

The previously outlaw gang, who had now cleaned up their act and were only skirting the law, not breaking it. Technically. Though throughout the last handful of years there had been kidnappings, drive-by shootings, bombs and oh, weddings. Apparently that's how they did things.

I didn't have anything to do with them, of course. But one didn't need to have anything to do with them to know everything about them.

They ran the town.

You weren't a resident of Amber if you didn't know who they were. And I also wasn't blind. Almost every single member of that godforsaken club was hotter than Hades himself.

And the one in front of me seemed to be darker and much more dangerous than the dark prince.

I sensed it in the air. In my bones.

Which was ridiculous, because I didn't believe in that stuff. It wasn't logical, and I worked with logic. Because only people who hadn't had the cruel awakening from a little thing called reality believed in fantasies such as a 'sense' of someone's evil.

But there I was believing it.

Because when you were presented with a man like the one in front of me, there was nothing to believe, to hold onto anymore. He ripped everything away and stomped over it with his motor-cycle boot. Yanked away the very air in my lungs and stared into me with an intensity I didn't think existed outside of horror movies and Stephen King novels.

Yet the first thing I said to him was "You should be wearing a helmet."

I must've been concussed.

Because me, the logical and previously dependable me, wouldn't've said this to a man who was staring at me while I was injured, alone and vulnerable in the middle of the night with no one else around. No man on a white horse to come and save the day. Because I wasn't under any illusions that this was him. This was most definitely the man I'd need saving *from*.

The villain.

Yet I didn't run.

Didn't move, actually.

"It's not safe riding a motorcycle on the open roads, at speeds in excess of fifty miles per hour, without a helmet." My mouth continued without any input from my logic- and fear-ridden brain. "Let's just forget that, in general, motorcycles are less stable and visible than cars. It is estimated by the federal government that per mile traveled, the number of deaths on motorcycles was 29 times the number in cars," I continued to babble, waiting for him to speak and stop me. Or shoot me.

Or kiss me.

Wait. Where the heck did that come from?

It was the middle of the night. I was injured and bleeding— almost certainly concussed—and I was thinking about the menacing and dark stranger, who was a member of a motorcycle club, *kissing* me?

Me.

No. No matter how hot I knew he would be in daylight—and I knew he would be because what the thin shadows masked was already something so beautiful it had to be sinful—he wasn't my type.

No way.

And more importantly, I wasn't his.

But he continued to stare.

And hurt, scared, and somehow turned on, I couldn't weather that stare.

Not in silence, at least.

So I continued talking.

"Helmets are approximately 37 percent effective in preventing motorcycle deaths and 67 percent effective in preventing brain injuries," I said, my voice somehow clear and logical, as if I was discussing this in my office in the middle of the day. I swallowed thickly. "And that means you're 63 percent more likely to die if you crashed, and if you didn't—die, that is," I corrected, somehow finding enough sass to raise my brow at him, regardless of the fact that he couldn't see me doing so in the low light, "you'll most likely have serious brain trauma since I would say you're the kind of guy who wouldn't be driving the speed limit."

The air snatched away all that foreign sass in my voice and my body in the seconds after I'd spoken my words. The man in front of me seemed to suck it all up, even the night itself.

And then he wasn't leaning against his bike. He was in front of me. Like *right* in front of me.

"You're right, darlin'," he murmured, his voice raspy and rough and somehow pouring desire into my bloodstream. "I don't drive the speed limit." His body almost pressing into mine, only the smallest sliver of air separating us. His breath hot and intoxicating on my face, smelled faintly of tobacco and whisky.

"I don't do limits," he continued as I forced myself to breathe and reminded my legs of their job to keep me upright. "But I don't crash." He said the words with a certainty that made me forget that a man couldn't control all the variables on the road to speak with that kind of certainty. Somehow he gave me the impression that if I were in a plane about to crash with him sitting beside me, somehow he'd make sure he'd control the outcome, and stop us from being bodies among the wreckage. He had so much power radiating off him, there was no way he could be bested by *anything*.

He'd keep me safe.

But there was no logic here.

Because I had a feeling my safety went out the window the second he stopped and dismounted.

Still peering at me, into me, his body almost brushed mine. "And it's mighty interesting that you're talkin' to *me* about my safety, or the perceived lack of it, focused on numbers and shit that don't have anything to do with me—"

"They have everything to do with you. Because statistics are made from people. You're a person, which means you're included."

The air changed and there was no longer so much as a hair separating our bodies. "Oh, baby, I'm not a person," he rasped, his voice a knife through the night. "And I'm never gonna be included in something made by the people who hold the keys to society's prison. But this isn't about me." He stepped back, and once more I could breathe without his... whatever was stopping me.

Still, I found myself craving it.

Grossly illogical.

"But we're not talking about me," he said, folding his arms. His head moved, and though I couldn't see his eyes clearly, I knew he looked me up and down. I felt his eyes on every inch of my body, making me feel like naked on the side of the road instead of in jeans and a sensible sweater.

"We're talking about the woman who is spouting safety statistics at me while she's walking down a highway, alone in the middle of the fucking night, and bleeding." His voice was mild. Casual even. But something rumbled underneath it. Something I couldn't catch, or couldn't understand.

He kept speaking so I didn't have the opportunity to do either.

"You want to know the statistics on that, *Good Will Hunting?*" he asked, stepping forward again.

That time I managed to have some kind of control over my motor functions, stepping back on an unsteady foot. The gravel crunched under my feet, my ankles rolling slightly, but I managed to keep myself upright.

"The chances of a beautiful woman, a fucking *injured* one at that, getting even more fucking injured while stumbling alone along a highway in the middle of the night are a *fuck* of a lot higher than me crashing a bike." He stopped advancing before our bodies touched.

The air thickened between us.

"Is this the part of the conversation where you say I'm lucky it was you who stopped and not someone who's going to hurt me?" I asked, my voice shaking slightly. I jutted my chin up to counteract it.

Which was a bad move because it made him all the more able to grab my chin between his thumb and forefinger. His grip was tight. Painful almost.

But I didn't flinch away from it. Didn't try to run. No, if anything I melted into that grip, into the pain.

He paused at my reaction. It was less than a moment, but I could tell my lack of resistance to his touch surprised him. "And who says I'm not gonna hurt you?" he challenged with more menace than before, as if to counteract his small pause.

My stomach curdled with a toxic mixture of fear and... something else.

Fear at the true promise behind his words, his eyes. This man would hurt me. I knew that. It was something even the most naive would see while looking into the abyss that was his eyes. The abyss that roused the intrinsic human fight or flight instinct.

I didn't fight.

Or take flight.

I just stayed, frozen in his grasp. Because of the something else.

Because of my body's other intrinsic reaction to his hands on me, eyes on me—gaze inside me.

Arousal.

Something that was *insane*.

The man grabbing me, without my permission, in the middle of the night, after he'd threatened me, basically ignored all my rather obvious injuries was *turning me on*.

I didn't get turned on by men like that. By villains.

I barely even *got* turned on. But when I did, it was by clean-cut, well-groomed, all-American men who radiated safety, or more accurately, dependability.

This man was not clean-cut. From what the dim light showed me, he had a beard, which looked somehow wild and yet well-groomed at the same time. His hair was long, though I couldn't tell specifically where it stopped, but it touched his shoulders for sure.

He was big.

Like *big*.

He towered over me; his sheer size and muscle mass seemed to have the ability to swallow up the night behind him. It was a presence of a *man*. And not a man who radiated safety and dependability.

No, one who radiated danger and chaos.

Everything I kept my well-ordered life away from.

Yet there I stood, turned the frick on. Finding it hard to speak, to *breathe* around the man grasping my chin in a border-line brutal grip.

His hand jerked, making my throbbing head move somewhat painfully in whatever dim illumination the moon offered.

I thought for a second—was actually certain—that he'd exposed my neck in order to slit it. Or was preparing to do that movie move where the hero—or the villain—cracked an enemy's neck in one swift jerk.

And yet I didn't resist his grip. Scream. Fight.

I didn't move.

Maybe I was holding onto the old advice that when you found yourself standing in front of a lion, you held your ground, stared it down.

Or maybe I didn't want out of his grip, even if it meant death.

But this was *insane*.

And after brushing off the spiky scales of insanity almost a decade ago, I've kept away from anything resembling it at all costs.

It soon became apparent he wasn't jerking my head to kill me in any number of ways I knew he was proficient in. No, he was doing it to inspect the gash on my head.

"Not likely to need stitches," he grunted, still holding my chin. "Might have a concussion." A pause. "You'll live."

There was no overarching concern in his voice. Nothing to betray the fact that he was overly worried about me bleeding from the head. He'd obviously seen worse. The casual way he handled my bloodied face told me that.

But I also knew my injuries weren't serious. They hurt, but like this dark man said, I'd live. I wasn't one to go for dramatics over a little blood. I was all about taking practical measures, keeping calm, and solving problems logically. It was logic that had me walking down the road in the middle of the night—however crazy it sounded—but all logic, and even God himself, abandoned me in the presence of this man.

Then again, God had abandoned me long ago.

When the man let me go, the absence of his grip almost hurt more than the throbbing of my head.

Almost.

But he stepped back from me, snapping me out of whatever kind of sorcery he had control over in the darkness. And my head started throbbing more than the need for him to touch me. My entire body ached, reminding me of why exactly I was there in the first place.

The blisters on my tender feet burned with the evidence of how far I'd walked.

Grabbing hold of my pain meant I got to grab hold of my logic, just before I could topple into the abyss that had nothing to do the inky blackness surrounding us and everything to do with the man in front of me.

"I don't think I have a concussion. Well, I don't have any signs of it, at least," I said, voice scratchy. "Symptoms include headache, confusion, lack of coordination, memory loss, nausea, vomiting, dizziness, ringing in the ear, and excessive fatigue, to name a few."

"You a doctor?" he demanded.

"No. I just..." I paused. How did I explain that I had no life, so in order to supplement the gaping hole that most people filled with friends and adventures, I read? Anything and everything. I also researched anything and everything regarding injuries and statistics. Sometimes it was fact-checking for a story, but most of the time it was to feed my logical brain.

Because I tried to keep my brain busy, full to the brim with as much asinine information as I could find so I didn't have time for it to wander. I structured my life so it was lived within the lower parameters of calculated risk.

I ate only organic, because pesticides had been linked to cancer, Alzheimer's, and ADHD, to name a few.

I didn't talk while charging my cell phone, because if the charger was faulty, it could burst in my ear.

I took aspirin daily for stroke and heart attack prevention, as well as reducing the risk of cancer and Alzheimer's. This was despite the fact that I had just turned thirty-one and it wasn't recommended to start doing that until you were sixty-five.

I wore SPF 50 sunscreen all year round. My skin was delicate and pale, and skin cancer killed more than people knew.

I did all these things and more because I made it my business to know what the numbers were on death, pain, and danger. And how to prevent it.

You didn't tell someone that in normal circumstances.

This was not normal circumstances.

So I didn't say anything else.

"So you're not a doctor, and you're not in a position to be diagnosing yourself, considerin' you're bleeding on the side of the road," the man clipped, saving me from having to explain why the heck I knew the signs and symptoms of a concussion. "Instead of you wastin' my time spoutin' bullshit, how about you get on the fuckin' bike so I can drop you off at the hospital and then go about my night?"

The words were harsh, hitting me harder than the steering wheel of my car when my airbags had malfunctioned.

I made a mental note to draft a strongly worded complaint to the car manufacturer. Then again, airbags could injure people in car accidents worse than the impact of the crash itself, so maybe I was lucky.

Or, depending on what happened in the coming moments, decidedly unlucky.

Then I digested his words.

"Get on the bike," I repeated, looking beyond him to the dark shape, silver glinting in the moonlight.

Or was it chrome on motorcycles?

That was one piece of information I didn't know.

His impatience radiated in what little I could see of his face. "Yeah, Will, for a rocket scientist, you don't seem to understand that I'm not hidin' my ambulance under my cut. Bike's the only option." He spoke slowly, deliberately, as if he was explaining something to a child.

I stiffened, not just at the tone but at the words. "Just because I know a couple of basic things about safety doesn't make me a rocket scientist. I'm a *sensible adult*," I snapped. "And a sensible adult does not get on the back of a motorcycle with a man she doesn't know. A man who is a member of a motorcycle gang. That's not rocket science. That's just common sense." I surprised myself with the clear bite to my voice that had never been there... well, ever.

"And common sense dictates you continue walking down the road, bleeding, hurt, still five miles from Amber?" he asked dryly. Unlike my own, his voice did not hold a bite. It was flat. "Fine." I almost heard him shrug, his disregard for me clear. "Don't confuse independence with stupidity, darlin', because one of them gets you killed. They'll both get you killed, eventually, as life has a tendency to be fatal. But suit yourself. I'm not a hero, so I'm not gonna lose a wink of sleep over leavin' you here. Mostly because I don't plan on sleepin' tonight."

I didn't see his wink like I had his shrug, but like the shrug, I heard it. There was something distinctly sexual to the words. Something that hit me low in my stomach, the place that warmed when I indulged in my fantasies in the dead of night.

But this wasn't a fantasy.

This was reality.

And the two never mixed.

After his words had tattooed the air, gravel crunched underneath his motorcycle boots as he turned, striding away to mount his bike. I chewed my lip, watching him, anxiety gnawing at me. And also panic at the thought of him roaring into the night, leaving me. Not just alone and hurt on the side of the road. No, just *leaving me*. Because then the visceral fear he roused in me would disappear too.

And that visceral fear had me feeling more alive than I had in a decade.

The roar of the engine replaced the debate I was having with myself over my options. Before I rightly knew what was going on, gravel was crunching underneath my sneakers and I was rushing over to the bike.

I stopped at the side.

He didn't speak.

Neither did I.

Nor did I make a move.

I expected him to roar off while I stood frozen, actually considering mounting a motorcycle, with a stranger, *without a helmet.*

But he didn't.

He just waited.

As if he had all the time in the world.

Almost as if he could sense that I needed a second because I wasn't a girl who made split-second decisions. I was a woman who made lists. A lot of them. And did research. A lot of it.

But I didn't have the luxury of lists or research right then.

I only had the handful of moments this man was going to give to me before he took off into the night, leaving me in silence and, presumably, safety.

Because there was only a short amount of time a man like him would wait. It was a miracle he hadn't left in the first place.

Or was it a curse?

Before I could decide what would save me or damn me, my leg was up and I straddled the motorcycle.

No sooner had I situated my butt in the leather seat did he roar off. No warning, no asking me if I was okay, no telling me to hold on. No, he just took off.

Instinctively, so I didn't fall off the back of the bike and onto the road, my arms fastened themselves over the middle of his body, wrapping around his torso. The second I realized what I was doing, the second my body pressed into his warm and muscled back, my palms grazing over his rock-hard abs, my body reacted.

Almost violently.

It was such a shock, I jerked my hands backward, momentarily forgetting that such a movement would send me toppling off the back of the bike and eating the asphalt. But I didn't. Eat asphalt. Because a firm grip atop of my hands stopped me from moving them.

The man with the muscled back and the rock-hard abs—as if it could be anyone else—was driving the motorcycle *one-handed*, the other working as a restraint to stop me flinching out of his grip.

Once I gained control of myself, I figured keeping my hands where they were was my best bet at surviving the ride—physically, at least.

But his hand didn't move from mine.

The whole ride.

TWO

Gage

He walked into the clubhouse early the next morning, though he hadn't expected to be doing so. No, he'd planned on coming to Amber, picking up some shit, tying up some loose ends, and disappearing into the night for as long as it took to get himself figured out.

Or as figured out as he could ever get.

But everything changed with the woman.

The woman who spouted statistics about fucking skull caps, who listed every symptom of concussion in an orderly manner while standing on the side of the road, in front of him, *bleeding from the fucking head*.

So yeah, everything changed with the woman.

With the fucking *damsel*.

He didn't fuck her.

No, he *saved* her.

Last night, at least.

He'd clutched her warm and soft body to him as he roared

into town. First, he'd done it because he'd felt exactly what she had the second she'd fastened her small arms around him. He'd felt it right in his fucking cock. And not because she was a woman pressed against him. That was in part true, but not all of it.

Because even in the dim light he could tell she wasn't his kind of woman. For starters, his type of women wore a fuck of a lot less than she did. And a fuck of a lot more makeup, enough so it would've been visible even in the dim light of the moon. Fuck, it would've been visible from space.

And the women he chose didn't argue with him.

Ever.

Nor did they smell like fucking lilacs and vanilla.

And they sure as shit didn't have brains in their heads. Not brains that could spout statistics and did so with a sophisticated curl to the words like she did.

Nor did they radiate a kind of innocence that men like him sensed from a mile away.

Horses smelled fear. Monsters smelled innocence.

Gage was the worst monster of them all, and her innocence sang to him like a siren's song.

So no, she was not his kind of woman.

But still, he had fastened his fucking hand over hers the entire ride into Amber, all the way to the hospital. He'd found himself wishing the trip was longer, despite the fact that she was bleeding, injured, and obviously in need of medical attention.

And needed to be as far away from his attention as possible.

Which was why he'd dropped her off at the hospital, gunning it as soon as her feet hit the pavement, before he could do anything stupid.

Before he could do what every fiber in his being told him to do.

Claim her.

Especially when the bright lights of the hospital illuminated her face and it punched him right in the fucking chest.

Blood stained half of her small and pale face, some glistening and wet, some dried and flaky. The gash on her forehead had bled like a bitch, as head wounds tended to do, but it wasn't life-threatening.

Gage knew life-threatening, and it wasn't.

To her.

To him, the cut fucking was. Because seeing blood staining her beautiful face made him flinch, his own blood boil beyond anything he'd experienced.

This wasn't going to kill her, but it had marked her. *Hurt* her.

And from what he could see from her peaches-and-cream skin, her large hazel eyes framed by thick and somehow sexy-as-fuck glasses, her full and quivering lips, she didn't need hurt. No way did she deserve to feel pain.

Which was why he'd roared off into the night before he could get off his bike and be the one to cause it.

First he'd taken a detour back where he'd come from, the road he'd found her on. Then he'd driven to his house—Rosie's house, if you wanted to get technical, but now that she was married to the fucking cop, it was his—and found comfort in the bottom of a bottle.

Usually his comfort came between the legs of a club girl, but the mere thought of polluting the scent of vanilla and lilac against his skin sickened him.

So he sat in the dark and drank whisky till the sun came up, snatched a few hours of sleep and then went to the clubhouse. Mainly so he wouldn't go to the hospital and see if she was still there. And take her home with him. Fuck her brutally and roughly, regardless of whatever injuries she'd sustained while crashing her car.

She didn't tell him that.

About the crash.

Granted, he didn't even fucking ask what had her out on the road in the middle of the night, bleeding. A good guy would've asked. Would've demanded an inventory of her injuries, would've made sure he'd catalogued them all. But Gage was not a good guy, so he hadn't asked. It hadn't mattered how she'd gotten there—it had just mattered that she was *there*.

But after speaking to her, smelling her, feeling her hot little body pressed against him, he'd needed to know what happened to her. Needed to find out if it was the work of another monster. And then he'd needed to kill them if that was the case.

It turned out it was no monster. Just a machine.

He'd driven out past where he'd found her to discover the car in a ditch, the front of the vehicle crushed against the curve in the land. Hence the whisky. Because she was lucky as fuck. She could've flipped at that angle if she'd been going faster—he knew she likely drove at or under the speed limit based on her tirade against him—and no way in fuck would he have found her walking down the side of the road with a minor head wound if she'd done that.

He'd likely have pulled her from the wreckage with not-so-minor injuries if she was lucky, or with a fuck of a lot of injuries and no heartbeat if she wasn't.

The mere thought of that grated against Gage's insides as he strolled through the doors of the clubhouse he hadn't planned on having on the bottom of his cut for much longer. He was only there to go Nomad for as long as it took to get his head right. Which was obviously never. His head wasn't ever going to be right.

She'd changed it.

Wiped out all the reasons why he was going Nomad in the first place. Scraped everything that had happened in LA from his mind like it didn't matter.

And around her, no other bitches mattered. Not even crazy, homicidal ones.

He didn't even know her fucking *name*.

But you didn't need to know the name of the woman who was going to destroy you. You just had to fucking brace. Destroy her first.

For her own good.

But if he'd left town like he'd planned on, he wouldn't have had to do that. But he didn't think about that. Because he was a fucking coward. Because he was making excuses for staying in town, trying to convince himself that she had nothing to do with it. And he was trying, and failing, to keep her out of his mind when he damn near collided with a bald-headed, tattooed, smiling asshole.

He wasn't really an asshole. He was actually one of his best friends—or as close to a friend as someone like Gage could get—but everyone who had the fucking audacity to be happy around his misery was automatically an asshole right then.

"Gage!" Lucky said, yanking him in for a rough hug before holding him at arm's length. "Oh, you've gotten so big since the last time I saw you." He put his hand on his heart like the theatrical bastard he was. "They grow up so fast."

"Go fuck yourself, Lucky," Gage grunted.

Lucky grinned. "I don't need to." He held up his tattooed hand, showing off the black ring on his fourth finger. "I've got someone who is legally obliged to fuck me from now until the end of time."

"You say that again, you'll be having blue balls for the end of time," Bex cut in, her eyes narrowed at her husband before giving Gage a quick arm squeeze.

She wasn't affectionate like her husband. Her demons gave Gage's a run for their money.

They shared that.

Demons so dark, they both sought not to fight them but drown out their screams with a needle. With a high.

The problem with highs was you came down eventually.

And the difference between Bex and Gage was Bex had managed not to come down all the way. Not into the grave. She'd always fight the low that came with the itch underneath her skin known as addiction, but she'd found new highs.

Found the smiling fucker who worshipped the ground she walked on.

"Glad to see you're back," she murmured, winking at him and ignoring her husband. "I'm going to work. You're going to think about what you've done," she addressed Lucky, turning to look over her shoulder, swaying her hips. "And think of the fact that I'm not wearing any panties."

Lucky groaned as she walked out the door, actual pain on his face, worse than any of the times the fucker had been shot. Despite his elementary humor, Lucky was one of the strongest people Gage knew. Apart from the bastard's wife. He had his demons too, but he just smiled at them rather than grimacing.

He watched the doorway for a long time before shaking his head and punching Gage in the shoulder.

"That's your fault, fucker," he hissed.

Gage grinned. It hurt, but he did it. "What comes out of your fuckin' mouth is no one's fault but your own and you know it."

Lucky scowled at him, then looked him up and down. "So you're back from LA? For good?"

Gage had helped Killian head up the chapter in LA, then had taken the VP gavel when Killian gave it up in order to head the security detail for his wife.

No way the kid was going to be apart from his wife after she'd been almost killed by a crazed stalker. She was one of the most famous people in the world, and the safest; not only would

Killian make sure nothing happened to her, but she had the Sons of Templar to back her.

But after that shit went down in LA, not even the worst of it, Gage had taken a vacation to someone else's hell to make sure he didn't end up in his own.

Rosie's.

He'd known she'd had something licking at her heels.

Something bad.

Because he'd moved into her place. And he'd seen the very effective cleanup job. Would've passed everything but a blue light. But Gage knew when death had touched a room. He knew even better when it had been covered up.

First he'd known she was okay because he'd made sure Wire tapped every fake passport she had, including the third one she thought the club didn't know about. Her brother might not have known, but Gage did.

He'd found Rosie in the depths of the underworld, using herself as bait to take down human trafficking rings. He didn't stop her though. She was more than capable, and he suspected it was the only thing that was keeping her together—killing monsters. He knew that better than anyone.

So he let her be.

And then shit had gone down.

Like it always did when people connected to the club had any kind of romantic shit going down.

It worked out in the end.

For Rosie, at least.

They still had the shadow of the Fernandez fucker hanging over them, though Gage was already exploring every option they had on taking him down. Because the fucker had tried to strike the club. No one did that and lived.

Not even one of the most dangerous criminals in the world.

Because Gage wasn't one of the most dangerous. He was *the* most.

Taking Fernandez down took time.

Patience.

So he took it.

Split his time between Amber and LA. More in LA of late because he got deep in some pussy he shouldn't have.

"Killian said you had girl trouble," Lucky said, a grin plastered on his face, as it always was these days. Especially with his wife around. "Now, I heard tales of shootings and explosions. Where is she?" He made a big show of looking around Gage as if he was hiding some bitch behind his back.

Gage folded his arms. "Who?"

"The woman, of course!" Lucky threw up his arms, his eyes touching on his wife, who was talking to Lily in the parking lot. Gage knew the fucker couldn't go ten seconds without making sure she was still okay when she was in his eye line. Like he was terrified she might fall off the face of the Earth if he didn't do so. Or maybe because he was terrified *he* might.

"There is no woman," Gage said. He did not need a woman who threatened to throw him off the face of the Earth if something happened to her. He'd already had that.

He was happy in Hell, as happy as a man could be being tortured. But he couldn't do any more. Because he was so fucked up now, the only way he could be happy was if he was being tortured. He wasn't wishing that on any bitch.

Wide eyes, pale skin, and lilacs entered his mind. He pushed the thought away with disgust.

Lucky frowned. "How is there no woman? There were shootings. Explosions," he said, speaking of some mild shit that had gone down in their LA chapter as though that explained something.

Gage grinned at his brother, clapping him on the arm. "Bro,

just because explosions and shootings meant *you've* found the right woman doesn't mean the same for me. Just means I've found *a* woman. Or that it was a Tuesday." He spoke with a careful, casual tone, making sure he didn't betray just how close that particular woman had been to fucking destroying him.

There was no point in talking of almost destructions.

Shit was put to bed.

She was, at least. The sooner he forgot her, the better.

He'd already fucking forgotten her, which was the problem, since the bitch from last night was proving hard—read: impossible—to forget.

Lucky regarded him, peering at him like he was trying to read Gage's fuckin' mind or something. He was convinced that "telepathy was purely a matter of concentration."

"Nope," Lucky said finally. "There's a woman." He shook his head, grimacing, not aware that he'd all but read Gage's mind that time. "I've got a feeling your courtship is gonna make the rest of ours look like a day at the park."

Gage narrowed his eyes and readied himself to make his point to Lucky with his fist in his face. It wasn't the first time, and it certainly wouldn't be the last.

A clap on his back was the one thing that stopped him.

He turned to meet the gray eyes of his president.

"You're back for good, brother?" Cade asked, the corner of his mouth twitching in what everyone knew was his version of a grin.

Before Gage could answer, the mouthy fuck spoke for him.

"He's got a woman," Lucky interjected.

Gage readied his fist once more.

Cade's eyes widened in shock.

Gage knew arguing with the fuck was pointless. Lucky was just as bad—if not worse—than any of the women around there. A dog with a fuckin' bone. Gage was sure he'd be pickin' out wedding china or some shit when he got back.

He'd get the picture soon enough.

When no woman entered the picture.

Especially not a fuckin' woman who smelled like vanilla and lilac, whose hazel eyes seared into him, whose skin needed to be marked by him.

The woman who made his cock rock-hard at the mere *thought* of her, even with her bloodied face, shapeless clothing and scrunched-up face as he'd roared away from the hospital.

No, not that woman.

Definitely not the crazy bitch he'd left behind in LA either.

"I need the tow truck," he said instead of replying to Lucky. He'd pretend to ignore him until the bastard started chasing a butterfly or remembered someone he forgot to kill.

Cade's eyes widened even more. "A tow truck?"

Gage nodded once.

"Why do you need a tow truck?" Lucky asked, raising a brow. "You haven't been behind one since you prospected, and you shot the last person who tried to make you do anything regarding work with the garage."

Gage rolled his eyes. "It was a flesh wound. When the fuck are you gonna let that go?"

Lucky folded his arms. "Right around the time you give me the name of your new sweetheart so I can stalk her on Facebook. And in real life if I'm not satisfied with the amount of pictures she has." He paused. "Or if she has too many. It's a slippery slope on social media. Too many consecutive selfies mean she's a narcissist, but not enough means she doesn't have a friend in the world and just sits in her room watching makeup tutorials on YouTube."

Gage ignored him and focused on an excuse as to why he needed the tow truck.

He didn't do mechanic work. Not when the garage was merely a front for the illegal gun running before the club went legit, and sure as fuck not now that they'd expanded to yuppie fucks—who they ripped off—with too much money and too much concern about image.

He killed people.

Tortured them.

Made them bleed.

Blew things up.

He didn't change fuckin' oil.

But there was a wrecked car on the outskirts of town that needed towing and repairing. And no way was anyone else touching it. It was *his*.

The thought was concrete in his mind without fully realizing it.

Instead of questioning him, Cade nodded once. Fucker knew not to ask questions when it came to Gage. Plausible deniability and all that. "Keys are in the office."

Gage didn't waste any time turning on his heel and striding out the door before Lucky could ask to be the best man at his fucking wedding or some shit.

He *liked* Bex.

He didn't want to have to explain to her why he'd shot her husband—for the second time.

Lauren

"Holy shit, Lauren!" Niles, my editor, gaped at me when I took off my dark glasses.

I didn't exactly want to take them off, but there was no obvious reason for me to be wearing them inside. Unlike Lucy, who had routinely worn huge shades until at least noon on a Monday to "hide the evil daylight," I wasn't known for hangovers.

Or drinking at all.

Hence me not being able to pull off the indoor sunglasses look.

I winced at the lights smarting against my eyes. Or more accurately stabbing razorblades into my eyeballs.

The doctors had been reasonably certain that I didn't have a concussion, though they'd kept me in for monitoring for the rest of the night, just in case.

I was thankful that my job included health insurance for that little stay. I had a sensibly sized nest egg for unforeseen emergencies, but hospital bills added up quickly, and a features editor for a small-town paper didn't exactly earn a lot.

In this economy, I was lucky to still have a job in journalism. It was a dying industry, and small-town independent publications were set to become extinct in the not-so-distant future.

The only reason why the *Amber Star* was hanging on was because Amber was different, and one of the many 'real' small towns left in America. Despite being in California and on the beach, we were far enough away from LA not to get sucked into *that* void. Almost all the businesses were owner-operated—we didn't even have a Starbucks. Every time a big conglomerate came sniffing around, offering too much money to yank away the personality of the town, we closed ranks.

I was sure the money would become too tempting in the future. It always did. Then big business would bastardize our town so it looked like the rest of the world.

And all the rest of the small-town newspapers in America were getting killed off in the name of progress. In the monopolizing of the media industry, the monopolizing of the freaking *country*.

So my job wasn't exactly secure; it was only a matter of time. And I didn't want to leave Amber. I loved my hometown, even if my parents had moved away... after.

There were too many memories for them there, they said. For me, it was the memories that kept me going, made that weight on my chest light enough to at least breathe around.

So I wasn't about to let go of my town, my memories. I was going to clutch onto them with vigor for as long I was gainfully employed and could afford to live in Amber.

Hence me walking into the office the morning they discharged me from the hospital with instructions to 'take it easy' and gave me a handful of pill bottles—all of which I'd thrown out. I wasn't about to miss a day of work when things were already precarious for every single person in the office. Niles had to lay off two people in as many months. We were down to a skeleton crew.

I had enough time to get a taxi home, having already called the sheriff from the hospital about my wrecked car sitting six miles out of town. It was only proper to let them know before someone happened upon it, abandoned, they looked up my plates, suspected the worst and then called my parents.

They may have recovered from the wounds of the past, but I didn't think they would've been able to handle a call from a police officer letting them know they'd found their daughter's crashed car with no sign of said daughter.

And it was also a hazard. I'd swerved enough to get myself fully off the road and fully into this situation in the first place, but still, it was a distraction. Even if that road wasn't exactly well traveled, especially in the early hours of the morning.

I'd been doing the last of my long-haul drive from Phoenix, determined to get home before work Monday so I didn't have to take a vacation day. I hadn't been overly tired, as I'd planned my stops well—I was overly *alert* if anything. Which caused me to notice the dog that had scampered onto the road to nibble on some roadkill and for me to swerve to avoid hitting it.

The number one rule my father taught me was to "never swerve for animals. They're not as precious as you are." But instinct had prevailed. This was not a raccoon or a squirrel. It was a dog.

One that was nowhere to be found after I'd wrenched myself out of my car and discovered that my phone had been smashed beyond repair in the crash.

Hence me walking.

Because the other option was to wait for someone to come by, and at that hour of the night, on that particular road, my odds were slim. I hadn't been severely injured, and the walk was roughly six miles. I was fit, and I could've made it.

Until—*don't think of him.*

The officer who'd taken my call assured me they'd get someone out as soon as possible to tow my car and retrieve my belongings.

Above and beyond the call of local law enforcement, but that was how things were done here. Especially since the local police had less crime to fight now that the Sons of Templar had gone legitimate. Well, they hadn't exactly fought it in the past, thanks to an uneasy agreement between Bill—the previous sheriff—and the club. The agreement that was shredded when Luke became sheriff. He had been determined to take the club down, but after a fair amount of drama, they were still standing and Luke wasn't the sheriff anymore. Now he was part of the biker family.

"Lauren!" Niles demanded, as I'd obviously not answered his first cried word.

I jumped, the movement sending shoots of agony down my aching body. In addition to the head wound, every single part of me screamed in pain. It was normal with a car accident, my doctor told me. I had known that already, since the trauma a body went through even in a minor car accident was enough to cause considerable pain for up to a month.

I merely had to grit my teeth through it.

Likely the medication I'd thrown out would've taken the edge off, but I didn't do *anything* to take the edge off.

I dealt. I was used to being cut from the hard edges of life.

"It's nothing." I waved in dismissal before the entire office crowded around me.

They were already staring, and I wasn't used to that.

I continued to stride to my desk, sinking down to hide while Niles followed and continued to gape at me.

"Nothing? You've got a gash on your head and a bruised eye. That's not nothing. Who did this to you? I'll kill them," he hissed.

I suppressed a laugh. My balding, fifty-year-old, tweed vest–wearing, spectacled editor was going to kill someone? The man had fight when it came to words and stories, but strictly on paper. Never in real life.

"Well my car is already pretty dead, so you don't have to kill it," I assured him, tapping at my screen and navigating to my email so I could inform my insurance company of my car's untimely death. Driver error was covered in my policy, which was comprehensive. Sensible.

I hoped they'd get it sorted quickly. I could technically walk from my apartment to the office—as I'd done after a lightning-quick shower to wash the hospital grime off me that morning—but I needed a car. We were downsizing at the paper, which meant I had to cover stories, which weren't always located within the town limits.

"You *crashed?*" Niles exclaimed, shock painting his face. "*You?*"

I smiled. He knew me well since I'd been working there almost straight out of college. Well, after my *break* from college, and reality.

Niles knew my thoughts about safety. He'd driven in a car with me once and told me that his "dead grandmother would not only drive faster, but she'd thank you for how safe you're keeping her grandson, since it's impossible to crash at fifteen miles per hour."

I nodded. "Me."

He leaned on my desk, taking his glasses off to clean them on the bottom of his shirt. "Well, who was the idiot who crashed into you?" he demanded. "Were they drunk? Are they paying for repairs? I hope the police brought them in."

I could see the wheels turning in his head as his cheeks reddened and he prepared for one of his famous rants.

He hated injustice, and he made it his mission to get loud and borderline hysterical in order to right it.

I smiled once more. "The idiot happens to be me and my aversion for killing canines," I told him.

He squinted at me through his newly cleaned glasses, pausing his temper tantrum.

"I swerved for a dog," I explained, sighing. "Not something you're meant to do, but I also couldn't handle killing a dog. I figured on that patch of road, going my 'dead grandmother speed,' my injuries wouldn't be serious." I shrugged, failing to hide my flinch at the pain that came with the motion. "And they're not. Serious, that is." I screwed up my nose. "Though I would like to find that dog."

I'd been worrying about it all night. Mostly in an effort to distract myself from being left bleeding at the curb by my not-so-shining knight in leather.

It had hurt more than I liked to admit.

And I was thinking about my body pressed to his more than I would like to admit, as well.

Hence distracting myself with worry for the dog.

It was too far out of town for it to have wandered off a property, and it had looked skinny in the small flash of my headlights before I swerved.

A stray that some careless owner had likely dropped on the side of the road when they realized what a responsibility dogs were.

My heart hurt for it.

"You're going home," Niles decided.

I frowned at him. "I'm not." I nodded at the computer screen. "I've got three articles to go through, one to copy edit, and one more to likely completely rewrite because Anna would've been too busy drooling at the college boys to get anything on the game itself," I listed. My responsibilities were more than mounting, as Niles had to continue laying off 'nonessential' staff in order to keep the doors open and the printers hot.

He straightened, folding his arms. "I'll take care of it. That's my job. And we've got unpaid interns from the high school. I'll put them to work. They fuck it up, we'll blame it on them." He narrowed his eyes when I didn't move from my chair, knowing me well enough to understand how stubborn I was.

"This is an order, Lauren," he continued. "Go. Home. You're no use to us if you pass out on your keyboard, and I can't afford the lawsuit if you do."

I stared at him, though I reasoned the power of said stare was hindered by the fact that my throbbing head stopped me from putting all my effort into it.

Which meant Niles won.

I sighed dramatically. "I've never taken a sick day the whole time I've worked here," I snapped.

He nodded in triumph. "Yes, which means you're well overdue for one. Take the day. And tomorrow if needed." He held up his hand as I started to protest. "And I know the idea of two consecutive days off is deplorable to you, so I'll allow you to work from home. Tomorrow. Not today," he clarified firmly. "Today you go home, get yourself situated on the sofa with bad TV and worse junk food."

I raised my brow. He knew me. Which meant he knew I didn't watch bad TV or eat junk food. I was more than a little obsessive about what I put into my body, determined not to poison it, to make it healthy and live a long life that wasn't short-ened by choices that brought about short-term pleasure.

"Up!" Niles demanded, shaking me out of my thoughts before they ventured to a dangerous place.

I did as I was instructed because he was right, I wouldn't be able to get any work done as I was right then. Even with my glasses, the computer screen was blurry at best; if I tried to edit anything, I'd likely make it worse than it was to begin with.

Niles squeezed my arm, his smile rare but warm when it appeared. He was a hard-ass, but he was also a good man. He'd treated me as somewhat of a daughter, since he made the paper his life and didn't have much outside of it.

"You call me if you need anything, okay? And I don't want to see you in here tomorrow if you're wincing at the fucking light like you are today, okay?" He didn't wait for my response. "Okay." Then he turned, storming about the office, shouting orders and chastising people for missing deadlines, telling them they'd be working at FedEx if they didn't "pull their fingers out of their asses."

My eyes touched Lucy's old desk, and inexplicably I missed my friend. She wasn't the closest of my friends—I didn't even *have* close friends—but she was important to me. She was kind. Cared about me. Didn't judge me. Had a great sense of humor. Was just a nice person to be around.

But she was in LA, living her journalistic dream, even if it had almost gotten her killed. It had gotten her stabbed, more accurately.

To me, getting stabbed on the street after a drug lord put a hit out on you for exposing him was nothing short of horrifying.

When I'd called her, she'd been light and breezy. "It's noth-ing, really. Just a flesh wound. And you're not a real journalist unless someone tries to kill you, anyway."

Yeah, she was fearless.

Maybe that's what I missed most, seeing that fearless, carefree aura around me. Pretending for a couple of moments that I might be like her.

Now I didn't have any illusions to cling to about what I was.

That was all on my mind as I walked slowly and carefully toward my apartment. It was just off Main Street, facing the ocean, and I loved it. An ocean-view apartment would've been out of my price range anywhere else, even here where property prices were modest, but I'd bought it when the market was good with the small inheritance I'd received from my grandmother when I came of age.

It was eight months after the thing I did not speak of or even think about, and I was twenty-one years old.

Maybe before things turned dark and gray and hellish, I might've used the inheritance to buy a backpack and a one-way ticket to travel the world like I'd always dreamed. Like *we'd* always dreamed. But then *it* happened. And things like taking off to Europe for a crazy adventure were more terrifying than staying in one place, which was bad enough.

So I shoved my dream away.

Or more accurately, reality did a good job of shoving my dream away, brutally and painfully.

Instead I made a sensible investment with a good mortgage rate, and had slowly been renovating my apartment above a small art gallery for the past ten years.

I gave myself exactly three seconds to look in past the glass of that gallery, feast on the paintings, the brush strokes, the pure *adventure* of the paintings. I gave myself two seconds to entertain other paintings hanging on the wall. Ones with familiar brush strokes, a little less adventure, more the longing for it.

And then I snapped my gaze back to my front door and forced my aching body up the stairs to my apartment. It was open plan as soon as you entered. The kitchen was straight ahead, in a corner where the windows faced away from the ocean, over the parking lot and then the town beyond. I had the back wall covered in pure white subway tiles with light polished floating wooden shelves displaying glasses and bowls on different levels with matte-black fastenings.

My fridge was my only little rebellion, my pop of personality. It was a vintage baby blue Smeg that sat at the end of my counter, by the window. The rest of my back wall had the same polished tiles, with matte-black racks hanging my matching tea cups at the perfect grabbing level. In front of that was a large square kitchen island with a huge deep white sink, matching the tiles behind it, and two black barstools tucked underneath the front of the island. There was always a vase of fresh flowers on the restored wooden coffee cart on the left of the island, and the shelves below were artfully stacked with all my favorite recipe books.

The kitchen itself was tucked away in kind of a nook, where exposed brick closed it off somewhat to the rest of the apartment, which was to the left of the stairs.

I had the original hardwood floors polished so they were gleaming and the whole space painted white, which gave my apartment a light and airy feel thanks to all of the windows. It was important to me, that openness. That brightness. I didn't do small spaces very well. Not... after.

My living area encompassed the whole room, and it had taken me years—almost a decade, to be exact—to get it how it was. I was picky with furniture, and my budget only allowed me to purchase sporadically. But it was my absolute sanctuary. The espresso leather sofas were domed and perfectly worn, with light fluffy blue afghans thrown over both. The cushions were white and fluffy, hideously expensive but worth it. A large white patterned area rug sat underneath my matte-black coffee table, another vase of fresh flowers set perfectly in the middle.

A bookcase spanned almost the entire wall behind my sofas.

It was stuffed with books I'd accumulated over the years, but there was still plenty of empty space I'd filled with photos and various knickknacks, spaced as not to look cluttered.

I threw my purse on one of the sofas, kicked off my shoes— not putting them in the wooden cubby I'd set beside the stairs for once—and padded over to my favorite area in my whole apartment.

My floor-to-ceiling windows boasted an unobstructed view of the ocean beyond, a well-worn leather chair with a fluffy white ottoman in front of it. Another afghan rested on the back of the chair. The small wooden table beside it always stored whatever book I was reading at the time.

My fingers trailed over the cover of *The Sword of Truth*—I was a fantasy junkie. Knowing I wouldn't be able to focus enough to read, I sank into the warm chair and let my eyes drift to the waves.

My mind wandered.

To eyes that were almost the same color as that ocean. Almost as wild. As unpredictable.

As dangerous.

A shrill ringing made me jump out of my thoughts before I drowned in them. It was somewhat of an effort—a painful one at that—to extract myself from the chair that was designed to swallow me up. I managed by gritting my teeth and rushing to the counter beside my sofa, where my landline—I was almost the only person left under fifty-five who still had one—was ringing.

"Hello, Lauren speaking," I gritted through my teeth.

"Lauren? It's Troy," a smooth masculine voice replied.

I walked back over to the windows, standing in the path of the sun's warm rays streaming through the glass and gazing out at the ocean once more.

"Oh, hey, Troy," I said. "You've got news about my car, then?"

Troy was one of the deputies at the Amber Police Department. We'd been in the same grade in high school, but he barely knew who I was—I was surprised he knew my name—since we didn't exactly hang in the same crowds.

I'd had kind of a huge crush on him back then. He was my ultimate type, after all. Quarterback. Square jawed. Dirty blond hair that was always cut and groomed perfectly. Tall, lean, but not too muscly.

Good smile.

Safe.

Evidenced by the fact that he was now a police officer.

I hadn't entirely grown out of the crush, merely pushed it to the back of my mind since it wasn't logical that the attractive police officer would be interested in the quiet, boring, glasses-wearing, beige-clad me.

But that didn't mean his voice wasn't comforting.

Though it didn't stir anything inside me quite like the rough growl that had woken my body the night before. That had stirred something I didn't even know existed inside of me.

Don't think of that!

"Well, that's exactly it," Troy said, voice hesitant. "Would you mind coming down to the station?"

I froze. "The station? I wasn't drinking or anything while I was driving. Heck, I don't even drink period. And I swear I was driving the speed limit, though that probably doesn't mean much to you, as people not driving the speed limit are likely to swear they were driving within it, but—"

A low and warm chuckle interrupted my freak-out and the visions of prison bars closing in on me. I logically knew that they didn't lock you up for speeding, or swerving for a dog and crashing into a ditch, but my mind was still conjuring up incarceration. The mere thought of it had me breaking into a sweat. Locked doors, enclosed spaces.

No.

"Babe, I know you. Which means I know for a fact that you were driving within the speed limit, and I know you sure as hell weren't drinking," Troy said, amused.

All thoughts of prison left my head, making room for Troy's words. "You know me?" I repeated on a whisper. I had been surprised he even knew my name and connected me to "the girl I had Biology with, right?" when I'd spoken to him earlier in the day.

"Yeah, Lauren, I know you," he replied, his voice low and warm and... something else.

Something my throbbing brain likely imagined.

"So I'm not going to get put away for swerving for a dog and, like, misusing police resources or something?" I clarified.

Another warm chuckle. "No, Lauren. You're not in trouble. And helping you out is definitely not a misuse of police resources. Best resource I've used in a long time, in fact."

There it was again, that strange tone.

Was he *flirting?*

No. That was insane.

"C-can I ask why you need me down at the st-station?" I stuttered, trying to regain my even voice. I pinched the bridge of my nose in an effort to somewhat alleviate the headache radiating to the front of my face.

The lack of sleep probably had a lot to do with that.

Oh, and the smashing of my head against my steering wheel.

"Well, I went out to the spot this morning where you crashed, and your car wasn't there."

I stopped pinching my nose. "My car wasn't there?" My previously quelled panic returned. "How is it not there? I mean, it's not even drivable. It was in a ditch. Do you think someone stole it? Why would someone want to steal a crashed *Hyundai?* It's one of the least-stolen cars in the country," I babbled. "Well, number seven, but that's still in the top ten. And that's when it's drivable—"

"Lauren, calm down," Troy said, a smile in his voice. "We don't know if it's been stolen yet. Could've been someone saw it, decided to do a good deed, towed it themselves. But I think it would be a good idea for you to come down and make a report anyway."

A good deed.

I froze on that thought.

An idea entered my mind. A much crazier idea than the police officer I'd had a crush on as a teenager flirting with me.

An idea about a certain motorcycle club and the garage attached to the clubhouse. The garage I assumed had the capabilities to remove a crashed car from the side of the road.

The motorcycle club whose patch was sewn onto the back of the leather I'd been clutching a handful of hours before. The man wearing the leather. The one who had held my arms pressed to his middle the entire ride into town. The one who gazed at me with a feral stare saturated with menace.

The man who'd left me on the curb at the hospital.

No, that didn't make sense.

He wouldn't leave me on the side of the road, anxious to get rid of me, and then do something *nice* like tow my car.

Troy had said "good deed."

That man did not do good deeds.

One just had to look at him, feel the air around him, to know that much.

"Babe? You still with me?"

I jerked out of my stupor in order to inspect the fact that Troy had called me 'babe' twice in a conversation that had lasted less the five minutes. The longest conversation we'd ever had.

'Babe' was a throwaway word for a lot of men. Best not to read into it. My brain wasn't capable of reading the pages woven by Terry Goodkind, so it definitely wasn't ready to inspect the complexities of a hot guy's lexicon.

"Yeah, I'm still here," I replied, my voice little more than a whisper.

"Good," he said firmly. "So you okay to come down to the station? Have a chat? Only if you're up to it. I know you're a bit banged up. I could come over to your place—"

"No!" I interrupted, horrified at the thought of the hot cop being in my space. And me being awkward and fumbling around like an idiot. Then the energy of my home would be stained with memories of my awkwardness and most likely embarrassing myself. "I mean, I'm okay to come down. Fresh air would be good for me since Niles sent me home from work. It'll stop me from getting cabin fever," I said, forcing my voice to be light and try to cover up the way I'd nearly shouted at him.

Another chuckle. "Well, I'd hate to be responsible for cabin fever. I'll see you soon?"

I cleared my throat. "You will be seeing me—I mean I'll, um, be down at the station soon," I stammered.

Speak like a human, Lauren!

"Okay, Lauren. Soon."

I hung up the phone and would've banged my head against the window frame if it didn't already feel like I was.

Some strange part of me knew there was more to come.

A lot more.

THREE

"Holy shit, babe," Troy said the second I walked into the station and pushed my dark glasses onto my head.

Before I rightly knew what was going on, he'd rounded the desk at the front of station and was in front of me. *Right* in front of me.

He grasped my chin much like another man had the night before. But his fingers were soft, gentle, barely gripping the skin— unlike the other man.

My skin didn't burst into flames from the touch, and my breathing didn't turn shallow.

That didn't mean I didn't react. My body warmed slightly from the touch and his scent of clean linen and some subtle man's aftershave that was classy and understated.

His green eyes zeroed in on the gash on my head, the bruising on my face.

"It looks worse than it is," I murmured shyly, not quite knowing how I'd managed to have two hot guys touching me in the space of twenty-four hours.

Two very different hot guys.

The man from last night couldn't have even be described as hot.

I didn't know how to describe him.

My mind went to the momentary glimpse I had of him under the streetlights outside the hospital. Everything about him was hard, rough edges. His large body seemed sculpted from steel as he'd clutched the bike, his muscled arms near bursting from the fabric of his long-sleeved henley, tattoos visible from underneath, creeping past his wrists. Tattoos that snaked up his neck, where they were buried by his blond beard. Not overly long, but a definite beard. Well groomed. Perfect, actually. Lumberjack meets biker. His hair was the same, brushing his shoulders. Or it would've if it'd been wild. At some point, he'd tied it into a messy bun at the back of his head.

I didn't think man buns would've done a thing for me, since I was all about clean-cut.

But the mere *thought* of that bun had me quivering under Troy's touch.

Troy, who was clean-shaven. Troy, who had short and expertly groomed dirty blond hair. Troy, who was tall, muscled, but leaner, a lot less imposing. Troy, who didn't radiate menace and wear a motorcycle cut. No, he exuded safety and was wearing a neatly pressed uniform.

He must've mistaken my quiver for a reaction of pain to his grip, letting me go and stepping back slightly.

His mouth was a tight line. "Well, it looks bad, Lauren," he said, answering my earlier statement. "The doctors clear you? Give you painkillers?"

I nodded once, ignoring the pain at the motion and deciding not to inform Troy of my stance on painkillers. He wouldn't understand. Not many people would. It was easier just to pretend that I conformed to society's habit toward swallowing a pill to forget pain instead of learning to live with it. Numbness was more dangerous than pain.

He held a hand out in front of him. "Want to come sit down and we'll chat?" he offered, eyes as warm as his voice.

I nodded again, lifting my aching feet toward the cluster of desks set apart in the wide room.

"You need anything?" he asked when I sat down. "Tea, water?"

"No, thanks."

He took a seat, sipping from a mug beside his computer.

"You didn't offer me coffee," I noted.

He grinned, showing gleaming white teeth. "You don't drink coffee."

My stomach dipped. "How do you know that?" I whispered.

His grin left him. "I'm a cop. It's my job to know things. Especially when it's things about the pretty features editor of the *Amber Star.*"

I stared at him. *He thinks I'm pretty?* Enough to somehow notice I didn't drink caffeinated beverages, at least.

I knew I wasn't ugly. My skin was pale but clear, due to being lucky with genes and not having acne in the family. Plus I didn't eat much sugar to promote that. My bone structure was relatively symmetrical, my features slightly too small, making me look slight and innocent. That was magnified by the thick glasses I was required to wear, as I was a little unluckier with my genes in regard to eyesight—both of my parents wore glasses too. I liked to think mine were nice, not fashionable but not geeky spectacles either. I didn't recognize my face without them—physically couldn't unless I wore contacts, and they irritated my hazel eyes.

My caramel hair was long and healthy because I took all the right vitamins and researched the best, paraben-free products to suit my slightly wavy locks. Though I almost always wore it up anyway.

No, I wasn't ugly, but I never thought of myself as overly pretty. More of a wallflower.

I shifted uncomfortably in my chair with Troy's attention.

He cleared his face to a slightly more professional expression. "Want to tell me what happened? Then we'll get to finding the car."

"The car?"

Another grin. "Yeah, your car. The reason you're here?"

I wanted to whack myself in the head. "Oh yes, my car. The reason I'm here," I muttered.

Idiot.

I tried to cover up my awkwardness by quickly and succinctly telling him what happened. That I was lucky someone stopped and drove me to the hospital—leaving out the 'who' of the situation. And not just because the resident reformed outlaw motorcycle club and the police didn't exactly enjoy a close relationship, despite the former chief of police being married to the biker princess, Rosie Fletcher, now Rosie Crawford.

No, it was more because I wanted to keep him to myself. Clutch that little sliver of beautiful chaos close to my chest.

I shouldn't be omitting that piece of information from an officer of the law. Especially since the very man who had picked me up off the side of the road was part of a club that also ran a garage.

But he didn't even know I'd *crashed.*

He hadn't asked what I was doing stumbling and bleeding down a highway in the middle of the night. As if the details weren't of consequence. As if it was something that happened every day.

Maybe in his world, it did.

"Jesus, Lauren, you're lucky someone picked you up. And that they weren't a serial killer," Troy said, his body tight.

I choked out a slightly hysterical laugh. I wasn't entirely sure the man who picked me up *wasn't* a serial killer.

He narrowed his eyes, obviously picking something up with his cop sensors. Or maybe he was trying to decide if he needed to take me back to the hospital for some kind of psych evaluation. My actions hadn't exactly been stellar examples of sanity.

So unlike me. I held on to my sanity with an iron grip. Because I knew what it felt like to lose it.

It was obviously the crash shaking me up. Not the man—who may or may not be a serial killer—affecting me in a way I didn't rightly understand.

Troy looked like he was about to press for the identity of my savior when a uniformed officer approached the desk.

"We've got something," he said.

Troy darted one look at me before he stood. "Excuse me for a second, Lauren."

I watched him move slightly out of hearing distance to discuss something with the officer I didn't recognize, inspecting him in his full glory.

He hadn't changed much since high school—he even had the same hairstyle. His body was slightly more muscled, but not by much. Same square jaw. Nice, tanned skin. Large and pleasing hands.

Everything about him was *pleasing*.

Nice.

But I noticed it with a kind of detachment that hadn't been present before that day.

Before last night.

Before I'd become aware of a hunger, a starvation inside of me that a *pleasing* and *nice* man could not sate.

Don't think about it.

Troy helped me with that by striding back over to the desk, arms crossed, face tight.

"We found your car."

I perked up, but he didn't give me a chance to answer him, or ask questions.

"It was towed into the Sons compound about an hour ago," he continued, voice hard and not at all the same as it had been before.

I gaped at him. "The *Sons* compound?"

He nodded once, obviously as unimpressed as I was, but likely for different reasons. "You want to expand on that?"

I stiffened at his pinched face and accusing tone. "Do *I* want to expand on that?" I hissed, surprising myself with the anger in my voice. "How would *I* expand on that?"

"How about by tellin' me exactly who picked you up last night?" he clipped, the warmness in his voice quickly dissipating. "'Cause apart from you, there aren't many good citizens driving down the highway in the middle of the night."

That rubbed me the wrong way.

I pursed my lips. "Well, considering the man in question picked up a bleeding and injured woman who he didn't know from Eve and took her to the hospital, I'd say he *was* a good citizen," I snapped, not really believing the words entirely, but I was angry. Plus I was feeling strangely protective of the man I'd been so sure was a villain until seconds ago.

"You caught up with them?" Troy demanded, changing his angle and line of questioning. "The Sons?"

I laughed. I couldn't help it. His granite expression and the question in general were ridiculous.

He did not appreciate me laughing if his scowl was anything to go by.

"You're supposed to 'know me,' remember?" I said once I'd gotten a hold of myself. "Well, knowing me, you've got the answer to your question whether or not I'm 'caught up' with the resident motorcycle club." I stood, my chair screeching slightly.

And the world might've tilted too, but I managed to recover before I could do anything embarrassing like faint.

"But I will be getting 'caught up' with them, as you say. As in going over there and educating them on how towing a car that doesn't belong to them is *so not freaking cool*," I hissed.

Troy's face had lost its marble by the time I finished speaking. He was grinning.

"This isn't funny," I snapped, hating that I couldn't command sass.

"I disagree. Never seen you pissed before," he replied, voice warm again. "It's cute. And funny."

I let the words deflect off me. I couldn't handle being called cute right then. "It's not *meant* to be funny," I sighed, my anger leaking out of me like I'd been a half-inflated balloon. "Now, are you going to kindly give me a ride over to the garage where my car is being held hostage?" The realization that I didn't have a vehicle and the Sons compound was all the way across town made me swallow my pride instead of storming out of there like I'd planned. Plus, I didn't do things like snap at police officers and storm off.

Troy's grin disappeared. "You're not going over there," he said, voice firm. "I'll handle it."

I folded my arms, narrowing my eyes at him. "Oh, you're mistaken. I'm going. This is my responsibility. And you're not 'handling it.'" I air-quoted his masculine words. "I'm quite capable of doing so. I was merely asking for a ride because my entire body feels like it was hit by a truck, not my Hyundai. But I'll walk if you won't give me a ride. And you're not stopping me. Unless you try to lock me up, and you've already promised you wouldn't do so." I gave him a hard look. "You don't seem to be a man who breaks promises, are you, Troy?"

He stared at me for a long moment, likely measuring his chances of being able to talk me out of it. He had probably thought me quiet and meek; that's how most people saw me because I didn't give them a chance to see anything else. I was quiet by choice, and definitely not meek.

Hence him sighing, snatching his keys off the table and muttering, "Let's go."

I followed him with a triumphant grin, trying to focus on the pain that came with walking instead of the butterflies crawling up my throat at the prospect of what I was about to do.

Gage

"Fifty bucks says there's a body in the trunk," Lucky said from where he'd leaned against the door of the garage after Gage unloaded the Hyundai and started assessing the damage.

He might not have done mechanic work on principle, but that didn't mean he wasn't good at it.

He was the best.

Gage made it a point to become the best at everything he did.

Mechanics.

Riding his bike.

Making bombs.

Killing people.

Becoming addicted to heroin.

Ruining his life.

He could've made a good living fixing cars. If he *wanted* to make a living. But he wasn't living. His demons wouldn't let him. They needed blood. Death. Pain.

"No, I think it's some industrial-grade plutonium," Brock said from across the car, assessing the trunk with a little apprehension. The fucker was never apprehensive, almost as ruthless as Gage when it came to killing. But even his brothers knew Gage didn't have control over himself completely. So even the most fearless of his brothers treated him like expired dynamite.

Which wasn't too far from the truth. Except expired dynamite was safer to handle.

"I'll raise that to a hundred," Brock said to Lucky, folding his arms and grinning.

"Done," Lucky replied. "I think it's to do with his woman," he guessed correctly.

There was a loaded pause. Gage focused on the car.

"Woman?" Brock repeated, shocked. "No way. There's more chance of the plutonium."

"Nope," Lucky replied. "It's to do with a woman. I'm almost sure of it. Or there's also a good chance of dead bodies in the trunk because, well, it's Gage."

Gage ignored them both.

He didn't trust himself to engage in the conversation.

Especially since his version of engaging would've been slamming his fist through Lucky's face to shut the fucker up. He didn't want to do that. He liked him. Respected him. And his wife.

His wife would also likely get up in Gage's shit for knocking her husband out. Bex may have been broken in a way she might never be whole again, but it was the most broken of people who were the strongest. To be feared the most. Especially in regards to another human who made their broken life that much more bearable.

Bex wouldn't stand for anything threatening that. Even if it was Gage.

He knew she was strong enough to make it through anything. Once you'd been through Hell and walked, crawled, or were carried out, there wasn't much more the Devil could throw at you to bring you to your knees again.

Apart from threatening the one thing that went through Hell with you. The one *person* who braved that Hell. The person who was damned too, for their own reasons or merely for their connection to you.

Hence Gage not speaking. Not addressing Lucky. Because if he did, he'd have to address why the fuck the car was in the compound at all. Why the fuck a woman—who even bloodied was still pure as the driven snow—had gotten under his skin so quickly. And by the look on her face when he'd pulled from the curb of the hospital, she was already damned. Because she'd felt it too. Whatever it was that had her scent imprinted on him, her warmth seeping into his icy bones.

He just hoped she was as sensible as her fucking statistics and lame-as-fuck car told him she was. Because that would mean she'd stay far away from him and the only person he'd be damning was himself.

And fuckers who deserved it.

A car entered the compound but Gage ignored that too. Probably some yuppie customer wanting to be treated like royalty. He trusted any of his brothers to rectify that quickly.

"What the fuck are the pigs doing here?" Lucky hissed. "Gage, hide the bodies. I'll take care of this."

At that, Gage looked up. Not because he was particularly worried about the cops; they'd never made anything stick, not for lack of trying. Even when Crawford was trying to take them down—fucker had been determined—they never found shit.

Now that they were basically legit, there was nothing to find. Because whatever laws they did break, they knew how to get away with breaking.

Gage wasn't legit, but he wasn't worried about the cops.

He knew they'd never trace him to any crime. Another thing he excelled at—covering his tracks. Not hiding his skeletons but destroying them.

The physical ones, at least.

No, he didn't look up because he was worried about the cops.

He looked up because of the soft voice filtering through the air after the car had stopped and the doors had opened and closed. The voice that yanked the air from his lungs and hardened his cock immediately.

His eyes met hers.

Then he realized she wasn't as sensible as her statistics and her car.

She might not know it yet, but there was no going back from this.

Not when he saw her in the daylight, not with the fire in her eyes when they found him.

She was damned too.

He'd make sure of it.

Because she was his.

And he should've cared that it meant she'd have to live in Hell instead of with a man who would try and give her Heaven, but he didn't fuckin' care.

Because the damned weren't concerned with redemption.

Lauren

The short ride from the station to the Sons of Templar compound on the outside of town was tense, to say the least. Troy obviously wasn't happy about bringing me somewhere he thought I couldn't handle.

It was becoming increasingly evident that he thought I was the quiet, bookish, timid girl from high school with glasses who had a delicate sensibility that would bruise easily, especially when faced with the big scary bikers.

It was hard to fight considering I actually was bruised and battered and about to face those big scary bikers.

But Troy had no idea what I could handle.

My sensibilities might've been delicate once, before the world showed me what it did to delicate and naive souls.

It stomped on them.

Shredded them.

And you had two choices after that happened.

You stayed naïve and delicate and barely existed in the world.

Or you dealt.

It might not have looked like it, but I dealt.

Because I was still standing.

Because I was still living. Yeah, it was a careful and structured life, but it was one I controlled.

As much as anyone could control their lives, anyway.

And no way was I letting the guy from high school turned police officer try to take that control. No matter how cute he was. No matter the fact that I used to have a crush on him. Or that he kind of might've been flirting with me.

Because I was learning that I didn't do cute.

Or crushes.

Or I'd begun to learn that last night.

It hit me then, physically, once we'd pulled into the compound and I'd jumped out of the car before Troy could try and stop me.

I saw my car first.

My fists clenched.

Then I saw *him*.

And my knees wobbled.

His crystal eyes met mine.

My body went aflame.

Just by meeting his fricking *gaze*.

In daylight, at a distance, it was jarring. Beautiful but ugly at the same time. Because he had to go through something ugly to become that harshly beautiful, so menacing that it floated across the parking lot and speared into my soul.

I ignored it because I had to. Because if I didn't I wouldn't stay standing. I would've been stomped on again. And that only happened once, or you could only get back up once. I had a feeling the people this man stomped on didn't get up.

I decided to hold on to the anger I'd been nurturing on the ride over, since I'd heard my car was there. *I planned to do the stomping.*

And I did.

Right across the parking lot, the thump of police issue boots behind me. I ignored it, just like I ignored my body's protests at my stomping. After a car crash, I guessed I was meant to be delicate with myself. My body. But as I got closer to the garage and the stare that was yanking me in, I became certain that delicate would never be a reality for me again.

"You!" I hissed, pointing at the man who had wiped his hand on a dirty rag and moved to clear the car completely.

My step stuttered only slightly when I saw him in his entirety. And he was an *entirety.* A presence that radiated even more than the two men watching me with rapt attention who I'd barely even blinked at.

And that was saying something, since the men in this club were a heck of a lot to blink at. Living in Amber all my life meant I'd seen them around, seen the effect the had on everyone around them. The very *air* around them. So making two attractive, tattooed, and menacing men obsolete was a feat.

And he—I realized I didn't even know his *name*—managed to do so.

Luckily my anger willed me forward instead of me sinking to my knees and offering to sacrifice a goat to him for his eternal favor or something equally crazy—like snatching his beautifully savage face and kissing him.

"Oh shit, it's happening," a deep voice whisper-yelled from the direction of the caramel-skinned, bald-headed, and tattooed biker to my left.

I barely heard it through the ringing in my ears that had nothing to do with my head injury and everything to do with *him*.

The him I had advanced on and whose chest I found myself jabbing a finger into. Yes, literally making contact. It was like pressing against iron. Warm, electric, beautiful, and tattooed iron, but iron nonetheless. I was surprised my finger didn't shatter.

"You!" I repeated, yanking myself away from thoughts of running my hands along his bare chest. "You have no right to just drag my car, my property, away in your little truck or whatever and put it in a garage without my consent," I hissed. "Especially considering you *abandoned* me outside a hospital in the middle of the night."

There was somewhat of a commotion behind me as the bald man moved in my path to, I guessed, block Troy from approaching.

Troy didn't like it from the handful of curses and a reminder to the man that he was an officer of the law.

"I don't care if you're an officer of Thor himself. You can't interrupt such a thing as a courtship between my brother and this little spitfire," Lucky—I remembered that was his name—said, smile in his voice. "Have you seen *Thor*? Great movie. But I'm thinking what's going on in front of us is better entertainment value than a big man with a big hammer. Just let it happen."

My finger was still pressed to the chest of the bearded man in front of me. His eyes were on mine, yanking all of my attention, every facet of my being to him.

It didn't make sense.

But it didn't have to.

We were close. Close enough for me to smell the tobacco and purely male scent that radiated off him and instantly awakened my desire.

Everything about him screamed *man*.

"Didn't abandon you considering I took you to the fuckin'

hospital," he clipped, his voice almost a growl. His eyes were daring me to lower my gaze in a way that I guessed was always successful for him.

He hadn't encountered someone like me.

My stubbornness kept me holding his glare even when everything else inside me—common sense included—urged me to run before it was too late.

"You're not a fuckin' child. A fuckin' damsel," he continued, voice still harsh. "By the looks of it, you were quite capable to walk the twelve feet to the door. Sure as shit didn't need me to be doin' it for you."

His words held something more, but I didn't have the energy to inspect that. My anger was still simmering. And he wasn't done, his own anger meeting mine.

"And you're an idiot to be mad about me getting your fuckin' hunk of shit off the side of the road and takin' it to a garage where it can be fixed," he continued. "A fuckin' thank-you would be appreciated. Not bringing the *pigs* to our property." He stepped even closer, his fury and danger enveloping me like a cape. "You'll be sorry for that, Will. Really fuckin' sorry."

People were talking around us. I was sure of it. From what I'd heard about Lucky, he didn't shut up. And I was sure Troy didn't appreciate me fighting my own battles, so he was likely having a lot to say about it.

But I didn't hear anything following the words that came out of *his* mouth.

The threat.

The threat that didn't insinuate bodily harm. The threat that was so saturated in pure sex that my panties dampened immediately, my breath coming in short pants.

I would've jumped him right there and then had I not let my anger grasp onto his words.

"You expect me to *thank* you?" I hissed, leaning back so I

wasn't choked by his pure presence. "Yeah, fat fricking chance of that, buddy. And in regards to the police officer who brought me here"—I pointed in Troy's general direction, not breaking eye contact with the icy irises—"he was doing his *duty*, you know, as a *protector of the law*, to help me. And I'm not a damsel, let me tell you that. I'm capable as all heck to take care of my own affairs—" I wasn't intending on finishing there, but the man in front of me did not seem happy that I wasn't cowering from his fury and his stare as he cut me off.

"That's why you were stumbling down the road in the middle of the night. Why you can't even say the word '*fuck*,'" he rasped, drawing out the last word, his meaning behind it very clear. The meaning that would have him taking me wildly. Brutally.

I swallowed and his eyes flared as if he sensed exactly what was going on between my legs.

But he kept speaking so I had almost definitely imagined the way his eyes flared.

"The woman who crashed a car that's basically un-crashable, and considering your stance on the speed limit, I'd say you weren't even going fifty," he guessed correctly. "Yet you crashed. A fucking *Hyundai*. And you need the boys in blue to come here with you, keep you *safe* from the likes of me? No, you're not a damsel."

It was a challenge. Plain as day. One he expected me to back down from. Because everyone probably backed down from him. Even those scary bikers who were currently watching us.

Because there was no threat in his words. In his eyes. Only promises. Somehow I knew he was a man with nothing to lose.

Because somehow I knew he'd already lost himself.

Maybe I recognized it because I'd lost myself too.

So I had nothing to lose either.

"For your information, asshole, I'm not afraid of curse words," I snapped, even though it wasn't entirely true, the word 'asshole' foreign and harsh on my tongue. "I just consider them to be a crutch for people who aren't intelligent enough to make their point with more effective words."

I made every word heavy. Even. It took everything in me not to rasp them, not let them shake like my knees did. But I managed.

"And I crashed my car because I was trying to save a life." I looked him up and down and was proud of myself for keeping my tongue in my mouth, not drooling while making it look like I wasn't impressed with the savage beauty before me. "I'm sure that's not something you're familiar with, but I didn't want to hurt an innocent. So I crashed. I'll heal. The dog wouldn't have."

He laughed. It was cold and somehow attractive at the same time. It didn't fill me with warmth like Troy's throaty chuckle. But it did fill me.

Every part of me.

He leaned forward, his body pressing into the air of mine. "Yeah, babe, you've got me pegged. I don't worry about protectin' innocence. I only ruin it."

Again, not a threat in the words. Only promise. Dripping with sex. The kind of sex that didn't exist in romance books or movies. The kind no one talked about. The kind I didn't let myself *think* about.

The kind I craved.

The kind that would ruin me for anything else.

But I had a strange feeling that I was already ruined for anything else.

"Ruin away, asshole," I invited, my voice slightly husky. "Because I'm no innocent, and I'm not scared of you because you growl like a dog, swear like a sailor, and dress like an outlaw. It takes *a lot* more than that to scare me." I glanced at my car, and the blond man beyond it who, of course, was muscled and attractive, covered in tattoos. Brock, I thought it was. And he was gaping at me. *Gaping.*

I didn't think these men gaped in surprise easily.

I ignored him and pressed my glasses up the bridge of my nose, where they'd fallen slightly during my tirade.

The man watched me do it, and every single part of me reacted to the way his eyes followed my hands, watching me as if I were undoing my shirt.

I ignored that too.

I had to.

"And you know what, speaking of innocence, and your lack of it, this," I said, pointing at my car, "is a crime. Troy?" I called behind my back. "Arrest this *criminal*. For theft."

The air around us turned to ice, as did the stare in front of me. But something else lurked behind those cold eyes. Sex. Definitely. Some kind of attraction so visceral and so animal that it was almost a physical thing.

But also... surprise? Did he not expect me to stand up to him?

I stood up to death itself when it ripped out my soul.

I wasn't about to succumb to a mere man. Even this man.

Brock burst out laughing.

Troy appeared beside me, though by the way he moved, I suspected he wanted to position himself in front of me. The giant before me tensed as if he expected him to do so and was ready to snatch me if need be.

"By all means, arrest me, Officer," the giant offered, but there was no surrender in his words. No, it was a threat. One that told me he didn't fear the law.

The air was wired. Just because the club and the police lived in strained harmony didn't mean the old dichotomy between the law and the lawlessness the man in front of me represented didn't exist.

A slow clap interrupted the moment and Lucky came into

view, grinning and slapping the giant on the shoulder. "Bravo. Better than *Thor,* I'll give you that." His eyes were on me. "You've got a Greek god beat for your bravery, darlin'," he said, eyes twinkling.

"Everyone knows *Iron Man* is better than *Thor,*" I responded, Lucky's easy smile somehow calming me slightly. Chris Hemsworth was hot and all, but I liked Robert Downey Jr better.

Lucky gaped much like Brock had. "Oh my God, you're insane," he all but breathed. "Therefore, you're perfect for Gage," he decided, folding his arms as everything was decided with the diagnosis of insanity.

One that usually would've speared through my memories and prodded at an old wound that wasn't healed.

But it didn't that time.

Because something else speared through me.

Gage.

That was his name.

I let the single word sink into my skin. It was perfect for the man in front of me. The man and *beast* in front of me.

The man and beast who were still staring at me, as if the two bikers on either side of him and the police officer in front of him didn't exist. As if nothing existed but us.

I didn't know if that was a good thing.

No, I knew it was a bad thing. A *terrible* thing. Because it excited me more than anything *good* ever could.

"I'll admit, I didn't imagine you exactly," Lucky continued, taking in my battered face, my simple white collared shirt, my dark blue jeans and crisp white tennis shoes with an appraising eye. It wasn't uncomfortable, his gaze. It didn't make me feel less, exactly. It made me feel more, if I was honest. It was appreciative, but not in a sexual way.

"Which is why I'm not surprised at all," he continued.

"Because it's always the ones who don't seem to fit that end up slotting in perfectly."

His cheerful tone was not at all home in the situation, nor did his words make sense, which was the reason I didn't respond immediately. And that was the reason someone else, someone who was not at all cheerful, answered instead.

"Walk. Away. Now. Lucky," Gage clipped through his teeth.

I watched the way he'd held himself since Lucky's eyes had been on me. He was reacting to the words. To the gaze. The one that was not at all sexual, only curious. A large wedding ring glinted on Lucky's left hand. Men didn't wear them that big unless they were proud to show the world they were taken.

And from what I'd heard about his wife, he adored her—it had taken a lot to get her down the aisle—so I knew he wasn't about to throw that away.

But it didn't seem to matter to Gage. Or the fact that Lucky was meant to be his brother. He looked ready to kill him for merely calling me 'not what he expected.'

That was when Brock entered the fold, right about when Troy's heat pressed into my side.

"Right, we need to take five here," Brock said casually, not even glancing at where Troy's hand had started to rest on his gun. His twinkling eyes met mine with the same amusement and interest as in Lucky's. "Darlin', I'm gonna first tell you that you've just earned my respect. Not one person, including myself, has managed to give Gage such a verbal lashing as you have. And I don't blame you for wanting to lock him up, because he can be a fucker." He glanced at the man in question. "But we're also the best garage in town, and by the looks of you, you're gonna be needing a car as soon as possible. I can't imagine walking after being in that"—he nodded to my ruined car—"is much fun at all."

"She's not walking," Troy interjected. "I'll take her where she wants to go."

"Right, I'm fuckin' *done*," Gage hissed.

"Oh fuck," Lucky muttered.

"You're not takin' her anywhere," Gage growled at Troy, ignoring Lucky. "And you're takin' *yourself* off our fuckin' property. And I'm not gonna stay here while you try and tell me that I can't threaten an officer. Because I did and I will. You touch her again, I'll kill you." He didn't even pause before he snatched my hand and dragged me out of the garage before I knew what was happening. "I'm taking you where you *need* to go, babe. Don't give a fuck about where you *want* to go."

I watched Troy try to go after me, but Lucky and Brock both managed to stand in his way. I wondered if Lucky would talk his way out of an arrest. I hoped neither of them got in trouble because of me.

Then again, I didn't need to worry about *them* getting in trouble.

I needed to worry about myself, and how much trouble I was already in.

Like being dragged across the parking lot by a man who looked like he may very well kill me.

"Let me go," I hissed at Gage. But I didn't struggle.

Why wasn't I struggling?

"No, you lost your fuckin' chance at that the second you put your foot in this compound," Gage said, his voice hard, flat. "Now you're in Hell too."

I screwed up my nose at his words, at the ridiculousness of them. The promise of them. Because his grip on my arm, his eyes on my body, sure as shit didn't feel like Hell.

It felt like Heaven.

But wasn't that the trick of the Devil? To make someone comfortable in their torment so they couldn't get out before it was too late?

It was only when we crossed from concrete to grass that I

realized Gage wasn't throwing me out of the compound as his face and brutal voice had communicated.

No, we were approaching the building that was off to the side of the garages, with a wide porch and grassed area, flying the same flag as the image on the back of the leather cut I was staring at.

"Where do you think you're taking me?" I demanded, still not struggling.

Why was I not struggling?

Maybe because it would hurt my aching body to do so. Though his face, his voice, and his words were violent, his touch wasn't. He was somehow grasping me hard enough so he could drag me, but not so much as to jerk my sensitive body.

I would not have expected that, a gentleness amongst the violence.

Yes, that's why I'm not struggling, to take care of my body, I lied to myself.

Because even if I was protecting my body by letting him drag me up the steps and into the clubhouse, I sure wasn't protecting my mind.

We entered a large living area that smelled faintly of smoke and spirits, but also tinged with lemon, telling me this was where the bikers partied, but someone cleaned it too.

Evidenced by the freshly vacuumed dark carpet. The relatively nice sofas surrounded a large television. There was a well-stocked but tidy bar off to the corner, some hallways leading to what I guessed were the kitchen and other rooms, and a large door with a sign reading 'Church' atop it.

The space wasn't full of people passed out or half-dressed as I had expected. Instead, there was a beautiful woman on the sofa, smiling at a little girl sitting on the floor and drawing in a book. The woman's emerald eyes went to Gage, then me, and instead of looking shocked by a large and menacing man dragging a woman kind of against her will, she smiled.

"Cade, honey?" she called. "You totally owe me. I *told* you Gage would be next." She had an unusual accent that curled around the words in a way I couldn't place. Or wouldn't have been able to had I not known she was from New Zealand. Because everyone knew about the beautiful Kiwi woman who had caught the most ruthless man in all of Amber and married him.

A man appeared from a hallway, a small child attached to his legs. Another man I'd seen around. And he was a man you *saw*. Because he was big. Tall. Tattooed. Muscled. Long, dark hair. Dark features. One of the most stunningly beautiful men I'd ever seen.

Before Gage, of course.

He was the president of the Sons of Templar.

You weren't a resident of Amber without knowing about Cade Fletcher.

He was notoriously cold and ruthless until his pretty wife had come along.

And now he was slightly less cold and ruthless, as the story went. He was a husband and father who had almost lost everything when someone tried to kill Gwen when she was nine months pregnant. They'd ended up shooting Steg, the previous president, and she'd had to kill the attacker. Before giving birth in this very clubhouse.

With *Cade* as midwife.

As the story went, it was one of the biggest in Amber.

Not just because it was about one of the town's most eligible and dangerous bachelors being taken off the market.

But because the most dangerous outlaw motorcycle club was rumored to almost completely take 'outlaw' out of their identity after the events that almost got this pretty woman killed.

And because it had changed the dangerous and ruthless man in question.

His entire form softened when he glanced from me and Gage to his wife. "Baby, that's not a bet I'm complaining about winnin', considering what I owe you."

Had I not been claimed—wait, did I think *claimed?*—by the man dragging me through the room, the erotic promise in Cade's words would've made me swoon, even though it was directed at another woman, the only woman he saw and would ever see by the looks of it.

But I was already claimed. And I was too busy trying to keep my thoughts in order and my breathing steady.

Gage didn't slow his stride, flying through the room so I could only see the pretty woman wink at me before we were out of the large hall and heading down a slightly dark hallway.

"If you're taking me in here to murder me, you've got too many witnesses," I snapped, covering my unease at the fact that he was taking me somewhere without witnesses. And I wasn't scared about him murdering me.

I was scared about what *I* would do when I didn't have people around me to remind me not to jump him and let him awaken every single one of my forbidden desires.

"If I'm killin' someone, I don't give a fuck about witnesses," he replied, voice cold, calm, and more unnerving than if he would've yelled. "What I do give a fuck about is having witnesses to what I'm going to do to you."

My stomach dipped once more, and I would've stumbled or maybe collapsed altogether with the combination of the dark erotic promise in his words and the pain ricocheting through my body.

But I didn't stumble because his grip tightened, keeping me upright. Then we were inside a room, the door slamming behind us, and his grip missing from my arm. I felt the loss in a way that didn't make sense for a man whose presence I'd been in all of two times, and for someone whose name I'd only just learned.

He paced the room.

I looked around it while he did so, mostly because I didn't know what the heck else to do and I needed to somehow calm my rapid heartbeat and breathing. So I did what I normally did when things started to spiral for me. When the past tried to wrench its way into the present.

I catalogued everything in the here and now.

Everything tangible, everything real, everything solid.

It was a bedroom. I guessed the large clubhouse had a lot of rooms like it, for the members who either didn't have their own homes or needed somewhere to crash after one of their famous parties... or to do something other than sleep.

I pushed away those thoughts, or I tried to, but it was hard to do with the man my body responded to in such a strong and terrifying way. Especially with the fury rippling from him. The brutal fury that didn't scare me like it should have.

It *excited* me.

I gritted my teeth and made myself look at the room.

There was a bed directly in front me. It was a small double, and surprisingly wasn't ruffled and unmade. It was tidied, military corners, dark comforter, nothing fancy but still of good quality. There was a bedside table only on one side. It had a lamp, a battered paperback—that surprised me too, especially when I glimpsed the cover, *The Road* by Cormac McCarthy. To the right of the bed was a closed door that I guessed led to the bathroom.

On the left of me was a large dresser with nothing atop it but a large collection of books spanning the length of the wooden surface, held upright by two bookends shaped like guns.

Other than that, the room was empty. Devoid of personality.

Well, it would've been if not for the bearded biker pacing the room. With him in it, the walls seemed to pulsate, trying to contain his presence.

And my usual routine of stilling those treacherous memories and calming my thoughts didn't work. Calm didn't work with this man around. He killed calm and birthed chaos.

I found myself not wanting to be calm. He was teasing out a part of me that I'd hidden from the world and, more importantly, myself.

The desire to be wild.

"You're callin' off the cop," he hissed, turning to stop and glare at me, as if he sensed that I was going to step forward, say something. Scream. Maybe try and get him to make good on those promises he'd structured as threats.

I blinked, the rapid movement of before and the stillness of now jarring me and my pounding head. "What?"

"The cop," he said through his teeth. "Call. Him. Off."

I folded my arms, mostly to make sure my hardened nipples weren't going to peek through my cotton bra and the linen fabric over it.

Gage's eyes immediately went there, and my nipples throbbed with his hungry gaze. I struggled to find words before I pounced him. "I thought you weren't scared of him arresting you. And I'm sure he's not actually going to, anyway, since I don't think this really constitutes as theft." I gestured out the window, which faced the garage. "Plus, no member of the Sons of Templar has had charges brought against them in roughly thirteen years," I added. "Which means the chances of you getting arrested for technically doing a job connected to your *legitimate* business are pretty slim. Even if Troy wanted to, he couldn't make anything stick."

It was his turn to blink, the desire leaving his eyes as his stare met mine. "How the fuck do you know that?" he demanded, his voice cold. Menacing. Accusing.

I shrugged. Mostly because I needed to do that or I'd flinch in very real fear at the change in the man in front of me.

From Dr. Jekyll to Mr. Hyde.

It wasn't like he was *hiding* the darkness inside of him. One needed only eyes to see there was something inherently wrong with the attractive, muscled, blond-haired, tattooed biker.

But the change at my words was something more than that.

And I needed to not show that it scared me. Because didn't monsters smell fear? Or was that horses?

"I'm a resident of the town," I said, my voice clear. "I'm an employee of the paper. I know things."

He stared at me for a long time, gaze ice, body taut, and hands curled into fists at his sides. The softening of his body, his gaze was barely noticeable, but I saw it. Saw him come to the conclusion that I was not some kind of spy sent in to bring them down.

Which he really only needed eyes to figure out.

Sure, spies didn't *look* like spies. But people with that much darkness and menace inside of them had a way of recognizing it in others. And to be a spy, I'd have to be cold, calculating and a killer.

None of which I was.

All of which he was.

And yet I wasn't running screaming from the compound.

Or at the very least briskly walking.

I was standing right there, in front of the man who looked like he might either kill me or kiss me.

And the logical Lauren who had ran the show for almost a decade was yelling at me that both options were unacceptable and I needed to get the heck out of there.

Like yesterday.

But that Lauren wasn't in control.

The biker named Gage was.

And he was looking at me with slightly less murder in his eyes at that point.

"Well you obviously don't know important shit," Gage clipped. "Like the fact that I'm not talkin' about a bullshit arrest I couldn't give two fucks about." He narrowed his eyes, still cold but hot with something else. "Talkin' about how the cop wants a piece of you. You're callin' it off right now. Unless you want me to do it for you." He grinned, and it wasn't a warm smile. No, it sent actual shivers down my spine to match the ice inside of it. "And you don't want me to do it for you."

My stomach dipped, but then my back straightened as I struggled to not let him affect me. "Troy does not 'want a piece of me,' as you so eloquently put it," I snapped, my backbone stronger than I had ever thought possible. "We went to high school together. He's a nice guy. He's looking out for me."

Gage folded his arms, and I failed not to notice the way his tee strained as he did so. The way the fabric clung to his arms. I found myself wishing those arms weren't covered by the long-sleeved tee so I could feast my eyes on them. Imagine them wrapped around me.

"You're not naive." His rough tenor jerked me out of my perusal of his arms. "Or innocent. As you made sure to tell me and my fuckin' cock not five minutes ago," he growled.

Another stomach dip, a much, much more intense one at the mention of his *cock*. I struggled to keep my eyes level with his stare. To keep my mind from going to what it would feel like inside me.

Too late.

My panties were soaked.

And I was obviously certifiably insane.

Maybe the crash had knocked something loose. Unhinged me.

But I thought back to a drawer in my closet. What I'd hidden in that drawer, stuffed out of sight, like I did with the thoughts that were harassing me right then. The desires I pretended I didn't have.

"So you're not convincin' me that you don't know he doesn't want in there," Gage continued, his voice thick. Rough. Full of sex. As if he could taste it in the air. His eyes roamed over every inch of me like a brutal and physical caress. Then they stopped pointedly on my hips before meeting my eyes. "And he's not getting in there." There was a promise in his voice, a concrete and certain one.

"And why is it that you think you have any say on who gets in where?" I demanded, my hackles rising on principle. I let my anger take the reins. It was rather welcome. Yeah, Gage was hot. Actually he was something else entirely. Just like whatever it was between us.

Inexplicable.

Impossible.

But that didn't change the fact that he'd known me less than twenty-four hours. So he didn't get to stare at my crotch—that was staring at him pretty freaking hard—like he owned it and then speak like he owned it too.

No matter how much I *wanted* him to own it.

That was not how I was going to let it go.

He wasn't going to own *me*.

He stepped forward.

I stepped back.

Because no matter what I wanted from the man, I wasn't ready for the promise in his eyes as he approached me.

"You know why," he purred, taking another step forward.

I took another step back and my back hit the hard wood of the door.

Just when I thought he'd cage me in with his arms, he stopped, eyes seeming to turn pure black. "You know there's only one man who's getting into that pussy that I'm guessin' is sweet as honey and as greedy as my cock," he murmured, his voice gravel, a freaking siren song to the pulsating need between my thighs.

My heart beat in my throat and my knees at the same time. I had never in my not-so-experienced sexual life had *anyone* talk like that to me. Not even when they were *inside* me. I didn't like dirty talk; I much preferred to seek out my orgasm in silence.

And I chose my men in regards to that preference. Sensible. Well dressed. Pleasing to look at. But safe.

Turned out I did like dirty talk.

It just had to come from the right man.

Or the so very *wrong* one.

"You can't speak to me like that," I breathed, my words a limp protest.

"Can speak to my woman however the fuck I want," he challenged. "However the fuck she wants me to."

He leaned forward and I couldn't stop myself from inhaling. He smelled of smoke, of soap, and of a scent that was so purely male, so purely *him*, I would've breathed it in my whole life if I could.

"And I know you want me to speak to you exactly like that. Can see it in your eyes." He paused, letting the words sink in. "I can fucking *taste* it in the air."

"I'm *not* your woman," I lied fiercely, clutching onto the last of my control. The last of my fight. Because I knew I was somehow his. Like in all those stupid movies and books I'd scoffed at, sure those things didn't happen in real life.

I wasn't entirely sure I *was* in real life.

In the real world.

Or maybe I hadn't been.

Until now.

Gage's face was granite. "You are. You know it. And I'm not doing this shit. Shit I've seen five times over, my brothers fighting

for bullshit reasons, running around wasting time with battles."
He narrowed his eyes. "I'm not afraid of a fight, or a battle. And
I'll fight for you, make no doubt about it. But there's gonna be
none of that shit. You're agreeing right now that this is somethin'
between us. That you're my woman."

His words curled around me, cutting at my skin. Because
they weren't gentle, tender, romantic. No, they were harsh, sharp,
almost ugly in their delivery. And that's how I knew they
were true.

Because if it wasn't ugly, it wasn't the truth.

Still, I was going to argue it. But of course he wasn't going to
let me.

"Now, you're gonna walk your ass out the door and get in the
car with the fuckin' pig—the very last time you're in an enclosed
space with an asshole who wants what's mine," he rasped, stepping forward so our bodies almost brushed.

Almost.

He caught himself just before that happened.

"You can educate him on how to back the fuck off. Maybe use
the numbers you're so fond of. Like how 100 percent of the men
who look at you the way he does die if they do it more than once,"
he continued.

I blinked. "You're not going to kill a police officer for looking
at me," I whispered. "You don't even *know* me."

"I know enough," he clipped. "I know you'd risk your life to
swerve for a fucking *dog* in the middle of the night. I know that
instead of sitting in the car and waiting for someone to help you,
you get yourself out of that car and prepare yourself to walk six
fucking miles, possibly battling a concussion and a hefty amount
of pain." His eyes flickered over me, as if he was cataloguing every
inch of that pain. And not just my visible bruises. "Then you
fuckin' sass the biker who corners you on an abandoned highway,
despite being vulnerable as fuck. You sure don't fucking *act*

vulnerable. You got on the back of my bike, even though you knew what I was."

He gave me a look as I opened my mouth, as if he knew I was going to protest his point. My mouth snapped closed.

"And you fuckin' *knew* the man I was, 'cause you know statistics about fuckin' helmets. You know about a motorcycle club on your doorstep," he said, showing me he saw a lot, saw me. "Then, knowin' all that, you could've let the cop handle shit for you. You didn't. You came here. Got in my face. Threatened to have me arrested. And I've buried a fuck of a lot of people for doin' a lot less."

I knew his words weren't an exaggeration to make a point. No, there was that ugliness injected in them which only came with the truth.

I swallowed razors. "Are you going to bury me?" I asked, voice low and timid. I hated it.

He smiled. And it was unnerving, because it wasn't a smile that came from happiness. The way his face moved with the expression, the hardness in his eyes told me it had been a long time since he'd smiled in happiness.

"No, but you know that already. But what you don't know is what I'll do for you already. Not knowin' everything, but knowing *enough*. And you don't know near enough about me, so here's something. I won't hesitate to put another person in the ground, whether they wear a uniform or not, whether this club walks on the right side of the law or not. Because that's the kind of man I am. And it's not good. But you knew that before your ass was on the back of my bike last night. And you got on anyway. You had a choice then. You don't have one now."

He stepped back, and I let out the rush of breath I didn't realize I was holding. He watched me exhale, his eyes hard, his body taut.

"So you get in the car with the cop. Let him down hard, or

easy, your choice. Because both ways end with him breathing. But you need to get the fuck out of here right now before I change my mind and do it my way." There was a long pause as his eyes devoured me, my body shaking under the gaze. "And my way is fucking you right here, right now." His fists clenched at his sides as if he was holding himself in place with great effort. "But you're hurt. That's what's stoppin' me from doing that. From taking you wherever you want to go in the way you'll be goin' once you heal. That's on the back of my bike."

I didn't move.

It seemed like I didn't *breathe*.

That was a lot of information to take in at one moment.

In one freaking lifetime.

Especially mine.

Because I'd crafted my life so I knew what awaited me around every corner. Planned my life that way. It *needed* to be that way. I didn't have many friends, but that was okay, because it meant I had more control over my life.

That meant I worked. Diligently. Efficiently. And then I went home. Read. Spent time in my studio. Cooked—something healthy and nutritious, of course—watched something on television—something informative and educated, of course—took myself out for dinner now and again, on a special occasion, obviously.

I went to the yoga class the little studio two doors down had on Sundays. Had a coffee afterward with one of the couple of women I was friendly enough to have Sunday morning coffee with. Then I'd get a pedicure. Every Sunday. Clean the house. Do a face mask. Exfoliate. Pamper myself.

Called my parents.

I did that every Sunday too. No matter how much it hurt. And it hurt so much that it was why my entire Sunday was spent being kind to myself, treating myself, because I knew what pain awaited me at night.

And then it was Monday and the routine started all over again.

No surprises.

Certainly no bikers talking about how I was 'on the back of their bike' like it meant something. Not before telling me they were willing to kill for me—after knowing me less than twenty-four hours and barely speaking to me—that they wanted to *fuck* me, and that I was *theirs*.

Certainly no *Gage*. The purest and most sinful antithesis of the order and safety of my life.

"You're not movin'," he hissed, my back still pressed against the door.

"Your name isn't Gage," I said instead of responding to that, or moving from the door.

He froze. Literally froze. Something cold and evil moved across his features like it had when he'd thought I was a spy. When he'd thought I'd known too much.

And I had a feeling that no one knew too much about Gage.

Because he buried the ones who did.

"How the fuck do you think you know that?" he demanded.

I blinked. "Because you're not a Gage. That's not a real name."

He stepped forward. "It's *my* fuckin' name. I look real to you?" he asked, his eyes never letting mine out of the shackles of his stare. And then he moved forward, kicking at my heels so my legs were splayed and he could press his iron body to my quivering one. So one very particular hard thing pressed against my stomach.

"I *feel* real to you?" he rasped, his lips almost against my mouth.

Every part of my body, every freaking cell cried out for him to kiss me. To do a lot more than kiss me. To soothe the ache between my legs that was more persistent and desperate than any of the pain in my body.

But he didn't.

He yanked my hips forward, moving me around with enough speed to jostle my aching brain in my skull. I was set on the floor, my back no longer against the door.

And I was facing the door.

"I'm fuckin' real, baby, and you're gonna find yourself wishin' I wasn't," Gage said, his entire body wired.

And then the door opened.

Slammed closed.

And I was left standing in the middle of the room, knees jelly, brain much the same.

FOUR

I didn't see him for two days.

Forty-six hours, to be a little more exact.

And yes, I'd counted. Through the work I'd forced myself to do—at home, per Niles's order—through the books I'd forced myself to read, the chores I'd made myself do, I'd thought of him.

Of the words he'd hurled at me. About us. About me being his. I mulled over the way he'd held his body, the way he'd structured his expression. As if it was painful to admit such things.

As if it was beyond his control.

But it wasn't. *He* was the one who chose to tow my car. *He* was the one to stop in the first place. Then *he* was the one to drag me into that room, stare at me the way he did. Say those words.

He didn't *have* to do any of it.

But neither did I.

I didn't *have* to go to the compound; I could've sacrificed my pride and let Troy handle it. I didn't *have* to get up in his face like I did—like I'd never done before—nor did I *have* to let him drag me into the clubhouse.

Because he would've let me go if I'd struggled. I somehow

knew that. Just like I inexplicably knew that he'd *wanted* me to struggle.

Because it was beyond his control.

Whatever it was yanking us together.

Again, it was the thing I'd scoffed at in every book and movie about romance. About two people being drawn to each other without logical explanation. *Everything* worked within logic, even love. It was pheromones, hormones, family ties, shared morals, shared interests.

For all the romance and 'magic' surrounding the sought-after emotion, it could be easily explained within the realms of logic.

But I was a fool to think logic could explain *this*.

Why my mind had been unwilling to let him go since he'd stormed out of that room. Why I'd gotten less than eight hours of sleep in two nights because the darkness was full of his shadow.

Of my own shadowed desires.

And it was why I lost the ability to breathe the second I opened my door forty-six hours after he'd stormed out of that room in the clubhouse.

Because he was standing there.

At my door.

Taking up every inch of it.

My eyes roamed up his body hungrily. Took in his faded jeans, his long black tee molded against the abs underneath it. The worn leather of his cut. The art covering the small amount of muscled skin on show. The beard hiding his jaw. The eyes that burned into my very core. The pure *air* around him pulsated with his presence.

And he was a total presence. Something that hit you physically. Painfully.

I let out a breath it seemed I'd been holding for forty-six hours.

I expected him to speak. Because a man who looked like that, a man who commanded the freaking air, who commanded the freaking *oxygen* I breathed, who threatened—no, promised to kill police officers, who turned up at a woman's door at eight o'clock in the morning, they did it because they had something to say.

But he didn't speak.

Not one word.

Neither did I.

I just stood there.

Like an idiot.

Staring at him.

To be fair, he was doing the same. Hence the reason I was having trouble staying upright, let alone forming words. Because his stare was like everything else about him: unyielding, destructive, unforgiving.

In these two days, I'd convinced myself that I'd imagined it. The power he had over me. What he'd roused in me. Because safe in my ordered apartment, in my ordered lifestyle, the memories could only have been a fabrication. When I took them out of the environment, out of Gage's environment and into mine, where logic ruled, it was impossible for a *man* to have that effect over me.

Or maybe it wasn't.

I reasoned that it might not be impossible for that particular man to have that effect over any living, breathing, hot-blooded woman. Or man, for that matter.

But it couldn't be reasoned why a man like Gage—who was not a biker version of a Greek god, unless you were talking about Hades—would be looking at me like he was right freaking now.

With pure, unadulterated desire.

Me.

No man looked at *me* like that. Especially not a man like Gage.

As mentioned before, I wasn't ugly. I was trim and fit because

I ate well and exercised slightly over the recommended amount for a woman my age. I took care of my skin, so it was smooth, blemishless, and lineless. Pale to the point of alabaster because sun protection was key.

Skin cancer killed almost ten thousand people per year.

I moisturized.

I went to the salon every eight weeks, had my mousy brunette hair touched up with some subtle honey highlights, got the ends trimmed, and light layers added to frame my face. But not too much, because I liked my hair long. Even if I rarely wore it down.

That day I had only just managed to carefully cover the fading bruise underneath my eye with an amount of concealer I'd never used, nor really needed. And since I hadn't used so much in the past, I'd taken longer to do my makeup than I allotted in my morning routine. Usually it was a dab of concealer, a swipe of blush—which I didn't even rightly need because my face flushed on its own. Filled in my eyebrows, which I didn't strictly need either, since they were full and dark and the perfect shape—not coming from me, but from the many beauticians I'd seen to get them shaped. A simple blending of eyeshadows, light because anything else made me look like a skunk. I'd perfected my 'usual' thanks to YouTube makeup tutorials. I itched to go wild and glam like the women—and men—in the tutorials did, yearning to let myself jump out of my carefully structured box.

But I never did.

So that day was no exception, even with more concealer than normal. I had mascara and a pale pink lip gloss but nothing else.

It was the ultimate 'no makeup' look.

But since it had taken longer, I hadn't yanked my hair up into the tight bun it was usually in for work. It was still tumbling in soft waves around my exposed shoulders.

I had yet to put a cardigan over the sleeveless blouse I'd tucked into my pale pink pencil skirt. It was modest, dipped only slightly at my chest, but not enough to show any of my cleavage, and was only a slightly darker shade of pink than my pencil skirt —which fit me well, but ended below my knees.

I was barefoot, my sensibly heeled pumps waiting for me in their spot in my closet, high enough to be flattering on my slim and short figure, but not enough to be uncomfortable.

It was my usual. And it was safe. Bordering on boring. I wasn't the girl next door. I was the girl who lived *way* down the road from her. The one men *might* pause their glance on, but not fricking *feast* their gaze on me like Gage.

My knees trembled at the way his eyes moved up, down, up again. He focused on my hair for the longest time, his hands shaking at his sides as if he was holding himself back from touching my tousled strands.

And then his gaze moved down again. Stuttered on my chest area, as if there was something to see there. As if I wasn't wearing a sensible cotton bra and he could see my nipples underneath the thin silk of my blouse.

Then his eyes moved farther down.

All the way to my brightly painted toes.

It was my one treat on my Sunday pedicure. Everything else in my wardrobe was muted, and the colors on my fingers were either a soft beige or a blush pink. But I always went crazy with my toes. Glitters. Neons. That week it was Barbie pink with little silver crystals on my big toes.

I was equally glad and embarrassed at my strict habit of going to get a pedicure every week. Glad because Gage was staring at my feet with a concentrated intensity. And though I didn't particularly like people looking at my feet—who did?—they were nice feet. Because of my weekly pedicures.

But I was embarrassed because a muscled, murderous, hotter-than-sin outlaw biker was currently staring at my hot pink, bedazzled toes.

And then he was staring at my mouth.

With a different kind of intensity.

One that had my inner thighs throbbing.

But still, he didn't speak.

"How do you know where I live?" I squeaked.

Yes, *squeaked.*

Like a mouse suddenly discovering it had vocal cords.

Mental forehead slap.

He folded his arms. "It's Amber. I'm me. Not fuckin' hard," he clipped, his voice full of anger, as if it was my fault that I was talking to him, as if he wasn't the one knocking on my door, forcing this conversation.

I blinked. Slowly. His voice was hard. Flat. But it was also raspy. Rough. Chiseled from smoking too many cigarettes throughout the years. That shouldn't have pleased me. Cigarettes killed almost half a million Americans every year, and the deaths weren't pretty.

The thought of Gage succumbing to a death like that had me tasting bile.

So no, I didn't like that he smoked.

But I liked the way it had deepened his manly rasp. The way it clung to his pores and mingled perfectly with his natural scent to create a cologne Armani would likely kill for.

But still.

"You shouldn't smoke," I said, surprising myself. Because I should've asked him what he was doing on my doorstep at eight in the morning. Or started the very well-rehearsed and efficient speech I'd drafted in case I encountered him again and he was still under the impression that we were *something.*

But I didn't do those things.

I said what I said because no matter what I loved about his smoky scent and voice, I did not love any single thing about something that increased his risk of dying early.

And from what I knew about the Sons of Templar MC, that risk was already pretty freaking high.

Gage's expression cleared completely, eyes wide in total surprise for a split second. Then he recovered. Of course he recovered.

"How the fuck do you know I smoke?" he demanded.

"I'm me, not freaking hard," I shot back, not resisting my urge to smile.

Something in his jaw ticked, the corner of his granite mouth turning up. "*Fuck*," he said, the curse somehow like ambrosia in the air coming from him.

I blinked again. "What?"

He stepped forward, slightly in my door but not in my space. That didn't mean my body didn't respond to his complete nearness.

It did.

Dramatically.

"The word you're lookin' for, baby, when you're cute as fuck and tryin' to mimic me but fallin' short when you can't even mutter the word 'fuck' from your sweet-as-shit lips," he said, eyes on the lips he'd just called 'sweet as shit.'

I struggled to keep my wits about me. He was making it hard as crap. "I don't need to curse to make my point," I said, hating that my voice betrayed exactly what he was doing to me. I sucked in a deep breath. "You shouldn't smoke. It's bad for you."

He leaned back, face hardening once more. "Do a lot of things that are bad for me," he replied. "Smokin' is just one thing on the list. Very near the fuckin' bottom. What's on the top is me standing right where I am now."

I screwed up my nose. "You standing on my doorstep is worse than you sucking on a death stick that boasts tar and carbon monoxide in its ingredient deck?" I clarified.

There was the mouth twitch again. "Yeah, baby. In my world,

there's something much fuckin' worse than suckin' on poison." His eyes were on my lips. "And that's tastin' something sweet."

His words struck me. Bodily. Struck me mute. But even his threats, his comments about violence and murder, hadn't made me mute. It was the way he talked about me being sweet. Like it was a bad thing, but a good thing too. Because his words, the low rasp of his voice, his gaze—they all told me that he was interested in me.

Me.

Luckily I didn't have to scramble a response, as he folded his arms across his chest. He was wearing a long henley because there was still a crisp chill to the air considering it was early October; even in California, the weather was turning slightly.

And he'd likely ridden on his bike.

"You gonna keep starin' at me, or you gonna get your shit together?" he asked, his voice hard but somehow amused at the same time.

My eyes jerked upward from where they'd been inspecting his pecs, wondering if they were as hard as they looked. And then wondering what they looked like without the shirt, if his entire body was coated in tattoos like his visible skin seemed to portray.

"My shit together?" I repeated, thinking that pretty much my whole life since that day almost a decade before was centered, almost violently focused on having 'my shit together.' I had excelled at that for nine years.

Apart from the past week.

Well, the past four days, to be exact.

Since this man came into my life.

My life since then did not have its shit together.

Or more accurately, *I* did not have my shit together.

How did he expect me to get it together with him standing right there? I wouldn't be able to get back to my carefully ordered life unless he was far, far away. And even then, the ghost of his presence was forceful enough to blow me off-kilter for the past two days.

"Yeah, babe." He looked pointedly at my toes. "Unless you're plannin' on going to work barefoot. And I'm guessin' you don't plan on that." His eyes went to my exposed arms. "And you're gonna need to cover up. It's chilly. Colder on the bike."

I was about to tell him exactly what I thought of his command to 'cover up' considering I was an independent woman, and I was barely showing anything but my arms. But the words that followed stopped me. And I forced myself to ignore the comment about it being chilly and the underlying sentiment that he didn't want *me* to be chilly.

"On the bike?" I parroted, painfully aware of the fact that I wasn't really speaking, more like echoing his words without the smoky, firm and very masculine tone.

He nodded once, jerking his head backward, and it was then that I looked behind him—such a thing only possible if I went up on my toes.

His bike was indeed on the curb behind him, which shouldn't have been a surprise because there was no parking on the curb in front of the gallery.

But what was a surprise was the helmet resting on the seat.

"You got a helmet."

He shook his head. "Nah, babe, *you've* got a helmet."

I stared at him. "I got a helmet."

Lauren! Stop repeating words he's already said and say something original so he doesn't go back to thinking you're brain damaged after the crash.

"I don't need a helmet. I don't have a motorcycle."

Great one. Just great. Stating the absolute obvious.

"But I do," Gage said, the corner of his mouth twitching as if he could hear my internal monologue. "And I meant what I said two days ago. Your ass is on the back of my bike from now on." His eyes flickered over me, as if searching for something. They settled on the spot on my face where I'd covered my fading bruises.

"You still sore, Will?" he asked, leaning forward, brushing his thumb over the area with the gentleness of a feather. Something I would've thought impossible, such a soft touch from a man who was not just full of hard edges, but *was* a hard edge.

"I really need to stop thinking everything is impossible. Because there's no impossible with you."

His hand paused and his eyes turned liquid.

I froze.

I'd said that out loud.

Holy freaking heck, *I'd said that out loud.*

Maybe I really did need to get my head checked.

"I mean no, I'm not sore," I said. "Well, a little, but that's normal in the days following the trauma a body goes through after a car accident. I was actually probably lucky the airbag didn't deploy, because my healing likely would've been much slower," I babbled, trying to cover up the words I'd previously spoken with sheer volume of nonsense. "At my low speed and lack of impact against anything solid, the airbag would've done more harm than good. It can cause temporary blindness, or permanent in some cases. Broken bones in the chest area, damage to the soft tissue. Broken bones in the face, the nose most common. And then there're the more serious neck and back and brain injuries."

Are you sure you don't have one?

I said all of that without taking a breath, which would've been nearly impossible regardless with the concrete that was Gage's gaze. Plus, his fingers were still brushing my face, the touch gentle, or it had been. Now it was heavier than his stare.

There was a long, painful silence after my words, mostly

filled with me sucking in an audible breath. Bad idea since I inhaled even more of his scent.

Maybe it had some kind of intoxicating quality.

Maybe *he* was just a totally intoxicating quality.

His hand was no longer on my face, having moved it the second his expression changed back to that vague and dangerous amusement.

"Well, since you're not blind and you don't have a broken nose—which I'm glad as fuck about, by the way—I'd say you're gonna be okay on the bike now," he said.

I gaped at him. "You want me on the bike?"

His eyes moved again. "Thought I made that pretty clear, babe."

The way he said that told me he didn't just mean today.

But I had to focus on today. Because that was all I had. Focusing on tomorrow was giving in to anxiety. Just like focusing on yesterdays—and the terrible yesterdays long before—was giving in to depression.

"I'm not getting on the bike," I said, my voice sharp and strong. Because there was no way I could get on that bike. No way I could press my body against his. Imprint his scent onto my pores. I'd be well and truly lost then. My shit would *never* come back together.

"You are," he replied, voice much sharper and stronger than my own.

That peeved me off. I folded my arms, but I didn't get the same effect as he did, though I did unintentionally push my breasts upward and cause my modest top to become not-so-modest.

Gage's eyes went there immediately and my entire body flushed.

"I've got to go to work," I said through clenched teeth, both from anger and from trying to fight the desire he awakened within me.

"That's why you're getting on the bike," he clipped, obviously getting impatient with someone not doing as he commanded. He looked like he might murder someone who told him no.

Murder was a pretty good motivation to say yes.

"You're trying to tell me that you're here at eight in the morning to take me to work on your motorcycle?" I surmised in shock.

He nodded once. "Figured you wouldn't be workin' yesterday considerin' fuckin' breathing seemed to hurt you, and I would've made sure your ass came home if that wasn't the case."

I blinked. "You would've made sure?" I repeated, not caring that I was parroting once more.

Another nod.

"And how would you have known I wasn't at work?"

"Told you, babe. This is Amber. I'm me. I'd know," he said. As if that was a satisfactory answer.

It was not.

"Okay, aside from the fact that that isn't an answer, you also don't have the right to make sure my ass is anywhere."

On the mention of my ass, his eyes darkened again and he stepped forward, fully inside my doorway.

I should've stepped back.

But I didn't.

I was hungry for his presence, the warmth that directly contradicted the icy resolve in his gaze.

"Oh, baby, you and I both know I have the fuckin' *biblical* right to say exactly where your ass is goin' to be. Where it should be right now. Which is on the back of my fuckin' bike. And it'll be over my fuckin' knee if you stand here arguing with me, wastin' both our time and not getting your shit together so you can get to work," he rasped, his voice pure sex.

He was talking about spanking me.

Spanking.

And my entire body responded to that prospect.

Biblically.

His entire body hardened, the cords of his neck standing out as if he was holding himself back. Then very slowly, purposefully, he took a step back. A big one. And it looked like his motorcycle boots weighed a hundred pounds as he did so. Like he was forcing himself backward.

And I just watched him, craving the promise of being across his knee. Of his hand coming down on me.

I shook myself—mentally, of course. Gage already thought I was crazy, so he might've had me committed if I did it physically.

"You don't need to drive me to work," I said, speaking slowly and making sure I didn't say anything stupid or embarrassing. Or something stupid *and* embarrassing. "It's less than two miles away. I can walk."

He narrowed his eyes. "You're not walkin'."

I narrowed my own. "Oh really? Is that your decision to make?"

"Yep" was all he said.

Yep.

"I disagree," I said through my teeth.

"You don't have a fuckin' car," he said. "And you were in an accident two days ago. Not serious, but also not minor. You're hurt. Not as bad as you were two days ago, but you're still hurtin'. I can't change that, but I can make it so you're not walkin' when you don't need to. Which is, unless I'm beside you, never." There was a heavy pause. "So for the foreseeable future, you don't go anywhere unless it's on the back of my bike. Until your car is fixed. Which is gonna be a week at the most, since I'm the one workin' on it and I'm the best. Even then, you need to go somewhere and I'm free—and I'll be free for you—it's on the back of my bike."

I blinked.

There were a lot of things wrong with that statement.

And worse, there were a lot of those wrong things that I freaking *liked.*

"We don't have time for this shit," he clipped, voice near feral. "You're gonna be late to work if you keep starin' at me like that." He paused, his hands turning to fists. "You're not even gonna make it to work, in fact."

Work? Who cared about work? Who cared about anything but those large, fisted, and tattooed hands opening up and coming down hard on my bare flesh?

"Lauren," he hissed between his teeth, "get your ass upstairs and get ready for work before I lose fuckin' control. You can't handle that right now."

The danger, the menace in his words had me moving, turning, and literally running up my stairs despite the fact that I was still aching. Nowhere ached as bad as the spot between my legs.

I stopped halfway up the stairs, the doorway still in my eye line. Gage still in my eye line. He hadn't moved a muscle, his entire form like a statue, his muscles bulging around the fabric of his shirt.

"Um, do you want to come in?" I asked, feeling strange about leaving him on the doorstep.

It wasn't good hospitality.

"No fuckin' way," he bit out through his teeth.

I didn't move, because his words were rough and harsh, and the way he said them didn't communicate that he really didn't want to come upstairs. It was that he really freaking *did.*

"Ass up the stairs, Lauren," he demanded, his words slow and heavy.

"O-okay," I breathed.

Then I turned and got my ass up the stairs.

I flattened myself against the wall in my kitchen once I was out of sight.

Took one breath.

Then another since the first one was shaky and shallow.

And then I recovered. Went to the kitchen, reached up to where I kept my coffeepot—strictly for guests I rarely had—did everything I needed to get it brewing, and then I went to quickly get the rest of myself ready.

Facing the mirror, I barely recognized who was staring back at me. My eyes, big and even bigger when magnified by my glasses, were almost glowing. Buzzing. More alive than I'd ever seen them. My cheeks were flushed a soft pink, lips seemingly swollen though they hadn't been kissed.

I touched them, thinking about Gage's lips on them. I had the distinct certainty that he would not be gentle. Tender. That my lips would be a lot more swollen than they were right then. That they would hurt from the force of his own.

And that excited me more.

"Get it together, Lauren," I whispered to my reflection.

Gage was downstairs, waiting for me so he could take me to work on his motorcycle. And I couldn't change that. He wasn't going to let me change that.

I didn't freaking *want* to.

So I quickly braided my hair into a single low plait, thinking about the helmet he'd pointed to. There was no way to really avoid helmet head—not that I'd ever had it, it was just an educated guess—but I hoped the short ride wouldn't do too much damage.

The smell of coffee filtered into my small bathroom at the end of my living room. It had a high window that was slightly frosted for privacy, but still gave a glimpse of the ocean and the horizon beyond. A vintage claw-footed tub took up a lot of the space. I'd had to knock down a wall that had once been a utility closet in order to get a shower cubicle put in. Not necessary, since I could've just replaced the bath with a shower, but I loved baths.

Evidenced by my huge collection of bath salts, bath bombs, and candles surrounding the small shelves around the tub.

My sink was also an extravagance I didn't need but loved regardless.

The surface was reclaimed driftwood that my dad had shaped and polished so it worked as a sort of countertop with matte-black legs and shelving underneath. It ran longer on the right side, where I had fresh flowers and an array of my modest cosmetics collection on a silver tray.

The sink was polished gray ceramic, set above the counter like a mini tub with a white tile backsplash that melded into the painted white brick of the wall. Mounted on which was my antique mirror. Dad had polished that for me too.

I took one more look in the mirror, then rushed to the kitchen.

It took me two seconds to pour the coffee, run down the stairs —carefully so as not to spill the hot liquid—and thrust a mug at Gage, who was leaning against my doorframe.

And he could *lean*.

His long legs were encased in black jeans, which were tucked into black combat boots crossed over each other.

His arms were folded over his chest, over his cut.

But then they were outstretched, taking the coffee I darn near threw at him in the midst of my drooling.

"Coffee," I explained, as if the black liquid in the mug needed explaining. "I didn't put in cream or sugar, because I suppose such condiments might totally wreck your street cred and you'll get kicked out of the club and then have to get a job at Best Buy and scare all the customers so bad the entire store will shut down, and I can't be responsible for that," I blurted, uneasy with his entire presence and my reaction to him freaking leaning.

He stared at me.

Then at the coffee.

Then he threw his head back.

And *laughed.*

I had been worried about my reaction to him leaning. It was nothing compared to watching him laugh. Really laugh. Something I sensed didn't happen often. Because those eyes, or more accurately what was behind those eyes, didn't let him. So it was something else entirely, watching the man in front of me laugh.

Beautiful because it didn't happen often.

Painful because it didn't happen often.

When he stopped, I was still staring at him in absolute wonder.

His eyes were light as his gaze went to where my hair was tucked over my shoulder. He leaned forward, grasping the bottom of my braid between his thumb and forefinger.

"You've officially saved the local Best Buy, baby," he murmured. "And the local biker club. So how about you get that ass up the stairs again and finish gettin' your shit before I make good on that promise of you not gettin' to work at all." He gave me a meaningful look that would've drenched my panties had they not already been soaked. "For the next week."

I swallowed. Hard.

I was tempted to tell him I'd quit my freaking job if it meant I could see his eyes easy and light like that, watch him laugh. But of course I didn't. I wasn't that far gone.

Yet.

So I went upstairs, once more ignoring the persistent ache in my body at making the trek that pushed my muscles to the edge.

I pulled my cardigan on, my hands shaking as I did up the buttons. Checked that I had everything in my purse. Swiped on some more lip gloss. Took three deep breaths. Checked that I had turned all appliances and lights off.

Even in my fluster, that was one thing I would never forget to do. It wasn't full-on OCD—I'd been checked for that—just another part of my need to make sure everything was orderly. That there was less of a chance of anything else in my life being destroyed. I was terrified of leaving the wrong switch on, forgetting to turn off the stove and coming home to see my entire sanctuary in flames.

Once I was satisfied, I made it to the bottom of the stairs, my purse on my shoulder and my muscles screaming at me for not treating them with the care they required.

I held out my hand to Gage. "Give me one second. I'll take the coffee cup upstairs. Then we'll go." I narrowed my eyes at him. "But this isn't me giving in, just so we're clear. This is me being professional and caring about my job. I'm not going to be late because I have to argue with you on my doorstep. It is *not* the beginning of a habit." I was pretty sure I was saying that to myself as much as to him.

Gage didn't speak, merely pushed off the door, staring at me.

I struggled not to squirm under his gaze.

"I got the mug, babe," he said finally.

I frowned, both loving and hating the idea of him being in my apartment. He would imprint his presence. I'd never be able to forget that he'd been there, even if it was the only time.

"I thought you had some strong reservations toward entering my home," I said, not moving to let him pass.

"I had some strong reservations toward entering your home with you inside it and the number of surfaces available for me to fuck you on," he growled. "So that's why you're gonna stay the fuck at the bottom of the stairs, because you've been comin' up and down too much as it is. You're hurtin'. Don't want you hurtin' more just because you want to take up my coffee cup. So I got the mug, babe."

My stomach was little more than jelly at his words.

"The number of surfaces available for me to fuck you on."

I had stepped aside before I actually realized I did so. And I realized right around the time his body brushed past mine, my nipples standing at attention underneath my cotton bra.

He grasped my chin, lifting my face to meet his gaze. "And you're already doin' enough in your fuckin' sexy-as-shit librarian outfit you've got going on to make me seriously consider hiking up that fucking skirt and taking you against the wall," he rasped. "Only thing stoppin' me is the prospect of you hurtin' more, and not in the way I'm gonna hurt you when I do finally sink into that sweet pussy. So how about you wait outside so I don't forget that by the time I come downstairs?"

He kept his grasp on my chin as I blinked at him, my eyes lazy, my entire body humming.

"Okay," I whispered.

He nodded once, eyes on my lips. There was a pause, one I was sure would be followed by a kiss.

And I was sure that would be followed by him hiking up my skirt and fucking me against the wall.

And I would let him.

But then he let me go, and all I saw was the patch on the back of his cut staring at me in accusation. As if the fabric knew I didn't belong there. That I wasn't made for the man inside that cut.

Or maybe you are. Maybe that's why it's staring at you, a voice whispered. *Because it sees all those dark and depraved thoughts you've hidden in the shadows of your mind.*

I shook my head, physically that time because Gage was out of sight.

Then I stepped into the fresh and salty air, needing something to clear my head, to cool my body. To calm my heart.

I stared at the bike on the curb in front of me.

All black. Chrome detailing—I'd looked it up.

A Harley. Obviously.

There were two saddlebags on either side at the back of it.

A replica of the Sons of Templar patch was painted onto the fuel tank, a grim reaper bearing a sword, riding on a road of skulls.

It shouldn't have been beautiful. It should've been ugly and unnerving. But whoever painted the image was talented. It seemed to jump off the bike itself, staring at me with almost the same intensity as the owner of the bike.

"Keys."

I jumped at the voice, at the closeness of it. Breath was hot on my neck, the entire back of my body electrified with the presence behind me.

Turning, I found Gage in my space. Way up in it. His eyes wild.

I didn't speak.

"Keys," he repeated, palm outstretched.

I looked down at it.

Keys. For my apartment.

"Right," I whispered, rummaging in my purse for the keys I'd remembered to take with me but forgotten I'd needed.

I placed them in his palm on instinct, forgetting that I was very capable of crossing the short distance to my front door and locking it myself.

He gave me his back before I could tell him as much.

And then I stared at that back. The knot of hair fastened into a messy bun at the nape of his skull. His wide shoulders that seemed like they could carry anything.

Like the world.

His muscled back, covered by that faded leather cut.

Perfect ass in his worn-in jeans. My fingernails bit into my palms as I clenched them into fists thinking about looking at all that without clothes on. About my nails raking down the bare muscled skin.

Lauren. Stop objectifying the biker, a voice inside me hissed. *You don't like it when men do that to women, and you don't do double standards.*

Extremely logical. I did find it annoying when women objectified men, like they didn't know what it felt like themselves. Then again, men had been doing it for thousands of years, so maybe turnabout was fair play.

And this change of heart had everything to do with the biker striding toward me after locking up my apartment, twirling my keys on his fingers.

His steps were long, fluid, purposeful.

Freaking hell, even the way he *walked* turned me on.

He held out my keys.

I robotically took them, putting them in my purse.

"No alarm," he said, eyes on me.

It took me a moment to figure out what the heck he meant. These bikers seemed adverse to complete sentences. "No alarm on my apartment, you mean?" I clarified. "Yeah, well, I've been meaning to get around it."

"How long you been in there?"

I chewed my lip. "Almost ten years." For someone obsessed about safety, an alarm system should've been the first thing I'd installed. But it wasn't.

His face went hard. "You're getting a fuckin' alarm. This week."

I wanted to argue with him, despite the fact that he was right. A woman living alone—even in a small town—needed an alarm for safety. Especially when said small town had a rather violent history. But that was mostly to do with Gage's club, which I'd had nothing to do with.

So no alarm.

But that wasn't Gage's business. And I was about to educate him on that, but he was already walking toward the bike, picking up the helmet and shoving it at me much like I'd shoved the coffee at him.

I took it on instinct.

And then I frowned when I watched him mount the bike. Not just because it turned me on even more than watching him walk. No, because he shoved on Ray-Bans that had been hanging off the handlebars—and he was lecturing me about security. Someone could've totally stolen them, if they were stupid enough to steal from a biker—and that was the extent of his protection.

He glanced at me. "Helmet works best on your head, Will."

I kept the aforementioned helmet clutched against my chest. "You don't have one."

He grinned. "Yeah, and I'm not gettin' one. Got *you* one, because I'm not riskin' the o.1 percent chance of me crashing and you getting a hair on that head hurt."

Okay, that was sweet. "It's illegal to ride a motorcycle without a helmet in the state of California," I continued, not knowing why I was even trying.

He was a grown man. A biker who belonged to a one-percenter motorcycle club. One that existed because they didn't want to follow rules. Society's. The law's. And I was sure they thought they looked so much cooler riding without a helmet.

Another grin. "Do I look like I give a fuck about laws?" he asked, reading my mind.

I chewed my lip, standing my ground for no other reason than because I hated the thought of that beautiful head smashing against the road with no protection. And I had to think of that because I always thought of the worst-case scenario.

Life was full of worst-case scenarios.

He sighed. "You get one, baby. Either cigarettes or the helmet. One. Take your pick."

I jerked back. Was he seriously telling me I got to choose?

His face had lost its grin and he was now watching me intently as I continued to chew my lip, his hands fisted atop his thighs.

Yeah, he looked pretty darn serious.

So I thought on it.

Weighed the options.

Riding a motorcycle was already dangerous enough. And that was if the rider had on all the right safety gear and kept within the speed limits. Gage was wearing a cut and a thin henley. His boots were the only thing that would've offered any protection, and I guessed that wasn't why he was wearing them. So driving at high speeds, without the proper gear, the helmet wouldn't do much more to save his life. There was a reason they called motorcycle riders 'organ donors.'

My stomach clenched at the mere thought of it.

"Cigarettes," I said quickly.

I loved the smell of smoke on him, the gravel in his voice, but I knew that even if he'd been smoking his entire adult life, stopping in his mid-thirties would decrease a lot of the risks of cancer and other health complications.

He only nodded once.

And I gaped.

He's going to give up smoking. For me?

I doubted he was a man who gave up anything for anyone.

"Babe, we've made our deal. That means you put the helmet on and get on the back of my bike," he barked.

And on autopilot, I did just that.

The ride to the office took a handful of minutes.

The entire time, I tried to think about what that morning meant.

A few minutes gave me no insight.

I reasoned a fricking lifetime wouldn't.

Gage

He had no fucking clue how he'd found himself parking his bike in front of her apartment, knocking on her door.

Not in the way he'd used to find himself in places not knowing how he got there. Not battling against the blackout brought on by booze and junk and the decisions he'd made when he mixed the two.

Or more accurately, the bodies he'd made. And then he'd have to bury the bodies without any memory of creating them.

Six years sober and he made sure everything he did now was purposeful. Planned. He created bodies. Plenty of them. And he had lucid and stark realness every step of the way. He liked to blow shit up. That also required presence. Planning. Sobriety.

Then again, his whole fucking life required sobriety. Required him to fight against that itch in his skin that he woke up with. That he slept with. That he fucking breathed with. It was his penance. His punishment. He wondered now and again what Hell would be like when he finally ate a bullet. Because there wasn't more to be done to him.

And maybe that's what had him in front of that door. Because when she opened it, Hell felt a little bit like Heaven.

Everything about her face had flushed when she locked eyes with him. She fucking brightened, from the inside out.

At *him*.

She didn't blanch. Didn't harden herself.

Not that he guessed she even knew how to harden herself. She was soft, beautiful edges. Her full curves that she tried to hide with her conservative fucking librarian outfit, but it did the opposite.

He was already hard as a fucking rock just staring into her eyes. Her fucking eyes framed by glasses that shouldn't have been sexy.

But they were.

Oh fuck, were they.

Her skirt, brushing over her knees, only showing a small length of her milky and lean legs shouldn't have either. But it hugged her long form, spanned hips that he wanted to bury himself between.

And then he didn't give a fuck how he got there, right where he shouldn't be, on her doorstep.

He knew he had to find himself there every fucking day. Because even if he was bringing his own Hell into her life, he wouldn't be able to deny her Heaven. He was already fighting too many battles of resistance. He should've fought against this one.

But he wasn't going to.

Especially not when her hot and soft body pressed against him on his bike—once she finally climbed on. When her skirt rode up and her fucking hot cunt was almost pressing into his back, he almost forsook it all and pulled over on the side of Main Street to fuck her on the back of his bike.

Regardless of who was watching.

He'd done shit like that before, with plenty of women. A blur of bodies, of fucked-up sex, of empty orgasms.

He could only find pleasure in depravity.

And that's what stopped him from taking her.

Not just on the street but at her apartment. When she'd run her eyes up him like some hungry sex kitten, not the shy librarian she convinced the world—and herself—she was.

There was something in there. Something wild inside her conventional and innocent little package. He saw it then. Fuck, he'd obviously seen it before. That's what had him coming back. That's what had him craving her almost more than junk these forty-six hours.

Almost more.

He'd never crave anything more than junk.

The roar of the bike left his ears when he pulled up outside her offices, which meant there was nothing but the itching need for junk to distract him from the way she was pressed against his back. The way her hands were interlaced at his midsection, how her palms were flat against his torso, almost brushing his belt buckle.

Almost brushing his fucking rock-hard cock.

He gripped the handles of his bike even tighter and was surprised he didn't shatter his teeth the way he was clenching his jaw, restraining himself from grabbing those tiny delicate hands and placing them on his dick. Not even caring about the fact that it was just past eight in the morning and there were people walking by.

But he was trying to remind himself that even if there was a little wild in her eyes, that didn't mean shit compared to his darkness. His demons.

He was playing with fucking fire already.

And he wasn't the one who was going to get burned.

So on the curb, with Lauren's soft body behind him, her hands near his cock, her scent pressing into his motherfucking bones, he was *glad* his body was crying out for junk. Never in his life did he think he would find solace in that filthy desire.

But it gave him something to grab onto. Something to distract him.

Lauren's body lurched, as if she was just now realizing that they were stopped and outside her building.

They had been stationary for eighty-eight seconds.

Gage had counted.

Because when shit got bad, like driving to the shady parts of Hope in search of a dealer bad, he counted.

Every second.

There were 86,400 seconds in a day. Sometimes, on those really bad fucking days, he counted every single one of them. It was his way of figuring out that time passed, and with every second, he was winning against the monkey at his back. Closer to the peace the grave might offer.

So he counted.

And he wanted more seconds with Lauren pressed against his back. He wanted 86,400 of them.

To start.

Then he wanted a fuckload more of her writhing underneath him, his cock deep inside her.

But he was glad that he didn't have another handful of moments with her pressed against him right then, because he couldn't take that shit.

So he exhaled when her heat left his back and she stood shakily on the curb. She had already taken the helmet off at some point and her cheeks were flushed, eyes bright, saturated with more of that wild.

He felt it in his cock, that brightness, that chaos he saw lurking in those eyes. His little librarian had liked being on the back of his bike.

No, she'd *loved* it.

His gaze didn't stay on hers for long, they darted to the fucker in a suit damn near walking into a door leering at her ass. Because her demure and hot-as-shit skirt had ridden up on the bike.

Way up.

She was now showing more of her shapely and long-as-fuck legs that no one but Gage should be seeing. He didn't even think on that strange and possessive thought before he was off the bike and on the curb, his hands on either side of her hem, pulling the fabric down to its rightful place.

She jerked again, in surprise, maybe. Gage was sure she hadn't expected him to move. He hadn't expected his movements to be pulling *down* her fucking skirt. But although he'd been into audiences before, hadn't given a fuck about people seeing—and taking—whatever bitch he had his dick inside, that was *before*.

That was with faceless women whose names he couldn't remember, who he hadn't given a shit about. Even the most recent bitch he'd tricked himself into thinking was something was really just him trying to pretend there was something he gave a shit about.

It had been a lie.

Until now.

He gave a shit about Lauren.

She blinked at him rapidly, her glasses magnifying the softness at the edges of her gaze when she realized what he'd done.

His hands moved from the bottom of her skirt, trailing up to rest lightly on her hips. Gage didn't even know he'd been capable of gripping *anything* lightly, let alone a woman he wanted so badly.

"I, um," she breathed. Yes, breathed. The air was hot and minty on his face, with a hint of cinnamon. He itched to taste it, to take her mouth. His body shook with the need to. But he wouldn't have stopped if he started. And no way in fuck was he having an audience for the first time he claimed his woman's mouth.

Not just because he'd be claiming her cunt shortly after.

"Thanks," she said finally, seeming to find her words. Her voice was light and husky, and Gage heard it right in his cock.

He didn't reply.

He couldn't.

"For the ride," she clarified.

He still didn't reply.

Didn't move.

Didn't fucking breathe.

Because this was one of the moments. One he was sure he'd

never get again. One of those simple, pure, perfect fucking moments that life gave you once in a while.

Her scent pressing onto his leather, over the stale smell of cigarettes and motor oil. Her bright eyes magnified in her glasses. Her hair, mussed and shiny, tendrils escaping from her braid. The softness of her hips underneath his palms.

Her minty and cinnamon breath.

Clean.

Pure.

A moment he never should've had again.

Not since he'd laid his daughter on his chest, smelled her head. Felt her skin.

Those moments were lost to him.

His fucking soul was lost to him, because he was responsible for that lightness in his chest that haunted him with the truth as to where his baby girl was. Who was responsible for that.

He'd resigned himself to the fact that he was in Hell.

Perfect and pure moments didn't exist in Hell.

But there he was, having one.

One he didn't fucking deserve.

With a woman he didn't fucking deserve.

So he broke the moment. Not just by breathing but by forcibly stepping back, releasing her hips from his grasp, and mounting his bike, then starting it in one swift move.

Lauren was gaping at him, her eyes dreamy, her body swaying slightly from the loss of his hands.

He should've left her there. Not said a thing. Just imprinted the moment on his memory as his one pure moment in Hell, and then go straight back to the pit where he belonged. Leave her up top, in the clean air, where she belonged.

"Be outside at five," he barked. "And if you fuckin' even *think* about walkin' farther than up those stairs and to your desk, I'll tan your ass."

Then he roared off.

Not in the direction of the pit.

Because Hell wasn't anywhere he could ride to.

It was something he carried around inside him.

Something he was throwing Lauren into.

FIVE

Lauren

"Lauren, am I having a stroke, or did you just get dropped off on a *motorcycle?*" Abagail, the receptionist, asked as I wandered past her, gripping the helmet I'd just realized Gage hadn't taken with him.

Marty, our sports editor, was leaning against her desk, as he always was at that time of the morning, trying to get her to go out with him. It was an ongoing thing that Abagail was too nice to end. She was pretty, young, kind, and Marty was older, sleazy, and wore more hair spray than a Vegas show girl.

"She did. Saw her with one of the Templar guys," he put in, his eyes running over the length of me in a way that made me need a shower.

And I didn't want a shower. I didn't want to wash Gage's presence off me.

But it had already seeped under my skin. His smoky scent. His desire that was somehow malicious, dangerous, and tempting all at the same time. His penetrating gaze the moment he'd climbed off the bike to pull my skirt down for me. To protect my modesty. Granted, him all but forcing me on the bike was the reason my modesty needed protecting, but he hadn't exactly forced me. I'd gotten on under my own volition.

Heck, I hadn't even noticed or cared that my skirt had ridden up almost to my hips. On Main Street. In broad daylight.

No, I was too busy trying to calm my heart rate. Do difficult things like breathe and blink at the same time after pressing against Gage, having the roar of the motorcycle underneath me, and not be distracted by a head wound like I had been the night of my crash.

It was magnificent. But I had wanted more. I'd bitten my lip to stop myself from squeezing his abs, from screaming at him to go faster, go farther.

And then there was the whole image of him just sitting on his bike, tattooed hands clutching the handlebars, eyes on me underneath his shades.

I'd never thought something would be so savagely beautiful.

So I'd been taken by surprise when he'd dismounted in one fluid movement, and in another he'd yanked my skirt into place. Then he'd gently, almost reverently, run his hands up the fabric, resting them on my hips, just staring at me.

I'd been frozen, eyes on his face, on the hard edges of it, thinking about how his beard would feel brushing against my cheek. What his lips would feel like against mine. I'd been so sure I'd find out, the moment so taut with sexual pressure that it drowned out the world around us.

But then he'd stepped back. Violently. In direct contrast with the gentle way he'd handled me seconds before.

And he'd climbed on his bike, shouted at me and roared off. I watched him till the blackness against the soft morning light was gone.

My core was still pulsating with his throaty and savage voice promising to "tan my ass" if I did any walking. Because he knew I still hurt. And technically the promise in itself was to hurt me more—on the surface, at least. But the way his voice melded around the words, I was certain it would be the best kind of pain.

I was tempted to forgo work and walk to the outskirts of town, to the Sons of Templar compound, so he could keep his promise. So I could demand he do so.

But I'd shaken such a reckless thought from my head and did exactly what I was supposed to do, opening the doors to our offices and walking up the stairs to the reception area.

The clock on the wall told me I was five minutes late.

Almost unheard of.

But that wasn't why Abagail was looking at me in shock.

Her widened eyes were on the motorcycle helmet I was clutching, before they went to me.

"The Sons of Templar?" she repeated. "You were on the back of one of their bikes? *You?*" Her words were not unkind exactly, just drenched with the rightful amount of shock.

Because I was somewhat of a staple in the office. I'd been there almost the longest, and had trained a lot of the staff— Abagail included, as I'd worked reception on break from college. They knew me. Knew I was a stickler for rules and being punctual. That I didn't drink coffee, strictly herbal tea. That my hair was always smoothed, my hemlines always low, as were my heels.

I contributed to all birthday cards, made all the birthday cakes, and stayed away from all birthday celebrations out of the office.

I was friendly, but I didn't make friends. Was nice without being warm.

And I did not ride to work on the back of a motorcycle. Especially not a motorcycle belonging to one of the patched members of the Sons of Templar.

Especially not one as beautiful and menacing as Gage.

So Abagail's shock was warranted.

Marty's eyes were fastened on my legs as he nodded. "Wouldn't have believed it if I hadn't seen it with my own two eyes," he said. "And I did see it. A lot of it."

His words and the innuendo behind them made my skin crawl.

My stomach swirled with the attention of his sleazy gaze. I had never attracted it before. Not once. There was always a prettier, younger, and bubblier woman in the office for him to prey on. I'd always thought he considered me part of the furniture, like the rest of the men around my age did. And I'd been glad of it.

I wasn't used to being looked at like he was looking at me right then.

Nothing like the way Gage had gazed at me, sending my hormones into overdrive and my brain into chaos. A much sleazier and emptier way than that.

"Are you dating one of them?" Abagail asked, as if me informing her that I was an alien from outer space was more likely.

I shook my head once, violently, a small lance of pain erupting with the movement. I still wasn't 100 percent healed from the accident. "No, of course not," I said, stepping forward in the direction of my desk, eager to escape the conversation. "I wrecked my car. Their garage is fixing it. Gage was giving me a ride since walking is... uncomfortable."

"Gage!" Abagail almost screamed.

I winced.

She pushed up from her chair, not even noticing the way Marty's eyes snapped from me to her skintight white dress with a much higher hemline than mine. She walked on her heeled feet to stand in front of me.

"Gage gave you a ride to work so you wouldn't be *uncomfortable*?" she clarified.

I nodded.

She continued to gape. "Gage has more of a chance of setting an orphanage on fire to roast marshmallows than doing something like that," she said, voice full of certainty. And worse, familiarity.

My blood ran cold as I thought of the young, blonde-haired, blue-eyed, tanned, slim, and adventurous receptionist I'd kind of liked up until that point.

Until the moment she talked about Gage with that familiarity.

What was I thinking? I wasn't jealous. I wasn't a jealous person. I didn't believe in jealousy. Nor did I believe in punishing other women because of the actions of men.

"You know him?" I asked, my mouth dry.

She grinned at me, showing off perfectly straight white teeth.

Bet she didn't even need braces.

I had. For almost two years.

"*Everyone* knows Gage," she said. "He's the most beautiful and insane of all of the guys there. He doesn't really take many girls to bed." She screwed up her nose. "But when he does, I hear he does some *fucked-up shit*. But, like, in a good way." She gave me a look that was meant to communicate something. "If you know what I mean," she half whispered.

I had no idea what she meant.

But I did know that my breakfast was about to come up.

And it had nothing to do with 'fucked-up shit' and everything to do with the thought of Gage doing it with other women and not me.

I smiled at her, the expression physically painful. "Well, I don't know anything about him other than he's fixing my car and gave me a ride instead of setting fire to an orphanage," I said blandly. "Now if you'll excuse me, I have to catch up on work. We're on deadlines, you know."

And I turned on my heel and almost sprinted to my desk, hoping Abagail wouldn't follow me.

She didn't.

But her words did.

I HAD BEEN EXPECTING the pounding on the door.

That didn't mean I didn't jump when it started. When my whole apartment seemed to rattle at the force of it. It had sparked a small slice of fear inside of me. Until I remembered Abagail's words and anger chased it away.

So I stomped down my stairs and flung my door open.

And I was presented with an angry biker.

No, a *furious* biker.

His gaze scanned over my body.

It hit me physically. The silence around it, around him. The fury inside of that silence was enough to make me shrink back into myself.

Almost.

Instead I jutted my chin up, folded my arms and met his stare with one of my own. It wouldn't have measured up to the menace in his, of course, but I also guessed it might be an anomaly considering he probably didn't get people staring back at him in such a way.

"Waited outside your work," he clipped, eyes stormy. But something had flickered in them when I'd refused to cower underneath his gaze.

I pursed my lips but didn't reply. What did someone even say to that as a barked greeting?

His entire being seemed to twitch as his eyes darkened. "Don't like to be kept waiting," he growled.

"Well I don't like being ordered around," I snapped. "Especially by a man who all but hurled me onto the sidewalk the night I was in an accident, *stole* my wrecked car, and then, without any proper conversation, without even knowing my fricking last name, spouts utter crap about *how I belong to him!*" I yelled, surprising myself with the volume of my voice. It was addicting, that fury, and nearly impossible to control now that I'd let it out of me.

"And then that man turns up on my doorstep two days later—two days of silence after saying I'm his, mind you—and orders me around some more," I continued, my voice slightly shrill. "Shakes up the life I've been very happy with up until now." I narrowed my eyes. "I know you're in a club that doesn't play by the rules, but *I'm* not. And that piece of leather on your back does not give you permission to break *my* rules."

I sucked in a rough breath at the end of my tirade, anger and arousal mixing together in a brutal marriage.

I'd never been attracted to a man like him before. All the men I'd been slightly interested in were all cookie-cutter versions of each other. The male version of vanilla ice cream.

There was only one version of Gage, and he was standing right in front of me.

And he was definitely not vanilla. In *any* sense of the word.

So my heart was slamming into my chest with the fear, expectation, and excitement swirling through me, waiting for a reaction.

But he didn't do anything. Didn't yell. Didn't growl. Didn't curse at me. His body had relaxed somehow during my little screeching session. That didn't make sense at all, since when I was silent he'd been as taut as a wire.

People were comfortable in silence.

They were irate when they were being yelled at.

But Gage was not *people*.

A small grin tugged at the corner of his mouth.

"And what, *pray tell*, Will, are your rules?" he asked, voice light. Teasing almost.

I hadn't been expecting it, so it took me by surprise. I digested his words, blinking rapidly. "I-I, um," I stuttered, nothing else coming out.

Didn't all those women in the movies have witty banter with the man looking at them in such a way?

Wasn't witty repertoire one of the building blocks of a relationship?

And yet I stumbled over my words like a fool.

"I suspect they're not too dissimilar to the rules of decency," I muttered, scrambling for something, anything, to say.

The grin remained but darkened in a way that made me very glad I had my arms crossed against my chest. Because I'd changed into my yoga gear after escaping work before five, intending on chasing some calm in the wake of the chaos that came with anticipating that very moment. My sheer white tee and flimsy sports bra were not enough to hide the way my nipples hardened at his grin. At the darkness in his eyes that once again roused that part of me I'd been pretending didn't exist.

"Oh, baby, I suspect they're *not at all* similar to the rules of decency," he said, his voice a low rumble. "I'm fuckin' certain that the rules you have, the rules I'll fuckin' break—and you'll love it when I do—have *nothing* to do with decency." He stepped forward, stealing all the oxygen from my lungs. But then I didn't need oxygen when he was that close, when he had that look in his eyes. "I can see it in you, Will. You might hide it from the world, but an immoral man like me can see the depravity that hides behind this." His hand went to the frames of my glasses, trailing along the frames in a motion that should not have been sexy at all. But it was.

"I'm not hiding behind anything," I whispered, my voice dry and croaky, my heart a hammer at my chest. Not just because of the dangerous erotic glint in his eyes, not his proximity, his scent, his presence yanking me in.

No, it was how he saw into me in a way that terrified me more than his soulless eyes, his muscles, his ink, his leather cut ever could.

"Oh, baby, everyone's hiding behind something," he murmured. "You're just doin' it better than most. And you're hiding a fuck of a lot more than most."

His eyes swam with something I recognized. A darkness. A sorrow.

"So are you," I said, my eyes searching his. "What are you hiding, Gage?"

I didn't know what possessed me to be so brash, so brazen as to taunt the man in front of me who could smash the glasses he was so carefully caressing.

Just like he could break the body he'd been so hungrily gazing at. The body that sang for him to do with it what he wished. Even if that meant becoming more broken than I already was.

His body jerked with my words, his eyes glazing over, shuttering. It was an instant and unnerving process, to see everything in him shut down, harden, freeze into something cold. Foreign.

A killer.

He stepped back the moment I shivered with fear. And something more than fear. A depraved kind of excitement. A little part of me that *needed* that cold and cruelness. That wanted to see more of it.

"Oh you'll find out what I'm hiding soon enough, Will," he clipped, the words structured like a threat. "And it'll be too late. For the both of us."

He didn't say anything, didn't move for a handful of moments, the words hanging in the air, tattooing themselves into it with a promise.

"And don't think I haven't forgotten what I said I was gonna do to you if you walked anywhere you didn't need to," he said, his voice melting slightly. "I always keep my promises, Will. Especially ones that cause pain."

Then he turned on his heel and walked away.

Gage

"Okay, smoke break," Brock said as he pushed up from his chair on Cade's right at the table.

"Thank fuck," Lucky muttered, following suit.

The shithead didn't smoke, but he also had his woman waiting for him outside. Gage knew because he'd arrived at the clubhouse with her.

They'd been at a meeting.

They went every week.

Sometimes more if Bex was having a hard week.

This was a hard week.

It had been two years to the day since she'd been taken by the Tuckers. Two years since she was strung out on the junk she'd previously kicked, chained to a bed. Raped. Beaten. For three fucking weeks.

Three weeks.

And no matter how many years went by, those three weeks would be the longest period of time Bex had experienced in her life. It would define her. Not as a victim—she would shoot anyone who called her that—but as a warrior.

She was strong.

One of the strongest people he knew.

But there was only so much a human could take. Especially with demons at their back.

And when things got intense, someone who'd survived a period of trauma that was lifetimes of Hell packaged into a cage called time, those lifetimes came back with a vengeance, clawed at the corners of a scarred mind, looking for the weak spots. Gage's mind was more scarred than most, the ruined skin on his arms only the tip of the iceberg.

Years had gone by without it being this bad.

But Lauren had changed everything. Because she was pure, she teased him with those moments he shouldn't have. Moments he never fucking deserved.

Moments that thrust the past back at him so his ruined skin rippled with that agony, so visceral he had to check to make sure it wasn't charred and blackened.

Hence them going to the meeting.

Hence Bex, the woman who abhorred physical contact, holding his fucking hand the entire drive to the meeting.

Holding his hand.

Gage wasn't about physical contact unless he was fucking some club whore. Even then he made sure all the contact was rough, brutal, painful for the both of them. He didn't do tender with bitches. Especially not with one of his brother's wives. But this was different. Gage knew she needed it, knew something was chasing her that day.

So he gave it to her.

And he fuckin' needed it too.

Because he'd nearly lost it at Lauren's door the day before.

Nearly taken her over his shoulder, gone up the stairs and done what he'd been waiting to do since he'd seen her on the side of the road, bleeding and beautiful.

Fuck her senseless. Fuck her into the Hell he was living in, so she was stuck there for however long he wanted her there. Until he ruined her.

And because he'd fought off that need, he was battling with a stronger one.

It'd been ninety-nine thousand seconds since he'd left her

standing on her doorstep in that fuckin' outfit that hid nothing and showed him exactly what he needed to stain with his soul.

Ninety-nine thousand seconds of the visceral need for a needle. For nothing.

So the meeting Bex needed was probably something Gage needed just as much.

"You seem different," Bex said as they'd pulled up to the clubhouse.

It was the first time they'd spoken since he picked her up. Neither of them were conversationalists. With him, it wasn't surprising.

Her, it was.

Because every other old lady—save maybe Lily—never fucking shut up. The bitches were always talking, always arguing, always seeing something they shouldn't see.

And it didn't annoy Gage like it should. Because they were all decent women. Good women. Women who could handle this life, even if it didn't look like it at first glance.

He was happy for his brothers.

But he needed respite from that shit. From their sweet and soft voices. The happiness that melted into the air from them. From them finding whatever fucked-up happily-ever-after landed them there.

He had landed there because he was fucked up. And because there were no happily-ever-afters for him. He'd been fine with that. Because there was nothing left of him to want that shit. The only thing he wanted was blood and pain.

It didn't stop those bitches from teasing him with something he would never have. Had never wanted.

Lauren's eyes surged into his mind.

"I'm not different," he barked.

He felt Bex's gaze on him, knew she was giving him an

eyebrow raise. His hand clenched on the steering wheel, the other still encircling Bex's tattooed one.

"So it has nothing to do with the woman Lucky said was screaming, 'all up in your business' and threatening to have you arrested before you dragged her off?" she asked sweetly.

Gage glared at her. The bitch didn't do sweet. Not when every inch of her was hardened by the world. Her arms were covered in tattoos that she'd started getting since they'd yanked her out of her Hell.

She'd used them like Gage had, to try to cover up the crumbling and decaying skin underneath. With her, it actually kind of worked. Because she had other shit to heal that crumbling and decaying skin—though not completely, as she'd always have it. The black diamond on her ring finger. The name 'Gabriel' on angel wings in the crook of her right elbow.

The light in her eyes that shone a little brighter than the stare of her demons.

But sweet wasn't something she gave often. She couldn't. There was only so much sweet left in a girl who had the bitterness of the world shoved down her throat.

"Your dipshit husband doesn't know what the fuck he's talkin' about," Gage snapped, forgetting how he'd told himself to handle Bex with care, today of all days.

She grinned. "Oh, that reaction tells me something else entirely." She didn't blanch at his harsh tone; it took a lot more than that to bruise this woman, even on her worst day.

Her grin disappeared as some true light, true sweetness flickered on her face. She squeezed Gage's hand. "You know I'm never going to ask you what gave you those scars." She looked down to the fabric of his henley, covering the ruined skin.

It burned with just her gaze.

Every single time a pair of eyes fastened on his arms, the pain intensified. Because there was always pain. He lived with it. Just like he lived with the ugly and ruined skin that the world gaped at when they got a look. And people stared. Because even though everyone was ugly on the inside, they tried to trick themselves into horror at seeing someone who wore their ugliness on the outside. Tried to use his pain to pretend they were somehow better than him. He didn't give a fuck about whatever lay behind the stares—it was the attention to them that made them burn. Because the more you fed a demon, the more it grew. The uglier it got. And eyes on his skin fed his demons. Hands on it was a feast for them.

Which was one of the reasons no bitch touched him there.

That was a hard fucking limit.

His only hard limit.

Bex had never mentioned his scars before. She was one of the few people who understood. Who knew you needed to starve the demons lest they take over.

Her eyes met his. "I know those gave you other scars that only certain people can see," she said, eyes on his arms. "I know that shit is locked up tight for a reason. I know it 'cause I'm using the same locksmith for my own shit. I also know there's only one person in the world with the key." Her eyes moved toward the windows of the clubhouse as they pulled up, softening at the edges. "The only one that doesn't create more scars when he opens that shit. And he was also the man I was sure I was going to damn. That I didn't deserve to have because I was too ruined for him." She gave him one last glimpse of that sweetness she reserved for her husband and her best friend. "Just remember that no one's too ruined for the right person." She paused, grinning slightly. "Or the wrong one. Because sometimes the wrong one is exactly who you need. We fucked-up people need the wrong ones to keep us on the right side of mental depravity."

She gave his hand another squeeze.

And because she knew when to shut her mouth, she got out of the car and didn't make him spew out a response.

Which was a good thing because he had nothing to say.

And she had hung around with the rest of the old ladies and their kids while Cade had held church.

It was a lot less chaotic than it had been for a good handful of years. It had a fuck of a lot to do with the fact that there had been no new partnerships between a patched member and an old lady. And those courtships always promised chaos. But after what happened with Bex, it had cut the club.

Deep.

And then the shit with Rosie.

She was the heart and soul of the place. Even Gage fucking saw that. And she'd been involved in some deep shit. Deeper than anyone thought she could be capable of. Everyone apart from Gage, of course. He knew his shit. He'd known it all along.

Because he excelled at seeing the shit people hid.

The dark shit.

And Rosie had dark shit.

She could also handle it.

But shit since then had been quiet.

As quiet as it could be, at least.

Partly because they'd stopped running guns and started going legit.

More or less.

They still took contracts out for some fuckers who needed to be put down.

Which was what Cade had given Gage.

A gift from the fucking Devil, as if the Prince of Darkness himself knew Gage needed to end someone if he was going to keep his shit tight.

"Not so fast," Cade said, eyeing Lucky and Brock who were nearing the door before he focused on Gage. "You need backup on this?"

He was talking about the ex-Mexican gangbanger Rosie had

sent them info on from LA. The bitch was a fucking *bounty hunter*, among other things. She and the ex-cop moonlighted, doling out vigilante justice.

Crawford.

Straight-laced fucker who'd tried to bring down the club for years. Now he was chasing—and killing—drug dealers and rapists with his wife.

Rosie had called in the club because she was unable to chase after a gangbanger turned pimp—one who specialized in underage girls—on account of being three months pregnant. Apparently Crawford had to detain her for a day because she'd been determined to take on the underworld, even with a baby growing inside of her.

Gage didn't doubt that she could've.

He wasn't of the same opinion of his brothers, who didn't seem to like their women foraging into the fray at the best of times, let alone being vulnerable. Gage knew fucking breathing was vulnerable, and he knew those women were stronger than most of the self-proclaimed badasses he'd taken down in his life. He also knew that women had demons too. Especially the ones within the club. And they deserved to fight them, to starve them in the best ways that worked. And those ways were likely to be dangerous. Because life was fucking dangerous.

But these fuckers didn't seem to like the idea of women fighting battles.

Cade, of all people, had driven up to LA to *side* with Crawford. That was all sorts of upside down. But the cop had proved himself.

So Gage didn't kill him.

It would've pissed Rosie off.

And Gage respected the fucker.

He cracked his knuckles, smiling at Cade's question. "When do I ever need backup?" he asked.

Cade shook his head, grinning.

Because Gage was right. He was the main member who dealt with the contracts. Sure, Bull would come along when he needed to feed his own demons. Sometimes Lucky, if it had shit to do with rape—his own demons were hungry still, and sometimes you needed to know when to feed the right demons and starve the wrong ones. But mainly it was Gage. Because he was the most fucked up of them all.

His brothers were strong motherfuckers who could stomach a lot.

But Gage could stomach *everything*.

And he didn't have a family to risk in case shit got turned around. There was nothing for him to lose. Which meant he was little more than unstoppable.

"All right, great, smoke time," Brock repeated, slapping Gage on the shoulder as if the matter were wrapped up.

Gage gripped the knife at his belt, more for comfort than anything else. Because in addition to craving blood, junk, and Lauren's body underneath him, he fucking wanted a smoke.

He wanted a whole fucking pack of them.

He'd hated them before kicking the junk. But they were the only thing that helped get him clean the first time.

And, eventually, the second.

Because you couldn't kick an addiction without starting another one. And he'd just fucking promised Lauren he was going to kick the addiction that'd had a big fucking hand in keeping him sober. That and killing people. And blowing shit up.

So he was going to have to take up a new addiction.

And he knew it was going to be her.

"Not smokin'," he replied to Brock.

Brock's hand paused, as did Cade from where he was getting up from the head of the table. They were the only two brothers—save Lucky—in the club who knew he was sober. Not that it was a secret; he just didn't go waving his chips like they were a badge of honor.

Because they weren't.

He wasn't *proud* of being sober.

Because it wasn't an accomplishment.

An accomplishment would've been never getting hooked on the shit in the first place. That might've saved them.

Might've saved him.

But there wasn't room for mights in his life.

Hence him not spilling his shit to the only family he had left.

An area in his chest burned with the fact that this wasn't quite true. He ignored it.

But Cade and Brock knew about the addiction. Nothing else though. No way were the words of his true past leaving his lips. It was too fucked up for even his brothers.

"Come again?" Brock asked, screwing up his face. "You're not smoking? What? You lose a bet with Lucky or something?"

Gage shrugged off his hand, pushing up to stand. "Givin' it up."

Brock gaped at him. Even Cade's eyes widened slightly, and the motherfucker had a notorious poker face.

"You're *giving up* smoking?" Brock asked in shock. "And taking up what? And don't say you're not replacing it with somethin' else, 'cause if you don't, I'm thinking you'll burn the fuckin' clubhouse to the ground just 'cause you're in a bad mood. Shit, you've done that before."

Gage gritted his teeth. "Wasn't our clubhouse, if you'll remember correctly."

Brock rolled his eyes. "Different chapter, still Sons."

Gage shrugged. "They were a piss-poor chapter anyway. Plus no one died. And no one traced it back to me."

"They never do," Cade said, eyeing him in that intense way the fucker did. He saw more than most men, but Gage hid more than most men, so he didn't really see shit. "You good, bro? Somethin' you want to share with us?" He eyed the door, the room now emptied of brothers who were in a hurry to get to their families, or a bottle, or between the legs of a club whore.

"Stays in here if you do. You know that," Cade continued.

Gage straightened his shoulders, reaching in for his piece, the weight of it in his hands comforting, calming. He checked the chamber before shoving it back into his shoulder holster. "Got nothin' to share. Got people to kill."

And he turned on his heel, planning to do just that.

Hoping—no, fucking *praying* he would be able to curb his need by ending some lives.

Not his need for the junk.

For her.

Lauren

I would've been lying if I didn't expect the person knocking at my door at eight in the morning on a Sunday to be Gage.

I wasn't just expecting it.

I was *hoping* for it.

Though I'd spent the time since he'd left pretending I wasn't. Convincing myself that the next time I saw him, I'd firmly tell him to leave me alone. Let him know I was so far from the woman for him it was comical.

He was a biker.

Even if he was your run-of-the-mill biker, it wouldn't work.

But he wasn't.

He was something so much more than those menacing men who threw society's rules out the proverbial window and lived hard and fast.

He lived hard and fast. But he also lived dangerous. He also had a kind of emptiness behind his eyes that chilled me to the core.

Then there was the other side of him that made me burn hot. That made me want things I'd pretended I'd never even thought about.

He was a killer. He didn't hide that from me. Freaking hell, he'd all but admitted it the second time we spoke—when he told me I was his.

And then there was me.

Me.

Who barely had any friends because she didn't do anything to put herself out there. Who never took risks. Who made sure her life was orderly, simple, safe. Who lived slow and gentle by design. For survival.

Abagail's reaction on Friday was right on the money. The mere thought of the two of us was comical. Like a mouse and a snake.

So using my precious logic, I should've been able to dismiss him, for my survival more than anything else. Because he was the antithesis of everything I'd insulated myself from. All the chaos, danger, and pain in the world wrapped into one man.

One man I couldn't stop thinking about.

So I both dreaded and awaited opening that door to him.

Only it wasn't him.

"Okay, she's alive and has all of her limbs and is cute as a fucking button," a stunning redheaded woman said into a phone at her ear, her emerald eyes going up and down my body in appraisal.

Usually when another woman looked at you like that—especially a woman who was tall, curvy, stunning with almost waist-length red hair and style that belonged on a runway—it was instinct to shrink back. To let anxiety and all those insecurities rise up and chew away at you, because certain kinds of women had a talent for pinpointing all those insecurities, bringing them to the surface with one look.

But it wasn't that kind of look.

Though her perfectly made-up eyes were appraising me, it wasn't sharp or mean like the way a lot of women did. Not that I had much time to deduce this, since she was somewhat of a Chanel No. 5-laden hurricane.

"Mhhm, yeah, babe, I'll pass on any and all goss, plus your little talking to. Okay, kiss your Kiwi for me, and give him a BJ too." She winked at me as she hung up the phone.

In a motion that she managed to not make rude, she pushed past me and started up my stairs, almost gliding up them in six-inch Valentinos.

The Rock Star Studs.

I nearly drooled.

Shoes were my weakness. Designer ones especially.

Not that I owned any. Of course not. They were a completely irresponsible purchase, and I didn't have anywhere to wear them. I merely admired them from afar. And here was an unknown glamazon woman, entering my apartment at eight on a Sunday morning wearing heels that cost more than my monthly mortgage payment.

I followed her up in a dream, my ballet flat–clad feet seemingly unworthy to step where those magnificent shoes had graced my floors.

"I need coffee, like yesterday. My baby decided it was okay to keep me up all night," she called from the top of the stairs.

The click of her heels on the hardwood followed her words.

She glanced over her shoulder on the way into my kitchen, grinning.

"Before I pushed that beautiful but fucking annoying human out, the only time I was up all night was when I was partying or my husband was giving me multiple orgasms."

Another wink as she started opening cupboards at random. I had stopped at my kitchen island, rather unsure of what to do.

She wasn't robbing me. It didn't seem like she was going to hurt me. But I was pretty sure I should've objected to a woman, no matter how friendly and well-dressed she seemed, walking into my apartment without introducing herself.

Though she did seem a little familiar.

"That was Lucy on the phone, by the way," she said, pausing at the third cupboard. "She heard about you crashing your car. I have no idea how, but her husband does own a security business, so I guess it would be weirder if she *didn't* know. Those badass motherfuckers have, like, I don't know, sensors or something." She shrugged. "And anyway, she was pissed. Because she tried your cell and it was disconnected—I'm guessing it broke in the crash—and then you weren't at work. She was going to drive up here, but of course, she has babies, like me. Well, hers is currently cooking in her stomach, but it's the same principle. They kind of stop you from doing anything spontaneous, like road-tripping to Coachella, or going to Paris to get drunk on champagne and shop at Dior." She sighed, her eyes dreamy, obviously not talking about Lucy. "Of course, we love our children dearly and all that." She waved her hand dismissively, but there was a warmth in her eye. "But they do tend to take a little more effort to rope into spontaneous road trips. And I mean *rope*. Have you seen those car seats they make?" She didn't wait for me to answer. "Honestly, you have to be a rocket scientist to figure that out. My husband isn't a rocket scientist, but he's got those badass powers, so he's in charge of all baby contraptions." She resumed her rummaging.

I was slightly relieved at the mention of Lucy, and I was beginning to connect the dots. There was only one redheaded, foulmouthed, beautiful and stylish woman in Amber who was married to a badass with "badass powers."

"You're Amy?" I said.

She looked over her shoulder. "Well, duh, of course I am. Who else would I be?" She looked back to my cupboards before sighing and stepping back. "Now, is there like some kind of map to get to your coffee?"

I smiled. "Um, I don't have coffee. I ran out."

She gaped at me like I'd just said I had bodies stuffed in the fridge.

"What do you mean, you 'don't have coffee'?" she asked slowly, as if she'd just stepped on a land mine and was hesitant to move too much, let alone speak quickly, in case the whole place went up.

I shrugged. "I don't drink it."

That time she braced herself on my island as if the very words struck her down. "You. Don't. Drink. Coffee." Again it was spoken like I'd offered her to become one of the severed heads in my freezer. "But how do you"—she waved her hands at me —"look like that and not have coffee in your life?" She pointed to her chest, covered in a green silk shirt, which was tucked into white drainpipe jeans. "I've had four coffees to make my whole situation happen and be fabulous." She narrowed her expertly manicured brows. "And you look like a damn vision of girl next door mixed with... hmm." She looked me up and down again, brows furrowed. "Something different but kickass. Something unique. And you've done this *without coffee*. I'm going to need the name of the demon you brokered the deal with to sell your soul. Because homeboy *hooked you up*."

I smiled wider, despite the way her words hit my exposed nerves. The way she spoke, a thousand miles a minute, was comforting. Calming somehow. There were people you just immediately clicked with. It had happened with me less than a handful of times, because I didn't *let* myself click with people.

Clicking meant caring.

Caring meant danger.

Because when you cared about a person, even a little bit, you gave them that little bit of yourself to hold onto, keep safe. And no matter how long it took, that little piece would eventually be destroyed. By that person themselves, or the world in general.

"You can tell me all about it at the coffee shop," she decided, closing my cupboards and snatching her purse off my countertop. "Because you might be some kind of human-demon hybrid, but we'll talk about that over my java, because I, sadly, am not."

She linked her arm in mine, directing us both down the stairs and outside before I knew what was happening.

"I don't have my purse, or my keys," I said as she dragged me along. She was a lot stronger than she looked.

"Oh, honey, you don't need your purse. It's only polite of me to buy you your unicorn tears or whatever it is you consume instead of coffee to make you this hawt at eight in the morning," she replied, her heels clicking along the pavement as we rounded the corner of Main Street.

"And no matter what those idiot alpha males say, you don't need to lock your fricking doors in Amber in the middle of the morning. Seriously. I've only been kidnapped *twice*. And neither of those times was from someone breaking into my house. So we're good."

Though I knew Amy had been kidnapped—everyone knew all of the things that had happened to the women tangled up with the Sons of Templar, as it was kind of hard to keep kidnappings and car bombs a secret—it was strange to hear her mention it so casually, like it was a trip to Bed Bath and Beyond or something.

She opened the door to the café, stopping and inhaling, her entire body sagging. "Lacey!" she yelled. "I need coffee." She looked at me. "I know what I said about the unicorn tears, but I don't think even Lacey is that talented."

I smiled. "Peppermint tea is fine."

She relayed that to Lacey by shouting it across the café in a way that managed to be not at all obnoxious. And by Lacey's reaction, I was thinking it was normal.

I had my butt in a booth before I rightly knew what was going on. Amy was a hurricane.

She clasped her hands together on the top of the table. Her nails were polished perfectly with the same green as her shirt, and most of her fingers were adorned with tasteful and obviously expensive gold rings. The biggest being the solitaire diamond on her left hand.

"So, Lucy told me to track you down in order to yell at you for not calling her about the accident," she began. "And sure, I'm happy to yell at people, but 'people' usually only include my husband and my best friend when she tells me I can't put makeup on her baby. And I have a feeling I'm going to like you, so I'm not yelling." Her eyes twinkled. "Plus, I didn't come on Lucy's behalf. That's just a ruse for me getting the 411 on you and Gage."

I blinked rapidly at her as Lacey set two mugs in front of us.

"I'm totally naming my firstborn after you," Amy said to her, snatching her mug.

Lacey laughed. "You already had your firstborn, and he's not named after me."

"Well, I'll change his name," Amy replied after sipping. "How important is it to have Brock's grandfather's name in there anyway? He's dead. He won't know."

Lacey laughed again before walking off.

Amy looked at me over her coffee cup as I was staring at my peppermint tea. "So," she prompted, "you and Gage. How in the ever-loving *fuck* did that happen? You are so *not* what I expected him to go for." She paused. "Not that that's an insult. It's a compliment, since I figured he'd snatch a black widow off death row to marry her." She screwed up her nose. "You're not a closet black widow, are you?"

"Well, if I was, I wouldn't tell you, would I?" I deadpanned.

She stared at me and then burst out laughing. It was throaty and melodic. And contagious, because it was real and true. When someone laughed like that, with a genuine happiness that didn't exist much in this world anymore, it was something that had to be joined in with.

"I take it back. You're perfect for him," she replied, wiping her eye.

I chewed my lip. "I'm not *with* him," I hedged.

She waved my comment away. "Yes, yes, he's a big stupid biker and you're not letting him boss you around and claim you. All about that life, girlfriend. But we're all friends here. You can tell me."

I gaped at her.

"How do you even—"

"Know?" she finished for me after gulping down the rest of her coffee like a frat boy chugging beer. "Oh, there're no secrets in the club. Especially when Lucky has anything to do with it. He has the biggest mouth of us all. He loves gossip more than Perez Hilton. We're like a hive mind. It's a bit crazy, but you'll get used to it. We're pretty fucking awesome too, if I do say so myself. And I took it upon myself to be the welcome wagon." She paused. "And I may be escaping my teething baby and letting my husband deal with it. But *I* was the one up all night and he was the one away on a run, so it served him right for having those fucking strong swimmers."

Her phone buzzed in her purse for like the hundredth time.

"Uh, do you need to get that?" I asked, hoping she would so I could escape the situation. Because I feared that this kind, beautiful, and almost definitely a little bit insane woman would yank the truth out of me. The one I'd been ignoring.

She grinned, glancing at her purse. "Oh no, that'll just be Brock freaking out about what diaper rash cream to use. For a big bad biker, he seems to get pretty stressed about such things. It's character building. Plus, he'll be pissed at me when I get home. And that means angry sex." She winked.

I blushed into my tea. Not that I was a virgin—that had been taken care of with an awkward, fumbling, and painful encounter in college—but I wasn't exactly open to talking about it in public with a woman I'd just met.

Not that I was judging.

I'd always kind of dreamed of having those *Sex and the City* moments with my girlfriends in a café, talking about men, supporting each other, and laughing over nothing, crying over everything.

But I wasn't a woman who had girlfriends. Nor was I a woman who had men to talk about. I didn't laugh over nothing, and I couldn't cry, because if I did, I'd never stop.

"So now that we've established that I know everything about you threatening to have Gage arrested—absolutely kickass, by the way—him dragging you into his room—that came from Gwen, not Lucky, and she thinks you're kickass too—and him picking you up and dropping you off at your place of work even though you can almost throw a stone and hit the offices of the *Amber Star*." She smiled as Lacey wordlessly placed another coffee in front of her and swept away her empty mug. "Definitely changing Elijah's name," she muttered, staring dreamily into the mug.

She jerked after a second of silence. "Where were we?" she asked, not waiting for me to answer. "Right, you were about to tell me about you and Gage. And just to let you know, this isn't because I'm nosy." A pause. "Okay, not *entirely* because I'm nosy, but because I've been through this before. And as much as I love my husband, and I really do, it's a hard road to get used to being an old lady. The title itself almost broke Brock and me. Calling me *old*. What are they, suicidal?" She shook her head. "But it's hard, and not something you can get through without emotional support. I'm here for that. And, of course, because I'm nosy."

She waited expectantly as she sipped more of her coffee.

I watched her, a little dumbfounded, but a warmth had settled around me at her constant and easy chatter. At the fact that she seemed welcome, opening. Not like those women who were polished and intimidating and judgmental. Who lived for pointing out other women's insecurities just because it made them feel better.

So I told her.

Everything.

And I had convinced myself it was nothing.

But I was on my second cup of tea and she was on her third cup of coffee—no idea how she wasn't shaking—by the time I was finished.

"And now, well, I have no idea what the heck is going on," I said, glancing down at the lukewarm liquid in my mug.

I looked up and she was gaping at me.

"Holy shit," she whispered. "I'm gonna level with you here, babe. This is gonna get worse before it gets better. Partly because Gage is a patched member of the Sons of Templar and this courtship hasn't had so much as a shooting, let alone a car bomb." The casual and serious way she said that disturbed me slightly, but Amy soldiered on. "But mostly because this is Gage, and he makes everyone else look tame and well-adjusted." She reached over to squeeze my hand. "He's a good guy, don't get me wrong. But he's fucking insane. The best ones are." She patted my hand. "I'm never gonna be about judging a book by its cover because I think it's a total dick move, but I'm gonna take a shot in the dark and say your life has not been about fucking insane but hot-as-balls bikers who like to blow things up."

I grinned weakly. "Not exactly."

She smiled warmly back. "But I'm also going to take some

more shots and say you're a good woman. And not because you have some kickass interior decorating skills and somehow manage to look like a goddess at eight in the morning without makeup or coffee." She narrowed her eyebrows as if that was some kind of crime. "And I also see that you've got some darkness in you too. Don't worry, I'm not going to be nosy about that," she said, as if she sensed my panic. "But you want to share, I'm always here. Despite how much I talk, I'm a great listener. I'm saying this because not every man can conquer your demons. In fact, no man can. Women are the best at conquering demons, slaying their own dragons and all that. But the right man with the wrong demons can show you that. And the right men don't always seem like that with their leather cuts, their motorcycles, and their monosyllabic declarations of 'mine.'" She grinned at me as if we were sharing a secret.

I liked that. Someone relating to me. Having someone to relate to. Someone to squeeze my hand and let me into a club I didn't think I'd ever be admitted to. One I'd never let myself be admitted to.

"Do they all do that?" I asked.

She grinned wider. "Oh, honey, I think it's a prerequisite to patching in. But you're the right woman, because Gage has been in a downright murderous mood all week. And that means good things. The greatest. Angry sex is the best, after all." She gave me another wink and her phone buzzed in her purse once again. "Speaking of that," she muttered, standing and snatching her purse. "I've got a husband to let ravage me." She exited the booth, leaning down to kiss me on the cheek. "We'll have drinks this week. I'll invite the girls, have an initiation or something."

Then she was gone.

But I wasn't alone in the booth.

No, her words stayed there with me.

"Women are the best at conquering demons, slaying their own

dragons and all that. But the right man with the wrong demons can show you that."

I DIDN'T GO to the right man.

Or the wrong one, for that matter.

And I didn't go to Gage.

He was separate from the two of those. Because I didn't know which one he was.

Neither? Or both?

But it wasn't about him. It was about what he awakened within me. What Amy wore better than whatever couture was on her body.

Strength.

And mine had a darkness to it that Gage woke up.

Which had me in Hope, at midnight, on the wrong side of town, looking at my brother's murderer.

Gage

Gage had wanted to ride out for the contract immediately. But Cade wanted him to wait another day, make sure payment was cleared, that everything was in place.

So he had to stay in Amber another night.

Fucking torture.

Because all he'd wanted was to go over to Lauren's. To kick her fucking door down if need be. Get rid of his bullshit conscience and do what every one of his instincts—which didn't give a shit about his conscience—was telling him to do.

Claim her.

Yank her deep down into the pit with him, make it so she would never get out. For all the selfish reasons, like not wanting to walk through the valley of the shadow of death alone.

And because he wanted *her*.

With more than just his cock—but fuck, did he need to sink inside her too.

That need had driven him nearer to true insanity than he'd been in a long time. So just when he was about to give in to that battle, he forced himself into another one. He drove to Hope, parking his bike outside the dimly lit dive bar in the shittiest part of town where shitty people did drugs.

Where even shittier people sold them.

And he sat.

Stared at the flickering light above the door, illuminating the alley to the left in a barely visible glow. But enough to show him the shadows of bodies. Of movements he knew all too well.

His entire body was wired, as if it could sense the junk, the proximity to near total oblivion. To that blissed nothingness that stopped time and sped it up simultaneously. Because that's why he'd started doing it. To stop time. To preserve the feeling of the high, the freedom, the nirvana of it.

But in the end, toward the grizzly, bloody, and fucking horrific end, he'd done it to speed it up. To try to hasten the sand in the hourglass, to bring him that much closer to death. To the death he was living but was too much of a fucking coward to make legit.

He wasn't sure which one awaited him if he crossed the street, made the deal and injected junk into his blood, but he didn't much care. What came after it didn't matter. He just wanted to sink that needle in. Fuck the consequences.

His entire body shook with the power of his restraint.

His leg twitched.

Later he'd tell himself it was just that, a twitch. Even though he knew it was really a small movement toward pushing off his bike and back into that sickening and pathetic life he pretended he'd escaped.

It wasn't willpower or strength that stopped him. Not the weight of the chip in his pocket nor the death on his bones.

No, it was catching a glimpse of a flash coming from inside a car parked up the street. One he'd been too fuckin' fired up to notice on first glance.

But he sure as shit noticed it now.

And the face that was illuminated by yet another flash of a fucking camera from inside the car.

Lauren.

He would've laughed if it weren't so fucking horrible.

Two of the things he craved most within almost equal distance to him. Both of which were already under his skin. Both of which promised pain.

He just needed to choose which kind.

There was no hesitation as he pushed off the bike and strode across the street.

SIX

Lauren

I wasn't going to *do* anything. Even in the darkest corners of my mind, where the darkest version of myself existed, I didn't have that hunger for vengeance in my bones. Or at least not the kind of vengeance that would get me out of the car to potentially get myself killed.

Even slightly out of my mind, I had enough self-preservation to realize that even trying on this new assertive and brave Lauren, I didn't have it in me to face off with a drug dealer. I barely had the stomach to lift my newly purchased phone and snap the photographs of the drug deal.

But I did it.

Because I might not believe in vengeance, but I believed in justice.

And no one was doing anything about the man in the alley dealing death in small vials, preying on people in the clutches of addiction. Yeah, maybe the blame didn't rest solely on him—

addicts still had responsibility—but he was helping feed an ugly and deadly illness.

I wasn't an investigative journalist. I was barely even a journalist. I didn't have the hunger or the stomach to go as far as people like Lucy did. To take those risks. I was safe behind my computer, correcting her hard-hitting stories, fact-checking, sometimes doing a feel-good piece on the elementary school kids volunteering at the local retirement home.

But I wasn't a good journalist. I wasn't good at talking to people, pushing past their boundaries.

I was too busy trying to protect my own.

And now they were falling down. With comments from a sassy redhead. With glares from a dangerous biker. With words that wormed into those dark corners in my mind. With his scent, my skin pressed against the iron of his muscles, the vibration of his bike underneath mine.

He radiated pure strength, like he would be able to save me from a plane about to go down. But I wanted to be strong too. I wanted to be a person to stop the plane from crashing in the first place.

In order to do that, I finally had to take notice of all those flashing lights and warning signals I'd been closing my eyes to.

Hence me driving to Hope, to the spot where my brother had bought the drugs that killed him. I'd borrowed Niles's car to do so, and he hadn't even asked a question when I told him the story, had just raised one bushy eyebrow and given me the keys.

So there I was, taking photos. I wasn't sure what I was going to do with them. I could take them to the police station, show them to Troy, even if Hope was outside of his jurisdiction. And if he couldn't help, I'd write an article. Niles thought I was already, but I'd kind of only said that to get his car. Kind of.

I'd already called Lucy about it earlier.

I waited for her to finish yelling at me for not calling her the second I crashed my car.

"I couldn't call you the second I crashed my car, since my phone kind of shattered on impact," I replied dryly, liking hearing Lucy's voice, even if it was yelling at me. I hadn't noticed how much she'd meant to me until she left. Hadn't realized that she was one of the closest things I had to a friend, one who never pried too much, who never judged, who just... was.

"Well, I didn't want to have to find out that my favorite and only friend not addicted to caffeine almost died in a car accident from Lucky, of all people," she hissed. "And that was only because he was talking to me about this 'sexy librarian' who almost had Gage arrested for stealing her wrecked car. And I've seen the town librarian, in real life and in my nightmares, and I only know of one sex kitten librarian type, and that'd be you. So you've been seriously holding out on me, girl. I'm hurt and offended that you decided to go biker after I left Amber. Seriously."

I smiled at the same time my stomach dipped at yet another sassy but kind woman demanding I tell her about something I'd yet to reconcile in my own head. It should've scared me, made me close down tighter than ever. But it didn't. It was like I'd been crying out for this kind of contact and I hadn't even realized it.

Which was why, for the second time in twenty-four hours, I spilled the entire story—so far—about Gage.

I expected more yelling from Lucy. Or at the very least a string of curse words. She cursed more than even the bikers I'd come across, but that was probably because she grew up around them.

But there was nothing except a slight crackle in the silence on the other end of the line.

"Lucy?" I asked after a couple of beats.

"No one has ever struck me speechless, but you have just done so," she said finally. "And I'm feeling like this isn't going to be the

last time you're going to be popping some cherries. Not that Gage is a virgin." She paused. "Wait, you're not—"

"No, I'm not a virgin. I'm not that tragic a case," I said, my voice a little lower.

"Honey, never in my life have I thought of you as being tragic," she said softly. "Just because you live life quiet and without caffeinated beverages does not mean your life is not important. That I don't admire it. Admire You. Always have, babe. Especially after what happened to David."

My blood froze. "You know what happened to David?" I choked out. I hadn't realized that Lucy even recognized me from high school, what with being years below her and the fact that I almost sank into the wallpaper. She and Rosie were too busy blowing things up to notice the wallpaper. "Why didn't you say anything?"

"Because, babe, I knew you didn't want to talk about it. You weren't ready for that. As someone who knows what it's like to hide from the past, and yourself, I know it's a choice you make on your own about when to confront that pain. I just hoped I'd be around to help you through it if you chose to trust me with that."

I blinked away tears that were unfamiliar to me.

"But I'm always here. Even if I'm technically in LA on damn near house arrest. You'd think a woman has never been pregnant before," she grumbled, as if sensing that I wasn't ready to say anything more about David.

"Well, how does a distraction sound?" I asked, taking considerable effort to brighten my voice.

"Dude, you already blew my fucking mind with the news that you're going to be the one who breaks in the wild horse that is Gage. Oh, and the crazy one. Not that I'm judging. He's hot as shit. The crazy ones always are. And I know that because Keltan is not entirely sane. I mean, he plays rugby. And he's married to me. He's got to be a little unhinged."

Looking out at the ocean, I smiled, and it was genuine. It was hard to believe David's name had been spoken in such close proximity to that smile.

"I think he's pretty darn smart, and I think you're pretty darn awesome, even if you're a little crazy," I said. "And I'm going to need some of that crazy for some journalistic advice."

I filled her in on what I wanted to do, and when I was finished there was more crackling silence on the other side of the phone.

"You've done it," she breathed after a long silence. "You've done the impossible, struck me silent for the second time in a handful of minutes. There must be some kind of trophy for that." She sucked in a breath. "And I'm not going to point out the obvious and talk about the dangers involved in trying to take down drug dealers, because that's just cliché and dull. And it's you, so of course you'll be careful. I'll just give you some pointers."

And she did.

Detailed pointers.

She also tried to convince me to get a gun. I had made all the appropriate noncommittal noises, but no way in hell was I getting a gun. I'd more likely shoot myself by accident before I shot anyone else.

Not that I had the stomach for shooting anyone.

The only shooting I was doing with my phone, safely in my car, prepared to start it and roar off into the night if anyone caught me.

Or I thought I'd been prepared.

Right up until my door was wrenched open, strong and firm hands gripping my upper arms.

I didn't even have the self-preservation to scream while I was dragged out of the car. Not that anyone would save me if I did. Not in that area. Not that I would *want* any of the characters who hung out there to save me.

My back was pressed against the car, another body hard and hot against mine as a large hand settled on top of my collarbone.

My heart was splintering my ribs, and I could barely suck in a painful breath until a familiar scent entered my system with my frantic inhale.

Woodsy. A lingering but old smell of smoke.

"What in the fuck do you think you're doing?" a voice growled, the fury in it rough against the night air.

I blinked at the beautifully savage face above me, his iron features painted in rage. His eyes were burning into me with more anger than I'd ever seen contained in them. It was dangerous.

He was dangerous.

I should've been more scared. I shouldn't have relaxed and tightened in his grasp at the same time, shouldn't have been slightly excited at the cruelty in his mere presence.

But I was.

"Gage," I breathed.

He pressed against me harder, his hand at my collarbone tightening to the point of pain. "I repeat, what in the fuck are you doing here?"

I blinked again, my mind trying to work against all the reactions that were scrambling for control.

"What are *you* doing here?" I snapped, anger I didn't quite know I possessed rearing up to strike back at Gage.

He froze, as if he was as unprepared for the violent bite in my voice as I was. Then he recovered, leaning forward so his mouth almost brushed against mine. "I'm here on club business," he murmured. "I fit in here. This place, in the dirty and depraved shadows, that's where I belong. That's where I operate. I make sense here. I blend into the darkness. You do not. You're a fucking beacon in this place. And the vermin around here can fuckin' smell your sweetness amongst the bitter."

His boots kicked my tennis shoes apart and I gasped as he stepped between my legs, his body almost pressing into the core of me, the part that was soft and craving his hardness.

"I'm not sure whether you need to consider yourself lucky it was me who snapped you up and not one of these other lowlifes." His lips brushed against my neck, and my entire body erupted into fire and ice at the same time. "I don't know if you're gonna thank me or damn me when I'm finally done with you." His mouth was gone and his eyes were tattooing his glare onto my soul. "If I ever decide to be done with you."

I wanted to escape his gaze. The brutal truth behind it. The way it snatched me, not gentle or tender, but rough and almost painful. But perfect in the pain.

"So I'm gonna repeat my question, baby, and maybe if you answer me now, I might go easy on you." His hand trailed up the side of my face. "Or maybe I won't, depending on what you want. What are you doing out here?"

I wanted to speak. To move. But I didn't want to run away. Didn't want to talk. I wanted to tell him to do his worst. To snatch his face and press it against mine. For him to take me, against the car, against the demons running around the street, running behind our eyes.

But I couldn't seem to speak, or move my limbs. It was all I could do just to inhale and exhale.

He let out a frustrated growl at my silence, and I was terrified at what was going to come next. But I was darkly excited for it too. I craved him to fulfill his depraved promise. Because despite all of our intense, erotic, and earth-shattering moments together, we hadn't even *kissed*.

But instead of crossing the short distance between our mouths, he yanked backward, the cold air a slap to my face.

I didn't realize he had a phone against his ear until he all but growled into it.

"Lucky," he clipped. "Need you to come out to hope in a cage. Bring whatever prospect is around." His eyes never left mine, his hand still pressing me into the car. "Lauren's boss's car is outside The Dive. Keys are gonna be on top of the front tire. You haul ass, 'cause it's only a matter of time before some asshole gets curious about a car like that on a street like this. And if I have to kill someone who thinks he can steal a car my woman's driving, I'll be dis-fucking-pleased."

He hung up and was dragging me across the street before I could properly understand what he was doing. The chrome of his bike glinted against the flickering streetlights that were few and far between. It wouldn't do well to have illumination when dealing drugs. Darkness was needed for dark deeds.

We came to a jarring stop beside the bike, my brain buzzing with everything and nothing at the same time.

"Get on the fucking bike, Lauren," Gage snapped.

I looked from him to the bike. "I don't have a helmet."

"Jesus fucking Christ," he muttered, running his hand through his hair, eyes darting over the top of my head to the alley behind me. "You on the back of my bike, without a helmet, is the safest place in the fuckin' world for you right now. Trust me."

There he was. The guy promising to protect me from the plane going down.

So I did exactly that.

I trusted him.

And I got on the bike.

GAGE NEARLY DRAGGED me off the bike the second it stopped outside of my apartment.

It was only then that I realized my apartment was locked and my keys were in my purse, which was sitting on the passenger seat of Niles's car. Which was sitting outside a dodgy bar in a dodgier area. Or, if I was lucky, Lucky himself would've shown up before someone could've snatched the car.

I wasn't sure if I was lucky right then or not.

I really hoped I didn't have to explain to Niles why I'd gotten his car stolen. But he'd probably make it into a story. Everything in life was a story. Even the bad. Especially the bad. Bad news was good for newspapers.

"I don't have my keys," I murmured as we reached my front door.

It was only then that I saw he was carrying my purse. I didn't even get the chance to be surprised, or find it funny to see my pale pink purse clutched in his large tattooed hands, because he was rifling through it almost violently.

He was a brave man to venture into a woman's purse without her permission. Then again, I wasn't exactly screaming in protest either. I was too busy trying to quiet my thundering heart.

Gage made quick work of doing one of the hardest things on earth—finding the exact object you needed in the depths of your purse. The door was unlocked and he was dragging me upstairs before I could catch up.

That's all I was doing, playing catch-up. I should've been trying to figure all this out on the ride, should've gathered my wits, my logic and started to make the important decisions I was known so well for.

But I hadn't.

I'd merely clutched onto Gage for dear life, pressed against his body, and let my mind think of something it had never thought of before.

Nothing.

Hence the reason I was still scrambling when the door slammed behind us and I was in the middle of my living room,

Gage pacing in front of me, his boots echoing through my apartment like harbingers of doom.

Then he stopped, turned on me, faced me fully.

"Thought I'd have time to lock it down on the ride here," he clipped. "Thought having your warm and hot little body pressed against mine would remind me that it was no longer sittin' in a car takin' *photos* of one of the biggest drug dealers in Hope, playing with her fucking innocent and precious life." His voice was low. Quiet. Dangerous. And his gaze a blade.

I didn't look away. Didn't move. Didn't speak. I just stood there, dumb and still, like some idiot.

"Thought I would be able to lock it down, standing in your house, surrounded by your shit. Surrounded by *you*," he continued, that voice still dangerous and low.

And then he wasn't across the room. In two strides, he was in front of me, clutching my shoulders painfully. "But I fucking can't!" he roared.

I jumped at the violence in his hands, in his voice, but more out of surprise than fear. Despite all of his unrestrained violence, I had some weird and unexplainable certainty that he wasn't going to hurt me.

"Do you have any idea how much danger you put yourself in tonight?" he demanded, shaking me slightly as he spoke.

"I wasn't putting myself in danger," I protested.

He gaped at me then, his face contorted in rage. "You're fuckin' kidding me, right? You know what you *look* like?" He leaned in. "What you *smell* like?"

My breathing shallow, I didn't respond because I didn't think there was an appropriate response.

Gage held me hostage with his grip, with his gaze, both bordering on pain. "Because I do," he said. "And I'm exactly like all those men. And looking at you, smelling you...all I want to know is what you taste like."

His mouth was almost brushing against mine.

Almost.

"And ain't nobody figuring out what you taste like," he continued, his breath hot against my face. "No one is putting their dirty fuckin' paws on you." One of his hands moved to grip my neck. "Except me."

Everything about his grip, his voice, his very stare was a threat. One I wanted him to carry out.

"You're mine, baby," he rasped. "And you're not playin' fuckin' games with your safety, with what's mine. You're not doin' shit like that ever again."

His voice was iron. A band against me. A fricking brand.

I was *his*.

That thought filled me with terror. And also something else.

Longing.

I *wanted* to belong to him. I wanted to feel like I fit in his arms, in his life. Let his violent gaze, violent grip, violent life envelop me.

But he was trying to take something from me. That control I clutched to my chest. The control I needed to keep myself together. He was trying to stop me from holding onto my strength because he thought I was weak.

It took all of my strength to yank myself out of his grip, and I missed the violent warmth of it the second he let me go. And he did let me go. Though his arms were vises, he wasn't going to hold me against my will.

"You know, this isn't how the world works!" I yelled, pacing the room like he had been moments before. We seemed to be trading fury, since his face emptied the second I raised my voice. "You do not just declare someone is yours and decide that you have a freaking right to tell that someone—me—what she can and can't do." I stopped pacing, turning to him and narrowing my eyes. "You can't just order me to be yours," I hissed.

I expected him to yell back. His eyes certainly told me he wanted to.

But he didn't.

Didn't even move.

Just regarded me with a cold gaze that would've frozen me to the spot if not for the pulsating heat inside me. It was empty, that look. Devoid of anything human. Any emotion. The gaze of a monster.

"Oh, I've got a fair idea how the world works, baby," he said finally, his voice as cold and empty and terrifying as his gaze. "Know it's ugly. Painful. Bloody. And there's no fuckin' way to control it."

He stepped forward.

I stepped back.

"For someone who knows shit, you don't seem to know that," he murmured, stalking toward me. "That this is not something I declared. Or something I fucking *wanted*." He reached me and I found no energy left in me to retreat. "I didn't order you to be mine. You just *are*."

There were a lot of things I could've said then. I could've continued to fight for the control I'd thought was so important to my survival moments before. That I thought I needed.

I could've told him to leave, take his dangerous menace away from my safe apartment.

It was the smart thing to do.

The logical thing.

I had a feeling it might be my last chance to get out of this, that I would be strong enough to do so. And Gage would let me. I had a strange feeling he *wanted* me to get out of this. That he wasn't strong enough to walk out the door he'd dragged me through.

That I might have to be the strong one if I wanted the control I'd thought was his.

"Kiss me," I demanded, voice hoarse and foreign.

It was like one of those sex goddesses from the movies came and took control of my vocal cords, because there was no way I had the ability to sound like a sex goddess. Then again, maybe there had been no man to awaken that ability.

"No."

The word was a slap in the face, a whip against that sultry voice that I had been so astonished by—and secretly proud of.

That single word did a lot of things.

Made me want to empty my dinner, right there at the top of his likely steel-toed motorcycle boots.

Cry.

Curl into a ball and die.

No, run far away, *then* curl into a ball in die.

I did none of those things. The only one I was happy about was the vomiting one. That would've added to an already insurmountable level of mortification.

The sex goddess disappeared, likely to never return again.

My awkward, stuttering, so-not-a-sex-goddess self took her place.

"Oh, um, that's okay," I muttered, eyes darting down to my palms, which were wringing each other out like a Russian housewife. "You—I mean I know I'm not what you're used to, not...." I trailed off, my voice rough and scratchy, full of unshed tears and unrealized insecurities. "What I'm trying to say is I understand. I was just..." What? Hoping this connection was actually real and not just inside my head?

Hoping something of import, *someone* of import might come into my beige life and splash it full of... something?

I tried to step back, desperate to engage in the running portion of the evening so the curl-up-and-die portion might come quicker.

An iron grip on my arm stopped me.

"Shut up," Gage growled.

My jaw snapped shut on his command, though my eyes stayed down and I kept wringing my palms.

A callused hand snatched my jaw, wrenching it upward so my eyes had no choice but to meet the unyielding pools of citrine in front of me.

"Whatever you were tryin' to say there, whatever you're tryin' to *think*, it's bullshit," he clipped.

"You don't even know—" I tried to interrupt, but his eyes stopped me.

"I know, Will. I know because it seeps from your every fuckin' pore. Your absolute blindness to what you are." The grip on my arm tightened. "What I'm fuckin' holding onto, somehow holding but not breaking." His eyes swam with something so dark it hurt to look at. "Not yet, at least," he muttered, his voice iron yet soft, like it had been under the forge for too long; it was melting, being molded by the heat—by pain.

"I don't want to kiss you. Well, I do. Fucking more than anything in this world. Then I want to eat your pussy for hours. Sink my cock into that pussy and fuckin' make you scream, make my fucking *home* inside that cunt."

My insides dropped to the floor with his words. My legs throbbed and my pussy clenched tight, as if expecting a release to come from the words describing the act itself. I didn't doubt that if Gage kept talking, kept *looking* at me like that, he'd make me come by just talking dirty. That was the thing about him. He was just so... visceral.

His eyes swam with the same desire that paralyzed me. Every inch of his body was held tight, the veins on his neck raised like he was battling with something.

He was silent a long time, just looking at me, fucking me with his stare. Then he leaned forward, inhaling roughly, sharply, sniffing me. My panties were drenched. He didn't take his eyes off me.

"It will start with that kiss you just asked for. The thing I'll give you, because I want to give you everything in this fucking world that you want, and it just so turns out that it lines up with my selfish desires," he murmured, his mouth almost brushing mine but not crossing that important and very tiny distance between our lips.

His eyes didn't let me go. "But it can't be yet. Because the second I lay my lips to yours, it's done. For both of us. I know it. You're not gonna be the innocent, beautiful, and fucking oblivious girl anymore. Because I'll worship every fucking inch of you to make sure you're not blind to yourself. But then I'll also fuck you so dirty that you won't even look innocent to the Devil himself."

Sweat beaded at my temples with the force of his words. He was penetrating me with those filthy and carnal sentences, my pussy wrapping around them like a physical thing. I'd never had such a reaction to anything in my life. I didn't think anyone had this kind of reaction to anything ever.

Gage watched me. He was my puppet master, yanking at strings I didn't know I had as he continued to speak. "I'm gonna tarnish you, dirty you, break you. I know it. Which means the longer I go without kissin' you, the longer I get to enjoy my little bird before I crush her in my hands. Make her broken like me." His hands tightened around me as if testing how much I could take.

His stare was unyielding. "And this isn't me sayin' I ain't gonna do it. Because I'm broken, baby. I'm bad. And not the good kind of bad that sees true beauty and lets it go before he can ruin it. No, I'm the kind of bad that will take that beauty, appreciate it, and then snatch it for himself. Turn it into something that means it'll never be the same again. Because you know you'll never be the same again. I sure as fuck won't." He paused, his hands still at my chin, his eyes still searing my soul.

My heart seemed to crack against my rib cage with the force of its beats.

"So no, I'm not gonna kiss you just yet," he rasped, eyes on my mouth. "I'm gonna let my little bird fly, enjoy the freedom she didn't know she had for a little while longer." He leaned in so his lips were almost—*almost*—touching mine once more. "But only a little fuckin' while. Because I'm a man of strength. I've made it a fucking prerequisite of my survival to resist the temptation of things I know will destroy me. But I ain't gonna be able to resist you for long, despite the fact that you'll destroy me. And I'll destroy you right back."

With those words spearing me right through the heart, he gave me one last moment, then turned on his heel and gave me nothing but the view of the death he wore on his back.

SEVEN

One Week Later

One week.

I hadn't heard from Gage in an entire *week*.

And I wasn't one of those girls who spiraled when a guy didn't call. Mostly because with me, after a point, the guy didn't call. My life was simple, structured, unexciting. But it wasn't that —it was because I didn't fawn at the feet of these men. I didn't yank my self-worth from inside me and hand it to them to do with what they wanted. I didn't change my whole life in order to make them comfortable, in order to 'keep them.' And with the guys I'd dated, that meant I lost them. And it never bothered me. In each of my very brief relationships, I'd made sure to distance myself, to not give them all of me.

And the men I'd been with didn't *want* all of me. They wanted the me I portrayed on the surface. The nice, plain woman who would make a good wife, a mother, and who would never speak up for herself. Who didn't have her own opinion.

I would *never* be that woman.

But to the naked eye, I looked a heck of a lot like her.

It was my own design, of course. To keep myself safe from pain.

And what those men couldn't even see in broad daylight, Gage saw completely and utterly in the darkness that night on the highway.

And I was no longer safe.

So before, I might not have been one of those women who spiraled when the guy didn't call, but I sure as heck was now. And my circumstances were kind of extenuating, considering what happened the last time I saw Gage.

Considering all the things he said.

I still felt his grip on me, even a week later. I still had the faint marks of how tightly he'd pressed the pads of his fingers into my soft skin.

And I was upset about that. Not about the marks being there in the first place, but that they were disappearing.

Because if the marks were disappearing, then he'd only become a ghost of a rupture in my smooth and utterly simple life. Something that might've cracked it slightly but then left me with the knowledge of how hollow I was.

Logically, it was a good thing, because everything about Gage was wrong for me. He was a biker who lived hard and wild. So hard that violence seeped out of his very pores. I wore cardigans and my life was all about order. Safety.

A man who lived for danger and excitement didn't end up with the woman who actively structured her life so meticulously that every second was designed to repel excitement. Danger.

So I should've been relieved, should've been settling back into the calm that came after a storm.

Though it didn't feel like the storm was over.

I didn't want it to be over.

But I had some distractions. One being Amy, who took it upon herself to show up at eight in the morning with two coffees for herself and a peppermint tea for me. She and her son, usually quiet in his stroller, would walk me to work every morning.

First I'd been a ball of nerves, thinking she was going to grill me about Gage and I'd have to say my greatest fears out loud—that he'd realized how wrong I was for him, how I was little more than a cardboard cutout of a human and I'd never see him again.

But she didn't so much as utter his name. Though she uttered pretty much everything else under the sun. By the end of the week, I could've written a book—heck, I could've written five and a half books—on the Sons of Templar, the men and their respective women.

It sure sounded like fantasy. Too crazy to be real. But I'd been in Amber when it went down. On the fringes, where I thought I'd always be.

Never did I imagine I'd be right in the middle.

Or maybe still on the fringes, with just a taste of what it was like to be part of a family like that. To be touched and looked at the way Gage touched and looked at me.

"Lauren?" a voice jerked me out of my melancholy.

I looked up from my computer, having stared at the screen for the better part of an hour. I'd managed to get the bare minimum done that day, and the whole week. Which was my version of spiraling. I was never happy with the bare minimum. I made sure I excelled at everything I did, put all of myself into it so there were no parts of my brain that could go wandering.

And yet it seemed that almost my whole brain had been wandering that week.

"Jen," I said, focusing on the woman leaning on my desk, smiling warmly at me.

Though I had no reason to think such a thing, the smile unnerved me. It was open, friendly, at home on her tanned and pretty faced, but there was something... off about it. About her entire presence.

Her presence that had been seemingly everywhere in the office for the entire week. I'd arrived at work on Monday after no sleep and my first walking session with Amy and I was not on my game.

Which was of course when Niles informed me of Jen joining the team as a new lifestyle columnist, and just a general reporter. Which in itself was strange, considering the current state of the paper and the journalism industry in general. We were laying people off, not hiring them.

But Jen was charming. Charismatic. And of course, beautiful, which I was sure helped with her hiring process. It was a catty thought, but it had merit. Niles was old-school in all the ways that were good, believing in journalistic integrity, like the muckrakers back in the day who were willing to sacrifice everything for the truth. Who believed journalism was the fifth estate, holding the powers that be to account. He worked independently and would never be bought. He rewarded talent.

But he was old-school in a handful of the bad ways too. When journalism used to be an 'old boys club' and patriarchy was as common as a typewriter in that old-school newsroom. He wasn't exactly sexist, and he always treated me like an equal, but he was a sucker for a pretty face. Which was why a large percentage of our female staff and interns were young and pretty. Talented too, but not hard on the eye.

And Jen was pretty. Tall, thin, with almond-shaped eyes and caramel skin that suggested an Eastern heritage. Long, shiny black hair that was always tumbling in wild curls around her face. She wore enough makeup to let you know she was a dab hand at it, but not enough to say she wasn't comfortable with her natural features. Her full lips were always smeared cherry red, and she always wore a garment of the same shade on her body.

Apparently it was her 'signature.'

That day it was a bloodred pencil skirt with a silky white shirt tucked in.

I wasn't jealous, not liking her because of her body, or style, or confidence—things I didn't have. But there was something about her efforts to talk to me, to be friendly with me that seemed disingenuous.

"Are you okay?" she asked, peering down at me with real concern.

Or maybe I was just so wrapped up in my own disaster that I'd been rude and guarded around her all week, and she was just a nice person who was new in town and trying to make friends.

I was never the woman who treated another person—especially a woman—badly because of my own personal turmoil. You never knew what battle someone was raging inside. I knew that all too well, and I made sure I would never be the reason that battle was harder to fight.

I forced a smile. "Yeah, I'm fine," I said, trying to get my voice to sound convincing. "It's just been... a weird week," I finished lamely.

Understatement of the century.

In addition to Gage's absence, my car miraculously appeared in front of my apartment one morning—right where you weren't allowed to park, of course, so it stood to reason that someone from the club had put it there. It looked good as new. Better.

Someone had rattled on about added features when I called the garage. Then they'd become pretty tight-lipped about how much those 'added features' were. And after not-so-gentle probing, it turned out he wasn't tight-lipped because of how expensive it was. No, because of how cheap.

As in free.

I did not do charity.

Especially from a man who'd rocked my world and then walked out of it, stomping on the ruins he'd made. That man did not get to fix the one thing that could be fixed and do it for free.

I was paying. I was adamant to the man on the phone, bordering on hysterical. The man in question clearly did not do well with borderline hysterical questions, because he muttered about customers and then hung up. And didn't answer when I called back.

Or return my calls.

I planned on doing extensive research that weekend, finding an appropriate sum and mailing them a check.

I jerked my mind back to Jen, who I was meant to be holding a conversation with.

She tossed her hair, her eyes twinkling. "Yeah, it's something, this place. Kind of hard to settle in somewhere where people are so nice. I don't trust it after where I'm from."

"Where is it you were from again?" I asked, trying to rack my brain and hopefully make sure she hadn't told me already.

She waved her manicured hand. "Somewhere *a lot* less nice than this. But it was home, and I had friends there." She paused. "I miss it, you know? Even though this is my fresh start, even though this is going to be good for me, give me exactly what I need."

I forced down my feeling of unease that something else laid behind her words. "What do you need from Amber?"

She showed white teeth, her eyes warm. "Oh, closure, I guess."

I blinked. It was a strange thing to say after talking about a fresh start, but then again, wasn't that exactly what a fresh start was? Closure?

I had no idea what the woman was battling, why that twinkle

in her eye was tinged with something else. But I knew a fair bit about hiding pain behind a smile, and she was doing that too.

I smiled at her, real that time. "I hope you find it here."

She stood, pressed her skirt down and smiled again. "Oh, I think I've already found it." She hitched her bag on her shoulder. "Want to go for a drink to help me celebrate my first week?"

I was about to refuse, the response robotic, since I'd answered all questions like that with a variation of the name answer. No.

But maybe I needed a fresh start too.

"Sure," I said, standing and getting my own purse.

She linked her arm in mine, walking us to the doors.

I attempted to shake off my unease, and push Gage from my mind.

By the end of the night, only one of those things was successful.

THE BANGING at my door woke me up. The sound sent me jerking upright, my spine straight and heart thundering in my chest. I felt like I'd just closed my eyes, and a quick glance at my phone told me I had; it was just after midnight, and I'd gotten home at almost eleven.

Unheard of for me, but I'd shaken off my uneasiness toward Jen to discover she was funny, warm, and easy to talk to. Plus she hadn't pried when I'd stuck to water, only nodded once when I informed her I didn't drink. That was enough for me to lower my boundaries and let myself have a good time. Engage. Maybe not as much as I did with Amy, but something similar.

And though I hated to succumb to clichés, the time did fly. And I almost didn't think about Gage every second.

Almost.

I'd obviously banished him from my mind enough to get

myself to sleep, if my brutal wake-up call was anything to go by. I was halfway down the stairs on instinct, not realizing that someone pounding on my door after midnight did not want to come around for tea. And no one came around to my place for tea, even at a decent hour.

My hand paused on the knob, and the wood rattled underneath my grip as a fist slammed against it. I jumped back, fear working to shake the last of sleep from my addled mind.

My grip tightened as I considered the option of running back up the stairs and hoping whoever was on the other side of that door would go away. It's what I *should've* done. I definitely should've snatched my phone from beside my bed and been prepared to dial 911.

Because whoever thought it was appropriate to bang on people's doors in the middle of the night was not going to contribute to my logical and calm life.

No, they'd smash right through it.

I didn't run up the stairs. Because I was quickly turning into one of the girls from all those books and movies, making stupid and perhaps dangerous decisions for men. Because I hoped the person damn near splintering the wood of my door was Gage.

So I opened it.

And I got my hope.

My calm world laid down in pieces at my feet. And it would stay there. I knew that somehow. Gage was no longer going to be a ghost in my memories, a crack in my life. He was there in the flesh and blood, and the view of him was splintering me to my very core.

"Oh my God," I breathed, gaping at the man in front of me in shock.

The man who was not just flesh and blood—he was *covered* in blood.

The man I'd been hoping for.

Along with the monster I knew lived inside him.

He didn't hesitate, didn't speak, didn't give any explanation for why he was there, why he was covered in blood that didn't seem to be his own. Because there was no way he'd have been standing in front of me if the blood covering his shirt, his face, his jeans was all his.

It was sick of me to find relief in that thought. To be glad that someone, somewhere wasn't standing, likely not breathing, but I *was* glad.

Gage gripped my arm, crossing the threshold and pressing me to the wall in my entranceway, slamming the door behind us.

The landing before the stairs leading up to my apartment was tight at the best of times. This was far from the best of times. Gage's expanse barely fit in the small area. But it did. And it fit so his entire muscled body was pressing against me. Blood that was sticky and fresh stained my white flannelette pajamas.

Shit, I'd answered the door in *flannelette pajamas.* I was pretty sure they had little stars and moons stitched into them. So not sexy. Why couldn't I be the woman who slept in sexy negligees for no one but herself? Why couldn't I be the woman who *owned* a single sexy piece of nightwear?

And why was I the woman worrying about such a thing when the man she'd been damn near obsessing over for the past week was pressing against her *covered in someone else's blood*?

Yeah, that needed to be the most important thing in the situation, not my body's reaction to his being against mine.

"You're covered in blood, Gage," I whispered when he didn't speak, merely held me to the wall, breathing heavily and devouring me with ice-blue eyes.

Those eyes glanced down between us, seeming almost surprised to see the crimson smear on the swell of my chest. But then they darkened, focusing on the fact that though my flannelette wasn't exactly sheer, I wasn't wearing a bra, and my body had a visceral response to Gage's pressed against mine, despite the circumstances.

His dark gaze shot back up to mine, and I felt it in my core.

"I am covered in blood," he agreed, voice rough. Brutal. "Always will be."

I blinked slowly as the tenor of his voice settled over my skin, electrifying every inch of it. "Whose blood are you covered in right now?" I asked, my own voice shaking.

He didn't hesitate. Didn't move a muscle. "A dead man's."

I flinched at the simple and emotionless response. I also read between the lines. He was wearing another man's blood. A dead man's. And it was not a dead man he'd tried to help, tried to save before he died. No, this was a man he'd *killed*.

But was I surprised? I'd known Gage was dangerous from the start. And not just because of his bike, his cut, the club he belonged to, but because of his eyes. I'd seen it. The death in them.

I should've recoiled at the mere fact that I was being touched by a murderer. That my crisp white pajamas, my crisp white life, were being stained with a murdered man's blood.

So why wasn't I?

"Who was he?" I asked, my voice small but not shaking as it should've been. I should've been terrified that he was so large he could snap me in two. That he was covered in blood. That it wasn't the first time he'd killed someone, if the still and resigned tone to his voice was anything to go by. And it wouldn't be the last.

His eyes changed, swirled, his body taut, humming. Something flickered over his iron features—surprise, perhaps. Maybe he didn't expect me to be asking questions like that. Not screaming. Not fighting.

I was surprised too.

"Does it matter?" he replied finally. It was a challenge, his gaze. His question. It was the crossroads where I was going to be forced to make a choice that would either change—maybe destroy —my life beyond repair, or would yank me back into my safe and boring existence with only the lingering aftertaste of chaos on my tongue.

I thought on it.

Yeah, it did. It really fricking mattered. This was a person's *life*. I was going to take an educated guess and say the person wasn't good. They likely swam in the underbelly of society, committed sins against that same society. Because I was taking the same educated guess in thinking that Gage didn't kill innocent people—if there were any of those left anymore. That he wasn't some kind of true monster who killed without conscience.

Or maybe that was just a prayer.

A prayer that no god would ever answer. Because I was looking at a man who had abandoned faith, and faith had abandoned him. Prayers weren't heard here. No way were they answered.

Or maybe this was the dark answer to something I didn't even know I'd been asking for. Something I'd been too afraid to crave. Someone I *was* too afraid to crave.

But no matter what, murder was murder. And it mattered. Because I wasn't a person who lived in the underbelly of society and regularly stained my clothes with blood. I wasn't used to violence. And I wasn't suited for it. This life would chew me up and spit me out. This life would destroy me.

This man would destroy me.

So I needed to say yes, that it did matter, and walk down that fork in the road that promised safety and order.

"No," I whispered. "No, it doesn't matter."

That time there wasn't just a flicker of surprise. Gage's entire body flinched at my words.

But I didn't let him speak. Didn't let myself think. I went up on my tiptoes and pressed my mouth to his so I wouldn't have to hear any more ugly truth. So there was nothing else stacking up as to why I should be running from things that were going to destroy me, not kissing them.

But *I* wasn't kissing them.

Because the second my lips pressed to Gage's, my actions stopped.

He froze for about a millisecond, one I was able to recognize because our kiss gave way to another cliché—time stopping. Everything seemed to move in slow motion between the moment my lips touched his and the small pause before he started to well and truly destroy me.

My heart was a roar in my ears, every part of my skin tingling with electricity, fear, excitement. Desire pooled in my stomach.

And then I couldn't recognize any of my feelings as a low growl in the back of Gage's throat drowned the thundering of my heart.

His mouth opened to me, and any control I had over the kiss disappeared as he clutched my hip with one hand and tore into my hair with the other, yanking our bodies together as he attacked my mouth with brutal ferocity.

The kiss was madness. There was only one way to describe it. A fall into insanity.

Pain erupted at my lips as his teeth crashed into them, warm metallic blood filling my mouth. Another growl as it filled his, the hardness at my stomach telling me he liked it, having my blood in his mouth.

The wetness soaking my panties told me I liked it too.

The kiss was nothing I'd ever experienced before. Nothing I didn't think anyone had experienced, because no way could anyone *survive* it. It was *wrong.* Depraved to be kissing someone moments after they'd confessed murder. While they were covered in blood.

But there was nothing on earth I could've been doing— breathing had never been as important to me as having Gage's mouth moving against mine. *This* was breathing, truly breathing. He wasn't giving me the kiss of life. It was the kiss of death, and all I could think of was *more.*

And the second I thought that, it was taken away from me, just as brutally as it was given.

I let out a little cry of protest as Gage's hands came up to either side of his face. The cords in his neck were tight, etched with evidence of the effort it was taking him to be still in the moment after the chaos of our kiss. His eyes silenced me, the beautiful cruel desire in them stopping my heartbeat. Or at the very least controlling it.

"This is it, Lauren," he clipped, his voice little more than a low growl. "The last moment I'm gonna give you to step away from this. The last moment I'm gonna be able to *let* you step away from this. Me. Us."

He didn't say anything else, his jaw clenched to the point of shattering.

But he didn't need to say anything else, because his words were clear. He was giving me one last chance to escape. To gather the ruins of the life he'd blown into, pick up the pieces that were still big enough to be glued back together so one day he would be but a ghost of a time when I could've taken a different path.

It was tempting. Safe.

And not at all an option.

I shook my head slowly. "I'm not going anywhere," I murmured, my voice throaty and raw.

"So be it," he rasped.

And then his lips were on top of mine, more brutal than before, because there was no end now.

This was the end.

Gage

She tasted like peppermint.

Fucking *peppermint*.

He still had the rancid taste of death on his tongue, but the second his mouth invaded hers, it was gone. Replaced with that clean and fresh fucking taste.

Replaced with *her*.

She was clean.

Or she had been until the moment she'd opened that door.

Fuck, until the moment she'd gotten on the back of his bike that night an eternity ago.

A good man would not have knocked on a clean and innocent woman's door at midnight. He sure as shit wouldn't be doing it covered in the blood of a man he'd killed. And no way in fuck would a sane man admit he'd killed someone when he held the most innocent and cleanest of women in his arms. Because that was a surefire way to make sure that innocent and clean woman would run.

But Gage was not a good man. Or a sane one.

So he'd come after finally ending the fuck he'd found raping a girl chained to a bed, while another one bled out on the floor beside him, after calling in someone who would disappear the girl who'd survived—though it was a shitty word for what she had done.

Survive.

She was not a survivor. Because shit like that killed a lot of important things inside a person. Shit like that pretty much killed everything that person would need to exist in normal society.

Whatever the fuck normal was.

Whatever it was, she'd never exist within the parameters of normal again. A trauma that dark guaranteed the death of the soul.

So she was not a survivor.

A zombie was closer to what she was at that moment and would be every moment after that. Gage wasn't one to save damsels, and even if he was, there was no saving that one. So he did all he could do, putting her in a car with a man he trusted to give her whatever life she had left, would ever have.

After that, he rode hard.

It was a dangerous and reckless thing to do, speed through the state wearing a well-known MC patch on his back and a pint of blood on his front. Blood that wasn't his. If he'd been pulled over, he would've been fucked.

But he was already fucked. And staying stationary with his demons clawing at his skin, with the images of those girls ripping at the flesh inside his mind—fuck, that was suicide. Because if he'd stayed even a moment to shower, change clothes, get sleep that had been absent for days now, he wouldn't have washed shit. Wouldn't have gotten clean. Nor slept. He would've found a needle, plunged it into his favorite vein.

There was only one destination that promised something other than that.

One woman.

And he knew what riding there would mean for her. What he was doing to her life. And he didn't fucking care. Because he wasn't good. Or sane.

It had taken everything he had to give her that last way out. Especially after seeing her answer the door in those stupid white pajamas that were somehow the sexiest thing he'd ever seen a woman wear. Her face was still flushed with sleep, eyes wide and bright beneath her glasses, hair wild over her shoulders.

And then he tasted her fucking mouth. She had fucking *kissed* him. Pressed her hot and soft little body against his. Her *clean* body. She'd stained it with the blood of his sins without hesitation.

And she'd fucking *kissed* him.

Gage didn't think there was a moment better than the second the junk hit his system, took everything away. Having her full and sensual lips press against his was fucking close. Taking her mouth hard and brutal and have her fucking *love* it? Yeah, it eclipsed that shit.

He hadn't even sunk his dick in her yet and she was more addictive than junk.

The junk had ruined him, and he'd beat it. As much as someone could beat it, anyway. The scars on his arms were a reminder that there was no such thing as beating it. He'd just found something to replace it with. *Someone.* And he knew for a fact that he was going to ruin her.

But he didn't fucking care. Because he didn't save damsels. He ruined them.

"I'm not going anywhere," she whispered, eyes on his, throaty voice touching his cock.

Gage's mind pushed away thoughts of what he was going to do to her in the end. It was easier than it should've been, because it was consumed with what he was going to do to her right fucking then.

"So be it," he murmured, his last apology to the gods for damning himself further.

Not that the gods even listened to him anymore.

The only one who heard him was the Devil, and he was doing more work in his name. That's what damned men did, after all.

He didn't hesitate in taking her mouth again, for good that time. She let out a sound that damn near made him cream his pants as he lifted her, fucking desperate to get her body plastered to his. She complied immediately, wrapping her legs around him, pressing her cunt into the hardness covered by his jeans, mimicking his desperation, challenging it.

She let out another cry in his mouth as he moved, creating friction between them while taking the stairs two at a time. He had never felt so wild, so fucking anxious to be inside a woman before. Like he would come out of his skin if he didn't sink into her cunt in the next five seconds.

And for him to be aware of how close he was to the edge, it meant something. Because he lived his life on the edge.

Her hands tore through his hair with ferocity, yanking at the strands with a violence he felt in his cock. He got off on violence, after all. There was a reason he only took certain bitches—the ones with hardness in their eyes and souls—to his bed.

When he reached the top of the stairs, his cock and whatever remained of his sanity couldn't take it anymore. Couldn't take the three steps that would put her on the sofa, sure as shit not the six it would take to get to her bed. No, nothing had seemed so urgent in his life as the need to get inside her.

So he went to his knees, Lauren still attached to him like a fucking sex kitten, attacking him with the same amount of ferocity that he was giving to her. He never would've expected that shit from her. Fuck, it was why he hadn't taken her earlier. He'd been so fucking certain that she wasn't going to be able to handle his particular kind of fuckery. And he'd known he would break her.

Now he was beginning to think she could handle being broken. Then again, this wasn't even the surface of his fuckery. He wasn't stupid enough, even insane with his need for her, to show her that shit right then.

Her back hit the floor and she barely noticed; he had to forcibly remove her legs from his hips, the pads of his fingers pressing into the soft skin through the fabric of her pajamas. In a motion that pained him, literally fuckin' pained him, he detached his lips from hers, flattening his hand against her chest and pushing her flat on her back.

Her hair splayed around her like a fucking halo, her lips swollen, bright red, begging to be wrapped around his cock.

And they would be.

Later.

But there was no time for that shit now.

"Gage," she whispered, her words only slightly more than an exhale.

His eyes darted to hers, which seemed to be glowing, her lashes hooding the pure fucking sex in her gaze. Underneath those glasses.

Fuck.

Yeah, she was gonna handle being broken.

"Shut the fuck up," he growled, unable to hear that voice and look at that face without exploding in his pants.

He'd never done that shit before.

Lauren was already creating a lot of nevers for him, but that sure as shit wasn't going to be one of them. Lotta people would've considered the shit he did to women as disrespectful, depraved. And it fuckin' was. But the bitches *always* got off before he did. He considered it disrespectful and depraved to rob a woman of an orgasm and whatever remained of her innocence when he fucked her.

His cock twitched as Lauren blinked rapidly, her mouth snapping shut, complying with his order. The hand at her chest rose and fell rapidly with her frenzied breaths, her body writhing underneath him, her fucking nipples pressing through even that thick and ridiculous fabric encasing them.

His palm moved before he realized it, buttons flying around them as he ripped the fabric apart, exposing her perfect tits. He let out a hiss between his teeth at the sight of them. Pink, hard nipples, begging to be put between his teeth. Full tits that would fit inside his hand perfectly. That needed his fucking marks pressed into them.

And she would be marked on the outside.

But right then getting inside was all that mattered.

And not just inside her pussy.

"Stay the fuck down," he commanded as she watched him with that hooded gaze.

Again she did what he said.

Again he felt it in his fuckin' cock.

He gripped the waistband of her pants and yanked, ripping the fabric right down the middle and exposing her bare cunt to him.

No panties.

A square of hair neatly covering her clit.

His cock pulsed again. He wasn't fussy with pussy, but he preferred hair. Fucking loved it, in fact. Not a lot, but exactly what Lauren had. A porn star strip. His quiet little librarian had a fucking porn star strip.

His fingers delved into it. There was no choice in that.

Her back arched up and she let out a low cry when he made contact, when he covered himself with her.

Soaking.

She was fucking *soaking*.

He lost it then. Well and truly. He yanked at his belt as he moved to cover her body with his, clutching her neck painfully to bring her eyes to meet his. She gasped when he freed himself from his pants to press his cock against her entrance.

It was pure pain to stay there, to feel her heat beckoning him, to be at the gates of Heaven and fuckin' pause.

But he did.

Because he was a man who was resigned to the fact that he

was in Hell. That Heaven would always be lost to him. He'd never wanted it anyway. Saints only showed him what kind of a sinner he was. The worst kind. He didn't want that shit. Didn't need anyone or anything reminding him of how blackened and charred his soul really was.

Not until right then.

He'd never craved Heaven more.

So he let that moment sink into his bones. Lauren's soft and wild gaze against his skin. Her hot and naked body writhing against his hard and scarred flesh. The blood from his sins smearing against her pale skin.

And then he surged inside.

She cried out the second he did so, her scream echoing off the walls of the apartment. Off the walls of his skull.

He wasn't worried about her not being ready. She was fucking *ready*. Fuck, he'd bet that she'd been ready since the moment she'd pressed her lips against his.

But she was tight. And he was big. So he took everything he had to pause once he was clenched in her tight heat. Once he was in fucking Heaven.

"Babe," he gritted out, his voice feral.

Her eyes, which had been squeezed shut, opened. He didn't see the pain he expected. No, he saw insanity, the wild need pulsating through his blood.

"Move," she pleaded, her voice raw.

And he obliged, setting forth to pillage Heaven for his own depraved desires.

Lauren

Was it possible to overdose on a person?

On orgasms?

Because I was pretty sure it was, and I was pretty sure that's what had happened when Gage started fucking me on the floor of my apartment.

And I wasn't a girl who 'fucked.' Or even used the word to describe the act.

But what we had done for who knew how long, down on the floor, had been *fucking*. Rough. Hard. Brutal.

And utterly freaking amazing.

Beyond amazing.

I didn't have words.

And I was going to be one of those cliché girls again, but it was life-changing. Something that shook me to my very foundation, yanked parts of me awake that had been banished to sleep lest they do something reckless. Dangerous.

Like let a biker covered in blood fuck me on the floor of my loft.

Yeah, that could be considered dangerous.

"Baby?" Gage murmured, bracing himself on his elbows, hovering over me, still inside me. The vibration of his voice traveled downward, like *all the way* down, and I jerked in pain and pleasure.

We had only just resumed this position of him on top of me. There had been many in the course of—four, or was it five?—orgasms. We'd been a blur of writhing bodies, my skin rubbing against the harsh fabric of his clothes, consumed with each other, consumed in our pleasure.

Another thing I didn't think happened in real life—multiple orgasms. I was sure they were something just dreamed up by someone to make women feel unsatisfied with the single orgasm a man may or may not give them. But I was wrong. My fried brain and ovaries were well aware of how real they were.

"Mmhmm?" I hummed, lazily blinking.

"You feel like gettin' off the floor?" His voice was thick, full of sex, like the very scent of the air around us.

"Does that mean you're going to have to get out of me?" I asked dreamily, not even realizing what I was saying until I said it. I didn't say things like that. I didn't say *anything* during sex. Though all the sex I'd had had been in a bed and in missionary position with men who were polite and gentle.

Gage was not polite.

Or gentle.

He had been brutal. From the way he'd spoken to me to the way he'd handled my body. Like he wasn't scared of breaking me. Like he'd *wanted* to break me.

And I'd loved it.

And I'd loved it loudly.

Gage froze and my eyes snapped open, fully alert, to see his face painted in an expression I didn't recognize. It wasn't the hard and dangerous intensity that had been there when he'd fucked me. That was still there, but it was mixed with something else.

I didn't have time to inspect it, because he moved and my legs instinctively went around my hips as he stood, the motion sending more shoots of pleasure along my sensitive nerve endings. Gage felt my reaction, if his hiss of breath was anything to go by. "No, baby, I'm not pullin' my cock outta you when you ask for me to stay inside in that throaty little voice of yours," he murmured, brushing his lips against mine as he strode across the short distance to my bedroom.

My apartment was originally all open plan, but I had a wall erected to section off a modest area to work as my bedroom, large enough for my wrought iron bed, distressed white dresser and a small walk-in closet. I didn't want the small number of visitors I had having to hang out in my bedroom. Plus, my bedroom was my space. Mine alone. No one had entered it, not even the few men who had taken me to bed. They'd taken me to theirs, not this one. It was an unconscious decision on my part, but I realized it was because I didn't want a man's presence in there unless I expected that presence to be permanent.

And I didn't even think twice about the fact that Gage was entering my room and what that meant about the permanence of his presence. Especially since he was entering it while still inside me. And I was naked, the remains of my tattered pajamas in shreds on the floor.

All his clothes, down to his boots, were still on, and he was still wearing his bloodstained white henley and leather cut.

It should've made me feel vulnerable, being naked while he was clothed, and covered in blood. But it didn't. It excited me.

He didn't lay us down on the bed, just stopped, standing in the middle of the room, one hand on my ass, the other at my neck. His cock was still hard inside me. I had known he would have stamina. The pure sex radiating off him the moment I'd seen him told me that.

I'd never felt so *filled*. So complete, despite the fact that he'd broken me into pieces.

"Gotta clean this blood off, Will," he murmured, eyes never moving from mine.

I glanced down to see the faint red streaks across my chest. Blood.

I had someone else's blood on me. It should've sickened me more than it did.

It didn't sicken me at all.

I glanced up, captured in his spell, my body crying out for me to damn myself further, for *more* of him. There was a hunger inside me I didn't even realize I had, and it seemed it wasn't sated, even though my limbs were jelly and I wasn't sure if I'd survive another orgasm.

"Later," I murmured, not recognizing my own voice, functioning purely on my need for him.

Surviving was overrated.

"BABY."

I had survived.

Barely.

Gage hadn't just taken me to the edge, he'd sent us both plummeting over it. My screams had bounced off the walls. His grunted and cruel demands snaked into the very air of the room. Not only was my bedroom saturated with his presence, it was tattooed with it. It had seeped into the foundation.

The evidence of the night would never leave. No matter what happened when the sun came up.

I didn't want the sun to come up.

I didn't want anything, my limbs screaming at me for the rigorous movements of the past few hours. My insides and outsides were aching from Gage's touch.

"Lauren."

Hair was brushed from where it stuck to my face with the thin sheen of sweat that covered my entire body.

It soaked through Gage's henley, the one that was somehow still clinging to his body, attached to those muscles that were made from hot iron.

I blinked at him as he came into brutal focus, his face carved so it was stark against the backdrop of the room. His eyes were glued to mine, his face blank, full of sharp angles. My own face stung slightly with the evidence of his beard brushing against the skin. The same sensation existed between my thighs, evidence of where his mouth had been, where he had devoured me with abandon.

I shuddered at the mere thought of it.

Men had done that before, because it was expected as polite behavior in the bedroom. And because they'd wanted me to reciprocate. I'd let men do it because it was what I was supposed to do. I hadn't enjoyed it. Ever. I'd felt uncomfortable, self-conscious, and was usually counting down the moments until it was over.

I had certainly never orgasmed with a man's mouth on me.

But I'd never had Gage's mouth on me.

And it was not uncomfortable.

It was explosive.

Glorious.

He'd eaten me like a starving man. Devoured me, swallowed my pleasure and my soul at the same time.

It wasn't polite. Or expected.

It was everything.

Gage's form tightened with my movement as he slowly pulled out of me.

I seemed to melt into the mattress without him to keep me solid, his hand at my neck the only thing holding me together.

The evidence of just how raw and naked our fucking had been slowly leaked out of me, and my entire form stiffened with realization.

I'd had sex without a condom. More than once.

Never, not once in my careful and safe life had I done that.

Never.

I was on the pill, had been since I was thirteen to regulate my periods, so I wasn't overly worried about pregnancy, though there was still a chance. I made a note to plot my cycle to make sure there wasn't even a possibility for me to be pregnant.

With Gage's baby.

I pushed away the strange warmth that came with that thought.

Because that was *insane.*

And I had more pressing matters at hand. Because Gage was not like me. He wasn't careful or safe. And I doubted his sex life resembled mine in any way whatsoever. The bruises that I guessed would be covering my body would be evidence of that.

Not that I was worried about the bruises.

I liked them.

The dark part of me loved them. Craved more of them.

"We didn't use a condom," I breathed.

The expression on Gage's face froze, as did the hand at my hair. He shuttered everything inside him, as if he'd only just realized it. It was a look that told me that he never in his dangerous and chaotic life had forgotten to practice safe sex.

Or maybe that was just wishful thinking.

"Don't expect you to believe me," he rasped after a long and uncomfortable silence. "Fuck, *I* wouldn't believe me. Very few instances where this word applies to me, Lauren. Only two, in fact. But I'm clean, baby."

His eyes flickered with something. Something deep. Something I wanted to swim in, but would likely drown in. I wanted to dive in just the same.

"Don't expect you to take me at my word," he continued, voice brusk. "In fact, I'm gonna insist that you don't. Give you my papers tomorrow. Proof." His hand tightened at my neck. "Don't know if you'll believe that I'm clean, but believe me when I say that I'd never risk shit with you. Not with you. Never would I ever fucking risk tarnishing you any more than necessary. I won't keep you safe in most ways, but in making sure I preserve you in the utterly beautiful and healthy state you are now, believe me, I'll fucking lose a limb to make that happen."

The declaration was so fierce it felt like he'd written it in blood.

Maybe he had. There was blood smeared between the two of us, after all.

He held himself so tight, so hard that it hurt me just to look at it. So I reached up, covering his hand with mine.

"I believe you," I whispered. "I trust you."

He flinched. Actually *flinched* at my reply.

A long and uncomfortable silence followed those words. Words that were tattooed between us. That meant something pivotal.

And then he moved, taking me into his arms, my head pounding at the brutal movement.

"We need to get you clean," he grunted, walking us out the door and across the living room toward my bathroom. He glanced down at me, his face still shuttered, as if it was a void for all emotion. "As clean as I can make you after that, at least."

The words were yanked out of him. Ugly. Full of self-hatred, like he was disgusted at what he'd done to me.

But my brain was still swirling. Still soft at the edges from everything that had happened. I couldn't process it all properly. I'd have to store it away for later inspection. Have to figure out a way to show Gage that I wasn't as clean as he thought I was.

But there wasn't enough room for more pain right then.

He set me on my unsteady feet, holding my hips for a long moment as if he sensed my need for him to anchor me. He kept eye contact the entire time. It was a strange thing, the way he did that. A lot of people—all of my lovers included—couldn't handle the intimacy of holding on to eye contact. A lot of Eastern cultures believed that a soul could be sucked out from the eyes.

Of course, in our Western society, we considered ourselves too dictated by science and logic to believe such things. But I'd always thought it was a throwaway from that 'illogical' belief when those in our contemporary society always seemed to shy away from constant eye contact, always breaking it when it went past the socially defined norms.

And I was right.

Because Gage was sucking out my soul with his eyes.

And I was letting him.

All I wanted was his in return. But I reasoned that it was going to be a lot harder than that, because he was more damaged than I was. That became apparent after he turned on my shower and his cut hit the floor. Then he peeled off his henley.

Then I saw it.

Saw him.

Not all of him.

Not even a majority.

Just the tip of his proverbial iceberg.

I may have been out of it, everything about me soft and falling apart at the edges, but the sight of his naked skin once he'd taken off his cut and shirt punctured my mind. It tore through it, brutally yanking me back to stark reality.

His arms were huge. Muscled. Carved from marble, it seemed. But not smooth and flawless like any kind of polished stone. No, it wasn't the absolute beauty of his form that jerked me into lucidity. It was the ugly, brutal evidence of what life had done to him, etched into his skin.

I'd always assumed his arms would be enveloped in the same tattoos that covered his hands, right up to almost his fingertips. I hadn't had much of a chance to inspect the designs on his skin, considering every moment with him up until that point didn't give way for calm inspection. Every moment between us was injected with brutal chaos.

But now the storm had hit, tore through everything inside me, though there was no evidence of it on the outside. The inside was that same chaos that lurked behind Gage's eyes.

That chaos I now knew went so deep that he wore it on his skin. There were tattoos, but most of them were obscured, slightly warped.

Because of what else decorated his skin.

Scars ribboned up both his forearms, starting just above his wrist and snaking almost to his shoulders.

I'd never seen anything like it in my entire life. A road map of pain. Of brutality. Because the puckered and raised skin communicated an almost unthinkable amount of pain to have that evidence carved into your skin. My stomach roiled at the utter agony Gage must've experienced to achieve that kind of scarring. On both of his arms. Some patches were fainter than others, and there were small areas of naked, untouched skin, but it was hard to look at. Almost impossible, but I had to. Because it helped me understand that dark emptiness in his eyes. Why I'd found his face, his entire presence something more than the beautiful masculinity people would see if his scars were covered.

I saw the pain in it because I recognized it.

Because I wore it on my skin too. It was just invisible.

He was watching me with that cold and cruel gaze that made him look like a psychopath. That made my intrinsic survival instinct flare up, telling me I was in danger, real and visceral danger.

He was waiting. When he'd peeled off his shirt, he'd known what he'd be exposing. And now he was challenging me, daring me to do something. I didn't know what. Likely he expected me to say something. To ask him something. Surely that's what people had done previously, wanted to point out the most uncomfortable part of his life, make it define him.

My feet were lead as I pushed them across the tile separating us, through the slowly thickening steam filling the room. Still his eyes were cold, deadly, his entire body wired.

My fingertips trailed down from the top of his shoulder, slowly, purposefully. He flinched as I did so, as if I was slicing through the flesh, opening the wounds. Every part of him was iron, his entire body shaking with my touch. I knew he was uncomfortable, wanted me to stop. Which was why I kept going.

I continued, my finger light, my eyes never leaving his. Pain reverberated up my hand, up my arm and all the way to my heart as my fingertip trailed the length of his trauma.

Then I reached the smooth skin of his hand and I tightened my grip, lacing his fingers with mine, bringing our intertwined hands together to lay a kiss on the top of his. His eyes lost all that cold menace, melting against the heat of his gaze, the naked intensity of it.

He was still waiting, I knew that. I could see it. He was expecting something. Because when you were disfigured or broken in a way that was obvious to the world, the world asked questions. Did everything it could to make sure there was no way to hide. To forget.

The world was cruel.

It made Gage cruel.

But it wasn't going to make me cruel.

So I slowly and purposefully opened the door to my shower, stepping into it and bringing Gage with me. His body was anchored to the spot for a moment, not prepared for me to move, to yank him to the shower to wash off what cruelty I could.

But then he moved.

And he *moved*.

The shower door was closed, water cascading off our naked bodies, coloring pink at the drain as the blood washed off us.

Gage's hands were at my neck, yanking me to him in the small space so our soaking bodies were plastered together. His mouth was attached to mine in the next moment, the kiss different than the ones we'd shared before. It wasn't soft or tender. I knew Gage couldn't give me soft or tender, had guessed it when I saw that coldness, that darkness behind his eyes. I was certain now seeing the scars on top of his skin.

But I had my own scars too.

And though they couldn't be seen, I realized they made it so I didn't want soft or tender.

So I sank into the kiss.

But it was more than just a kiss.

It was Gage showing me that I'd tilted his world too. That I'd shaken it to the core.

It was a harbinger of the destruction we'd bring one another.

EIGHT

A knocking woke me up.

Or more accurately, a *banging*, since the sound traveled all the way from the door, into my bedroom and punctured what had been, until that moment, a pretty deep slumber.

The knocking teased me out of sleep, and then the incredible heat covering every inch of my body fully woke me. It took me a couple of moments to realize the source of that heat. To remember who was holding me. Why every square inch of my body ached underneath the grip of the scarred arms atop mine.

Gage.

He was in my bed. He was *cuddling* me. My chin was using his muscled pec as a pillow, my leg cocked up and slung across his body. I was draped over him, my naked body pressing into his skin. In his sleep, he didn't seem to be complaining, holding me so tight against his chest it was hard to breathe. How it was the knocking and not the struggle to inhale that woke me up, I had no idea. Or maybe I did. My body was willing to forgo oxygen in order to have Gage.

That, of course, was insane.

But it was also *right*.

Because had there not been a knocking at the door, I wouldn't have even *entertained* the idea of moving. Who needed their full lung capacity anyway?

I'd always considered Gage to be hard. Everything about him was. His eyes. The angles of his face. Whatever darkness and evil lay behind his eyes. His muscles, sculpted from pure stone, the scar tissue rippling across those muscles, melding into them with a permanence that showed his demons would always live on his skin.

But sleeping in those arms was one hundred times better than my Tempur-Pedic pillow that took three months to pick out. In his sleep, his body was still hard, but it was relaxed, almost bordering on vulnerable. But not quite. The way he clutched me to him seemed like he was expecting someone to try and wrench me away while he slumbered, and he was ready to wake up and fight whoever tried.

I toyed with the idea of ignoring the not-so-gentle knock at my door, curl into Gage—who was still asleep, if his relaxed breaths were anything to go by—and pretend the sun wasn't up, that it would be as simple as staying in bed, naked and safe in the arms of the man who was the antithesis of safety.

But the knocking persisted.

And I was one of those people who, when I was awake, I was *awake*. Once I had abandoned my dreams—or more accurately, my nightmares—I was ready to proceed in getting through another day.

For once, I wasn't just ready to *proceed* and *get through* another day.

I was *terrified* of what the day would hold.

And it meant something. That I was alive. Properly and truly alive.

Gage was little more than a dead weight, and it took considerable effort and jostling just to get myself from under him—yet he stayed asleep. I wondered how tired a person must need to be to sleep that deep. Something warmed my terrified heart, because a person can't be just *tired* to sleep that hard. A person had to feel safe, utterly and completely safe, in order to render themselves so vulnerable.

And a lot of people might argue that something like sleeping deeply when one was super tired wasn't something you could control. I disagreed. Because I had the sense that Gage controlled *everything* about himself. His violence and menace weren't borne out of chaos. No, it was structured. Controlled. He controlled it because if he let his guard down, his demons would eat him alive. So he chose to live in danger and violence in order to keep the demons at bay.

Much like I controlled my safety and logic in order to survive.

He just went a different way.

Okay, maybe a *way* different way. On a different planet type of way.

And yet somehow he was there. Naked in my bed, the sheets riding low on his hips so I was treated to the full glimpse of his muscles from the sun streaming in the windows. I didn't think men had eight-packs in real life.

Gage did.

I doubted he had any body fat percentage, he was that ripped.

His entire chest was tattooed in such an intricate design, the art of it beyond anything I'd ever seen. And that was saying something since art was my life. My secret life, but my life nonetheless.

Though I knew I had to get up before the knocking finally woke Gage, I paused to feast my eyes on his chest.

It was like Gage himself, beautiful and ugly at the same time. Savage in its construction but painfully stunning to look at. From shoulder to shoulder, spanning his entire chest to the middle of his ribs, were the gates of Hell. It couldn't be anything else. A hooded skeleton with illuminated eyes was perched in the middle, his hood and plumes of smoke snaking up toward Gage's neck. Shadowed clouds were the background of the piece. Then, downward, merging into the skeleton's body were two open large gates, their light giving way to darkness. Right in the middle of them was the Devil himself, holding a sword in one hand and beckoning with a clawed talon with his other. He stood on a floor of flaming human skulls.

That was the tattoo on close inspection. At first glance, the entire design and the details within it were in the shape of a human skull. The talent was incredible.

What it meant was horrifying.

Gage was literally wearing Hell above his heart.

And if that was on the skin above it, it was agony to think of what lay underneath.

But I couldn't think on that now.

Not with the morning sun illuminating the darkness.

So I forced my eyes down, to not linger in the pit of pain.

His glorious abs had no ink and I was glad of it. Right where his hips went into that delicious male V was where the tattoos started again. A dark garden of decaying roses and crumbling ruins spanned his hips and moved downward.

My stomach hungered to yank the sheet down, expose the tattoos and more of the dark hair creeping upward from his groin.

I ached to explore him in the sunlight, to trace every inch of the beautiful artistry with my fingers. And my aching and ruined body craved something else. I clenched my tender thighs at the mere thought of it. The memory.

Desire for him consumed me in a dark way that definitely wasn't healthy.

My eyes jerked to his arms, splayed along the bed now that I wasn't encased in them. In the harsh light of day, the scars were just that—harsh. Brutal. Evidence of something literally ripping at his flesh, grinding it up. It didn't look real.

It *couldn't* be real.

But it was.

Because reality was always stranger than fiction. And it was always uglier. Harder to swallow. That's why everyone preferred the candy cane fiction. Why happy-ever-afters always earned more than the tragic endings.

Because people didn't want to be reminded that reality was harsh and cruel. They wanted to pretend, until the last possible moment, that life was like a Disney movie.

But there was no Disney here.

A tear ran down my cheek. I knew, was certain those scars—and the story behind them—were the key to him.

To unraveling him.

To destroying us both.

Because scars like that never healed. Neither did the person wearing them. I knew that better than anyone; I just didn't have to look at my scars in the mirror every day.

My hands itched with the need to hold a paintbrush. To immortalize this moment, the way I felt living within it. To communicate it the only way I knew how. To hold onto this feeling, to put it somewhere tangible where I could revisit it after Gage's chaos had torn out of my life. Because he *had* to tear out of it. He was a fire, an inferno, and I was shutting out all his air with my calmness. Fires needed oxygen to burn.

It was only a matter of time.

Hence my need to make this moment count before it was stolen away from me by that tragic reality everyone pretended didn't exist.

But the person outside my apartment was obviously not going away, and I didn't want Gage to wake up. I wanted to continue to keep him safe here. To let him sleep without demons.

For as long as I could, at least.

Because there was no way to fight off the demons. They always won in the end.

I padded quietly to my closet, yanking at my robe, hating that I didn't have time to put anything on underneath. It was... *naughty* being naked underneath the fabric—no matter how thick and unsexy—and answering the door to an unknown caller.

The pure thought of such a thing would've had me erupting in hives in any other situation. I wouldn't have been able to walk through my living room and down my stairs in normal circumstances. But these circumstances were far from normal, so I did walk through my living room and down the stairs, pausing to kick my ripped pajamas underneath the sofa and not entirely unpleasant pulse in my core.

I went downstairs, the ghosts of last night caressing me and abusing me at the same time.

I turned and yanked the door handle backward just as the knocks paused.

The second I opened the door, I smiled.

It was instinctive. Habit. A calm happiness settled over me at the sight of the person I would've said personified chaos—until I met Gage.

"Well, finally," a voice snapped. "What do you think you're doing, leaving your poor old grandmother freeze in the cold? I could catch my death out here," she accused, rubbing her arms across the smooth cashmere of her sweater to make her point known. My grandmother committed to her theatrics completely and fully. Always.

I smiled, knowing the sharpness in her voice was as fake as her hair color. But like her bright red locks, it was flawless. Only those who knew her best—me, in other words—would recognize the slight warmness in her tone and in her eyes.

I leaned back on my heels and folded my arms. "We're in California, so I'm thinking you catching your death is one of the least possible outcomes of you standing out here at eight in the morning. I haven't heard about any persons reporting anything more than a slight sniffle from exposure in Amber, and that's more likely to do with the ease of the spread of the common cold than the actual temperature," I said, my voice calm and orderly.

My grandmother pursed her lips, eyes warm. She didn't speak; she was used to this kind of stuff from me and knew I wasn't finished.

I wasn't. "And a certain woman, perhaps even the one standing in front of me, told me that age was just a state of mind. She also threatened to scalp me if I ever mentioned the word 'old' in any kind of proximity to her." My eyes flickered upward in a poor imitation of her practiced sharp and teasing gaze "As for the 'poor' part of that little statement, you're wearing a fur vest and your purse is worth as much as my mortgage payments," I commented, my voice dry and my words accurate.

My grandmother was old money with a decidedly new age state of mind. It was a chaotic and dueling marriage, but she made it her own, like she always did.

She scrunched up her barely lined face—thanks to one of the best cosmetic surgeons in the country, she looked at least twenty-five years younger than her eighty years. "Oh, are you ever just going to let me be wildly dramatic and wildly fabulous without hindering me with such things like *details*?" she snapped. "Plus, this purse could be a knock-off, the fur could be faux and I could've lost all my money in a poker game that I played with a Calvin Klein model with a decidedly deceiving poker face."

I smirked. "You don't play poker."

"Exactly. Which was why I might've lost all of my money

purely because I was bored and it was a Tuesday. You don't know that."

"I know your poker face is better than anyone in the world's, despite the detail that you never play poker," I replied, quirking my brow. "And you told me that you were more likely to fight a crocodile in the wilds of Australia than be seen dead—or alive— wearing anything fake. Including your fur. Which isn't politically correct anymore, in case you were wondering," I added, though I knew it was a vintage piece belonging to her mother, not something she purchased on a regular basis.

She rolled her eyes. "Not once in my life have I wondered or cared about what's politically correct, Lo," she replied, using the nickname one of only two people could call me. The other was dead, so I guessed it was only her who could call me that now.

"Why are you leaving me standing on the doorstep like some common *postman?*" she added, spitting the word out as if it weren't the champagne she drank from France and merely a cheap imitation.

Her turquoise-painted eyes flickered over me in suspicion, as if she was only now noting my attire—or lack thereof. She knew me almost better than I knew myself, so she was aware of how out of character it would be to answer the door in a robe, something she did all the time. Though she would be wearing a silk kimono and cradling a glass of wine with a splash of orange juice. Or a martini with no orange juice to be seen.

"You're about as likely to answer the door in a robe as I would be to be wearing *faux fur,*" she said, voicing my thoughts. Her pink-painted lips parted to reveal sparkling white teeth as she smiled wide. "Has it happened?" she asked, voice hopeful. "Has Hell finally frozen over?" She scrunched her nose up again. "I hope I'll get a full refund. I had a prepaid one-way ticket there. It's a prestigious place, you know, and I wanted to know I got the best real estate."

I rolled my eyes to hide my growing discomfort at her advancing years. No matter how good her plastic surgeon was, or how hungry her energy for life was, life was finite. The thought of her light going out filled me with so much dread, I could barely breathe around the pain.

Because that's when I would be truly alone. When the second and last person to truly understand me, to accept me, left this world. I'd have my parents, whom I loved, but it was different. Like life, the number of people in this world who truly saw you for who you were and celebrated that were finite.

"You're never going to die, Nana," I said, forcing the bitterness of the words and their untruth from my tongue. "You already said you were going to do the whole *Vanilla Sky* thing, despite how badly that turned out for Tom Cruise." I wasn't lying. She had all sorts of harebrained schemes—this was only her latest.

She waved her hand. "Well obviously I'll have you for company, I've already got plans in place to kidnap you when you're in your early sixties and freeze you. I won't tell you the exact date because that would spoil the surprise." She narrowed her eyes. "Stop stalling," she demanded, as if *I* were the one talking about future kidnappings. "Have you got a dead body up there or something?" Her eyes widened like a kid in the proximity of ice cream. "First of all, if you do, I'm so proud. You're finally breaking free of those shackles constructed by society. And second, shame on you. You always promised you'd call me when you needed help burying a body," she chastised.

I shook my head. "And I always promised that it was not a matter of *when* I killed someone, considering burying a body— or creating one—is not on my bucket list," I replied, gritting my teeth at the fact that my grandmother was saying all this in jest, yet she didn't know how close to the truth she was. A naked man lay in my bed. One who had created a body. But I doubted he'd need help burying it. Especially from an eighty-year-old woman.

"Whatever." She waved dismissively, her jewelry glinting in the morning light. She uttered the word with the same attitude of a teenager.

And my eighty-year-old grandmother had the mindset of one. As well as the personal style of a fashionista in their early twenties.

She had on a bright pink beret, somehow not clashing with her expertly styled and curled crimson hair. In addition, she was wearing a matching pink fur gilet. Large diamonds decorated her ears and neck. She never left the house without diamonds. She sometimes left the house in a silk kimono, but never without diamonds.

My grandmother had never grown up and was always of the opinion that normalcy was death. How my father had turned into the ordered and sensible man he did was beyond me—maybe from the grandfather who died before Dad finished high school. But maybe his orderly life was the ultimate act of rebellion that he'd found some kind of solace in. I knew he resented his mother for not giving him the upbringing he gave me. The nuclear family. The white picket fence.

My grandmother once said, "I'd rather be impaled on a white picket fence than live behind one."

I'd gotten my sensible and ordered traits from my father.

But I had a wildness in me that I knew I'd inherited from my grandmother. She knew it too, which was one of the reasons we got on so well. She was always trying to coax it out of me, urge me to do something 'fun,' and doing something fun with my grand-mother more often than not meant doing something illegal.

I was more inclined to let her lead me astray *before* me clinging to my sensible roots was for survival instead of habit.

And for the past ten years, it was for survival.

She understood that. Let me be. As much as someone like her could, at least. Because she was hurting too. Bleeding. Not like me, but she was wounded deeply. Though she didn't let those cuts fester, bleed, continue to drain the life from her like I had. She'd only thrown herself into life more, with fewer reservations —if she'd ever had any in the first place.

But she didn't abandon me, despite the fact that my coping mechanism was the polar opposite of hers. She never called, never planned visits—since she never usually planned, because "that's not how fabulous things happen." She would just turn up on my doorstep, like right now.

And usually my lack of a life meant that was never a problem. She was never interrupting plans because I never had them, though not for the same reason as her.

"So," she jerked me into the present. "Why are you guarding the door like some Brit outside Buckingham Palace?" she demanded. "Well, not *exactly* like one of those pompous pricks, because you're moving and talking and wearing a lot less." She waggled her eyebrows.

"Oh my gosh," she exclaimed, her eyes going wide in realization and peering up the stairs. "You've got someone up there. And not a dead body. A *live one*. A *man* one." Her eyes went over me, electrified with a youth that not many had when they were young, let alone eighty. "You finally got laid!" She clapped in glee.

Heat crept up my neck. "Not finally," I snapped. "I'm not a virgin." She knew that because she was the one I'd told about the fumbling encounter that was my very first time. I hadn't gone into details, because I didn't do sharing of such personal things, but I told her enough to let her know the experience was not one I was keen to repeat.

"This is a different kind of virginity," she said, waving in dismissal. "There's the first time and then there's the *last* time.

You know, the time that changes everything and you'll never be the same again?" She nodded, not to me but to herself. "You've had it."

I groaned, palming my forehead. "Can we please not talk about this?"

"If you can't talk about life-changing sex with your grand-mother, then who can you talk to?"

I raised my brow. "Um, anyone else on the entire planet? Or no one?"

She winked.

"And *you're* the one not letting me in and causing me to come to such realizations on the *street*, so you've really only got yourself to blame," she continued, her sly grin still in place. "You've got to learn how to lie better, my darling." She patted my hand, and then, with a strength that surprised me, she pushed past me and damn near skipped up the stairs. "Now let's see this hunk of man. And find out if his grandfather is single. And still alive," she sang while ascending.

"Shit," I muttered, closing the door and resting my head against the wood. It wasn't that I was embarrassed of Gage. It was the exact opposite. I knew my grandmother would approve, wholeheartedly, especially given the fact that he was in a motor-cycle club that may or may not break the law on a daily basis.

She'd never been impressed by my previous boyfriends. Not that she said as much, but she did go to great pains to call them all 'Chip' and ask them about their 401(k) the way a parent might ask an ex-con how long they were in prison for. To her, their sensible investment portfolios and five-year business plans were worse than a rap sheet a mile long.

So yes, I had the strong inkling that my grandmother would be delighted at a muscled, dangerous, and savagely beautiful biker here to shake up my life. But that wasn't the problem. I didn't know how long my life was going to have him in it for. I was on borrowed time as it was, before he realized exactly what I was—boringly sane, completely and utterly wrong for him.

Dealing with that heartbreak would be bad enough in my private sorrow.

Having to tell my grandmother would be worse.

But there was nothing I could do about it now.

The cackling of my seemingly elated grandmother coming from up the stairs told me that. And the low rumble of Gage's voice that hit me right between the legs.

Yes, the biker I'd *fucked* last night after he'd finished *killing a man* was now making my eighty-year-old grandmother *laugh* at eight in the morning.

I was not a person to use this term in the sense of the word, but I was fucked.

And I had no choice but to go lumbering up the stairs like I was the eighty-year-old in the equation.

The sight upon entering my kitchen stopped me in my tracks. I literally slammed into the air like I'd hit an invisible wall.

Because Gage was in my kitchen, pouring coffee—I always had some on hand for Amy these days—for my grandmother, who was sitting on a barstool with her back to me.

That in itself wasn't exactly an earth-shattering thing.

It was Gage.

In my kitchen.

Doing something as domestic as pouring coffee. After turning up on my doorstep hours before covered in someone else's blood. After he'd fucked me on the very floor I was standing on right then.

Now he was in my kitchen, making coffee, making my grandmother laugh.

Oh, and he was shirtless.

Shirtless.

It was impressive last night. Feeling the ridges of his abs, raking my nails down them—my stomach dipped with the faint red scabs on his midsection serving as evidence of it—feasting my eyes on them in the dim light. I hadn't exactly been in a position to study them correctly since I'd been half insane with desire the entire night. And I'd been rushing this morning.

But now, with the sunlight of the early morning streaming in, illuminating every ridge, every inch of his exposed and ink skin, I didn't quite know what to do with myself.

Actually I did know what to do with myself. My fingers itched to hold a paintbrush, charcoal, a freaking Magic Marker, anything so I could reproduce this moment a thousand times over.

He was art.

There was no other way to describe him.

Not beautiful.

No, he was too hard for that. Not in a way that described his sculpted muscles, but in the way pain had etched itself into his skin.

The scars decorating his arms were so ugly that they had a rhythm to them. A flow that turned them hauntingly beautiful on his sculpted arms. Something so hard to look at it caused me pain. A kind of pain I would be loath to live without.

A pain that would become an addiction.

Yes, he was art.

Of the most brutal and horrible kind.

The greatest art was always created with the greatest and deepest kind of pain, after all.

His eyes met mine in a way that told me he'd known I was there for far longer than the seconds he held my gaze. Though those seconds could've been lifetimes. Not full of that strange awkwardness that came with the morning after. When every-thing was strange and impersonal—in my past experience, anyway—and the fact that you had been intimate the night before only created more distance in the morning.

No, there was none of that distance, though I might've craved it because of the intensity passing between us. One that scared me more than anything ever had in my life.

"Will," he said, his voice low and husky.

I jerked in response. My entire body actually spasmed with the muscle memory of that rough voice in my ear while he pounded into me.

He saw it, my reaction, seemed to sense the erotic direction my mind had gone, because his eyes darkened and his jaw hardened.

"Babe, come here," he demanded with a tone so dripping with sex it should've been illegal. Especially with my freaking *grandmother* sitting between us.

That should've given me pause, her presence. Should've made me hold onto common logic and appropriate behavior and seat myself beside her, be pleasant, civilized, and with the island between Gage and me. A physical barrier.

But there was no pause after his command.

I moved immediately, my body responding to his order the exact same way it had last night, without hesitation. I was rounding the island before my mind could catch up with me, and I stuttered in my step just before I made it to Gage, intending on stopping short of the muscled, scarred and shirtless Adonis in my freaking kitchen.

Of course he wasn't going to let that happen, his eyes narrowing, moving so his hands circled my hip and yanked me into his side, his mouth coming down on mine.

I stiffened when his intention became clear. Yes, my grandmother was pretty worldly and easygoing, but I wasn't about to kiss a shirtless man she'd just met right in front of her. Plus, I hadn't brushed my teeth.

But the second his mouth hit mine, everything in me melted. I forgot my grandmother's presence. Forgot the possibility of morning breath. Forgot the freaking *world*.

The kiss was quick, hard, and closemouthed, but it was firm. It communicated something.

Ownership.

"Gage, you can't kiss me in front of my grandmother while shirtless, seconds after you've met her," I hissed when he released my lips, my voice not as sharp as I would've liked thanks to the fact that his kiss had the same qualities of Xanax. Well, the qualities I imagined Xanax might try to mimic poorly.

"He can and he did," my grandmother interjected when Gage didn't respond, merely stared at me as if he was etching my face into his mind. "And boy, do I approve." Her slow clap echoed in my head as I tried to pull away from Gage.

He merely pressed his lips against my head and tucked me into his shoulder. My body sagged against him, coming alive at his touch, inside his embrace.

My grandmother's face was beaming behind her coffee mug. Yes, she was delighted at seeing me be ordered around and manhandled and kissed in front of her.

"This is like Christmas, Easter, and Mardi Gras all rolled into one," she exclaimed, then focused on Gage. "You don't know how long I've been waiting to see a man abandon the laws of decency and french my granddaughter in front of me."

Gage's chest vibrated with his low chuckle.

"Glad I could be of service, ma'am," he replied, his voice a low rasp, but also somehow lighter than I'd ever heard it. Almost playful. Almost carefree. But it would always be almost for Gage.

That thought was a razor against my soul. The scarred arms, brutal and stark in the morning light, showed the truth. They would be the immovable force, creating the *almost* happy, *almost* carefree, the *completely* broken.

The lightness on my grandmother's face disappeared and she narrowed her eyes at Gage's words, but not for the same reason as me. "Now, I like you, so I'll not be scooping your eyeballs out with my sugar spoon for calling me *that*," she said with distaste. "I give one free pass. Don't make me do it. I'm sure you're attached to your sight."

Gage's eyes found mine, twinkling and hard at the same time. "Increasingly so," he murmured.

A blush crept up my neck, his words and gaze almost chasing away the pain of before.

Almost.

"SO HE LOST THE BET, I got to use his private jet for a month, and I thought what a perfect place to make my last stop," my grandmother said, sipping at her second cup of coffee. The one she'd put a serious dollop of whisky in, from the bottle she always carried in her purse "for emergencies."

She winked at me. "And don't worry, I got you some great souvenirs. Asia has some excellent skincare and makeup. And I know how much you love those products, even though you don't buy them for yourself, because you're so *sane and sensible*." She groaned the words like they were worse than eating non-dolphin-safe tuna.

Her eyes touched on Gage, who, surprisingly, was still there, chatting with my grandmother, sipping on his own coffee—sans whisky—and holding me like it was natural. Normal.

But there was nothing normal about the two people in my kitchen.

Two people who were important to me.

Grandma had been in my life for as long as I could remember, so that made sense.

Gage had been in it for less than two weeks. That did not make sense. But he was still important. Gaining more crucial status with every minute those scarred arms stayed around me. With every second he didn't make his excuses and escape. Because it was what most men would've done. Most men who didn't plan on being permanent.

My heart fluttered at the thought.

"Well, you're not *completely* sensible and sane," Grandma murmured, eyes still on Gage. "And it's just wonderful."

Gage's arms flexed around me, the energy coming off him changing slightly.

"I can't wait for you to tell me all about this," she said, waving her free hand at us. "When the man in question is out of earshot, of course."

That strange energy coming from Gage dissipated slightly and the corner of his mouth quirked. "Is that your way of tellin' me to fuck off, Anna?" he asked.

I jerked. "You can't curse in front of my grandmother!" I hissed before she could answer.

"Of course he can. I expect nothing less," she interjected. "Not everyone has a mouth like a choirboy, Lo," she said. "Swearing is *fabulous*. You should try it some time." She winked. "And yes, young man, as much as I *thoroughly* enjoy the company, and the view"—her eyes pointed to his torso in a way a grandmother should not look at the man her granddaughter had slept with the night before—"I need some serious deets, and it won't work as well with Lauren being all awkward and quiet with you here. She's already going to be awkward and quiet enough *without* you here. I've got my work cut out for me." She winked at me again as I pressed my head into Gage's shoulder for some kind of solace. "But I expect you back here so I can take you out for dinner." She paused. "That's unless you have some kind of rival gang to give a beatdown to, or something to blow up. In that case, we'll make it a late dinner and you can take me along. I do love an adventure."

"Oh my God," I whispered into Gage's shoulder.

"No bombs to make tonight, I'm sorry to say," Gage replied, not missing a beat. "But I'll be sure to let you know if something comes up while you're in town, Anna."

Grandma nodded. "You be sure to do that, though I'm thinking it's going to be a flying visit so I don't cramp your style. Plus, I've got a meeting with a Calvin Klein model," she replied. "You'll be free for dinner, then?"

I was about to open my mouth and say that men like Gage, who radiated danger, who lived life hard and chaotic, were not about to go to dinner on a Saturday night with an eighty-year-old and the boring woman he'd slept with the night before.

Gage's arms flexed around me, and he spoke before I could. "Yeah, I'm not likely to want to be anywhere else."

I let out a strangled breath. "This is too much to take in the morning," I murmured to no one but myself.

Gage's hand went to my chin, making my eyes meet his. "You can take it, Will," he said, voice lower than a whisper.

The sex barely concealed beneath the words sucked away the oxygen from my lungs.

"Breathe, Lauren."

I gulped in air on his command. Air saturated with him. With the sheer unbelievably of the moment.

My eyes stayed captured in his stare for a beat longer before he stepped back. I sagged slightly with the loss of him, and his hand steadied my hip for a moment before he let me go.

"I got shit to do, anyway," he said, voice louder now. "But I'll be back, tonight." The words were a promise for *a lot* more than just dinner.

The tenderness between my legs pulsated with the craving for more.

With my freaking grandmother right between us.

"Oh don't worry, I'm not staying here," Grandma said. "I don't like the rules."

I turned to face her fully to give her a warning look.

I now had my back to Gage, so he couldn't see this look, nor understand the warning it conveyed.

"Rules?" he repeated, voice low and raspy and slightly amused.

Grandma nodded. "Oh yes, and curfews."

"Curfews?" His eyes darted to me before he yanked me back into his arms as if he couldn't be without my touch. There was definite amusement in his voice now.

"There are no curfews," I hissed, still fighting to get out of Gage's embrace. It was distracting. "Just exit and entry preferences."

Gage's body vibrated with a chuckle. "Babe. 'Exit and entry preferences?'"

"What are you today, a parrot?" I hissed, my face flushing. I glared at Grandma. "You *need* entry preferences since, on more than one occasion, you've lumbered in at 4:00 a.m."

"Lumbered?" she said, hand to her chest. "I do not *lumber*. Imagine a thing to say to a grandmother. If we're talking about lumbering, what is it you do during uncivilized hours on a Sunday?"

"I go to yoga," I snapped. "And eight in the morning is hardly uncivilized."

"In my world it is. Especially when you've just gotten home at four." She glanced to Gage. "She's a tyrant."

I let out a sound of exasperation. "It's my house!"

Grandma narrowed her eyes. "You know what *my* house is? My vagina. And your father came out of it. And his sperm went into your mother's. So I'm responsible for giving you life. How about a bit more respect?"

My head found my hands. "Oh my gosh, my grandmother is talking about her vagina at nine in the morning when my man is right beside me," I muttered, mortified.

The air had been light, pleasant, easy, and I'd sunk into it without hesitation. That was my mistake. Because my words tore through that energy with a serrated knife, Gage's body stiffening behind me.

And then I wasn't tucked into his embrace any longer, because he was dragging me across the room.

Yes, *dragging* me across the living room, without a word to my grandmother, who didn't seem concerned at all, if her faint giggle was anything to go by.

I didn't really have it in me to struggle. There was never a time I had struggled against Gage. Never a time I *wanted* to struggle.

The door to my bedroom slammed behind us. The scent of our coupling—of pure *fucking*—permeated the air, the rumpled and blood-smeared sheets assaulting me with beautifully brutal memories for the second I looked at it before I was slammed against the closed door.

Yes, *slammed.* My body protested at the impact, as the tenderness of my muscles cried out from the brutal handling. Gage didn't seem to notice, since both of his hands circled my neck in a grip that so wasn't gentle as his entire body pressed against mine, plastering me to him.

"Gage, what are you—"

"Shut the fuck up," he ordered.

And then I did shut up, because his mouth was on mine. His kiss wasn't tender. It couldn't be. Not with the wildness in his eyes, the violence in his body. The kiss was as painful as everything else.

And it was also as beautiful.

Soul-destroying.

Time and space disappeared for the moments—or was it years?—his mouth moved against mine.

My breathing came in shallow pants when he finally released me, the darkness in his eyes seeping out and covering every inch of my skin. Every inch of my freaking soul.

"Want to fuck you right now," he growled. "Want to sink my cock so deep inside you that I'm fucking *imprinted* on your insides like you are mine." The grip at my neck tightened and his hardness pressed into my stomach. "Gonna punish you for sayin' that shit at a time when I can't do that," he murmured, teeth brushing my lips, pressing down so they drew blood.

Wetness flooded between my legs.

My blood stained Gage's lips. His tongue flicked out and tasted it.

His hardness pulsated inside his jeans and his grip tightened even more, to the point of pleasurable pain.

"You're gonna *pay* for makin' me hold back right now," he hissed.

"For wh-what?" I stuttered.

"You called me your fuckin' man, baby. *Yours.*" He ground the words out like they were painful.

I froze.

I had. Without even thinking about it. There wasn't a question. With what we shared last night, there was no option other than that Gage was unequivocally mine.

He was broken. And mine.

He'd be a battle.

One I was going to fight.

I hadn't even realized I'd decided that until right that second. Because it was in that second that it became very apparent that everything with Gage was a battle. Merely breathing was a battle for him.

"You are mine," I whispered, gaze never faltering. "Because

you're broken. Like me. And I want to be yours because you won't try and fix me. Because I'm broken too."

He turned to marble with my words, his eyes the only thing still active, still alive, still devouring my soul.

He didn't speak.

Not for a long time.

He just kept staring. Kept sucking me into him, burrowing under my skin.

Then he released me, stepped back so I was no longer pressed against the door, but I stayed there, still glued in place by the coldness of his eyes. Of the weight of the moment.

My eyes followed him as he snatched his cut from where it was draped over the chaise lounge in the corner of my bedroom, slipping it over his bare torso.

I was about to comment on that, though seeing him wear that piece of leather against his muscled, tattooed and scarred skin was probably one of the hottest things like ever. But it wasn't exactly a practical thing to wear in public. And not just because I was getting all sorts of unfamiliar and rather violent feelings toward other women having the same reaction I was. It wasn't safe riding his bike with so much of that skin showing.

Skin that didn't need any more scars.

So primarily, I was going to comment out of worry for his safety, because his safety was now inexplicably connected to mine. And some of that comment was going to be motivated by a possession I felt toward that scarred skin.

I was going to, until I realized he didn't have any other option besides wearing his cut on top of his bare torso. His shirt, which was still lying on my bathroom floor, was covered in blood, not something he could likely wear in broad daylight.

A bloodstained shirt would raise more questions than a scarred and beautiful body, obviously.

It was once I came to that conclusion that he was in front of me once more, still silent, still taking in every part of me with his violent gaze.

I expected him to say something. Because he was obviously leaving. And he couldn't just walk out without saying something. Without addressing everything that just happened.

But that's exactly what he did.

Right after he surged toward me, yanked me into his arms, pressed his mouth to mine in a violent, closemouthed kiss and set me on my feet facing the door he then opened and strode out of.

Without a freaking *word*.

NINE

"I'm planning on a dastardly early takeoff in the morning, so I'll say my goodbyes here." A cloud of Chanel enveloped me as my grandmother yanked me into her embrace with surprising strength. "I approve, my dear," she murmured in my ear. "And you know David would've too."

I was frozen as she gently extracted herself, giving me a kiss on the cheek and a wink before focusing on Gage, who was at my back, most likely stoic and blank-faced like he'd been most of the night.

He'd turned up at my apartment right on time. I was worried he wouldn't turn up at all, and I didn't even freaking have his number to call.

After everything that had happened with this man, and I didn't freaking have his *cell phone number*.

There was no way to contact him, short of humiliating myself and driving my newly repaired car over to the Sons of Templar compound. He held the control; he could've just left today, and that would've been that. Everything was on his terms.

There was no control for me.

Me, the woman who needed to control her life in order to survive it.

But there was no surviving Gage.

Not after today.

I had expected a thousand and one questions from my grandmother when I'd finally emerged from my bedroom, dazed and confused from Gage's exit. But I didn't get a thousand. Or even one. I got a cup of peppermint tea all but thrust at me and a pat on the cheek. My grandmother's warm, dry hand stayed there for a beat, her eyes twinkling, giving me silent support I didn't know I needed and didn't know she was capable of.

Then she demanded I drink my tea, then change out of my birthday suit and get into yoga gear so I could stretch.

She gave me a knowing look. "I'm thinking you need it."

I didn't even have time to blush or cringe a thousand and one times because she was already breezing down the stairs, yelling how she'd meet me at the yoga studio and not to "dillydally."

So I didn't.

I drank my tea, changed into my yoga clothes, and did yoga with my grandmother. And she was right, I totally needed to stretch. My entire body ached like I'd run a marathon.

Upon inspection while I was changing, small bruises of varying colors covered my body. Fingerprints on my breasts. Hand marks on my hips. More fingerprints on my inner thighs. Faint marks on my upper arms. It sounded like a catalog of abuse. Instead, it was a road map of worship.

Gage's worship.

And I needed *more*.

I forced my aching body into healthy exercise in order to try to distract it from its need. From its fear. Because fear was my default. There were two states of human emotion, only two. Everything else was a byproduct of one or the other. Those two states were love and fear. Both lived within the other. One was magnified by the other.

I didn't love Gage.

Not yet.

But I feared him.

Worse, I feared loving him.

Because I would.

Despite how utterly insane the certainty of that thought was, I knew it to be true. In my bones, the ones I was sure held the evidence of Gage's touch, I knew it.

My grandmother must've seen something in my actions that communicated how delicate I was. How fragmented my normally ironclad state of mind was. Because not a word was spoken of him until the early evening, when she was curled up on my sofa with her glass of wine and me with my coconut water.

Of course, that was after she'd ruthlessly made fun of me for drinking coconut water.

"It's not fortune that's given me this carefree, crazy life, my dear. It's tragedy," she said, after I'd listed the health benefits of coconut water and she'd pretended to go deaf.

My body jerked at the words, because they weren't spoken in the same tone as the ones moments before. They didn't even seem to be uttered by the same person.

No, it was like my grandmother had aged ten years in the ten seconds between topics.

I blinked at her.

She smiled sadly, taking a hearty gulp of her wine. "I know, you've known me as fabulous, funny, beautiful, and adventurous your entire life," she said, her voice only holding a hint of that lightness that usually burst from every syllable. "But I've kept things from you. Because that's what grandparents do. Keep their trauma from their young, fresh-faced, naïve grandchildren so they don't tarnish them with the ugly truth. No, that's not the grand-parent's job. Or a parent's. The world does that well enough. And the world has done that to you. In the most brutal and ugly way possible. In a way that made me lose not only one precious grandchild, but a large piece of another too."

My hands shook as I set my glass down beside me, afraid of squeezing it too hard and smashing it in my hands.

My grandmother never spoke of David.

Never.

I used to think she did it because she wanted to respect my wishes. Because she knew I couldn't talk about him when every breath I took was him. Because she saw how tenuous my grip really was on sanity.

But now, her eyes, the absolute and utter sorrow entrenched in them, told me something different. Told me I wasn't the only one holding onto sorrow.

"I was terrified that I had lost my lively, adventurous, spirited Lauren. I was heartbroken by the thought that David's death would not just happen once, but a thousand times over forever," she continued, voice sounding older and more tortured than I'd ever heard it. "I had faith though. I had to, because there wasn't a thing I could do to bring you back to yourself. I know that because I'm wise and worldly and I've had tragedy in tenfold. I'm not talking about us losing our beautiful David, because that's something more than tragedy. There isn't a word for the pain of such a thing. There shouldn't be a word. It shouldn't happen. But this world is ugly and cruel, so it did. My heart breaks anew every single morning when I wake up and remember it wasn't a terrible nightmare."

Tears fogged my glasses. "Me too," I croaked.

She smiled, sad and full of pain. "I wish I could tell you that was going to change, say it would get better with time, but that's not true. And I never lie to you. I don't tell you everything though, because I'm a woman of many talents and just as many secrets. Ones I keep like baubles to hand out to you when you need them." She paused. "I'm being metaphorical right now. You're not getting any of my jewelry until I croak. I need it all."

I choked out a hysterical and tear-filled laugh.

"But I'm talking about little pieces of my life I've collected and kept, despite the pain in doing so, in case they might help my beautiful and tortured granddaughter." She sipped her wine. "And as much as it hurts to remember, I'm glad I have to, because it means good things for my Lo. The best. And it's in the shape of a rather delicious man, if I do say so myself. Shirtless was more than impressive, so I can just *imagine* him pantsless." She winked at me.

I rolled my eyes. Of course my grandmother had to get lewd in the middle of a heart-to-heart.

"Beautiful he may be," she continued, "he's broken. Dangerous. Any fool can see that. And your grandmother is no fool. I don't just mean those scars and that motorcycle cut. That's just surface. It's nothing compared to what lies beneath."

She took another sip and I thought on how much my grandmother saw. And my heart hurt because I knew that if she saw that much in such a short amount of time, she was battling more pain than I'd realized. Because it was almost impossible to see true pain—ugly, true, visceral pain—unless you knew what it felt like.

"I loved a man like that once," she said, her voice quiet.

I jerked. "Grandad?" I asked, squinting and trying to remember the blurry man from the photos of him where he always seemed to be surrounded by cigar smoke and wearing a frown.

Grandma rolled her eyes. "Heavens no. I *despised* your grandfather," she said conversationally.

I blinked. "What?"

"Ugh," she groaned like a teenager. "He was such a *bore*. I would've ditched him the second I realized he had as much personality as a two-bit vibrator."

I nearly choked on my coconut water.

Grandma continued, smirking. "Anyway, I didn't ditch him because I had a little boy whom I adored. And I loved him more than I loved myself. Which is a feat. Your grandfather had much the same opinion. We lived different lives, with different lovers—me at least. Who knew what that piece of cardboard did?—and put on a united front. Obviously I still escaped as much as I could. Still was me. Your grandfather worked too often to disapprove too loudly. I tried to give your father the most exciting life possible, but as you're aware, he wanted a stable one. And stability and excitement are not conclusive. I wore myself out giving him a pair of—on the surface—stable parents. So we gave him that until cancer took away his father, and then he did everything he could to escape his now fully insane mother."

"He doesn't know?" I whispered, thinking about my father's resentment toward my grandmother, wondering if it would change if he'd known what she'd done for him.

Grandma shook her head. "Of course not. As I said, it's a parent's job to keep all the ugly secrets," she said, confirming my hunch. "But we're not talking about that," she continued with a raised brow, as if she knew I was about to push the subject.

"We're talking about Mick—not Jagger, though I may or may not have been there and may or may not be legally bound not to talk about it." She winked. "But my Mick was it. You know the it." She gave me a shrewd look. "He gave me *my last time*. And he gave me knowledge of how beautifully wretched love was. Because he had darkness. Different than your Gage, but then everything's the same in the inky blackness, isn't it? Painful, ugly, torture. It was torture loving him. But I would've lived it my entire life." She looked at the windows, but she wasn't seeing the ocean.

Her eyes sparkled with tears.

My grandmother never cried.

Never.

Not even at David's funeral.

Well, I wasn't entirely sure, as I wasn't in a state to notice other people's emotions since I'd been drowning in my own, but I was pretty sure.

And now she was almost crying.

"We only had six months together," she whispered. "Six months of the most beautifully ugly love I'd ever experienced." Her voice broke and she snapped her gaze away from the window with a force that told me she was yanking herself back from the past before it swallowed her up. "And I lost him. In something as utterly common and cliché as a car accident, of all things. Someone ran a red light. He died on impact. Thankfully, I guess, since his life had been so full of pain that it would've been cruel if his death was too." She leaned forward and topped off her wine from the bottle on the table.

I watched, frozen. "How come you never told me?" I asked, my voice little more than a whisper.

She smiled. "Because, my dear, the pain was so great that if I uttered the truth, I was worried I might just fall apart and never find myself back together again." She said the words lightly, almost casually, and that made them that much more painful to hear.

I leaned forward. "Grandma," I croaked, wishing I could find something to say that would take away the pain on her beautiful face.

She waved me away. "I'm not telling you this for sympathy," she said, almost dismissively. "I'm telling you this because that's what pushed me to live. Really *live*. I know your father disapproves of the way I live my life. My carelessness, as he sees it. But my chaos is careful in its construction. Designed to ensure I make it through the day without falling apart. That's what we're all trying to do, get through the day. Sometimes the ones who seem to make life harder are the ones who make the days that much easier."

She let her words sit, crowd the room, crack my heart. She wasn't bothered by my silence, my inability to figure out what to say to that. I didn't think she even expected me to say anything; what I had to say wasn't what mattered.

She just sipped her wine.

And then she looked at me. "You know, honey, you're not him if you want to have a sip of wine," she said gently. "And this isn't me pushing this on you just because I want a drinking buddy. I have plenty of those. It's actually *nice* having a sure-thing sober driver, so it's to my detriment that I'm speaking on this." Her eyes twinkled. "But I will speak on it because it's apparently the night for a purge. You've been too hurt to live your life because of how David's ended."

I tried not to flinch at the way the words grated against the air.

I was sure Grandma saw my reaction, but she continued. "I see there's a man who will show you something more than fearing death. Who might teach you how to live. You might resurrect him," she murmured, confirming that she saw everything on little more than a glimpse.

"David had an illness, honey. A chemical imbalance. And he had troubles. Bone-deep troubles that he saw as insurmountable mountains. And he found something to turn them into molehills. And it was his end."

She paused, taking a huge gulp of her wine.

"It's an illness you *don't* have," she said firmly. "You might have the mountains, honey, because everyone does in one way or another, but you're willing to climb them. Fuck, I think you've found a man who would carry you over them. Who would walk through fire. But I don't want him to do that. I just want him to show you that *you* can walk through fire. *You* can *live.*"

Again that heavy silence settled over the room.

"I think I might be starting to," I whispered in response.

She grinned. "I think so too."

And then, not long after that, Gage arrived.

Right on time.

He'd barely looked at me all night.

Apart from the way he'd devoured me with his carnal glare the second he turned up, yanked me into his arms for a brutal and closemouthed kiss, of course.

He'd done that in such a way that it seemed like it was beyond his control, like he was *angry* he was doing it.

Or maybe that was my overactive imagination.

I hadn't been angry that he did it.

My lips had been craving his all day. Every single cell of my body had been. And my blood roared in response to his touch, his kiss, even if it was considerably inappropriate in front of my grandmother.

"Hey," I whispered when he yanked his head back, glowering.

He didn't answer for a moment, his eyes searching my face. "Will," he murmured, tone deeply intimate and yet coldly detached at the same time.

I would've said such a thing was impossible before.

But with Gage there was no impossible.

Because *he* was an impossibility. His very presence. The ghost of his touch on my lips. We'd driven to dinner on the bike, him wordlessly shoving the helmet at me serving as him telling me as much. My grandmother had not made a tut of disapproval at that as my mother would've, or a load protest like my father.

No, she literally *clapped.*

With *glee.*

I was lucky I'd worn a motorcycle appropriate outfit, considering I'd stupidly hoped I'd need to wear one. I'd gone for my black capris, skintight, ending just above my ankle so I could match my light pink booties to them. The heel was higher than I normally wore, but it did something good to my legs. Which was why I'd bought them in the first place.

And never worn them before. It had been a rare impulse purchase at the mall.

Because I didn't think I was the person to wear lace-up, blush-pink suede booties.

Because I'd never thought I was the person to feel at home pressed into one of the craziest bikers in Amber. The biker she belonged to. The biker she'd had sex with moments after he confessed to murder.

I would've said such a thing was impossible.

But *Gage* was impossible.

So I did ride on the back of his motorcycle to dinner at Valentines.

He didn't speak to me when we pulled up, just rested his hands lightly on my hips once I'd climbed off, kept me rooted in place while his eyes ran over the V-necked cami underneath my blush pink jacket. It was black silk with a lace trim, the lace covering the fact that it dipped *way* low.

Another thing I didn't think I'd wear.

Didn't think a man as sinfully hot as Gage would be gazing at it with pure and filthy hunger.

And he was.

Of course, that was when my grandmother pulled up.

I was glad, because I loved my grandmother and her company. And because it meant I could exhale with the moment broken.

But *I* wasn't broken.

Not in the way Gage's gaze promised.

And I *wanted* to be.

I wanted him to break me in.

But he didn't.

Instead he listened to my grandmother's crazy story about "that time at Studio 54" as we walked into the restaurant, pointedly ignoring me, apart from the fact that his strong hand was wrapped around mine for the entire journey to the table. Then it rested on my thigh as soon as we sat down.

For the *entire* dinner.

He ate with one hand just so he could keep the other on my leg. Normally the lapse in table manners would've gotten to me, because my father had stressed the importance of such things. And because it was what my 'safe' men had. The set of skills utilized by those living within the confines of a logical society.

But something as menial as proper table manners at a nice restaurant didn't mean much at all when he'd murdered a man the night before.

Obviously they didn't mean anything to me either, because I'd known he'd murdered a man and I was letting him have dinner with my grandmother. Letting him keep his hand tightly gripping my thigh.

Loving the thought that I'd have fresh bruises in that spot.

He wasn't exactly the most articulate of company—definitely not to me—but he had engaged my grandmother in his version of polite conversation, which of course meant he used the word 'fuck' as a comma.

That did not bother my grandmother.

In fact, it amused her greatly.

Gage himself seemed to both amuse and impress her.

As did the club, when she asked about the leather at his back and what it represented.

I expected him to give her the sanitized version. This was my *grandmother*, after all. And we were both 'civilians' and not sanctioned to know too much information about the club. I knew because Niles had tried for years to get Lucy to do a piece on the Sons of Templar. She never had. They were family.

Her loyalty was ironclad, and despite her position 'on the inside,' which could've taken her right to the top, she didn't use it. It said a lot about her. But I also thought it said a lot about the club that everyone thought was a gang full of murderers and lowlifes.

The past, present, and the future were all leading reasons why I thought Gage would give my grandmother the publicity statement that they were just a club of motorcycle enthusiasts and mechanics.

But Gage didn't give way to reason.

And he wasn't about publicity statements.

He was about the truth.

No matter how ugly.

"Club started as a place for disenfranchised Army vets to find a home. A family. Somewhere that made sense when they realized the freedom they'd fought for, their friends had died for, didn't exist," he said, just after our meals had been delivered. He'd put down his utensils down in order to give Grandma his full attention. "So they made their own freedom. Away from the bullshit life that had no place for the damaged." His hand at my thigh tightened as he paused, as the words out of his mouth described not just the men from the past but the man sitting right next to me.

The damaged man.

The dangerous man.

The one I was falling for.

Or maybe I'd already fallen. Hit the ground, shattered at the bottom, and now I was just waiting for him to pick me back up.

"Freedom isn't cheap," he continued, eyes still on my grandmother, but every bit of his energy was focused on me. I knew because my entire body was focused on him, despite the fact that I was making a serious effort to focus on toying with the straw in my drink.

Because his hand was no longer clenching my thigh at that point but creeping up my leg. Every single inch it moved closer to the throbbing core that was crying out for him was a moment my breathing shallowed. That the blush crept up my neck.

Gage's face was marble.

And he continued to talk, as if he wasn't almost at the apex of my thighs. As if every inch of my skin wasn't on fire.

"And the price you pay for freedom isn't something that can be earned through honest channels," he finished.

"Of course," she said, nodding and taking a sip of her wine. "The best things in life aren't free. They're usually very expensive and very illegal." She smirked.

The corner of Gage's mouth turned up and his hand reached the top of my thighs, mere inches away from my core. It was covered with fabric, but Gage's hand seemed to sear that away, his bare palm scorching into my skin.

I gripped my water glass and counted myself lucky that my grandmother was focused on Gage; otherwise, she would've spotted my discomfort and connected the dots immediately.

But he had that affect. He was the puppeteer of every room he walked into, commanding the eyes of all. You wanted to stare at him all day long but also avert your gaze because you knew there was something about him that repelled humanity. That welcomed pain and danger.

That was what drew me to him in the first place. But I was learning there was so much more to him than his pain. Than his scars.

Something changed in my grandmother's expression, something that distracted me enough from Gage's teasing fingers, inching toward the apex of my thighs. Her words even stole away the blush, the need that was coming from his brutal touch.

"So you sell drugs?" she asked, her voice bland. Casual. As if she were asking if they sold car parts.

But there was nothing casual about my grandmother's question. Nor about her thoughts to the answer. Because she was okay with a lot of things. She was okay with outlaws, with illegal activity, with people who operated outside the normal parameters. She preferred those people, in fact.

But not those who peddled the substances that stole my brother away from us.

Gage's hand froze at my thigh, and the pads of his fingers pinched painfully into the soft skin underneath my pants. I didn't notice the pain. No, I was too busy focusing on the white-hot agony that came with her question. With the fear of what the answer would be.

I noticed the change in Gage's demeanor immediately. He had been hard, cold, and menacing so far. But not completely. His edges were purposefully dulled, obviously as dull as they could be for the situation. But now they were razor-sharp. Now he was ice, wearing that cruel mask he yanked on to keep the world from seeing his monster.

The silence following Grandma's question was long. Yawning. My heart was pounding in my ears. Gage's jaw was clenched tight enough to shatter his teeth.

"No," he ground out with enough force that it hit me physically. He sucked in a rough inhale and the fingers at my thighs relaxed. Slightly. "Club doesn't fuck with drugs. Not now. Never."

Grandma smiled, as if the moment wasn't strained, as if the air weren't laced with razors. "Oh, well that's nice, then," she said mildly.

Her response and light and airy tone did a lot to ease the tension. Gage's mouth didn't twitch up, but his jaw relaxed.

She leaned forward, eyes bright and curious. "So, if not drugs...?" she prompted, not addressing Gage's intense and dangerous reaction to her previous question.

She did that, my grandmother. Had a sixth sense for pain and exposed nerves and deftly avoided such subjects where most people would prod, hungry for someone else's pain. Which was why I'd guessed she'd failed to ask a single question about Gage's past. Or his family.

Because she knew they were land mines.

I hadn't even realized how big until her sense exposed them. Until I realized I knew nothing about Gage, the man. The man underneath the cut. Underneath the scars. The reasons for his scars, not just the ones on his arms but the ones etched behind his eyes.

I ached to know his pain, to feel it myself just so I could know him more. Get closer to him. I knew that if he ever told me, I'd hurt for as long as I was in his presence. His pain would be added to what I carried around. It would be agony.

And I craved to share it.

For now, I had to do what everyone was doing—dodge the emotional land mines. Until the right moment. Or the wrong one. Then everything would explode. I just hoped enough of me—and more importantly, Gage—would remain when it was all over.

"Guns," he said, his rough voice cutting through all other thoughts in my mind, yanking me to the present.

"We ran guns," he continued, thumb rubbing my inner thigh, almost brushing the area where my drenched panties lay beneath my pants.

Almost.

Then he moved downward. Rubbing.

Bruising the skin, no doubt.

But still not looking at me. Not speaking to me.

"Used to?" my grandmother asked, her voice still easy, curious, not a hint of disapproval. Though it took a lot to earn my grandmother's censure. Or a little, depending on how you looked at it, considering her tone had been saturated with it when she'd been talking to my last boyfriend about his job in investment banking.

Gage nodded once. "Characteristic of the life. Blood. Pain. Death. It's the price of freedom. Every single brother wearing a patch knows that. Willin' to pay that price in order to live the life we want. To live the life you want, you gotta be willing to die the death you don't want." His words were no-nonsense, flat, as if he were speaking about stock options.

A vision of Gage bloody and lifeless assaulted my mind, and I tasted bile from the mere thought. It was so real that I had to shove my hand atop his on my thigh just to remind myself that he was warm and alive.

His entire body tightened with my touch, his jaw hardening, his breath pausing. But he still didn't look at me. After a beat, his hand lifted slightly so I could snake mine into it.

"Patched members are willin' to die for the club," he continued. "But we're not willin' to lose something more precious than our lives." He paused, his hand tightening around mine to the point that my very bones protested. "That's our heart. The innocents." His hand relaxed on mine slightly, but I didn't find relief in the receding pain. Because I wanted to feel more of it, because Gage needed more of it. I wanted him to give it to me. To hurt me in ways that made him hurt less. Or at least feel less lonely in his pain.

"One of my brothers lost his woman in a club war over territory nearly seven years back," he said, voice hoarse.

I knew that. Everyone in Amber knew that. It was a blow that wounded the entire town. The beautiful, innocent woman named Laurie who was brutally kidnapped, tortured, and finally killed. It was barely healed, that scar.

The club had been a fixture in town since before I could remember. And they had been loud. There had been violence. Some deaths. Blood. But nothing that really stained the town in a way like Laurie's death.

Because this was violence that even the men with chaos in their blood couldn't handle. It had given way to an ugly and dark time for the town. Not long after which Gwen, Cade's wife, had entered the picture and things began to change.

There was still violence. A lot of it. Most of it centered around the new women entering the club, trying to fit around the wound made by Laurie's death. There was still pain, but there was also more light and happiness. Even an outsider like me could see that.

"My president, Cade, almost lost his own woman to this shit," Gage continued. "Price for that kind of freedom became too high, so we stopped runnin' guns, started runnin' legit. The club, at least."

My grandmother's eyebrow arched. It wasn't hard to read between the lines. "The club?" she repeated, her question clear.

Gage nodded once. "Price of *my* freedom is still high enough for me to need to pay it in ways the club doesn't."

He didn't say anything else on the subject.

And my grandmother didn't probe.

Because of the exposed nerve.

The huge freaking land mine we'd stumbled onto that would level everything and everyone around it.

The night lightened after that.

As much as it could.

And with my grandmother around, it was a lot. Though not enough to make me feel at ease around Gage. Not enough to shove away the bone-deep fear that his silence and coldness toward me was a harbinger of doom.

So my smile was bright and totally fake when my grand-mother released me from her embrace in my doorway at the end of the night, once we'd gotten back from the restaurant and she'd informed us that she was off on the next adventure.

"Please be careful, and call me often," I asked, my voice low.

She grinned, squeezing my arms. "That's supposed to be *my* line."

I smirked. "Well, *I'm* not the one who gets wild hair and goes running with the bulls at seventy-nine years old."

She winked again, releasing me. "Hmmm, I think you're running with something a lot more dangerous than the bulls," she murmured, eyes on Gage, who was returning from putting her suitcases in her trunk, her car was idling in the 'no parking' spot.

"Love you, Lo." She leaned in for one more kiss, rubbing her lipstick off my cheek with her thumb before stepping back and looking at Gage, who was standing in front of us, arms crossed.

"You take care of my granddaughter," she demanded. "And I don't mean keep her safe. I mean show her a little danger. She'll show you a little safety."

And on that, she blew Gage a kiss and sauntered to her car with a speed that shouldn't have been possible from a woman her age, and in five-inch heels.

But she was kind of like Gage in that respect, making anything and everything possible.

Her car roared into the night at a troubling speed, both of us watching the headlights disappear. The stillness of the night took over, silence heavy and painful between us. My heart splintered my ribs as Gage's eyes ran over me. I continued to stare at the empty road, too cowardly to meet them. Because I was too terri-fied to face a goodbye that I knew was inevitable.

But my choices were taken away from me when the dim glow

of the moon was blacked out by something much darker than the night.

Gage.

Fingers bit into my hip as the other hand gripped my chin painfully.

I expected him to speak immediately. People who demanded attention in such a brutal and physical way usually did it because they had something urgent to say.

But Gage was not *people*.

So he didn't speak. He just stared at me.

Gone was the cold blankness that had been present all night. The cruelty.

There was violence in his gaze, because there was violence in his soul. It roused the part of me he had awakened that night on the side of the road. That he had fed with every touch, every kiss, every brutal grip, every intense gaze, every uttered word.

The part of me that would starve without him.

The part of me that I was terrified of.

Silence yawned on. Silence that was louder than anything I'd ever heard in my life.

"Lauren, get in the fucking apartment. Now," he ground out, letting me go and stepping back, his body so tight it was shaking.

My body cried out in protest from the loss of his touch. From the loss of his violence. And then my body responded to his order, my brain registering his barely restrained chaos.

So I got in the apartment, taking the stairs nearly two at a time, overcome with fear. With erotic excitement. I expected the slam of my front door to follow me, the thud of motorcycle boots against my stairs to vibrate my bones with the echo of his approach.

But there was only silence. Apart from my rapid heartbeat and shallow breathing, of course.

I made it to the middle of my living room, unsure of what

exactly to do with myself without Gage's order. I wasn't a submissive. I didn't want to follow a man's order. Bend to a man's will.

But this wasn't a *man*.

This was *Gage*.

And I wasn't going to bend to his will.

It was going to break me.

Fear clutched my throat at the thought of him *not* slamming
my apartment door. *Not* entering my apartment along with his
fury and violence. Of *not* controlling my body with his barked
and brutal commands.

Maybe that's why he wanted me in there, so he could roar off
into the night and leave without me doing something mortifying
like cling to his motorcycle boot and beg him to stay.

I wasn't entirely sure I wouldn't.

Because he had been in my life for mere moments, in the
grand scheme of things. But there was a lifetime in those
moments. A dark and painful one, but one I wanted to live in.
Die in.

When had I welcomed such dark thoughts? Or maybe they'd
always been there and I hadn't let them actualize out of fear.

My entire body jerked with the slamming of the door. I
blinked as the sound of boots on the stairs crashed into my stomach, stoked the burning fire in my core.

My knees shook.

Gage reached the top of the stairs and his gaze found me. It
fricking *devoured* me. He had pushed his sleeves up, exposing the
rippled and scarred flesh of his forearms. His hands were fisted at
his sides, veins pulsating within his rippled flesh.

His hair was no longer in the bun that melted my panties the
second I saw it. No, it was wild around his face, smooth and
messy at the same time, as if he'd been running his hands
through it.

My palms itched to clutch it, to fist it while he pounded into me.

His gaze was pure sex.

And pure pain.

His eyes had been doing the same inventory of me as I'd been doing with him, the fire in my body evidence of his stare.

Then he moved.

Not fast and violent like his stare might suggest.

No, his steps were slow. Measured. Almost painful with the lack of speed in which they brought him toward me. He didn't let my eyes go the entire time it took to cross my living room and stop in front of me.

He didn't snatch me into his arms. Didn't rip at my clothes like I ached to do to him. He didn't touch me at all, and I almost screamed in the frustration of it.

My body jerked forward as I prepared to pounce on him, to assert myself in a way I never had before.

"Don't fuckin' move," he growled.

My entire body obeyed.

My core pulsated with his command.

His eyes darkened as I snapped back to stillness, the cords of his neck carved from steel, his reaction to my obedience stark and immediate.

I wasn't a submissive.

I wasn't *submitting* to Gage.

I was *surrendering* to him.

And he liked it.

He loved that.

But something mingled with the sex in his gaze. Something that had been underneath the cold and cruel man who had been present tonight.

The man who wasn't entirely Gage.

The man who was both something more and less than the Gage on the surface. The Gage I itched to know.

"You don't drink. Alcohol. Coffee. Fuckin' soda."

It was a statement. And at the same time, there was a question in it, even if there was no inflection at the end.

I was beginning to understand that was how Gage worked. He didn't ask questions. He watched. Came up with his own answers, and then, if he wanted to know more, he'd all but force more out of you.

It was becoming apparent that he didn't need to force anything out of me.

Not even my heart.

It had been his for longer than I cared to admit.

Longer than was sensible—two freaking weeks, if you wanted to get specific.

But I didn't know about his.

Because I may have known that one thing about Gage and his questions that weren't questions, but that didn't mean I knew everything.

Or anything.

I still didn't know what those brutal scars on his arms were from. But just like Gage didn't ask questions, he didn't answer them either. He didn't even *invite* them.

But even though he was unwilling to give me something, anything, or everything, there he was forcing everything out of me.

And there I was letting him.

"How do you know that?" I asked, trying to delay my answer. But I couldn't delay forever, and Gage wouldn't wait forever.

His gaze was unyielding. "Notice shit about people," he said, voice still hard and empty. "Handy, knowin' how they tick. Especially if I'm plannin' on destroying them. Considering you're not *people*, and I'm makin' it my life's mission that no one—including me—destroys you, I notice more shit."

Holy. Crap.

The words screamed in my mind as the silence after them screamed around us.

What the freaking heck did I say to *that?*

"No, I don't drink soda, coffee, or alcohol," I responded to his question, cowering out of doing anything else.

Like jump him.

I was also trying to leave it at that, draw out his curiosity, make him show something more than his eyes betrayed.

Make him ask me a fricking *question.*

So maybe I knew something about him.

Like he thought *I* was something to him.

Something enough to change the formula he had with every single other person in the world.

But he didn't.

He just watched me, eyes drawing out my soul like venom from wound.

"I keep away from anything mind-altering," I said, proverbially blinking first.

He raised his brow. "Soda is mind-altering?"

I shrugged, picking at a loose thread on my pants while my mind began to pick at the loose threads of my soul.

No, while *Gage* picked and yanked at those threads with little more than an eyebrow raise and an intoxicating stare.

I could've told him I didn't like soda. Or that drinking my calories didn't line up with my diet. Or that there were studies showing how sugary and caffeinated drinks accelerated tooth decay. The increased risk of diabetes. Or any of the number of excuses I'd memorized and rattled off to whoever decided to comment on the fact that I didn't drink coffee or soda.

Like it was the same as being a murderer.

Or worse.

Murderers were much more common in our country than people who didn't drink stimulants, something to keep them awake, alert, get them through the day. Or get them through their life.

I had so much practice at my many excuses, I almost fooled myself.

Almost.

I might've been able to fool Gage, if I'd wanted to.

But I didn't want to. "My twin brother, David, died of a drug overdose when we were twenty-one years old," I said, my voice flat. Empty.

I was surprised.

Because it was the first time I'd said it out loud. Ever. I'd excelled at avoiding all conversations about family and siblings when I had to exchange pleasantries with people. And since both David and I had somewhat kept under the radar at high school, then gone off to college out of state, not keeping in touch with the few friends we had—we had each other and that was enough—it wasn't really 'big' news in Amber.

It had shattered my whole world.

But in Amber, it barely made a ripple.

Mom and Dad had friends, of course. But the circle was small, and though they were respected by people who knew them in the community, they also kept to themselves. When David died, they pretty much folded in on themselves, shut everyone out and moved out of Amber within months.

And when I came back, the few friends I'd had from high school had moved on. A couple of people recognized me, maybe in passing, enough to screw their noses up trying to figure out where they knew me from. Some gave me a smile and a nod. Very few actually *talked* to me.

I could count on one hand the number of people who had not

only talked to me, but expressed their condolences for David's death.

And I'd barely spoken through the shards of glass in my throat when they did so. I usually nodded, garbled out a "thanks," and escaped as soon as it was socially acceptable.

But those people had already *known*.

I hadn't had to lay it out for anyone. Because I didn't have friends, people I opened up to over cocktails, made bad decisions with. I had my grandmother, and she made enough bad decisions, so when we were together, I forced her to make some good ones.

But she already *knew*.

And she knew my policy on talking about it—which was not at all. Apart from her most recent visit, when she'd opened up her pain and my own. Even then, I'd never actually spoken the words.

And when people asked me if I had siblings, I'd shake my head and then escape the conversation. There wasn't a single photo of him inside my apartment. There were other things in the room I hid from everyone, the room meant to be a broom closet, but instead of brooms it held chopped-up pieces of my insides.

But no photos on display. On the rare occasion someone came into my apartment, photos would raise questions.

It was like I'd erased him, my brother, the other piece of me, right off the face of the earth. Outwardly, at least. I might not have said his name in nine years, but I thought it. Every single day. Didn't look at a picture of his face in around the same amount of time, but I didn't need to. It was seared into my brain.

So I was surprised that the first time I'd ever uttered the words cementing his death into the air, my voice was so foreign.

So cold.

Maybe because it was me realizing that not saying he was

dead out loud didn't keep him alive somehow. I'd known it all along, but it was the final nail in the coffin.

I hadn't expected Gage to react.

He was Gage.

But he flinched.

Visibly *flinched* at my words.

Maybe it was the tone.

Maybe it was the one thing I'd been waiting for. That he knew the pure absence of emotion in my voice showed him just how much hurt was shattering my bones at that moment. And that he cared. That my pain hurt him.

"I've never said that out loud before," I whispered, somehow aching to give him more of me, even though it was one of the most painful things I had ever done.

Wasn't that what love was? Giving someone everything, no matter how much it killed you, shredded your insides to do so?

"I don't know why. Maybe because I didn't have the energy to, because I've been screaming it in my head for ten years," I said, eyes faraway. "Because saying it out loud, I'd have to admit that ten years haven't passed. At least not for me. Because if I told people, they'd expect me to be healed, by time and all that." I shrugged, hating the phrase 'time heals everything' with a passion.

"They'd expect me not to still be bleeding from a wound that was sustained a decade ago," I continued. "But it's not a *wound*. It's a complete fricking leveling of me. An entire chunk of myself just... gone. An important chunk. One that doesn't grow back. Because it doesn't come from me, you see? I wouldn't know how to grow it back if I even wanted to. It was him."

I screwed my face into a frown because that was the only way to stop myself from crying.

"We weren't two different people. We were the *same* person." I held onto Gage's gaze like an anchor. "Each of us holding vital parts of the other. And that's what makes it worse. Because I didn't even *notice* the vital parts of me being slowly poisoned. David slowly poisoning himself. I didn't notice him freaking *killing* himself."

A tear rolled down my cheek and I was surprised at it.

I'd screamed that day.

Wailed.

Rivaled the ocean for sheer volume.

I'd had to be sedated.

The one and only time narcotics had entered my system.

After we buried him, there was not one tear.

Because he was gone. Buried.

And life went on.

Without him. Even the six months of my life that I didn't think on, that my family didn't speak of, that were etched into the concrete of my soul.

It was so freaking tragic, so painful, it was beyond the point of tears.

"I had to be sedated," I continued, my voice still cold. Robotic. "I was the one who found him." I forced myself not to look at the image the words shoved to the front of my mind.

The image of my beautiful brother's dead body.

I hadn't let myself think of it in ten years.

Not awake, at least.

My nightmares showed it to me often enough.

But I couldn't handle it now. So I didn't. Such things usually weren't conscious choices. You couldn't just choose not to be confronted with your worst horrors. In fact, your brain consciously chose to put them in front of you. Because life without pain didn't exist. The very environment we lived in nurtured pain, multiplied it.

"I found him, called 911, even though it was obvious he was already dead. I didn't believe it. I couldn't. How can you believe that half of you is lying dead in his own vomit with a needle sticking out of his arm?"

The image assaulted me now. Tore pieces of my flesh from my very bones. I bit my lip, hard, so bitter metallic blood flowed into my mouth.

"I'm not quite sure how long it took for paramedics to come," I continued. "It could've been five minutes. Five hours. Five years. Time doesn't mean much at the end of your world. I wouldn't let anyone touch him," I said, my voice cold and foreign again. "Apparently I became violent." I screwed up my nose, trying to grasp onto those foggy memories, isolate them from the horror. "I still don't remember that. I just remember thinking that those people were going to take him away from me, and I knew I'd never see him again, you know?"

I paused, though Gage didn't answer my question because it wasn't really a question. He didn't do anything, in fact, just stood there, staring, yanking at those threads in my soul even harder.

I sucked in a ragged breath. "They were going to tear away half of me." My voice broke ever so slightly, and I straightened my spine so I wouldn't break along with it. "So I had to fight for him. For me." My voice was firmer now. Nothing else was. "Because if they took him away, how was I supposed to survive? How did half a person go on?"

He didn't answer, but he flinched, not as violently as before but still visibly.

"So yeah," I whispered. "I was fighting for David's life. For mine. And I fought hard. Hence the sedation." I thought back to the sharp prick of the needle, which was all surprise and nothing to do with pain. There was no physical reproduction of the pain of a soul being torn apart. The prick in my skin meant nothing.

Less than nothing.

Then, quickly with the force of the chemicals being introduced into my bloodstream, everything was okay.

No, everything was *nothing*.

My brother's wide-open eyes, staring at me with no soul.

Nothing.

His cold body, covered in grime and vomit.

Nothing.

The paramedics zipping him into a body bag and shoving him in the back of a truck like he was no longer a human being, just a sack of meat to be buried in the ground.

Nothing.

And then they wore off.

And then there was *everything*. A pain so harrowing that each breath I took was a shock because I didn't realize a human being could continue breathing, continue surviving while in that much pain.

"I swore I would never let a substance take me away from myself the second I became lucid," I whispered. I didn't add that the six months after that contributed to my determination. It wasn't a lie, but I just wasn't ready to bare that piece of myself too.

"The second the pain came back, I told myself that I'd never let myself do anything to take it away again," I continued. "Because there's only one thing in the world that's worse than your soul being ripped apart, and that's not caring that it's happening. That's what those sedatives did." I shuddered at the thought of that numbness, moreover at how *tempting* it was. I continued to hold onto Gage's image, my hands fists at my sides.

"And I *have* to care," I whispered. "David deserves for me to care. Every day. Because somewhere along the way, something happened to him to make him not want to care anymore. And not only do I have no idea what that was, but I didn't even *see* him fade away to nothing until he *was* nothing."

My thoughts wandered to that horrible image of my precious and beautiful brother's body being hurled into a bag like trash.

"So no way am I going to ever introduce something that could take me away from that. From my sober and lucid everything. Because I don't deserve that. Not now, not ever," I vowed.

Gage

The second she had spoken in that cold, fucking bone-shattering tone, he had frozen.

Every fucking part of him.

Because no way should this warm, complex, and cute-as-shit woman *ever* sound like that. But she did. And it was worse, because *his* warm, complex, and cute-as-shit woman felt that every fuckin' day.

Someone didn't speak of trauma with such cold emptiness unless it was a trauma that had scraped their souls from their bones.

And he'd known there was something underneath all her soft. Her glasses, her statistics, her reserved smiles, her fire, her quiet. He knew there was something loud underneath that. Something screaming.

Gage knew demons. Excelled at recognizing other people's. Or he thought he had. But fuck, hearing her talk, every word ripping at his skin, flaying him, he realized he didn't know shit. Because no fucking way had he expected Lauren's demons to be *that* dark.

Only because someone with demons that dark didn't rebuild their life. They didn't smile, didn't live in a fucking apartment radiating light. Didn't do kind shit for other people daily, like Lauren did.

The people with those demons, they withered. Escaped into the bottom of a bottle. Fucked their way through half a state. Gambled. Hurt other people so they didn't hurt themselves. Caused other people pain because they wanted someone else to experience the utter agony they carried around with them every day. Because they wanted to spread that pain so the whole fucking world could *pay*.

Gage had done all of that.

And more.

Yet Lauren didn't touch anything that might offer her even a moment of respite. Not even a fucking *soda*.

He'd encountered some fucked-up people in his life—not including the most fucked up of them all, the man in the mirror. Had also seen some of the strongest human beings to walk the face of the earth.

People who gathered the ashes of their lives, carried them with them, but also used them to fertilize, grow something new.

Bull.

Bex.

Lucky.

Mia.

Gwen.

Rosie.

Not many people knew, but Ranger.

People usually showed him their fucked-up shit because he wore his depravity on his sleeves. Literally. When you showed the world you were crazy, most people shied away from it, crossed the street to avoid it. But not because they were afraid of him. No, because of what he would make them see about themselves.

Only the bravest of people wanted to open up with their crazy, and they did it with him because it didn't seem as bad to expose those demons to someone who had bigger and worse ones.

So he had a list.

The list went on. In fact, it included almost everyone in his club.

The men, not so surprising, since they had to be strong in order to keep drawing breath, keep from eating bullets.

The women were a little less obvious, but not by much. Their struggles were laid out for the world to see, because they'd had to fight a war to get them to where they were. Gage had seen a lot of it.

A lot of it—like Bex, chained to a bed, strung out and being *raped*—was burned into his brain.

The rest he'd heard about, seen the aftereffects of.

But with Lauren, it blindsided him.

"Because there's only one thing in the world that's worse than your soul being ripped apart, and that's not caring that it's happening."

The words were rebounding inside his head. One of the strongest and bravest sentences he'd ever heard someone say in his fucking life.

And it was coming from his woman.

His little woman who wore skirts that never brushed higher than her knee. Who talked about the dangers of fuckin' *subway grates*. Who still bitched at him about wearing a skull cap.

He knew she was special. Fuckin' priceless.

But he'd still been a fool.

Because she had done something he'd been unable to do—live with the pain. Grit her teeth against it and not succumb to the temptation of nothingness.

He was frozen as she spoke.

Cataloguing every inch of her pain, sorrow, and then feeling it tenfold. Adding it to his own. Because that shit was his now. Every inch of her pain.

And he was also cataloguing every inch of *her*.

Because the second she fuckin' spoke, he knew it had to be done. The thing he'd been stewing on all day since leaving her. The thing that had him physically unable to look at her during dinner. He had to get the fuck away from her before his poison polluted her life.

His fucking *addiction.*

The one that had killed her brother. He had survived, with no one to mourn him, no one to care—his parents were better off without him in their life, because it would kill them to see the monster he'd turned into—and her brother, the other fucking *half* of her, had let the needle drain away his life in the pursuit of a high.

Gage had overdosed in the midst of the worst time in his life.

Been legally dead for two minutes.

But he'd survived.

And for what?

So he could send more fuckers to the grave? Cause more pain?

He'd held himself back from taking her. From snatching away those bleeding words with his mouth. With his cock.

He itched to fuck the demons out of her.

But he was frozen.

So she kept speaking them, and they kept eating at her soul, right in front of him. And there was nothing he could do about it.

Talk to an addict. Any recovering addict. They'd tell you that at any moment of any given day, they were thinking about a fix. Their skin was itching, crawling with the need for something to get under it, something to take it away.

The ones who said they had days—fucking moments—when they weren't thinking about junk were fucking liars.

Because every fucking second of Gage's existence had been resisting the urge to shoot up. Never had he enjoyed a fucking moment of *not* wanting it. Not when he was killing a man, fucking a woman, or blowing shit up.

Not a *second.*

But the moment his woman began talking about finding her overdosed and dead twin brother, her voice so saturated with pain that it was a wonder the air she breathed wasn't drenched in crimson, he found himself not wanting a fix.

Never in his life since he'd started junk had he been disgusted at the thought of shooting up.

Sure, he'd been disgusted at himself for *wanting* to. Disgusted at the fucking *world* for being so depraved that drugs had to even exist.

But never at the junk.

That was the only shit that didn't make him want to hurl.

The high.

But right then it did.

Because it was the reason the magnificent creature in front of him was shredded, torn, scarred beyond belief. Beyond what Gage could realize. Fuck, she had scars just like his, despite her milky smooth skin.

And then she stopped speaking.

And thank fuck for that, because Gage didn't know how much longer he could've handled that cold and detached voice.

He'd handled torture. Both giving and receiving. He'd seen the aftereffects of what happened to human bodies after being blown up. *He'd* been the motherfucker to blow them up. Heard the ones who weren't lucky enough to die immediately. The sound of a human being burning to death while missing some vital limbs was an exquisite kind of horror. One no one in the world should ever hear if they expect to keep vital parts of their souls. The sounds Gage had heard. More than once.

So he could handle shit.

What he could not handle was another fucking second of his woman's voice like that.

This was his time to get up. Leave her.

He knew it would hurt her, and he fuckin' hated that shit. But hurting her now was better than destroying her later.

But then he spoke, the words out of his mouth in the same breath as he'd been preparing to walk out of her life forever.

Lauren

"I'm not going to be able to give you what you need," Gage said, his voice flat but not empty.

It was after silence had descended, apart from my heavy breathing. Because spewing all that out felt like running a freaking marathon.

Gage had been unreadable during the entire thing. And I think that was the key to him. When he didn't look like he was feeling anything at all, he was feeling *everything*. So I found the strength not to let the words level me, and I answered them. Challenged them.

"And what, pray tell, do you think you know I need?" I asked.

His gaze was hard, unyielding, bordering on cruel. The gaze of a man going to his execution. And he was gripping me, holding my arms tightly like he was going to take me with him.

"A normal fucking life, Lauren. A normal *anything*." He was yanking the words out, throwing them at me in some kind of desperation. His eyes melted my bones. "I'm broken. And not in those ways that everyone is a little bit broken. My past, it shattered me, then forced to me construct a fucking Frankenstein outta the pieces. I'm a monster, babe. There's no denying that. I'm not stable. Not gonna be able to provide a life that's certain. Life that's good. And you might be broken, but not in a way that deserves a fuckin' life like mine." He gripped me harder, even though the words were trying to make him let go. Make me let go.

I placed my hand atop his. "You may have pain and darkness in your heart, but you've got sunlight in your bones," I whispered. "And even if you didn't, I wouldn't let you walk away."

His face hardened. "You don't know the things I've done, Lauren," he said harshly.

I didn't waver. I had a newfound strength now, after spilling something that I thought would kill me and remaining breathing afterward. "I don't need to know the things you've done to know the man you are."

His brows narrowed, as if he was expecting me to ask questions, to force things out of him. "Baby, I'm too fucked up for you. For this fucking world."

I smiled, sad and melancholy, as my fingers trailed his jaw. "We're all a little fucked up, Gage. That's the big secret. Some people hide it better than others. But this world is fucked up, and it's a side effect of survival to get scars from that." My eyes touched his arms. My fingers followed suit.

He flinched, his entire body tensing. I knew that it was difficult, bordering on impossible for him to handle me touching them, even with the lightest of fingertips. But I didn't stop.

"We all have scars, Gage," I murmured. "You just have no choice but to wear them. I have the luxury of hiding mine." I stepped forward, leaning up so my lips almost brushed his. "I don't want to hide mine with you." My fingers snaked underneath the fabric of his tee, running along the smooth and hard muscles of his stomach.

My other hand left his and did the same thing, only it went downward, to the hard length inside his boxers.

Gage let out a harsh hiss.

"I want you to see all my scars, Gage," I whispered.

He grunted as I circled him with my hand, squeezing just tight enough to cause him pain, pain I knew he liked. Pain I knew he needed.

He responded by tightening his grip on my hip as the hand at my face fell. He knew I needed pain too. Or maybe he didn't. Maybe he was just figuring that out.

I stepped back, struggling to let him go. He was the port in my storm, but he also *was* the storm. I didn't want to let him go, but I did it. Because I was doing all sorts of things I didn't think I could do tonight.

Gage let out another hiss of air as I left him, though that time it was more a growl in protest, in warning, than a sound of pleasure.

I was sure he was going to surge forward, to snatch me into his arms and fuck me into oblivion, but once he saw what I was doing, he froze.

My cardigan fell to the ground.

"I know the world can't see my scars, Gage, and it can see yours," I whispered, clutching the bottom of my shirt. "But I know you can see mine now." I whipped my top upward, hoping it didn't get caught in my hair or something equally embarrassing. The air brushing my face as the fabric fell to the floor told me it didn't. My eyes caught Gage's hungry stare immediately. He was eating up every single part of my exposed skin.

But he wasn't just seeing it, he was *seeing* it. Those places beneath that I was letting him see, that I was hoping he would understand after I'd painted the words of my soul in the air.

I made short work of my booties because there was simply no sexy way of divesting myself of them. But Gage's eyes weren't on my boots. No, they had migrated from my eyes to my chest, circling over my plain white cotton bra with an intensity that would've been surprising even if I'd been wearing sheer lace.

He found me sexy. Me. Not what I wore to cover my body but what was underneath. What was *really* underneath. My nipples hardened into stiff peaks, aching to be let out from the fabric encasing them. My eyes on Gage, I reached around to unclasp my bra, the fabric falling to the ground.

Gage's body pulsated in front of me, his jaw iron with the strength keeping him in place. I hadn't verbally commanded him to be still, but he knew I needed him to be. And even though it looked to be physically painful, he obeyed my silent command.

It took great effort to slowly peel my pants down my body and step out of them once they pooled at my feet.

Instinct had me wanting to stop there. To move forward, give in to my visceral need to have Gage's lips against mine, his hands all over me. I literally shook with the need for it. But I fought. Because this wasn't just about succumbing to my need, succumbing to Gage. I needed to succumb to my demons, to let them in.

So I didn't move. Instead I hooked my thumbs around the edges of my panties and moved them down, a lot quicker than I did my pants. Then I straightened, naked, in every sense of the word. My skin burned with fear, and with something else too. Something with Gage's gaze that made me feel safe and wild at the same time.

My nipples throbbed painfully as the hardened nubs were exposed to the air, my core pulsating as Gage's eyes went to that forbidden spot between my legs. That time, he did growl. So loud it shook my bones, warmed me to the very core.

"You are the most beautiful thing I've ever seen, Lauren," he choked out. He still didn't move. Still let the distance yawn between us in order to make us closer than I'd been with any other human in my life.

He let me live in that moment. The one where I'd told him one of the most harrowing and painful things that had ever happened to me, the thing that defined and broke me in a way I'd never be whole again, and he stayed standing in front of me, worshipping me with his eyes. With everything that was broken within him too.

I had not had many truly beautiful moments in my life. Not for the years I'd been living without David. I made sure to eliminate risks, the possibility of pain—but doing that meant I took away the possibility of true happiness, of beauty.

Because happiness and beauty were never possible unless one accepted that risks, pain, and ugliness had to be part of your life too. Had to mix perfectly with all the good things, so the beauty could outweigh the pain.

And then came Gage.

With pain.

Ugliness.

And true beauty.

That's what this moment was. After I had just laid my broken, severed, and utterly ruined soul in front of him—one of the most horrible things I'd had to do because it was the first time I was seeing it for myself—and my reward was him.

The moment was so delicate, so beautiful, I was scared to breathe, to blink, because I was terrified I'd alter it, pollute it, and it would crumble away into obscurity.

But delicate things were made to be broken. And I wanted this one broken. Because that would mean Gage was about to break me.

And he did, surging across the space between us.

I expected him to take my mouth, to run his hands all over me. I needed his mouth on mine so I could breathe. Needed his hands on every part of me—inside of me—so my heart could beat.

One of his hands clasped my bare hip. The other clutched my neck, yanking our heads together so our mouths almost touched.

Almost.

"I'm not gonna be a hero, babe," he growled. "Because heroes, their playbook is narrow. Limited. They're predictable. Play by the rules." His mouth brushed against mine as he rasped the words. Then his hand left my hip, traveling downward, over my sensitive clit and then going inside. *Right* inside.

I cried out a little, my knees weakening at the beautifully brutal intrusion.

Gage's eyes flared. "And you know as well as I do that this is a world where the rules don't mean shit, and the heroes are the only ones who don't know that. That means they lose. No matter what shit you read about in the books, the villain *always* wins." His fingers moved in a violent rhythm, coaxing me to climax, yanking me to the edge. "'Cause their playbook is endless. 'Cause they have no rules. Heroes lose everything. Villains get it, and they get it bloody. And I'll be a villain one hundred times over because I'm damn sure not losing everything, not again." The grip on my face was painful, his fingers inside of me pure nirvana. "And just so you know, baby, *you're* everything."

And just when my heart was about to explode, when *I* was about to explode, his fingers left me and I sagged, almost crying with the loss of him. With the loss of what promised to be one of the most intense climaxes of my life.

I wasn't disappointed for long.

Because, eyes still on me, Gage lowered and knelt at my feet. His large hand circled my proportionally tiny ankle and lifted so my knee hooked over his shoulder.

I let out a harsh breath at the angle, at how open, how exposed I was to his eyes.

But then I didn't think of that, because his mouth was there, right there. And I didn't say anything.

I screamed.

I fell over the edge.

He caught me.

TEN

I was late to work the next day.

Really freaking late.

The reason was obvious, if Abagail's sly grin was anything to go by as I passed reception. She had been warmer to me after her initial shock at me, of all people, being with Gage. Not that she was cruel about it in the beginning; she just didn't have that in her. She didn't have the tact to keep the hurt of her surprise from smarting though.

I'd forgiven it, because she had no malice, only youth.

"Morning, Lauren," she said, sipping her coffee.

I smiled wide. "Good morning."

"Late start?" she prompted, eyes wide and knowing.

"Oh no, very early start," I said with a wink and a tone that I didn't recognize.

The way her eyes popped out of her head, Abagail didn't recognize it either.

And the start to my morning *was* early. The sun was only just kissing the horizon when Gage's heated half woke me. Then the hardness pressing into my hip *really* woke me. And I decided to do something I had done but not enjoyed up until then—wake Gage up with my mouth around him.

Turned out I hadn't enjoyed it because I hadn't been doing it with Gage.

It was nothing short of life-changing.

The utter and complete control I wielded over the strongest man to enter my bed, my life. One of the strongest men in the most ruthless motorcycle club in the United States was at my mercy.

Yeah, I liked it so much that I finished myself with my hand while I finished Gage with my mouth. It was safe to say he'd liked watching me do that. And that it had driven him insane.

Hence me being three hours late in walking out the door, Gage's hand on my ass.

And however long we'd been outside, leaning on his motorcycle, making out like teenagers. But teenagers didn't kiss like Gage.

The Devil didn't kiss like Gage, and I bet that guy was the king of seduction and eternal damnation. Gage had him beat on both.

So no, I didn't care that I was late.

Didn't care that Abagail knew why.

And the whole office, based on the sly looks. No one was pissed. Not even Niles, who merely raised his coffee—probably his fifth of the day—at me in a salute and then resumed reaming an intern for some "colossal fucking fuckup." It was only Jen who regarded me with something that looked like contempt. Like fury. It was so deep and uncomfortable that it crawled at my skin. But then she jerked a little and that look melted away, warmth spreading in her eyes as her mouth turned up into a sly grin.

The change was so drastic, so quick, I must've simply imagined the pure hatred on her beautiful face. Maybe it was my mind twisting things, because it had too many good—freaking amazing—moments happen at once that there couldn't possibly be more. Like me making new friends.

And that's what Jen was. A friend.

She stood from her cubicle, picking up a cup. "Got you this," she said, nodding down to the cup in question. "But I'm thinking it's going to be cold now, since I got it for you precisely when you arrive at work. A time, I'm told, you haven't deviated from in almost *six years,*" she continued, voice teasing.

I took the cup off her, smelling the liquid that was resoundingly peppermint and realizing that it was indeed cold. I grinned, walking over to our small kitchenette, and poured the liquid down the drain. "I'm sorry you wasted a tea on me," I said, throwing the cup in the trash. I turned back to Jen, who had a slightly puzzled look on her face, eyes still on the trash. I hope I hadn't offended her.

I could've just microwaved the tea.

Shoot.

"How about I buy you a coffee to make up for it?" I asked, hoping to remedy the situation.

Her face jerked up in surprise. "A coffee? Now? You're late to work *and* you're playing hooky?" Strange look gone, her voice was playful again.

I grinned, thankful I hadn't offended my one new friend. "Yeah, I totally freaking am," I decided, walking forward and hooking my arm through hers. Her sharp and floral perfume overpowered me as soon as I did. It itched my nose, but I ignored that. "It's a morning of trying new things. It seems only apt."

"WELL, well, well, look who *finally* decides to show up," a terse voice said as Jen and I arrived back in the office, laughing about an ex she had who "got what was coming to him." I didn't even know why I was laughing, but it was just the mood I was in.

The mood that only improved at the sound of the reproachful voice.

And not because it was coming from my pissed editor.

No, it was coming from the woman who was sitting in my chair, her heeled shoes propped up on the draft of my latest story. One she'd helped me research—in secret and not getting stabbed or anything. "I've already done that, so I'm an expert at knowing how to avoid it" were her words on the phone a couple of days before.

"Lucy!" I yelled, surprising myself.

I didn't yell or scream at the sight of old friends.

Maybe because I didn't have old friends, not counting my grandmother, and she'd skin me alive if I called her old.

But talking to Lucy, realizing how important she had been to me, how much she'd known and chosen not to pry about, how much she'd helped me with, I couldn't not yell and beam and damn near sprint over to the beautiful and glamourous pregnant woman pushing out of my chair.

Even at what looked to be six months, she was polished, wearing her signature *Breakfast at Tiffany's* all-black elegance. Her turtleneck was skintight and showed off her beautiful baby bump, the rest of her tiny body encased in skintight leather pants.

The woman was noticeably pregnant and still pulling off leather pants. And bright red Manolo mules.

She was a superhero.

Or at the very least a witch.

Her eyes widened as she took me—and presumably my uncharacteristic yell—in. "Oh my God, someone got *laid*," she breathed, yanking me into a somewhat awkward but warm embrace.

She held me back at arm's length to run her eyes over me.

"Yeah, you got laid *good*. I'm so happy for you." She pulled me into her arms again before releasing me completely. Her eyes went behind me, locking in on Jen, and all warmness of before seeped out of them as she transformed her friendly and welcoming gaze into something else.

Lucy had the power to be intimidating. Very freaking intimidating. She was tall, absolutely beautiful, and a total ass-kicking babe. But she hadn't utilized that power. Not in front of me, anyway.

She was utilizing it now. And it made me uncomfortable.

"Lucy, this is Jen," I said, trying to warm the air. "She's the new columnist. Jen, this is Lucy. She used to be the best journalist in Amber, but then she moved to LA and took down a drug lord, so she's pretty much the best journalist in the US right now. And obviously pregnant. And her ankles aren't even swollen. So she's definitely a witch," I babbled.

Jen was smiling warmly in the face of Lucy's slightly chilly expression. "So nice to meet you," she said. "I've heard a lot about you."

Lucy smiled in a way that made it look like a scowl. "So nice to meet you too. And I don't mean to be rude, but I've heard *nothing* about you. I'll be rectifying that, obviously, because I'm nosy and also protective over my girl." She nodded at me. "But right now, I've heard almost nothing about my girl breaking Gage in, so I'll be needing everything on that, like yesterday."

Lucy gripped my hand before I could try to say something to Jen to lessen the blow of Lucy's words, her pretty face scrunching up in hurt.

"Niles, Lauren's taking lunch," Lucy yelled in his general direction.

Then she proceeded to drag me toward the stairs I'd just come up. You wouldn't think such a feat would be possible since she was really pregnant and in towering heels.

But nothing seemed impossible in my life now.

"COME ON, babe, you've *got* to come to girls' night," Lucy whined, making her eyes big and clasping her hands together in a prayer. "You're officially an old lady now. And you need to be initiated. And don't worry, it's not anything to do with hoods, daggers, or animal sacrifice. I'm sure Gage has that covered."

This was after we'd taken a long lunch, like a really freaking long one, during which I told her everything about Gage and me. Well, not everything, but the important parts. The important part being that he was mine and I was his.

She had cried.

Actually *cried*.

Then she'd scowled as she snatched the tissue off me. "Fucking hormones," she hissed. "I can't hear one piece of good news without blubbering like a fucking disgraced celebrity who 'forgot' to pay their taxes." She narrowed her tear-filled eyes. "And you and Gage being together is a good thing. Like *good*. But not me crying good. The only thing I should ever be crying about is the moment Karl Lagerfeld names a purse after me." She paused. "Or when I finally pop this thing out of me, I guess," she said, pointing to her stomach.

She reached across the table to squeeze my hand. "But I'm happy," she murmured. "And I'm going to tell you that, because this is a Sons of Templar relationship and he's Gage and there hasn't been an ounce of drama, things might get bad." Her eyes clouded over slightly. "Bad," she repeated.

My stomach dropped thinking of everything the women had gone through.

"But this man and this club will protect you with their lives," she promised. "And the bad is worth it, for the good. And you and

Gage deserve good." She smiled wickedly. "Or at least the best kind of bad."

I thought about that morning.

My stomach dipped.

Then it dipped more thinking about the fact that I knew there was more coming. More of the best kind of bad. I knew Gage was holding back. Waiting. But I didn't want him to. I needed him to give me that bad.

But not something I should've been thinking about in front of my pregnant friend, even if she did just ask me about length and girth over salad.

Of course, while I retreated into my thoughts, she'd been deciding I had to come to the night out all the women were having tonight.

"Pleeeeease?" she whined, taking my silence as a no.

I smiled, despite myself. Lucy and I were complete and utter opposites. She was drop-dead gorgeous, with style and confidence radiating from her very pores. She was outgoing and liked to party hard—well, she had until the big bump protruding from her stomach stopped her from imbibing alcohol. She had a huge group of loyal girlfriends that included the wives of some of the most feared and respected men in Amber. Of those women, I'd only met Amy, but I felt like I knew them all already, and they were both intimidating and impressive.

But they weren't *my* people.

No matter how much I wished they were.

I didn't have girlfriends. I wasn't outgoing, confident. And I definitely didn't party. A lot of people would've thought my shyness was snobbishness and my avoidance of any mood-altering drinks—including coffee—was boring and that I was a wet blanket.

Not Lucy.

She didn't do judging.

Not since the second she'd walked into the offices at the *Amber Star*, when she'd treated me with a warm smile and asked me if I wanted to go eat an entire day's calories with her on her lunch break.

She was thin, beautiful and most likely a size two. So she counted calories. Well, before.

I did not.

But I went anyway.

And we'd become unlikely but firm friends since then.

She'd lumber into the offices in dark glasses, muttering about regrets encouraged by "too many cosmos and my fucking insane best friend" or lamenting, "Why don't cars burn as well as they used to?" while drinking coffee after coffee and still managing to look like a runway model.

I'd listen to all of her stories with wide eyes, thinking about how she'd spent the night blowing up the car of a man who'd broken her sister's heart, and I'd been getting my heart broken by Jane Austen.

We were worlds apart. Not just me and Lucy, *all* of the women. They had caused somewhat of a stir in Amber, with kidnappings, car explosions, weddings, births, and rock stars, something right out of a soap opera.

Me? I literally watched soap operas and got too nervous to finish them out. No way I could even be on the sidelines of what-ever ended up happening tonight, and something would happen. Even being a bystander, I knew there was no such thing as a 'quiet girls' night' with these women.

I was going to say no.

That's what the old Lauren would've done.

It was safer.

"Okay," the new Lauren found herself saying. "What's the worst that can happen?"

Lucy smirked, rubbing her stomach. "Oh, I'm sure you'll

find out."

Gage

"*Oh my God*," Lucky breathed after Gage had spoken. "It's happening. The apocalypse. I knew it, of course. I'm not an idiot, I watch the *Walking Dead*." He rose. "I'm going to have to buy a crossbow before they're all sold out."

No one even blinked at Lucky and his fucked-up words. Everyone was used to the fucker spouting shit that didn't make a lick of sense.

Lucky grinned at Gage, deciding to answer the question that no one had asked, that being what in the fuck he was talking about. "Because it's gotta be the end of the world if Gage, of all people, is turning down a job where he not only gets to blow things up, but he gets to kill things."

Lucky was talking about the new contract the club had gotten for a pack of lowlifes cooking meth. Some rich fucker's son had been killed by a bad batch of the stuff. That same rich fucker had connections and pockets that led him to their door. And he was offering them a fuck of a lot of money for a lot of blood.

Neither money nor blood was going to bring his son back, but it was a good distraction.

Gage had used all sorts of bloody distractions in his life.

But he had a far deadlier one now.

Hence him not taking a contract that would take him away from Lauren. Something simmered underneath his skin. An uneasiness at how easy things had been between them. Well, things hadn't been easy, because he was in love with her already. And that shit on its own wasn't easy. It was the most complicated thing on this planet. The most painful and the deadliest.

So it hadn't been *easy*.

But he also hadn't been faced with the violence that had

stared every single one of his brothers in the eyes. Showed them how their life could snatch away the most precious of things.

Kidnappings. Bombs. Shootings. Fucking *rapes*.

Actual bile burned at Gage's throat with the utter thought of Lauren having to go through any of that. And the odds were against her, as it was with every single woman connected with the club. And that was with his other brothers.

With him, it was worse.

He should've done what he wanted to do the second she'd revealed her pain to him. He should've let her go so he didn't cause her another second of pain. Because he was going to, he knew that. But he was also too fucking selfish and cowardly. He was yanking her further into his life, burying her in the good things so when the bad hit, she was in too deep to crawl out.

It was fucked up.

Cruel.

But he was doing it anyway.

"Got better shit to do than blow things up and kill things" was Gage's response to Lucky.

Understatement of the fucking century.

Lucky grinned at him, slapping him on the shoulder. "My little psychopath is growing up. I've never been more proud."

Something was changing now that he had Lauren. He was part of something that he'd always been on the outside of. The thing he'd been glad to be outside of when he'd witnessed his brothers going through Hell in order to get to their own versions of Heaven.

But there he was, fucking glad about being inside it.

So he didn't stab Lucky.

"All right, Bull, you gonna tap in for this one?" Cade asked, ignoring Lucky as he always had to in order to get anything done.

But Lucky was not to be ignored, directing his gaze at his president. "Why is it automatically the next psychopath in the group who gets all the fun stuff?" he demanded. "I want to blow something up. Becky doesn't let me do it to the cars anymore."

The fact that his wife had to dictate that particular edict to him was why they had taken so long to have kids when every other fucker was popping them out like candy. Well, one of the reasons. The scars that Bex wore—rivaling Gage's own—were a huge contributing factor.

Cade sighed. "Fine, you can go. Bull will go to supervise. Surely one of your boys needs a field trip."

The corner of Bull's mouth turned up in response.

His two sons took after both him and Mia. In other words, they were fucking insane. Gage took it upon himself to teach them all the best ways to incapacitate someone, steal things, and generally just encourage what was already there. They were Sons, after all.

Cade looked around the table. "That all?" He didn't wait for a response, just smashed the gavel down. "Good, I've got a wife and kids who are a lot prettier to look at than you fuckers."

Brock clapped him on the shoulder. "I would agree on that score, but the kids are currently under the care of their grand-mother, along with mine. Since it's girls' night."

There was a collective groan around the table.

Girls' night was never just *girls' night*. No. Not with their women. Shit went down on those nights. And not normal shit. No, Gage wouldn't be surprised if there was some kind of national emergency as a result.

Gage shook his head, feeling sorry for the poor fuckers and readying himself to get out of there before shit started going down.

So he could go home.

To Lauren.

"Ah, don't you go looking so smug," Brock said, focusing his attention on him. "I have intel that suggests your woman is now firmly part of the posse, being that my fucking woman won't shut up about how 'kickass' she is and how she'll 'cut the balls off that mad motherfucker if he does anything to fuck this up,'" he air-quoted.

There was a collective chuckle around the table.

Gage's body tensed, and not for entirely bad reasons. He knew Lauren kept to herself. Knew the reasons why. The fact that she didn't have a lot of friends filled him with a sick satisfaction at first, because that meant he didn't have to share her with anyone. He was a greedy fucker; he wanted all her time.

But he wanted that shit for her. All the shit she'd been hiding from because of her pain. These women were crazy as fuck—arguably crazier than Gage himself—but they were good women. And they would look out for Lauren. More people caring about the most precious thing in his world was a good thing.

Her being at girls' night was not a fucking good thing.

"Fuck," he hissed, standing and intending on riding straight to Laura Maye's bar, since the bitch was crazy too, and crazy tended to group together in places that served alcohol.

"Hold up, brother," Cade said, stopping him from striding out the door. "You'll likely get skinned alive by my wife if you interrupt too early. I don't fuckin' like the prospect of whatever crazy shit's gonna happen tonight, but take it from me, it's better to leave it for a bit. Have a beer. Give them a second to initiate Lauren to the fold."

Gage was tense. Because he wanted that for her. But he wanted *her*. And he sure as fuck didn't want her in danger. And the girls' night was about as dangerous as a two-year-old with nuke codes. Or Lucky with anything that could explode.

"One hour," he relented.

Brock smiled.

Cade's mouth turned up.

Asher shook his head.

Bull clenched his fists.

Steg, who was now used to this kind of thing, gave a weary shake of his head, something that was decidedly too old for the man who had held the gavel for years before Cade.

Lucky gave him a fucking thumbs-up.

IT HAD BEEN AN HOUR, and he'd been counting the fucking seconds. For a slightly different reason than usual. Not just to distract him from the aching need for a fix—that was still there, of course, always would be—and not just to be pleased that another second of his life was over. No, he was counting down to when he could see her.

It was just him and Cade at the bar now. Gage was still nursing his first beer. He and alcohol enjoyed a careful and dangerous relationship. He didn't cut it out like the junk because people needed vices. And it was only slightly less dangerous than junk. There were points though, after too much whisky and not enough blood, that his resolve wavered in the haze of alcohol. But he never gave in. Not in seven years. But the hangover was that much worse because the pain of how close he'd come was lingering.

And since he was with Lauren, he didn't want to seek solace in a bottle. Not when he had *her*.

Brock was readying himself to come with him, though he'd had to go home and check on the baby. The fucker was more maternal than Amy. Though that wasn't hard.

"She's too good for me," Gage clipped, his words razors, cutting only as the truth could.

To the bone.

To his utter fucking surprise, Cade grinned. The fucker *grinned*. He never smiled unless it was at his kids or his wife. And it had taken his wife a long time to tease that smile out of him. They'd been through enough to wipe that smile off permanently.

"Of course she is," Cade said. "They're *all* too fucking good for us. As it should be. We should be aware of that shit, so then we make sure we always do whatever we can to make sure we're good enough for them. That every fucking day's goal is winning them over as if we don't have them."

Gage glanced at his president. Tasted the words. The truth in them.

Then he got up off the stool.

To win Lauren over for another day.

Lauren

"I'm so happy we've got a fresh face!" Gwen screamed, grinning at me above the rim of her glass.

It was a grin that hadn't left her face since I'd entered Laura Maye's bar with Lucy. A bar I'd never set foot in in my whole life. Despite that, the infamous Laura Maye rounded the bar with vigor and yanked me into her perfume-laden embrace.

I was surprised that I didn't sink into the masses of choco-late-brown hair teased around her head. I was also surprised that I relaxed into the embrace, something I didn't do with many people. Especially not strangers. But she didn't exactly feel like a stranger. The way she looked at me to babble on about a new courtship and about how excited she was to *finally* have me in the circle, as if it had been somewhat of a foregone conclusion.

Each of the women waiting at the best table in the house—the big booth with a stunning view of the ocean setting—gave me versions of that same welcome.

Some were more exuberant—Gwen and Mia—while others were more subdued—Bex and Lily—but all were warm. There were no uneasy glances, no cooling toward the new woman in the group, something I'd been terrified of.

Not a single one of the women blinked when I'd refused the cocktail Gwen had all but shoved in my face. Something crossed Bex's pretty but hard face with my refusal. Something like understanding. Or maybe respect? But of course, she hadn't been able to get a word in edgewise, not with Amy, Mia, and Gwen in attendance.

Amy looked over at her beautiful friend. "What do you mean *fresh?*" she demanded. "My face is plenty fresh. It's fresh as fuck," she snapped, palming her cheek. "I spend thousands on face serums in order to make sure Botox isn't in the picture... yet." She narrowed her eyes at an amused Gwen. "And don't you fucking dare utter a word to Cade about that. He and Brock natter like old women, and Brock has some strong feelings about me maintaining my youth."

"He has strong feelings about you injecting poison in the face he loves so much," Mia corrected, sipping from her own glass. "I'm much older than you children and I'm yet to need that stuff. Age gracefully, like *moi*." She waved over her flawless face. It wasn't lineless—small creases edged her almond-shaped eyes, but they were evidence of happiness. Of a perpetually smiling life. It only added to her beauty.

Amy scowled at her. "Oh shut the fuck up. You're not aging gracefully. You've got a famous daughter who's most likely a member of the Illuminati now, and she's given you all the secrets about living forever and becoming a reptile and whatnot."

A gaggle of laughter erupted around the table. I was surprised to find myself laughing too. Really laughing. With my whole self. I hadn't done that, not properly, in almost a decade.

I realized Gage hadn't just given me the gift of sharing pain with me. He'd given me these women too.

I also realized I loved him.

Had for a long while.

———

"HEY, honey, can I buy you a drink?" the low drawl sounded from behind me. Like right behind me, up in my space, an unfamiliar and uncomfortable warmth spreading from the closeness of a stranger.

I was at the bar getting another round. The women had protested heavily, since I wasn't drinking, but I'd insisted and then Amy had shouted above everyone else, "If she wants to buy us drinks, let the bitch. It's free cocktails—who says no to that?"

And the matter had been settled.

It wasn't hard, considering most of the women, save Lily and Bex, were well on their way to being blotto. I sensed that they rarely all got together at the same time, considering they all had small children and really, *really* attractive husbands to keep them busy.

The man's breath was off my neck and his presence out of my space before I even had a moment to breathe, or more likely to panic and figure out what the fricking heck to do.

I whirled to see Gage yanking the man by the lapels of his jacket, eyes wild.

Brock, Amy's attractive husband, folded his muscled arms and grinned behind Gage.

I was wide-eyed and blinking rapidly as he shoved the sandy-haired man against the bar. I didn't know what I expected from Gage—a lot of profanities, of course, a warning, some shouting. Because he was Gage and protective, and he was bound to do one or all of those things.

But I got none of that. Well, the sandy-haired man got none of that. Instead, Gage pressed the man's palm flat on the bar and, in one fluid motion, embedded a knife into the top of it, spearing him to the wooden surface.

His screams echoed through my ringing head.

"You come near her again, you won't be walking home with a hole in your hand. You won't fucking have one," Gage said, voice hard yet somehow businesslike, calm.

And then, in another smooth movement, he yanked his knife from the bar, wiped the blood on his jeans and turned to me, snatching me by the arm and dragging me toward the bathrooms.

I let him drag me, because when Gage wanted someone to be somewhere—especially when the someone was me, who was five-foot-nothing and weighed the same as one of his thighs—they were somewhere Gage wanted them to be.

The screams followed us through the now eerily silent bar. I craned my head over my shoulder to see Brock, still grinning, but now doing it with his wife in his arms. She was grinning too.

Mia lifted her drink to me in a 'cheers' motion.

Gwen gave me a thumbs-up.

The rest of the women were doing variations of the same thing, none of them looking at all alarmed that my boyfriend had just stabbed someone in the middle of our girls' night.

And then I lost sight of them as Gage locked us in a bathroom and slammed me into a wall.

"You just stabbed someone in the hand, in public," I breathed, my voice much lower and calmer than I'd expected it to be.

He didn't say anything, merely continued to stare at me.

"He could press charges," I continued, not knowing why I didn't focus on the stabbing part of the equation and instead worried about Gage getting in trouble.

"He won't. He knows what's good for him," Gage growled, pelvis pressing into mine. "And if he does, I don't give a fuck. He was touching what was mine. Needed a lesson."

I swallowed roughly around the desire that snatched hold of me with Gage's body against mine, his eyes devouring me, his breath hot and minty on my face. It no longer smelled of smoke considering he'd quit, for me.

I tried to hold onto my constant logic, but it was hard with the adrenaline and desire pulsating through my system. Even if I never drank a drop of alcohol in my life, I'd always be fully drunk on this man in front of me.

"You couldn't have given him, I don't know, a verbal warning?" I asked when I finally had a somewhat tenuous control over my logical brain.

"Don't do warnings," he grunted. "And I'm not going to give any fucker a second chance to touch my woman."

"But no one even knows I'm yours!" I exclaimed, though it was kind of a lie, because all the women watching the exchange knew I was Gage's—and more importantly, Laura Maye knew, which meant the whole town likely did by now.

His callused hand brushed my cheek in a tenderness I didn't think was possible from a man who'd just stabbed someone. "Well, they know *now*."

I swallowed again, trying to remind my knees that they had to hold me up. "You could've communicated that without stabbing someone," I rasped, a snip in my voice.

"Could've," he agreed blandly, eyes flaring at the bite in my tone. "But I'm not fuckin' going to. You're mine. Someone touches what's mine, I don't fuck around. I take blood."

As if he sensed that I was about to go into a tirade about how I was my own woman and didn't need bikers stabbing men for me, his mouth covered mine, stealing the words from me.

Stealing the breath from me.

Not that it was mine to give anyway.

I understood that after he broke the kiss and my entire soul protested his mouth leaving mine.

"We can have the fight about how you're a strong independent woman later," he murmured, twinkle in his eye as his fingertips moved up my skirt.

"How did you know that's what I was going to say?" I asked, voice dreamy as he trailed the outside of my thigh, his fingertips at the top of my panties.

"Been around the block, babe. Seen the courtship process from the sidelines. I know how this goes. It's going to be a battle. One I'm happy to fight." He yanked his hands downward, my panties going with them, and I'd stepped out of them before I rightly knew what was going on. Gage brought them to his nose and inhaled deeply.

Yes, inhaled.

My stomach burned with shock, and desire.

His eyes didn't leave mine. "But I'm gonna fuck you first."

And he did.

Against the wall in the bathroom in a bar.

Crazy. Wild. Brutal. Freaking *public*.

And I loved every second of it.

Two Days Later

"Late again," Jen said, smirking. Though again, her smirk was slightly empty.

I winked at her, holding up a coffee for her and a tea for me.

"Yes, but it was because I was getting us drinks." I paused, thinking about how Gage and I had been about to open the door to leave my apartment and he'd slammed me against the wall.

"Can't do it," he rasped, mouth against my neck, bunching my skirt with one hand, yanking at his belt with another.

"*Do what?*" *My words were broken by the stabbing need in my soul.*

He pushed my panties to the side, delving into my drenched core.

I let out a moan.

His eyes met mine. "Can't let you walk out the door lookin' like that without fucking the life out of you." *He plunged into me again and hissed out a low growl.* "And then fuck you back to life."

And he had done just that.

Hence me being late.

Jen lifted a coffee tray.

I laughed. "Ah, great minds." I handed her one from mine. "I'm sure mine's a little hotter since you likely got yours a while ago."

She took the cup, sipping. "Yeah, I'm thinking you're not going to be predictable anymore?"

I sipped my tea, thinking of the delicious tenderness between my thighs. "No, I think not," I murmured.

"Look, Lauren, I don't know you very well," Jen said, interrupting my sex flashback, "though I hope that's going to change because I like you. And I'm saying this because I like you, and please stop me if I'm crossing the line," she said, putting the coffee down. "But this new guy... he sounds great."

"Great is an understatement."

Her eyes flickered. "Obviously, since by the looks of it, he's changing everything about you in such a short amount of time."

I stiffened at her words.

She smiled as if it would reduce their sting. "I'm not saying this to be cruel. I'm saying it because I've got experience with this kind of thing." Her eyes went faraway. "I know what it's like to have someone unlike anything but a tornado come into your life and blow it apart. And at the time, it seems like a good thing. The best. Destruction of who you were before doesn't matter because of who you are with them." She paused, eyes zeroing in on me. "But tornados leave as quickly as they come, and the destruction they leave in their wake isn't as exciting as it seemed in the middle of the storm. That's all I'm saying. Make sure you know him well enough that you know what he's taking from you. So you know he's not taking everything and going to run off when the storm's over."

She sipped her coffee, glancing at her computer as if her words hadn't just hit me and touched all the fears I'd been ignoring.

"Shit, I have a deadline and I just realized I didn't fact-check this," she said, glancing back up to me. "I'm sorry, babe. We'll talk about this later, okay?"

I nodded and wandered to my desk, relishing the tenderness that came with sitting down, trying to hold onto that pain instead of the pain that had just come with Jen's words.

But I didn't.

I held onto them both.

All day.

I LET Jen's words eat at me for the rest of the week.

The week that was little more than a blur of work—I was trying to do all my normal duties and finish the story that wasn't anywhere near normal—and Gage.

Well, work was a blur.

Gage was hot—sometimes cold—stark, beautiful reality.

He had been busy with the club and didn't come to my apartment until late most nights.

But then he made me come.

Continuously.

He broke me with his body. With his presence.

But he was holding back. I could tell. His darkness was lurking, waiting to strike. It terrified me, but I wanted it to strike.

I just had to wait.

But then I needed something else.

Something that all but burst out of me on Sunday morning.

The Sunday morning that did not consist of yoga. Or tea with acquaintances. Or pedicures.

It consisted of Gage.

It was almost noon and I'd only just managed to get dressed in frayed denim cutoffs and a flowy halter, Gage wearing jeans, unbuttoned at the top, no underwear.

I was trying to make lunch.

But he was standing there, like that, in the kitchen. Shirtless. His muscles, his scars, his art.

In my kitchen.

Tearing through my routine. My life.

"Make sure you know him well enough that you know what he's taking from you. So you know he's not taking everything and going to run off when the storm's over."

The words bounced around in my head as they had all week. I'd been unable to banish them, even with Gage filling me up.

So I had to get them out.

"This doesn't make sense," I whispered, taking the bacon off the stove and staring at Gage. "This, us... what we have, after..."

"After what?" he demanded, his body iron, his face blank. I hated that I had torn that slightly easy look from his face.

I struggled to find words, usually having them stored and planned. But all plans went out the window with us. "After nothing. We haven't been on a *date*, or met each other's parents or... I don't know, *traveled* together. You can tell a lot about a couple by the way they manage airports."

My words sounded totally freaking lame to my own ears, but it was true. My parents didn't know about him—nor did I plan on telling them anytime soon—and he never talked about his. Or anything about himself, for that matter.

He stared at me. And stared. "After *nothing?*" he repeated.

And then he wasn't across the kitchen. Neither was I. I was in his arms, his body pressed against mine. "This isn't nothing," he growled, clutching my face. He pressed his lips to mine, and I opened to him without hesitation, letting him take whatever he wanted. Anything.

My breath was strangled in my throat by the time he separated from me.

Then again, he never really separated from me.

Not really.

"That isn't nothing," he rasped. "And we don't make sense. Because we live in a fuckin' world that doesn't make sense. And I know you need it. Logic, sense. Because that's what you've built around you. I'm here to knock it all down. Destroy that. Because we're never gonna be logical. You know that. But it doesn't matter. You know that too. Because you fuckin' feel this too." He gripped my hips. "And there's not gonna be dates, or flowers or anniversaries. You know that too, because that's not how I work. That's not how *we* work. But you're gonna be the fuckin' air I breathe. My sun and my moon and my everything in between. So I don't give a fuck about airplanes and sense. I give a fuck about you. And that's all that matters. 'Cause you give a fuck about me too."

I blinked as he brushed away Jen's words. Obliterated them.

Because she was right. She didn't know me well.

No one really did.

Because I hadn't let them.

Until Gage.

And he wasn't telling me much about himself—yet—but he was teaching me everything I didn't know about myself.

"Yeah, Gage," I whispered. "I give a fuck about you."

His hands flexed around my arms.

"You want a date?" he asked, voice even and calm like it was when he had something wild on his mind—in other words, all the freaking time.

I nodded slowly, even though I knew I was agreeing to some kind of deal with the Devil. No, a date with the Devil.

He grinned, and I knew I was damned.

Because there was danger in that grin.

He grabbed my hand and yanked me toward his bike.

"If my woman wants a date, a date is what she'll get. Gage style."

***

"DATES USUALLY TAKE place at movie theaters. Restaurants," I said after the roar of the bike had surrendered to the quiet surrounding us.

What I was looking at was not a restaurant. Or a movie theater. It was an abandoned warehouse in the middle of nowhere. Gage had ridden twenty minutes out of town, stopped at a locked gate, unlocked said gate, and then rode another ten minutes down a bumpy dirt road that he'd navigated without hurling me off the back of the bike.

And we were here.

"Is this where you're taking me to kill me?" I asked when he didn't answer.

Of course I was joking. Kind of.

Gage's hands went to the clasps underneath my chin since I'd dismounted while still wearing my helmet. He brushed the sides of my face, taking off the prescription sunglasses I was wearing and deftly swapping them out for my regular glasses he'd had stuffed somewhere.

The gesture was small. Tiny. But it hit me square in the

chest, the absolute smallness of it. He'd known I needed my glasses to see, remembered to bring ones for inside—when I hadn't even thought about it, which was unheard of—and slipped them on my face.

I love you.

I almost said it right there and then, because he remembered I needed two pairs of glasses.

"Not in the habit of killin' beautiful things, babe," he murmured, eyes dark. He cupped my face after he'd put my glasses on. "You know I don't operate on the usual," he said, responding to my initial statement. He stepped back, letting my face go but snatching my hand and walking us toward the building.

Gravel crunched underneath my shoes as butterflies swarmed in my stomach. I was never settled with Gage. Never complacent. Because he was always doing something to shake me up. He did that just by freaking *looking* at me.

And now he was dragging me toward an abandoned building in the middle of nowhere for a 'date.' What was inside could range from a picnic lunch to a pile of dead bodies. That was Gage.

"Nervous?" he asked, eyes twinkling as he stopped us in front of rotting wooden doors.

I jutted my chin up. "No," I lied.

He full-on grinned, yanking me forward for a rough kiss.

My butterflies went wild for an entirely different reason once he let me go.

He seemed to sense the need flooding between my legs, his eyes darkening. "Later," he promised.

Then he opened the door.

It took a few seconds for me to adjust to the grainy light inside, the smell of dirt and metal mingling with the fresh air from outside.

There was a thump and rattling of chains as Gage shut the door behind us, grabbed my hand and walked me to the middle of the room.

I had expected it to be messy. To have random motorcycle parts lying around the place. Torture devices.

Dead bodies strung up from the rafters.

But it was clean.

Meticulously so. The concrete floor was slightly dusty, but not as much as it should've been, which meant it was regularly swept.

There was a desk running along the length of the building to our left. Most of the surface was clear, and I couldn't see exactly what lay atop—tools of some kind—but they were all neatly bunched together. There was also a sofa, small coffee table, an old TV, and a white mini fridge.

But that wasn't the focus of what was in the room.

No, it was the table that Gage stopped us in front of. More accurately, what was on top of that table. Gage yanked a string attached to the ceiling when an electrical buzz sounded for a moment, a bright almost blinding light illuminating every detail.

I gaped.

It wasn't hard to put the proverbial pieces together and realize what was in front of me.

"Okay, for our first date, you want *to build a bomb?*" I asked, looking to the mess of wires in front of me and then back up at Gage. "And that's not actually a question, since it's pretty freaking clear we're making a bomb right now. It's just a clarification of reality."

He grinned, cupping my face. "We make our own reality." He nodded to the table. "Sometimes I destroy mine." He laid a gentle kiss on my lips. "You said you could tell a lot about people about how they manage airports," he repeated my ridiculous words, made all the more ridiculous by the fact that we were standing in front of a half-built bomb.

I merely nodded.

"Well, I'm not people. You know that by now. But you want to know more, so I'm giving you more." His eyes shadowed with something. Something dark. "As more as I can right now. So you can tell a lot about me by how I build a bomb. You up for it?" It was a challenge and also something else. He was showing me his life, not hiding the more dangerous parts of it. Because everything was the ugly truth with Gage.

That's what made it so beautiful.

"Yeah," I whispered.

His eyes flickered and he laid another kiss on my mouth that was not at all gentle. "That's my girl. And just so you know, I'm teachin' you. Because my woman is gonna know how to blow shit up, just in case she feels the urge."

ELEVEN

I opened the door with a smile because, well, I was smiling a lot these days. Even though life with Gage wasn't exactly conventional—we'd built a *bomb* together for our freaking first date, for crying out loud. A 'conventional' person wouldn't consider our thus far rocky and pain-filled relationship—if that's what it was—a reason to smile.

But I was quickly learning that I was far from conventional too. And Gage and conventional didn't even live in the same zip code. Or the same country.

He certainly wasn't smiling when I opened the door not long after I'd gotten home from work. Not even his version of a smile—an attractive mouth twitch. No, it was the exact and utter opposite of that, in fact. He was glowering, his fury pushing past me and polluting the very atmosphere of my apartment.

And then he slammed the door behind me, threw me over his shoulder and stomp up the stairs. I let out a surprised squeak that wasn't at all cute.

"Gage!" I cried, not struggling even though the motion wasn't sexually motivated. I should've been very, *very* scared by that look on his face.

I was.

But that same fear excited me in equal parts. Because Gage had awakened that in me. That reaction to things that scared me. That *craving* for them. Since he scared me most of all.

Once at the top of the stairs, he plopped me down unceremoniously and rather roughly, telling me that his carrying of me was because it was the most efficient way of getting me up the stairs and not because he wanted to throw me on the bed and ravage me.

Part of me—a lot of me—was disappointed. But there was also a lot of me left to be freaking terrified, since I really hadn't gauged the full range of his anger in the fleeting glimpse I got of him at the door.

He. Was. Mad.

"You went to the fucking *cop*?" He spat the last word at me with such force that it hit me physically, like a bullet.

My brow furrowed, understanding his anger but not realizing the source of it. "Come again?"

Me not immediately knowing the source of his manly and oh-so-visceral anger was obviously not the right reaction because his stare darkened and his fists clenched harder at his sides, the veins of his arms sculpting themselves even more sharply from the scarred flesh.

He stepped forward, body brushing mine in a threat, not a caress. "Oh, I'll make you come. Again. And again. And *a-fucking-gain*. Until you're tortured with the amount of attention I'm showing that pretty cunt of yours. Until you think you can't take any more." He grasped my chin roughly. "And then you'll take more." His eyes were black. Cruel. "And that's gonna be your fuckin' punishment for this shit."

The air thickened between us until I could breathe nothing but pure sex in the air. Then he stepped back and I exhaled in relief. Or in disappointment.

He folded his arms across his chest, the muscles underneath his scars moving the puckered skin. "But for now, you're going to explain why the fuck you went to the man who not only stands for everything we don't but who also wants a *piece of my fucking woman.*" His voice held no more of that erotic threat. No, this was pure fury, the tenor beginning to rise to an almost shout. Something Gage rarely did. Which meant he was really mad.

I struggled to capture my thoughts under the torture of his glare. Then I realized why he was mad. Because I had gone to Troy. About the photos I'd taken on the night Gage had dragged me from Niles's car and onto his bike. I expected him to ask more about it. He didn't. Though I guessed he'd come to the right conclusion after I told him about David. Maybe he thought he didn't need to say any more about it, since he'd already expressed his disapproval and thought that would work to stop me from doing anything further.

I was almost finished with the story I'd begun writing because of the reaction I got from Troy a week ago, which was not a lot about my pictures and a heck of a lot more about my relationship with Gage.

I pursed my lips. "I'm not here to talk about my personal life, Troy," I said, my voice sharp, like it'd been the second he'd started to tell me how dangerous the men of the Sons of Templar were, and how Gage was most of all. "And I'm reasonably sure that it's of little import when measured up to these." I nodded to the images on my screen. The images I'd put in front of Troy after initial strained pleasantries—I hadn't spoken to him since that awkward car ride back from the Sons of Templar compound when I'd brushed off all questions pertaining to Gage—were done.

He wasn't looking at the pictures. He was focused on me, all softness gone from his face, his expression hard and grim. "I beg to differ, Lauren," he clipped. "One of the sweetest and most innocent women I know getting tangled up with one of the most dangerous men in the Sons of Templar MC is a hell of a lot more important than a fucking lowlife selling to other lowlifes."

I flinched. Not because of the harsh tone, nor the sheer disgust with which he spoke about Gage, nor the truth of his words about Gage.

"Lowlife selling to other lowlifes."

His face changed the second I flinched, softening with the realization of what he'd said, and the implications.

"Shit. No, Lauren, that's not what I meant." He leaned forward, as if to grasp one of the hands I had lying on the desk.

I sat back, taking my hand away from his reach, snatching my phone as I did so. "No, it's fine. I understand," I told him curtly.

I stood. Troy did too.

"You consider this less of a crime because it's happening to people who only have themselves to blame. Who live outside the proper society you protect from drug-addicted lowlifes. I get it." My voice was flat because I was trying not to scream.

Troy rounded the desk and got in my way as I turned to leave, battling at the sharp prickling of tears behind my eyes.

"No, Lauren," he protested. "I do not consider it that way. I treat these dealers with the same harshness as I would murderers. Because they are. I can't technically do anything because Hope isn't my jurisdiction, and a photograph that doesn't explicitly show drugs being exchanged isn't grounds for an arrest. But," he continued as I tried to speak, "I do know a couple of guys in Hope who can set up surveillance, try and get this guy." He stepped forward and grasped my elbow. "But there's something in my jurisdiction that's worrying me more than that. You're my jurisdiction, Lauren. And I don't want to see you hurt if I can stop it."

I yanked my elbow out of his grip. "You can't stop me from

being hurt," I said coldly, his words doing little to lessen the sting of the previous statement. "And I wouldn't want you doing anything even if you could."

Then I turned on my heel and walked out.

I didn't tell Gage because, well, I wasn't an idiot. I might not quite understand the why of our connection, or his violent protectiveness, but I knew it was there. And if his reaction toward Troy before we had even become a thing was anything to go by, I knew it was in Troy's best interest to keep the communication under wraps. That, and nothing had come of it apart from a fresh tear in a wound that would never quite be healed.

He wasn't going to do anything about the dealer who sold my brother his last hit. But *I* was.

"Women are the best at conquering demons, slaying their own dragons and all that. But the right man with the wrong demons can show you that."

Gage was looking to be a dragon I needed to slay myself, if the savagely angry and beautiful man in front of me was anything to go by.

Hence me deciding that this—or any point in the near future —would not be a good time to tell him about the story due to go to print in a week.

"How do you know about that?" I asked. *I* obviously didn't tell him. I was pretty sure Gage and Troy didn't have weekly knitting circles, so I knew Troy didn't tell him, and no one else knew.

"How do I know?" he repeated, voice slow and dangerous. It was a warning. Probably for me to ask another question, or plead forgiveness from the almighty being in front of me.

But no way was I asking for forgiveness. Gage might've scared me, but he wasn't going to scare me into submission. Not when sex wasn't involved.

My stomach did an involuntary flip with the promise of punishment Gage had tattooed onto my bones moments before.

I didn't let it distract me... much. I jutted my chin up in defiance, waiting for the answer to my question in silence.

"I know because I know shit," he seethed. "Because this is *my* fucking town, and when things have to do with the local boys in blue, I know a lot." He placed his hand on my hip and yanked me to him. "And when it comes to you, I know fucking everything. Consider me the all-seeing fucking eye of Sauron."

I blinked. His tone was deadly. "You like *Lord of the Rings?*"

Silence followed my words. Dangerous silence.

Gage's face wiped of all expression for a moment. And then it changed. "Of course I fucking like *Lord of the Rings!*" he bellowed, right in my face. "It's a work of fucking cinematic genius, and one of the best pieces of fantasy ever written. But that has nothing to fucking do with this." He was still yelling, which was the only reason I didn't smile at the contrast between the words themselves and the tone in which he uttered them.

And he wasn't done.

He leaned forward, his hand still biting into my hip while the other grasped my chin. "You still haven't answered my question as to why you went to the cop when I explicitly told you not to."

With great effort, I yanked myself out of his grasp. The effort was not due to Gage holding me against my will, but because even when he was in the grips of fury, yelling at me and saying things I *so* didn't agree with, I still didn't want to be outside of the cocoon of his arms.

But I had to. My point was not as easily made if he was clutching me as he was, holding all the power. I at least needed the illusion that I had a grasp on some of it.

He glared at the distance I'd created between us but didn't try to cross it, though his jaw twitched in obvious frustration.

I ignored how sexy I found that twitch. "For a man who's

structured his entire way of life outside the bounds of society-created rules, you seem very fricking determined to create them."

His eyes narrowed. "Not asking you to follow society's rules, babe," he clipped. "Fuck, do what you want with them. Lie, steal, cheat, murder. I'm right by your side with you breakin' society's rules. But you're gonna live by mine."

I folded my arms, no longer finding the jaw twitch sexy because I was getting seriously pissed off. "I'm *gonna* live by yours?" I repeated.

He nodded once, as if it were a completely reasonable statement and not out-of-this-universe insane.

"You're insane!" I yelled.

"You're right, Will, I am," he said, his voice a low rasp to juxtapose my near screech. "I'm insane, and therefore I will do fucking anything to keep you safe. *Anything.* I'm insane and my feelings for you are of that vein. It's only a matter of fuckin' time before you realize that."

The words were a premonition. A dark one.

"You don't think I'm strong enough for this, for us," I accused.

His stare was unyielding. Cold. Unfeeling. Cruel. "No, I *know* you're not strong enough. Don't take it personally. Most people can't handle this life. It's a compliment that you can't. Means you're not broken beyond repair. Means your soul isn't so fucked up that even the Devil wouldn't take it." He said it with the vacant humor I'd noted he'd clutched to in times of turmoil. Basically all the times we were together, since turmoil had become the norm for me. Turmoil was his constant. Chaos his companion. Pain his captain that steered his life.

I pursed my lips as I digested all his words. As they created little papercuts in my skin and his stare pressed salt into those wounds.

He wanted to hurt me with this indifference, drive me away.

He was succeeding.

"Right," I said, my voice husky.

Then I turned around and walked calmly to my closet. He stayed where he was; I knew that mostly because I didn't hear the low thud of his motorcycle boots on my polished wooden floors.

He was standing in the exact same position when I exited my closet, holding two things in my hands. Two things I'd bought in the middle of the night after a terrifying and erotic dream, my hands clicking 'add to cart' and typing my credit card info before I'd even fully woken up.

When the UPS guy had dropped them off two days later, my cheeks had flamed with shame, somehow certain he knew the contents of the box and was silently judging me for it. Not so silently judging myself, I'd buried it in my closet, telling myself I'd never use it but hoping that one day I would.

Not me. Someone else. The man who existed not in my dreams but in my nightmares. Not the hero on the white horse I'd read about all through childhood, had fantasies about in adolescence and said a sad goodbye to on my twenty-first birthday when I realized he didn't exist.

No, this was the man I didn't even let myself think about because he was borne from a dark and deeply unsettling part of me.

His eyes flared when he got a look at what was in my shaking hands. Every part of him turned wired.

I held out the objects, barely able to keep them in my grasp.

"Show me," I whispered.

His eyes glued into mine. "Show you what?" he demanded, voice hoarse.

"Show me what you're so certain I can't handle."

His eyes snapped down to the handcuffs, then back up to me. His body was shaking, taut, almost transforming with his need. With that dark need that had been lingering beneath the surface every time he touched me. What he had been holding back, even as he fucked me more brutally than any man had before.

Because that brutality was beautiful, perfect, wild, but I knew there was more. Something that wasn't perfect. Wasn't beautiful. Something he was locking down because he didn't think I would survive it.

I wasn't sure if I would either, but I was sure I wouldn't be living, really living, if I let him walk out the door, out of my life.

Gage moved in a blur and pain exploded in my throat as his hand bit into it enough to steal almost all my oxygen. His cold eyes ran over me as I struggled to breathe. But I didn't struggle out of his hold as I was sure he expected me to do.

This was a challenge. He *wanted* me to be scared. Think he was going to hurt me. He wanted me to escape that. Escape *him*.

But I didn't. I just stared at him, my eyes a silent dare to squeeze harder. Fury and arousal danced in his eyes at my reaction. He held me for a beat longer, and then his grip loosened. He didn't completely let go, still held me in place, but the pain was mostly gone and I could breathe easy.

In theory, at least. No one could breathe easy with Gage's eyes on them.

"You don't fuckin' know what you're asking for," he growled, voice feral.

"Yes I do. I'm not afraid of you," I said, slightly raspy.

He looked at me as if trying to find the cracks in my words. "Yeah, babe, because you're brave in ways I'm not," he said finally.

I wasn't prepared for that response, not in the midst of his fury. "What are you talking about?"

"Because *I'm* afraid of *you*," he ground out. "Only thing in my life I'm afraid of. Because you're the only thing in my life that's priceless." The grip on my neck tightened once more. "And you askin' me to show you what's inside, what's *really* inside, that fuckin' terrifies me, because I can't fuckin' control that shit. And once I let it out, I can't rein it in. I'm terrified that I'm gonna be responsible for ruining the only thing left in my life that's priceless. It's been ten years since I've touched some-thing—someone—and not wanted to cause them pain." He paused. "Not *needed* to cause them pain. I don't fuckin' want to do that to you, Will. You're the first person in a decade I've wanted to touch with something resembling tenderness. But I don't have that now. It's gone, that ability. It died. There's only pain left."

I didn't let his gaze go, though I was sure he wanted me to. He wanted to scare me away with his admission. His threat.

"You're not going to ruin me, Gage," I whispered. "The world has already done that. And even if it hadn't, I want you to ruin me. There's something inside of me, not something you created but something you *awakened*. It's a darkness, maybe not as black as yours, but one that wants you to drag me further down. Wants you to show me everything depraved in your head. I want you to do things to me that you've been too scared to do to anyone else." I paused. "In fact, I'm going to have to insist that you do." My voice was husky, the being inside me that I'd silenced for so long finally getting her say.

The knife he always wore on his belt was out of its sheath and running down my body before I even knew what was happening. The tearing of my clothes was a roar in my ears as he literally cut my shirt off me.

And my bra.

My core pulsated with the violence, with the sharp and deadly weapon being so close to my skin.

Not the knife.

Gage.

He had transformed since he'd unsheathed his knife.

Because at the same time, he'd unsheathed his monster.

My need was almost painful as my eyes locked on his, the flat edge of the knife pressing into one of my hard peaks.

Gage's gaze didn't leave mine.

The knife circled one nipple.

Then another.

"Your cunt dripping wet, Will?" he asked, voice little more than a growl.

I gasped as the sharp edge of the knife pressed into the swell of my breast, almost tearing at the skin before Gage flipped it and ran the point down my midsection.

His hand came up to shackle my neck when my answer was a succession of sharp breaths. "I asked you a fucking question. When I do that, you answer."

The tip of the knife pressed into my lower stomach in warning.

"Yes," I breathed.

The knife ran along the waistband of my skirt. "Yes what?" Gage demanded.

He wanted me to prove something. To shed the skin that covered what was really underneath. "My cunt is dripping wet for you, Gage," I whispered, my voice throaty. Raw.

"Christian," he said, his voice feral. Throaty. "I'm Christian to you when we're like this. Never outside of this. Never. I'm always Gage then. I have to be. But here"—the flat of the knife pressed into my soaking panties—"here, I'm Christian."

I jerked, and the movement pressed the tip of the knife into my skin, enough to draw blood. Gage hissed as though it had cut through him, his eyes flaring in panic.

I snatched his wrist, the one holding the blade now stained with my blood, stopping him from yanking it away.

"No," I demanded, not breaking his gaze. "Don't stop."

It took pain, brutality for Gage—*Christian*—to slice off a tiny piece of himself and hand it to me. And I was willing to go through anything to get more.

His eyes flared and the knife paused for a moment more. Then it tore through my panties and I was standing there naked, exposed, and bleeding in front of Gage. He lifted the knife and licked the small amount of my blood off the steel, not breaking eye contact with me the entire time.

I watched, rapt, hypnotized and terrified by the man—the monster—in front of me.

The knife moved down to the sheath as he grabbed one of items from my hands.

"You trust me, Will?" he asked, stretching the blindfold over my head.

"Yes," I said instantly.

His eyes flickered with menace. "You shouldn't."

And then everything went black.

My first instinct was to panic. My vision had been taken from me, and I stood naked in front of the most dangerous man I'd ever met. Instead of fighting that panic, I gave in to it, let it sink into my bones.

"We're all monsters," Gage murmured, lips against my ear. His entire body pressed against my naked skin, the rough leather of his cut grating against me.

The handcuffs left my grip.

My heartbeat intensified.

My breathing shallowed.

My pussy clenched with utter desire. Utter pleasure. Already, I could feel my orgasm building within me, threatening to level me.

"There is a small number of people who will look in the mirror and recognize they are one," Gage continued—not Christian, no, this was still Gage—the rattle of the handcuffs an omen of what he was going to do with them. "The rest of the world won't believe what they see, so they make up a mask for the world, for themselves, and make excuses." His hand ghosted between my breasts, his palm atop my heart for a moment before moving to take my nipple between his thumb and forefinger. He tweaked it. Hard.

"Pain is the only way we know we're alive," he murmured, letting my nipple go. "It's the only constant in this world. It's the only way to make sure we're living." A hand circled my neck. "And Lauren, you're about to find out how alive you are."

The hand tightened once more, every one of my senses intensified with the theft of my sight. There was no darkness. No abyss. Only Gage. He was the abyss. His hand at my neck, the pain of the grip was the only thing keeping me grounded.

He yanked at me so his mouth landed on mine, brutally laying waste to my soul with his violent kiss. I matched it with violence of my own, until blood from both of us flooded into our mouths.

I lifted my hands to tear through his hair, the skin of his back, to hold on tighter.

The loss of his mouth was immediate, and I stumbled forward slightly as he stepped back and there was no longer anything keeping me grounded.

"No," Gage's growl came from somewhere in the darkness. "There's no fucking touching me."

He paused, and I floated in the nothingness of the silence. Pressure circled my wrist as he dragged me across the room. Disorientation had already set in; I was in my home of ten years, but somehow I had no idea where he was leading me.

I guessed he was taking me to the bedroom, though it felt like the opposite way based on the hard floor under my feet and not the plush carpet of my bedroom.

We stopped and the grip left my wrist.

"Lie down."

I immediately complied with the harsh command, though slowly, because I didn't have anything to hold onto and Gage didn't offer me anything. Chivalry may or may not have been dead, but it hadn't even been born with this version of Gage.

The wood floor was cold against my flaming skin, a shock against my sensitive nerve endings.

The thump of his boots against the floor were earth-shattering rumbles in my sightless world. Beads of sweat rolled down my temples as my heart beat with excitement and fear.

Pain exploded at the back of my head as Gage bunched my hair into his fist and yanked me back so his teeth brushed my exposed neck, then moved up to my earlobe.

"You should be a fucking sin," he hissed.

I relished the pain, the violence. It hurt, but I loved it. The wetness between my legs was proof of that.

"You are a sin," he said from above me, releasing my hair. "But I'm the worst sinner of them all." The handcuffs rattled, and I twitched as I felt the sound in my core.

"On. Your. Back," he bit out.

Shaking, I complied.

I was lying naked, blindfolded, on my floor.

It was wrong.

It should've been demeaning.

But it wasn't.

"Hands above your head."

I did as asked.

Gage clasped my wrists together in one of his hands, the cold steel handcuffs clicking around my wrist and then something metal.

I tried to move.

I couldn't.

He had cuffed me to the bottom of the banister that ran along the top of my stairs, serving as a barrier from someone falling down them. Now they were serving as an instrument of my torture.

My worship.

Gage's lips landed on the spot just below were the metal was biting into my skin.

Then he was gone. I heard his boots, circling me. I traced his movements with my ears until he was standing at my feet. My nipples throbbed, my entire body aching with need. I was almost coming out of my skin with desperation for his touch.

But I wasn't going to move without his permission. He had snatched my power away. I was at the mercy of his cruelty.

"Spread your legs," he commanded.

My breath hitched with what I imagined him seeing if I did so. Him, standing, fully clothed. Me, naked, blindfolded, and cuffed on the floor below him.

"You want me to make you?" His whisper carried over the air, caressing and abusing me with its threat.

I spread my legs slowly, exposing myself to him.

He let out a harsh hiss.

There was a long silence. One I spent inside my protective darkness. It should've terrified me more, but it didn't. It gave me permission to give in to Gage's commands, to my own desires, using only instinct, without barriers. Without reality surrounding me.

Gage knelt between my spread legs, his fingers spreading my sensitive skin so I was completely and utterly exposed to him.

My back arched violently with the touch, my climax threatening to explode through me. Gage's hand against my stomach pressed me down gently.

"Your cunt is beautiful, Lauren," he murmured, his fingers probing, exploring, worshiping.

My breath was strangled with his words, with his touch.

His hands left me and I wanted to scream with my desperation.

His fingertip traced my curls, the small strip my waxer always left despite the trend to take everything off.

"Beautiful," he repeated.

Then his finger moved up, over my hip bone, the side of my body, circling my breast with a gentleness that was in direct conflict with everything else. With Gage himself. The touch was reverent.

Then his mouth followed the journey of his finger, first pressing a slow and gentle kiss to the hair covering my pussy before he inhaled deeply and audibly.

My stomach dipped and flames crept up my neck.

He was smelling me. There. It was wrong. Dirty. And it caused wetness to flush between my legs.

He growled. "Can fucking smell you getting turned on by this, Will. You're a devil too, disguised as an angel."

The vibration of his words traveled to my clit, jerking my body with bouts of pleasure.

My hands became claws, straining against the metal of the cuffs.

Then, just as I was convinced I needed Gage's mouth on me more than I needed my next breath, it was gone.

I exhaled with a violent pain I didn't know was possible without actual injury. He was hurting me, causing pain by depriving me of pleasure.

His mouth moved slowly, torturously against my hips, my navel, up to the underside of my breast. Finally his lips circled my nipple and he sucked at it, causing me to cry out, my thighs clenching to the point of pain. His teeth grazed my nipple so sharp pain mingled with pleasure.

And just as I thought he was going to make me come, it was gone.

I let out a hiss between my teeth.

His hand circled my neck, then moved up to cup my cheek as he pressed me against the floor. "Oh, don't worry, baby, I'm gonna make you come," he murmured against my mouth. "I'm gonna make you scream. Just needed to make sure you know you're at my mercy. And I don't have fucking mercy."

And then he kissed me.

But it wasn't brutal and hard like I expected.

I didn't know anything else, because brutal and hard was all I had experienced from Gage. It was all I knew.

But he was showing me something else. Someone else.

He moved leisurely, slowly, cupping my face like it might shatter if he gripped it too tight. My heart crashed against my chest as the slow and gentle kiss didn't do anything to slow it. No, it only made it more frantic.

His mouth left mine.

"Gonna eat your cunt now, Lauren," he murmured, voice less than a whisper, the crude words working to raise it to a yell.

I couldn't speak.

But he didn't need me to.

He moved down my body.

And then I could speak.

And then I screamed.

GAGE MADE good on his promise.

He made me come. Again. And again. He tortured me with pleasure until my body was little more than liquid, my arms screaming from the angle they were forced to keep, my wrists burning with evidence of me trying to escape the cuffs.

But Gage didn't show mercy.

He only showed more.

And I wasn't sure if I could take more. But I wanted it.

I needed it.

He had taken off his clothes.

I wasn't quite sure when that happened, but he was now naked, lying atop me, his skin bruising mine, pressing into me.

I needed him inside. Even though it would ruin me, I *needed* it.

He paused at my entrance, torturing me some more with just how close I was to being full. Complete.

"It was Gage that did all this to you." His finger brushed my neck, where I imagined small bruises were already blossoming. "It's Gage whose bike you ride on the back of. Who you wake up to. Sleep with." The darkness was snatched away, but I still saw the abyss as I blinked Gage into focus.

He was held with violence.

With utter agony.

With painful beauty.

Demons clawed at the backs of his eyes.

"It's Gage you're gonna share your life with," he growled. "Your pain." He moved, just slightly, so he probed my entrance, teased inside.

I let out a harsh moan.

"But in here, and only in here, I'm Christian," he said through clenched teeth. "He's dead and buried, Lauren. And you're an angel, but you're never gonna resurrect him." He pushed into me with a brutal beauty and I screamed, seeing stars.

Gage didn't move as my pussy clenched against him.

He merely stared at me, waited for my vision to clear.

"Christian comes to life inside your pussy. But he dies outside of it, and there's no saving him. You need to know that. It's important, fuckin' vital. He's dead and gone. But here?" He moved slowly.

I bit my tongue.

"You get that, Lauren?" Gage—Christian—asked, voice strained.

"Yeah," I rasped, at the edge of ruin. "Yeah, Christian, I get it."

He twitched inside me as I said the name of the man he used to be. The name of the man the world had killed. I got it. This wasn't the story where love saved something inside each of us.

No, it wasn't that kind of story.

He moved, slow, beautiful, as if tenderness were the only way to fight the demons between us. I arched my back, straining against my shackles, meeting his thrusts, moving my lips against his.

It wasn't that kind of story, but it didn't matter because this was the only one we were going to get.

And it was everything.

TWELVE

"There's a club party tonight," Gage said.

He was Gage now.

He was always Gage. I knew that, because there was no way he could be anyone else. I understood Gage was who he had built together from the skeletons of the man who had been Christian—the stranger who made love to me in the darkness—and I couldn't think of him as being anything but Gage.

I glanced up from the pot I was stirring—I was melting chocolate for brownies because it turned out that Gage had a serious sweet tooth—and still, even now, seeing him and all his chaos in my ordered life was jolting. Like an earthquake that people were convinced meant destruction, but really it was nature's way of shaking things into place.

I'd been so surefooted for so long, I forgot the excitement that came with unsteady ground.

Gage was on the other side of the kitchen island, watching me bake, talking to me. Whenever we were together, there was nothing else—no phone, no book, no TV. His intense attention was focused completely and entirely on me.

He was growing his hair. I liked that. He knew I liked it long and wild, running my fingers through it, tugging at it when he kissed me. When he was inside me.

"You gotta stop lookin' at me like that," he growled, rounding the kitchen island.

I put down my spoon just in time for him to snatch my hips and yank my body to his. "And why, pray tell, do I need to stop looking at you like that?" I asked, my voice husky. "It seems it's got you right where I want you."

His hands tightened at my hips, dancing to the point of pain. Because he did that now that he knew I could handle it, knew I liked it.

And I didn't just like it.

I *loved* it.

"If it's wrapped around your little finger, then yeah, babe, I'm right where you want me," he murmured against my mouth.

I smiled, my heart beat increasing with his proximity, his hardness pressing against me. "No way could anyone wrap my big, bad, scary, all-powerful biker around their little finger," I whispered.

His fingers clutched my chin so I met his eyes. "You're not anyone, babe," he said, his voice thick.

The words curled around my heart, settling there, warming it. That's what this ice-cold, menacing man was doing to me, warming places I'd been sure would be frozen solid forever.

"But you can't wrap me around your finger right now," he said, leaning back, breaking the moment and turning off the stove.

I folded my arms, a little pissed, and hurt, but still turned on. So the folding was mostly to communicate the pissed part, and partly to hide the turned-on part.

Gage's eyes went to my chest, flaring with desire, the corner of his mouth turning up in his version of a smile.

He totally had my number.

"The club is having a party. And you're not luring me into that sweet, hot cunt of yours," he rasped.

My stomach dipped.

A lot.

"Well, not yet at least," he continued, folding his own arms, splaying his legs and pretty much dripping sex all over my kitchen floor. "I'll be takin' it before the night is out," he promised. "Maybe even before we go, if we're quick."

"I'll be quick," I blurted, my desperate need for him speaking before my brain had time to catch up and realize how pathetic I sounded.

Instead of putting him off, my words made his eyes darken more, the corner of his lip twitching again. "I know you will, baby," he growled. "Can't promise I will be when I know how hungry that pussy is for my cock."

My knees trembled.

"You're fuckin' looking at me like that again," he accused.

I bit my lip. "Well, you're the one who has control over the sex god thing. I'm just a mere mortal. My reactions cannot be held against me."

I was in his arms again before I could even finish my sentence, his hand cupping my chin. "Will, there's no fuckin' way you're a mere mortal." He brushed my hair from my face, eyes reverent. "Nothing but a fuckin' angel can tempt a devil."

I moved my hand up to brush the scars on his arms—I had made a point to touch the ruined skin often, hoping it would speak its secrets to me. "You're not a devil."

"How do you know that?" He shuttered his eyes, as he did when things got a little too close to those demons he wore on his sleeve yet hid in his soul.

"Because I love you," I whispered, uttering the words that had been stuck in the back of my throat for weeks. It was terrifying, letting them out. But I had to. "And devils can't be loved. Only men can. And you're my man."

He froze, the hand playing with tendrils of my hair pausing in midair. Never did I think there would be a time when I'd strike Gage immobile. The only inkling that he hadn't turned into a very lifelike statue was the hot breath on my face and the way his eyes moved over me, as if he was memorizing me.

"But baby, I *am* a devil," he said finally, his voice rough. Rough enough to cut through my soul with the burn of an unreturned 'I love you.' I tried not to let the sting get to me. I knew Gage was different than any other human being on this planet. Knew this wasn't going to be easy.

But it was going to be worth it.

I smiled and reached up to stroke his face. "Well, then you're the exception to the rule, and you're my devil *and* my man."

The hands at my hips tightened and I was in the air, my skirt pushed up and the cold counter kissing my exposed thighs. Gage had spread my legs and was standing between them, his denim-clad hardness pressing into the perfect spot at the apex between my thighs.

I hissed out a harsh breath, his hand grasping my neck, yanking my mouth to his, while the other plunged right inside me. I cried out into his mouth at the exquisite intrusion, and the expert way he knew how to move within me—fluid, perfect.

His fingers left me, and the rustling of his jeans told me exactly what he was doing. "My angel," he murmured, pausing at my entrance for a sliver of a second, his eyes on me, before he surged in.

Then the world ended, and Gage fucked me in the ruins.

"SO WE'RE GOING to the club party," he said after cleaning me up, setting me down on unsteady feet and rolling my skirt down tenderly, like he hadn't just fucked me hard, fast and brutal on my kitchen island.

I blinked at him, trying to make sure my knees were steady and my mind was clear before I replied.

"I know it's not the good guy play," he continued, watching me. "I shouldn't be bringing you further into this world, tarring you with its brush. But fuck, I'm not the good guy. And I want to bring you in further. I'm selfish, and fuck do I know it. But I want you in my life. I fuckin' need you in it. Even if you don't belong."

His last words smashed out whatever calmness his previous ones had settled in my chest.

"I don't belong," I whispered.

His eyes narrowed. "No, fuck, Lauren—"

I held up my hand and stepped out of the way as he tried to snatch me into his arms again. "Seriously?" I hissed, rounding the counter so it was between us. "After *everything* between us, after everything I've told you about myself, shown you about myself, you seriously think I don't belong?" I yelled.

He was watching me, face blank, guarded, as it always was when we weren't having sex. "Lauren—" he tried again.

"No!" I screamed. "No more talking and weaving words that distract me. It's Lauren's turn now, and yes, I'm quite aware that I'm referring to myself in the third person, but that's how freaking *pissed* I am right now!"

His mouth twitched, and I hated how sexy I found it. "You're cute as fuck when you're angry, baby."

I let out a little scream. Both at him for saying the words and myself for finding them so freaking sexy.

"Well, hands inside the ride, buddy, because I'm about to get fucking adorable," I hissed.

I stomped around the kitchen, forgetting about my need to

have a large slab of furniture between us, advancing on him and jabbing at his chest. "You do not get to tell me the *one place* you consider home, with the people you consider *family*, is somewhere *I don't belong*," I shouted.

The smile left his face, his body going taut.

I ignored it. "I do not deserve to fall in love with you and then have you slap me in the face with shit like that, Gage. It's cruel." My words seemed to actually hit him, and I battled to stop that from affecting me.

I had to continue with this. My anger was a physical, living thing.

"Crueler than you trying to scare me with blood and murder and that darkness you think I can't handle. Crueler than you feeling like you have to hold back with me because you think I'm a delicate flower." I glared at him. "Newsflash—the world has already stomped on this flower, shredded it. You're not so high and mighty that you're the first person to show me how ugly things can get. The problem is you're so focused on that that you don't realize how fucking beautiful I find all your ugliness. You're too busy telling me I don't belong. And if that continues, you'll do what you're so sure you're already doing." I yanked my shaking hand back, Gage still frozen. "You'll destroy me," I whispered.

Then I turned on my heel and stomped off, pausing to snatch my purse off the table. And ignoring the fact that I had no idea where the freaking heck I was going.

"HOW DID you know I'd be here?" I whispered to the wind when a heat kissed my back. I didn't turn as I spoke. Didn't need to, because I knew it was Gage. His scent—cigarette smoke nearly absent now—pressed into the wind like my words.

I expected him to snatch me into his arms, force me to face

him physically like he normally did, but he didn't. He sank down on the slightly damp grass beside me and stared at the hunk of rock that stared harder than even him.

Only the dead could stare harder than the Devil.

"Told you, babe, I know shit about people," he murmured, eyes forward, voice gravel. "You're not people." He paused. "Didn't think there would be many places you'd go. Thought about where *I'd* go. And I come here."

His words made me jerk my gaze to his beautiful profile. "You come here?"

He nodded once.

"Is there anyone... here for you?" I asked gently, despite my pain and anger, hoping I would finally get a little bit of his pain so I wasn't drowning in my own.

His body stiffened for a millisecond. "Nah, Will," he all but whispered. "No one here for me but you."

My heart skipped a beat.

"But then why do you come here?"

He waited a moment. "'Cause sometimes you need the company of the dead," he said. "Like to look at the tombstones. Used to be a comfort to me, knowin' my name would be on one one day."

I flinched at his words. The way he spoke, it was like death would be a relief.

"I'd walk around here for hours, countin'," he continued.

I blinked. "Counting?"

That time he did turn and face me. He reached forward to gently push my glasses up my face, since they'd dropped slightly down my nose. The gesture was so tender it hurt. Even when Gage was being gentle, there was pain.

"Counting the seconds left in the day. In my life," he replied. "The seconds until I'd be here, buried under." He nodded to the grass where my brother's skeleton lay.

"You were counting down the seconds *until you died?*" I whispered, my voice breaking.

He nodded once. "Don't count when I'm with you."

My heart didn't miss a beat then. It freaking stopped.

"You belong, baby," he growled, snatching my chin in his hands. "Me sayin' otherwise was me tryin' to be the good guy. Remembered I'm not that guy. And I remembered that you're not the good girl the world thinks you are either." His eyes darkened. "So you belong."

Tears streamed down my face.

"I lost a half of myself when he died," I whispered, shifting my eyes from Gage to the slab of rock that held a handful of words supposed to immortalize my brother. "What is a twin without the other half of them? What is a person with only half of their soul?"

He surged forward, gripping my hips, eyes on mine. "I know what it is, because I don't have *anything* left of mine, Will." His hand moved to cup my cheek. "Or I didn't think I did. Till you. You've got enough soul for both of us. That makes you not just half a person. That makes you fuckin' everything." His hand tightened almost to the point of pain. "Everything."

I WAS nervous as Gage unclipped my helmet and laid it on the seat of the bike. We were in the parking lot of the Sons of Templar compound. The last time I was there I'd been shouting about having Gage arrested. I'd been doing that in front of Gage's brothers.

I knew they didn't hold it against me, because Brock and Amy had been around to my place for dinner.

I didn't ask, of course. Amy just informed me.

"I don't cook, but I'll bring great wine." There was a pause.

"Shit, you don't drink wine. I'll bring something else great. If you don't want to cook, or can't, like me, I'll order takeout."

"I can cook," I told her, not at all insulted at her inviting herself and her handsome husband over to the loft I'd pretty much barred from the world. No, I was excited.

"Great, I'll see you tomorrow night, then."

And then she hung up.

It was the best night ever. Conversation was easy. Natural. Laughter filled the loft that had been silent. Warmth that couldn't be mimicked by any heating system burst from the walls.

So it wasn't as if I was being thrust into the lion's den. That had already happened the night I got onto the back of Gage's bike.

Voices and music carried over the parking lot.

This was different. This was a club party. This was me being firmly tattooed into this world. And I wanted that. More than anything.

Gage cupped my face. "Been a big day for my girl," he murmured, searching my eyes.

We'd come straight from the cemetery.

"We can get right back on the bike, go home and I can fuck you till you pass out?" he offered.

My thighs quivered and I swallowed my desire. "No, Gage. I want to."

His eyes lightened and he laid his mouth on mine. Brutal, and like we weren't in the middle of the parking lot.

"But hold that thought," I whispered against his mouth. "I'm not adverse to getting fucked till I pass out... later."

Darkness floated in his eyes. "Oh you will, babe. That's a promise."

Then he slung his arm around my shoulders, yanked me to him and walked us to the party.

"WHY DON'T we ever go to your place?" I asked, my head in Gage's lap, peering up from the page of the book I was doing a very good job at pretending to read.

We were naked.

I'd spent hours tracing the design on his chest, his 'safe' area. My fingertips could brush down his arms sometimes, when his eyes weren't full of shadows. They might even clutch them during sex—no, during *fucking*—because at that point, pain had become just as important as pleasure for us. Ever since I'd showed him that I wanted depraved and dark and not romantic and soulful, he'd shown me all sorts of depravity.

All of which I loved.

We were exploring each other's capacity for pleasure as well as our capacity for pain.

Gage was a man without limits, both inside and outside of the bedroom.

Well, almost.

Those scarred arms were a hard limit.

But we were working on it.

After him literally holding his breath as I'd trailed the map of pain etched into his skin, I gave him respite by looking at the artistry of pain on top of it.

"Why the gates of Hell?" I asked, tracing around the hooded skeleton.

His body, still taut from my fingers on his arms, tightened even more. "Because, Will, despite what Shakespeare said, Hell isn't empty. It's full, too many damned souls and not enough real estate," he murmured. "And maybe that's why all the devils are here." His arms tightened around me. "Present company included."

I glanced up. "You really think you're a devil?"

"*Awkward, I was talking about you,*" he teased.

I rolled my eyes, smiling slightly. He chose the strangest and most inopportune—some might say inappropriate—times to inject his dark humor into situations. Mostly when those situations got a little too close to his exposed nerves.

But I was getting bolder, stronger, more willing to risk brushing against them, causing us both pain.

"*We've all got our demons, Gage,*" I whispered. "*I just learned to live in a distorted harmony with mine.*" My eyes never left his. "*You chose to become yours.*"

He stiffened as he had when my fingers had been tracing his scars. Because my words were doing the same.

He didn't speak for the longest time. Long enough that I'd resigned myself to the fact that this was just another time when Gage spoke with his silence.

"*You looked at my demons, saw me without my mask, and somehow you fell in love with the beast instead of the man,*" he rasped. "*What made you stay was the very thing I thought would chase you away.*"

I glanced up, tears prickling behind my eyes at the emotion rattling in his tone. "*Nothing is going to chase me away.*"

He didn't meet my gaze. "*That's what I'm afraid of.*"

And he hadn't let me respond to that troubling statement. Instead he fucked me into silence. Into oblivion.

For the time being.

And then we landed on the sofa, with Gage's 'naked' edict fully in place. I'd thought in theory that such a thing would be uncomfortable. That I'd be crippled with anxiety about those dimpled spots on my thighs, that little pooch in my stomach that never went away. The way my breasts had started to drop, just slightly, almost magically when I'd turned thirty.

Wrong.

Those little insecurities still whispered at me, but Gage's gaze, *his worship, quietened them, much like he did my demons. And I quickly found the benefit to the edict when he bent me over the kitchen counter, slamming into me while slapping a wooden spoon hard and fast against my ass.*

The spot stung with every move.

And it was glorious.

"Why don't we go to my place?" Gage repeated my question, hands running lazily through my hair. Where I had a book, he did not. I knew he loved to read, because I remembered his shelves at the club, and his intense perusal of my own collection. He'd run his eyes over it for at least a solid fifteen minutes. He didn't touch a book, just looked at the spines. And only a true book lover knew the joy that merely looking at the weathered spines of classics and favorites could provide. A book lover also knew that you could tell a lot about a person by their collection.

But he wasn't reading. He was just sitting, running his hands through my hair. He was a man content with just sitting. I asked him about it, and he said it was a new thing.

"Because I don't count when I'm sitting with you. And I like to bathe in those little moments, those pockets of peace a man like me has been starved of."

Hence me finding it hard to read because my boyfriend—such a lackluster word for what we were—was running his hands through my hair, the same hands that killed people, that provoked violence, that built fricking bombs, and was at peace.

Because of me.

"We don't go to my place because we're *at* my place," he finally answered.

I blinked. Did we move in together without me noticing? It had only been weeks. Less than that since Gage and I finally had sex. Granted, he'd stayed over every single night since then, showered here. But he went home to change.

To the home I'd never seen and was infinitely curious about, hence the question. I was pretty sure we hadn't moved in together—though the thought filled me with warmth and comfort —and I was about to query his response when he kept talking.

"*You* are my place, Lauren," he said.

He obviously didn't notice my heart fricking stopping, because he kept talking.

"And this place, it's saturated in you. I know you've worked fuckin' hard to make it your sanctuary from the ugliness of the world. Somehow you've made it mine, not because of your fuckin' ridiculous pillows or kickass sofas, though I do approve, but because of you."

"But I want to see you," I whispered.

His face changed, turning unreadable, as it had now and again throughout the past week. Something flickered, something I itched to tease out of him. A pain that ran along his arms, that ran inside his soul. But it was gone too quickly to hold onto. And I couldn't force it. I knew that. If I wanted to know Gage's pain, I had to wait until he was brave enough to show it to me.

He was the bravest man I knew, but standing up to the horrors of the world took a different kind of bravery than standing up to the horrors of one's soul.

"You see me, babe," he murmured, yanking me to his body. "You see me better than anyone else does."

Again, as if he sensed my broken heart could take no more, that he'd found the limit of my pleasure and pain in his words, he gently pushed me up so he could stand.

My book went tumbling to the floor.

Not because of the motion of him pressing me upward, but because he was standing in front of me.

Naked.

And it was the most beautiful sight, like ever.

He grinned, eyes running over me. "Now, I've explored every inch of *you*," he said wickedly. "But not this apartment. Because you're distracting and much more pleasurable to explore." His eyes moved. "But there is one door that I've been wondering about."

"No, wait, you can't go in there!" I cried, jumping up and rushing forward. But it was too late. He'd opened the door, and his body was barring me from doing anything about it.

He hadn't turned to face the room; instead his eyes twinkled at me. "What? Is this where you hide the bodies?" he deadpanned. "Because you know that's no reason to be alarmed. It'd turn me on that you'd be so brazen as to not even bury the bodies of those who've wronged you. Even *I'm* not that badass." He winked. "Oh, and for the record, I'm already turned the fuck on without even knowing what's inside this room."

I could've fought him on it, if I'd really wanted. I would've lost, of course. Because when Gage wanted to be somewhere, he was there. But it was an instinct to hide another part of myself that no one had ever seen. And Gage wanted in there, to those parts. And he was there.

That wasn't why I stopped fighting. It was that twinkle. That wink. It was something that he had done often in the time I'd known him. But it was the first time he'd *really* done it. Done it without that inky blackness that came from inside him tainting it. A small sliver of a moment that he wasn't fighting his demons. He was just... Gage.

So I didn't fight it, wanting to keep that sliver alive as long as I could. Not forever, because I knew that was impossible; no one could hide from their demons forever. But you could find someone who scared them off long enough for you to be happy in moments without them. Then, after a time, you'd be happy in moments even with those demons.

I hoped I'd be able to be that for Gage.

Because he was already that for me.

He gave me one more moment of naked twinkle before he turned, stepping fully through the door.

Then he froze.

Every part of him.

I just stayed rooted in my spot, staring at his back. More accurately, staring at the reaper covering the large expanse of his back. Tracing my eyes around the lines of the patch, the piece of fabric that held him together.

"Baby," Gage rasped, turning to circle the room, his eyes touching every canvas, every piece of paper, everything cluttering the room.

The one area in the house that didn't surrender to order, that didn't have to know order. The one area in the house I didn't make myself control.

His eyes met mine. "These are fucking amazing, Will."

People had told me things like that before. In art school before... everything. Before I dropped out. My grandmother. My brother.

I wasn't blind I knew the way a paintbrush, a stick of charcoal, a pencil—anything in my hand—was an extension of me meant something. The way art, creating it, made my heart beat and my blood flow.

But the simple and visceral way Gage said those words hit me somewhere, told me what he was seeing. He wasn't just saying it because my paintings were good. He was saying it because he saw what my paintings were—pieces of my broken soul wrenched from inside of me and thrown onto square scraps of fabric.

He saw that, beneath the beauty of the paint and pencil, there was ugliness.

"You need to be doing this full-time," he continued. "This is you."

I blinked. Opened my mouth. Closed it again.

"Will, why the fuck aren't you?" he demanded, gesturing

around the room. "This needs to be out there. You need to be doing this for a living. You're good with words, babe. I know it. But this isn't good. This is something more than that. You need to be doing *more*."

"I can't," I whispered.

He was on me in two strides. "Why the fuck not?"

I stared up at him. "Because my job, with the words, it's logic. I know how it needs to be. It has order. It's... safe."

His hands tightened around my neck. "We talked about safety the first night we met, Will," he murmured. "And the only compromise I'll make on that score is having a helmet on your beautiful head when you're on the back of my bike." He stroked my cheeks with a gentleness I didn't even know he was capable of. "But that's it. The second your life mixed with mine, you stopped livin' safe. More accurately, you started living. Because I know this isn't me forcin' you into something. This is me showing you who you are. Like the day you showed me those handcuffs." His eyes darkened. "The day you showed me just how wild and fucking *dirty* you are. And I'll need a reminder of that in a couple of minutes. But for now, I'm tellin' you that safe? That's out the window. I'm not lettin' you live safe anymore, baby. I'll keep you safe in respect to makin' sure you'll never get hurt, but respect to keepin' you wild? That's just as important as your safety."

His words blew me away. But he wouldn't get it, wouldn't see until I showed him one more thing.

The darkest thing.

No matter that he hasn't told you a thing about himself, a voice snarled in my ear.

I ignored it. It hurt, thinking Gage didn't trust me enough to show me his darkness. But he'd shown me what he could. And it wasn't because he didn't trust me—it was because he didn't trust himself.

I got it, because I was having trouble trusting myself right then.

"I was in a mental institution," I blurted.

All expression left Gage's face.

"Well, that's not what they're called, obviously," I continued. "Not the politically correct term for them. *Rehabilitation facility*. For people with minds not poisoned by drugs but something much more dangerous. Life." I forced myself to keep Gage's gaze, even though it hurt. "It was after David's funeral. I didn't take his death well." I laughed coldly. "Or a lot worse than well, considering I was checked into a facility for six months. I had to be fed intravenously. A few doctors reasoned it was because I was suicidal. Obviously they could only speculate since I stopped speaking for six months too. I think that might've been a contributing factor in my parents committing me."

"Baby," Gage murmured, his voice breaking as he grasped my hips.

"It was easier to be around strangers than my own family," I whispered, needing to say it all before my throat closed up. "I couldn't be around them, which is why I let them commit me. Because I knew I couldn't be fixed. There's only one thing worse than being broken—people you love thinking they can fix you."

My eyes roved over him with meaning I didn't have to convey in words.

"Anyway, I wasn't suicidal. I knew that much. Sure, I wanted to die sometimes, but not with a permanence. I just wanted... respite from life, I guess. And the only respite from life people get is death. But the no-eating thing wasn't from wanting to die. I just couldn't. I didn't have an appetite for life. It was hard enough sucking in oxygen—how the heck was I meant to swallow food?" I shook my head. "I began eating soon enough because getting force-fed was not a fun experience."

Gage's jaw clenched but he was silent.

"Still didn't talk, though," I continued. "Not for six months. A lot of people tried to make me. The doctors, my parents. Not my grandmother though. She'd come to visit, sit there talking to me, acting as if I responded to all of her questions and stories. Then she'd yell at the doctors for trying to 'push me.' She always told them 'She'll talk when she's ready, and not with ducks quacking at her.'"

I smiled.

"Truthfully, I didn't talk when I was ready, because I'd never speak if that was the case. There was no great epiphany—I just realized I couldn't stay in a silent tomb forever. Something almost clicked inside me, and I just said, 'I would like to go home now,' one day. Obviously it wasn't that easy, but I did get out and my parents didn't speak of it again. It was something we swept under the rug. Not because it embarrassed them, but maybe because it was more evidence of the gaping hole in our life."

I let out a large sigh, the kind a furniture mover might exhale after carrying a large sofa up many flights of seemingly endless stairs.

I'd never told anyone that. Maybe that in itself was why I'd never gotten close to people. Because in order to get close to people, you had to share your secrets. The one about David was bad enough. Not because of how it made other people think of me—I knew any decent person wouldn't judge me for my twin brother dying of a drug overdose—but more about my utter inability to utter it. My refusal.

But then there was also the prospect of having to tell these people about being committed for six months. People were a lot less sympathetic about crazy than they were about death. Death was uncontrollable, could happen to anyone, but it was a tragedy that needed kindness.

Insanity was also uncontrollable, and under the right—or wrong—circumstances, it could still happen to anyone. But people didn't like being confronted with that fact; therefore, they didn't like being confronted with insanity. They preferred to believe it was a choice of people who weren't *right*, people to be kept away from, avoided on the street.

So yeah, I didn't tell anyone.

But Gage didn't just know the truth about insanity. He lived it. He wore it.

"Anyway," I said, "there's a reason I'm telling you this, apart from the fact that if you intend on staying in my life, this is something you need to know."

"I fucking intend on staying," he growled.

Forever was the unuttered word.

I smiled. "That was a reason, and that's also a reason for this." I gestured around the room at the paintings. "There isn't much to do when people think you're crazy. I read a lot, but books are always full of other people's sorrow. I couldn't live in theirs and my own, not unless I really wanted to cross that threshold of insanity, one I couldn't come back from. So I ripped my pain out of myself and put it on paper. Then canvas. And it's just a... habit I've continued."

"This isn't a fucking habit, Will," Gage declared fiercely. "This is more beautiful than anything I've ever seen. And that's sayin' a lot, since I've seen you writhing underneath me. Seen you wake up in the sunlight." He cupped my face. "But these are the broken and ugly pieces of the soul you've been brave enough to yank into the light and turn into something." He leaned forward and pressed his lips to mine.

"This is all my pain. How am I going to show it to the world?" I whispered when his lips left mine.

"Take it from someone who knows. The only thing worse than showing your pain to the world is hiding it."

The truth lingered underneath his words.

He was still hiding his too.

THIRTEEN

The roaring of the bike chased me up the street as I dawdled past the gallery, spending longer than my allotted three seconds entertaining a fantasy.

But even now I couldn't just break out of a lifestyle I'd clung to for nigh on a decade. It didn't work that way. Gage was making me wild, and I loved it, but that didn't mean I wanted the logical and sensible part of me to die. I wanted to be able to live in harmony with the two sides of myself. Or at least that's what I was telling myself.

Luckily such thoughts were interrupted with that faraway rumble of the motorcycle that I knew belonged to Gage.

Our connection wasn't that intense that I could hear a motorcycle and *know* it was him. No, I knew it was him for other reasons. Primarily because my story had gone to print today.

And I hadn't even told Gage I'd written it.

Because I was a coward.

And also because I knew he'd not only try to stop me from writing the article, but he'd also try to 'take care of' the problem for me. As was his way.

He'd done that with the car. My car. The one he'd fixed and refused to let me pay for. It was somewhat of a fight. Not our first one—our whole fricking relationship was a battle—but our first semi-normal fight. Because regular couples fought about things like money. Not exactly about the man fixing the car the woman crashed and then refusing to let her pay for the repairs, but something similar, surely.

Gage scowled at the check I was trying to hand to him, then folded his arms across his chest, obviously trying to distract me with the flex of his muscles.

It kind of worked.

"Gage," I huffed, tearing my eyes from his arms and chest. "You're being ridiculous. This is my car. I pay for the repairs."

He narrowed his eyes. "You're my woman. I fix shit that gets broken. The stuff I don't break myself, that is." His voice dripped with delicious darkness.

"Don't use sex to try and distract me!"

He smirked. "You do it to me all the fuckin' time. Turnabout's fair play."

I glared. "I do not. Name one time I've used sex to distract you."

"Any time you fuckin' breathe. Any time I inhale and taste your sweet cunt calling to me."

I clenched my thighs together at his words.

What was I talking about again?

"Gage, just take the money," I demanded, hating that my voice was now husky.

"No."

I stared at him.

He stared back. "You know I'm not gonna be the one who blinks first here."

Crap. He was right.

"Okay, you might blink first, but I'm also dedicated to my deci-

sions. And I will stuff this money in your jacket. Into the saddle-bags of your bike. I'll make sure it gets to you. You know it."

He glared at me. "You're fuckin' frustrating, Will."

I smiled.

Hand still outstretched, he snatched the envelope off me.

But then he yanked me onto his knee while he sat on the sofa. My core pulsated with exact and intimate knowledge of what he was about to do. My bare skin kissed the air as he yanked my skirt up, exposing my ass.

There wasn't even a pause, a warning.

Gage didn't do warnings.

A sharp sting erupted on my left cheek moments after a resounding slap echoed in my ears and inside my pussy. I moaned in both pain and pleasure, clenching my thighs together, fighting the orgasm that was already building.

"You may be able to get what you want this time, but I always get what I want," he growled as his hand came down again.

It just so happened that what Gage wanted was to give me multiple orgasms.

And I was totally okay with that.

The next day, I figured out why he'd taken the money so easily.

Well, easily for Gage, at least.

There was a strange man inside my apartment when I got home from work last night. And he wasn't there to try to kill or kidnap me like Amy was convinced someone would "eventually, because you two have been together for weeks without it happening. It's an enigma that it's been this long."

I'd always thought someone trying to kill or kidnap me was an enigma, not an eventuality. But I hadn't missed how Gage was always looking around, always checking in. He was waiting for something. Bracing.

I understood it. Because of the club's past.

They expected the drama.

But for me, Gage was the drama. Living through him. Surviving him.

But obviously he was expecting more. Hence the strange man in my apartment installing the alarm system.

I hadn't screamed because it was rather obvious what he was doing and who'd directed him to do so. The man sitting casually in my living room reading leisurely.

I dropped my purse to the floor with a thump to get his attention. Though I knew I'd had his attention the second I entered the room.

"Seriously?" I snapped at him as he dog-eared the book and put it down.

"What?"

I rolled my eyes. "Don't play innocent, Gage. You know what."

He was on his feet and across the room in a blur. "I never play innocent, Will. You know that better than anyone."

He gripped my hips tightly, his mouth on mine and hungrily kissing me before I could answer.

I blinked a few times once he'd let me go. "You can't silence me with a kiss," I snapped, my voice free of the bite I'd intended.

He raised his brow. "Oh, baby, a kiss is the only thing I can silence you with. As soon as my cock is inside you, there's no silencing you."

His words were a punch to my stomach. But a good one.

"Gage," I hissed. "Stop trying to distract me. There's a man downstairs installing an alarm that I didn't order or pay for."

"You did pay for it."

I jerked. "What do you mean?"

Gage pressed his body against mine so there was no air between us. "I mean I took the check you gave me and gave it to him to purchase the security shit, then install it."

I gritted my teeth. "You're impossible."

The teasing left his eyes with a quickness that chilled my insides. "No, what's impossible is me trying to live in a world where something happens to you and knowing I didn't do every fucking thing in my power to prevent that. I've seen my brothers go through this shit, babe, and I'm bracing to go through it too. Because with the way we live, bitter and ugly, sweet and beautiful don't come easy. Without a fight. Without a fucking battle. You're my battle, and I'm gonna do everything I can to make sure you're the only battle. So let me fucking install the alarm."

I let him fucking install the alarm. Because each of his words hit me. Hard. They were saturated in fear. For me.

So I knew me writing a story about one of the biggest drug dealers in Hope and then publishing that story wouldn't do much for his fear.

But it was something I had to do.

For David.

And I was sure Gage would understand that.

But he would want to do it for me. And he would do it with blood.

That was his vengeance.

The roaring bike acted as an omen.

I'd been so busy fearing his reaction that I didn't notice the police cruiser pull up half on the sidewalk until the slam of the door drew my attention.

Troy was stalking toward me with a hard jaw and a purpose.

A purpose that was obviously clutching my arms and shaking me.

"Are you *insane?*" he hissed.

I didn't answer immediately, shocked at such behavior from Troy.

It wasn't the pressure but the grip itself. Troy wasn't a man to touch a woman without permission. I was pretty sure police officers weren't allowed to do that.

I guessed Troy had read my story too.

The roar of Gage's motorcycle was louder now, and I didn't think this was going to end well.

"Lauren," Troy demanded, shaking me once more.

I tried to wrench from his arms but his grip tightened. "Troy, let me go."

"Are you determined to end up like all those other women?" he demanded. "I told you I would take care of the dealer. Told you not to do something to put yourself in danger."

The roar of the bike was now chattering my teeth. I wanted to glance toward it, but I forced myself to meet Troy's eyes. "I'm not the one in danger right now," I said, forcing my voice to calm as I saw a flash of black out of the corner of my eye and the roar of the motorcycle was snatched away. "You are if you don't let me go."

His expression tensed. "Are you *threatening* me, Lauren?"

I obviously didn't get to answer, because someone ripped Troy backward and then punched him in the face.

More specifically, my boyfriend, the member of an outlaw motorcycle club, punched a police officer in the face in broad daylight.

"You're in so much fucking trouble," a feral voice growled.

Not directed at Troy.

But at me.

GAGE WAS ARRESTED.

That was after Troy had taken a long time to push himself off the sidewalk.

It felt like forever.

Because after Gage uttered his threat, he had just stared at me. Hadn't spoken. Hadn't touched me. Just stared, promise of punishment radiating from every pore.

I'd expected him to fight when Troy drew his gun, cuffed him, and placed him under arrest.

He hadn't.

He hadn't said a word, just continued to stare at me until Troy closed the back door of the cruiser after shoving Gage inside.

Troy's nose had finally stopped bleeding at that point.

"This really the life you want, Lauren?" he asked softly, giving me a look before getting in the car and roaring off, leaving me standing on the bloodstained sidewalk.

Obviously I'd called Amy.

Who called Brock.

Who called me and told me, "Don't worry. This isn't the first cop Gage has punched, and it won't be the last."

I was worried.

Enough to drive to the station, even though Brock had urged me the club "had it sorted" and to "sit tight."

No way I could sit, tight or otherwise, in my freaking apartment after my boyfriend had just been arrested.

So I went to the station.

"Oh shit," Lucky said as he watched me storm in.

Obviously I had a certain look on my face. Hence the "Oh shit."

I ignored him. In fact, I ignored the whole sea of leather congregated in the precinct.

Until a large body stepped in front of me, a 'President' patch on his cut.

I'd met Cade briefly at the party the week before.

He was intimidating. Not because he was hot—which he freaking was—but because of something else. The darkness that rippled out from around him. Not like Gage's. No, nothing could be like his. Because his was chaotic, unrestrained.

Something about Cade was controlled, chaos somehow tamed.

Still menacing nonetheless.

But I was feeling pretty menacing myself, having worked up to it on the drive over.

Hence me jutting my chin up and meeting his steely gaze.

"Lauren," he began, likely to try to relegate me to the place of the woman, which was fretting someplace where she couldn't do something like get in the way.

I wasn't one to be relegated.

"Okay, I know you're the president of the club, and therefore your word is law." I glanced around at the uneasy officers in the precinct. "Or the exact opposite of it. But I'm not here to listen to laws, on either side. I'm here for *my man*. And with all due respect, Cade, I'm not about to let you stop me from doing something because of your position at the top of the club. My position is at Gage's side. And right now, my position is yelling at the cop who put my boyfriend behind bars."

My voice rose to a yell at that point, my eyes catching the man in question and my anger getting the best of me.

Cade, who had approached me with an iron face, was now looking at me with something resembling shock, though the corner of his mouth was turned up in something resembling a grin.

I pushed my glasses up the bridge of my nose. "Now, if you'll excuse me."

He stepped back, giving me a clear pathway to Troy, who was emerging from one of doors off the side of the large room.

"This is not going to end well," Cade muttered at the same time Lucky declared, "This is going to be *awesome*."

I was in front of Troy before I actually knew what happened.

"Let him out right now," I hissed, not worrying about the audience.

Troy's expression hardened. "Lauren, let's talk in the office," he said, gesturing to a door I knew to be an interrogation room, based on previous stories I'd written about renovating the precinct.

I anchored my feet to the floor. "No. I don't intend on being here for long, so we're talking here. And you're letting Gage go."

"He assaulted an officer, Lauren," he sighed. "You know, since you were *a witness*."

I arched my brow. "Yes, I do know. Since I was a *witness*," I sneered. "And I was a witness to a police officer grabbing me, touching me without my permission and not letting me go when I told him to take his hands off me."

Troy's eyes widened in shock.

"I know my boyfriend saw *me* being assaulted by a police officer, and he likely was *witness* to my pleading with that same police officer to take his hands off me. Therefore he did what he could to forcibly take those hands off me. So unless you want me to press charges, then write a story on an outlaw coming to the rescue, I suggest you drop the charges and *let my man go*."

Anger flowed through my body like fire. I was no longer forcing myself to act like the quiet and meek woman who had been in that precinct only a handful of weeks before.

This woman had been here too.

Troy just hadn't known it.

Pure silence followed my words.

Utter silence.

Obviously my yelling had meant that everyone in the open-plan bullpen had heard my words, my accusations. I had Troy in a bind, I knew. I watched the fury and resignation mix in his eyes.

There was an echoed slow clap from behind me.

"Bravo," Lucky yelled. "Bra-fucking-vo."

GAGE WAS RELEASED.

I was swallowed by that same sea of leather I'd waded through, Lucky being the first one to yank me into his arms. Well, the only one, since he was the only one exuberant—and suicidal— enough to do such a thing to Gage's old lady, but I did get smirks and nods of approval.

"Didn't know you had it in you," Brock muttered with a smile.

"I did," the scary and attractive Bull said with a knowing mouth twitch.

But that was silenced with the slam of a door and a change in the air.

My eyes found Gage's immediately.

No, those eyes weren't entirely his.

They were filled with something else.

Something so menacing that every single man who'd been crowding around me collectively stepped back to clear a path. Some of the most dangerous men in the country stepped out of the way because of a *look*.

I didn't.

Even though it terrified me.

He stalked toward me with the grace and purpose of a panther.

I expected him to snatch me into his arms, drag me from the precinct.

But he didn't.

He stopped in front of me. And not inches away, snatching my personal space and taking it for himself as he normally did, but a good two feet away, like I had some kind of force field around me.

His entire form was iron.

His stare melted into me for thirty-eight seconds.

I counted.

Because that's how long I lost my breath for.

His eyes released me and went to someone behind me. "You bring my bike?"

"Surely did" was Lucky's cheerful response, but even it held a slight bit of apprehension.

Gage's eyes snatched me back into his possession. "Lauren. Get your ass on the fucking bike. Now."

"Brother, maybe you should—" Brock stepped forward, as if to come to my aid. As if he, one of the big and scary bikers, was afraid for me.

Gage's eyes didn't move. "Tell me one thing I should be doing to my woman, I'll shoot you," he promised, not seeming to mind that we were in the middle of a police station.

There was a heavy pause.

"Ass on the bike, Lauren."

I turned to get my ass on the bike.

I SHOOK THE WHOLE RIDE.

Actually *shook*.

From fear. And from arousal.

Because something in Gage had snapped.

It should've made me want to run.

But I wanted to see it. Feel it.

And then we were in my apartment. I wasn't entirely sure how we got there; it was all a blur of Gage damn near ripping me off the bike and dragging me up the stairs. He let me go the second we reached the living room, and then he started pacing.

I stood in the middle of the room, still, waiting.

"You're going to fucking regret this," he growled, stalking

toward me with such menace that I backed up, hitting the wall roughly, the wood hindering my retreat.

He caged me in, his entire presence a prison, towering over me as his palms rested on the wall behind me.

"Regret what?" I whispered.

He leaned forward, his hair like a waterfall around his beautifully savage face. "Making me fall in love with you," he murmured.

My body froze like someone had poured ice water on me and my cells were too shocked to react for a split second. Then they did, and warmth spread to my toes as my heart beat in my throat.

"How did I make you?" I choked out.

His eyes searched mine. "You fucking *looked* at me, baby."

I swallowed, my stomach a mess of elation and fear. "And why am I going to regret it?"

His hand moved from the wall to circle my neck. "Because, baby, I'm not gonna love you gentle, or sweet, or in a way that's gonna make you happy. I'm too fucked up for that. I'm gonna love you the only way I know how, the only way this fucked-up soul lets me. It's gonna be hard. Brutal. Maybe unpleasant. And I'm not gonna fucking let you go. So you might regret it because this isn't what movies or books promise a girl like you. What a girl like you dreams of. What a girl like you deserves. No, it's gonna be the stuff of nightmares."

The words echoed around us for a long while, hitting me constantly with their weight. With their glorious weight and ugly truth.

He just stared at me, making good on his promise that he'd never let me go.

Which was good, because I didn't want to entertain the idea of what my life would be like if he did.

No, I knew *exactly* what my life would be like if he did.

Exactly the same as it had been before him. Structured. Logical. Sensible.

In other words, a slow fucking death.

"You're angry at me for making you love me," I whispered, my throat struggling against his grip.

"Of course I fuckin' am," he hissed. "I'm not *meant* to love you. You're not meant to love me back, but you do, and every time I hear you say it, it hits me in the cock." He paused, pressing the cock in question against my body, and my skin answered his call. He moved his hand so it no longer gripped my neck but caressed it. "It hits me fuckin' everywhere," he murmured.

"You're angry that I gave you something to love when all you wanted was something to hate," I surmised, unblinking and taking in all of his feral beauty.

"I don't deserve somethin' to love," he growled, his body shaking.

I could sense his need to stalk away. To inflict violence on something, someone. I knew it in his eyes, saw his beast itching to come out.

I hooked a finger into one of his belt loops, yanking him in and making sure he wasn't going to inflict pain on anyone but me.

He let out a harsh hiss as his hard length pressed against me once more.

"It's not up to you to say what I deserve. Nor is it up to you to say what *you* deserve, because I know you don't think you deserve anything but a lifetime of punishment. That's not happening. I won't let it."

His jaw tightened as he battled with something behind his eyes, and then he backed away.

"You might change your mind after this," he said.

I froze, knowing exactly what he meant. What he was going to do. He was going to show me the scars beneath his ruined skin.

"You know how you said it broke your mom thinking about

how your brother never had a reason to go down the path he did? How she tortured herself, blamed herself for maybe doing one minute thing wrong?"

All I could do was nod, remembering the conversation we'd had a handful of nights ago, Gage's arms around me, darkness surrounding us.

"I had a mom like that too," he said, his face so blank, so calm, it hurt to look at. Because I knew when Gage looked the calmest, that's when he was hurting the most.

I'd wanted this for so long, but now, seeing the beginning of it, it terrified me. And I wasn't sure I wanted it anymore. Because I was scared I wouldn't be able to be strong for him. Terrified I'd break down in the face of his demons, and he'd realize I wasn't strong enough for them.

"I don't know if she was wonderin' the same things, if she's still wondering the same things, my mom," he continued. "I'm sure she is, 'cause she's a good person. The best." He paused. "Didn't know that when I was a kid. Didn't appreciate that. That when I started to get wild, wilder than a teenager should, they punished me because they loved me. They were terrified that road I'd somehow found myself on would swallow me up. So they tried to stop that. They couldn't."

His fists were clenched at his sides.

"They kicked me out, hoping that would jerk me out of my bullshit. That I'd man up. But I didn't man up, just used that as an excuse as only a cowardly boy could. Let the underworld yank me down. Ran with some bad people doing worse shit for a couple of years. Then I met her."

I instantly hated *her*. I couldn't explain why—she was one fricking word, a woman without a face, without a *name*. She could be completely and totally innocent. But I knew better. Because there was a lot poured into that one single word, and none of it had anything to do with innocence.

"She didn't have the same problems as me in the beginning, but we had the same problems at the end." His voice was still flat and cold. "I was under the impression that no one in my life gave a shit about me because they weren't enabling my destructive behavior. She was *born* out of destructive behavior. From people who didn't give a shit about her, only so much as the paycheck from the state she'd given them. She was more lost, more damaged than me, and fuck if I wanted to fix her. That was my first mistake. You can't fix broken people."

The sentence hit me in the heart, so much so that I flinched. Gage saw it, of course. Gage saw everything.

His jaw tightened, but he continued.

"So we started giving a shit about each other." He gave me a look, one I was supposed to find something in, but I could barely blink through the pain. "It was the wrong kind of love. It wasn't natural. Organic. Especially not since we both loved each other only slightly more than we loved the junk. Or slightly less. Which was worse?"

The realization of what he meant, what he was saying, hit me so hard that it seemed my very bones shattered.

Junk.

Drugs.

The addiction that stole my brother away from me.

That was the reason for Gage's hard looks, that distance that yawned between us when he retreated into his darkest of places.

He was a drug addict.

And I could taste his fear at the confession. I knew why he'd kept it from me, because he felt this insane connection too. And I imagined after what I'd told him about David, he thought the truth would sever it.

But it only made it stronger.

I wanted to tell him that. Wanted to salve that obvious fear lingering behind my strong man's eyes. But I didn't have the words. And Gage didn't let me try to find them.

"But then she got pregnant," he continued, his words razors on my soul. "And I found something I loved more than the junk. A fuck of a lot more."

He paused, the silence long. And painful. Daggers in the air. I itched to go to him. To touch him. To somehow take away the utter destruction in his eyes. But there was nothing that could touch that kind of pain.

"My daughter."

The two words bowled through my soul. Shattered my bones. Tears streamed down my face before I could even fully realize it.

Because I knew this story didn't have a happy ending.

Because there was no way sorrow could inject itself so deeply, so profoundly into those two words if it did. And the man in front of me was someone who'd convinced himself that he didn't have happy endings. Because of what the world had shown him—or more accurately, what the world had taken from him.

"She was the most beautiful thing I'd ever seen in the shit-filled and ugly life I'd been livin' the years after my folks kicked me out," he said, voice empty. Because I knew that was the only way he could speak of her, with that detachment that was so cold it almost frosted his breath.

Because there was no other way for him to speak and stay standing.

"A whole head of dark curls the day she was born. Biggest eyes I'd ever seen. Saw fuckin' *into* me. Like a baby seconds old somehow knew the fuckin' secrets of the universe. Well, she knew the secrets of mine, at least. She was mine."

My face was soaked, the tears like acid, searing through my skin.

"Those eyes alone, those curls, they were what I needed to get my shit straight," he continued. "Because my girl deserved beauty every inch of her life. I didn't know how the fuck to create it, since ugly was all I knew. Junk does that, takes away the beauty from your memories, erases it. But I tried. Stayed the fuck away from junk. Thought Missy did too. How could you want to touch that shit with the same hands that touched our *daughter*?" He shook his head, clenching his fists at his sides. "That was my mistake. Not my only one, but fuck, my biggest one. Thinking my wife would love my daughter, *our* daughter, more than a fucking *high*." He hissed the word through his teeth and it seemed to turn to fire.

"Didn't notice because I was busy. Too busy trying to create beauty by livin' ugly. And in the end, that's what killed her."

His eyes were dry and empty and bowling through me.

"It wasn't *my* life that killed them, both of them. I've always found that darkly ironic," he said, voice still clear and flat. "I was running with some bad fuckers in those days. In order to run with them, I needed to rule them, so I became worse than all of them. I'm not gonna say I had good intentions beyond trying to stay clean and give my daughter a life that would one day not be stained by the filth of her parents."

He glanced to the door to my studio that was no longer closed, where some of my paintings were visible, namely the reproduction of Gage's chest tattoo I had just about finished.

"The road to Hell isn't just paved with good intentions, and there's more than one way to get there," he said. "My intentions were all bad—when they weren't connected to my daughter, at least—and they brought me to Hell." He gritted his teeth. "Didn't notice my woman was still using. Or maybe I did and didn't want to notice. I was clean from junk but not a fuck of a lot else. Drank a lot. Dove into toxic pussy because my woman was starting to disgust me. But *never* around my daughter. My princess. I'm not a good man, so I wasn't a good father. But I loved her. Fuck, did I love her."

His voice broke then.

Literally broke.

Like shattered into a thousand pieces at the truth that Gage likely hadn't faced in years. It was the single most horrifying thing I'd ever heard, save for the story, because the air was bleeding with this wound.

I wondered why the whole fricking world wasn't bleeding.

How in the heck Gage was standing there in front of me.

Not quite whole. Not even a lot whole.

Broken.

But still battling through life.

Gage reached forward to brush a tear away with his thumb. He looked at it blankly for a beat, then put it in his mouth, as if he was tasting his pain within my body.

"I protected her against everything in my world," he continued, voice little more than a rasp. "Everything I could control, which I made sure was almost fucking everything. They went anywhere, they had tails. House was Fort Knox. She got her checkups every fucking month. I was neurotic about that shit, terrified of some illness ripping through her tiny body, something I couldn't control." He paused. "Turns out it was an illness that killed her. One I couldn't control but shoulda noticed. Because if I'd noticed, my little girl would be ten years old right now. She'd be smilin', doin' whatever the fuck it is that ten-year-olds do."

His eyes were faraway, as if he was looking into the future. One not burdened by the horrors of the past.

He physically shook himself, the motion violent and agonizing.

"But she's not, because the illness she was born out of, what brought her parents together, is ultimately what killed her."

It was an unnerving thing to have a devilishly attractive man stare at you straight in the eye. It was even more unnerving to have the Devil himself look you in the eye. I still hadn't gotten used to Gage's intense and almost violent gaze. But I loved it. Loved what it shook up inside me.

But this wasn't that.

This was something else entirely.

This was exactly what Nietzsche was talking about when a person stared into the abyss. When the abyss stares back at you.

"Bein' frank right now, the reason I haven't told you 'bout this is partly 'cause of your brother," Gage said, not breaking eye contact, his irises flickering with something that looked like shame. "Also 'cause I haven't told a fucking *soul* about it. For much the same reasons you kept quiet about David."

He twitched then, as if he was going to come forward, snatch me into his arms. I braced for it, needing it. But he didn't, just stiffened and kept talking.

"'Cause our demons have good ears, and they come runnin' when we come callin'," he murmured. "But there's also another reason. 'Cause even if all of this didn't scare you enough to run away from me forever, which would be an utter fuckin' shock, there's *more*, and it's definitely gonna chase you away." His resolve was firm, as if it was already decided. "This isn't 'cause I don't think you can handle the truth, babe. I *know* you can. This is 'cause I don't want you to handle this truth. My truth. Didn't want you finally realizing that you're lying in bed with a murderer. An addict. A demon wearing a man's skin."

I tried to speak, to protest the fact that I wasn't going to leave him because of an addiction. Certainly not because of his daughter's death. That was only going to make me hold him tighter.

He didn't let me protest. Silenced me with a look. Because he wasn't Gage now. This was the abyss.

"You don't get to speak until I'm done," he said. "And you'll know when I'm fuckin' done because you won't wanna speak to me again."

The certainty in his voice chilled my soul.

"Gage," I whispered, "there can't be more."

His gaze was ice. "Baby, when it comes to horror and pain, there's always more."

The words hung between us.

"She was high when she did it. When the mother of my child drowned my baby girl."

The words hit me like a slap. No, like a punch to the face.

"Don't know what was goin' through her mind," he continued. "Bad junk gave her a bad trip. Bad enough she was convinced our daughter was a demon. Our fuckin' ten-month-old daughter was a *demon*. But that's what junk does, turns angels into demons and then makes the demons think they're angels." His fists were clenched. "I was already a demon. To protect my angel, I turned into one. Turned into the Devil to avenge her." His stare yanked at my insides. "Drowned the mother of my child in the same tub she'd drowned my baby in. Did it the second I found her floating there. After, I took my little girl out, laid her gently in her crib, like she could feel me. Of course she couldn't. The dead don't feel anything. The dead *aren't* anything."

I visibly flinched at his words.

He eyed me, stare cold and empty. "To the living, they're everything," he murmured. "Lost my everything in a tub that day. Cunt who killed her not included. Don't regret ending her life. Not to this day, and won't till the day I die. She was sick, yeah, I'll admit that. But she made a conscious decision to shoot poison into her arm. The same one she held the whole world in. She didn't deserve to be in the world when she let the junk take mine away. There's no way to package that, Lauren. No way to spin that to make me come off better, less of a monster. I killed her. She's not the first person I killed, and she wasn't the last. Because that day broke me. Broke everything inside me that's needed to function as a human being. I'm not that now. I'll never be capable of living a life without blood, pain, killing. That replaced the junk. That's my life now. I can't fuckin' let it be your death."

It was then that I moved, despite everything in his body repelling me, repelling any human touch. That's exactly why I did it.

He flinched when I put my hands on his neck, his whole body stiffening as if he was expecting me to strangle him. I stroked his beard and braved the demons in his eyes.

"You're not my death, Gage," I said, voice clear. "And I'm not going to let you convince me of that. I'm sorry about your daughter."

He flinched again.

"I don't even know how you're standing here after that," I continued, going up on my tiptoes and laying my mouth on his. He didn't respond to my kiss. I knew he couldn't. "I don't know how you're standing, but I thank God you are, here, in front of me. And that's where you'll be for the foreseeable future. Hopefully forever."

His eyes widened as I spoke, in pure shock, as if he'd truly expected me to be disgusted. To throw him out of my apartment and out of my life.

"You should hate me," he hissed finally.

I tilted my head. "And why is that? Because you hate yourself plenty for the both of us. And that already broke my heart before I knew this." I stepped forward, clutching his face. "And it shatters it now."

He stepped from my grasp. I let him.

"You should fuckin' hate me! You need to!" he roared.

I jumped slightly but didn't retreat. "No, *you* need me to," I argued softly. "And you know that's never going to happen. If David had died from cancer, you think I'd hate you just because you survived it? Or if he'd died in a car crash, I'd never want to see you again because you walked away from one?" I shook my head. "That's not how I work."

"But you don't fuckin' get it! I'm not *recovered*. I haven't walked away. I haven't *survived*." His eyes zeroed in on me with a force akin to a tornado. "Addiction doesn't work that way, baby. For all your knowledge, for all your faith, I'm glad as fuck that you don't know that truth intimately. But I do. And if I stay around you, then you will too. Because my monkey is never getting off my back. It's hooked into my flesh, my bones. Tattooed onto me more than the ink I've tried to cover it with. It's always there. I just have to choose not to feed it. Every day, for the rest of my fuckin' life, I have to fight against that bone-deep hunger." He stepped forward. "And you're dangerous, you see. Because I never thought I'd have to fight against something stronger than that. Never thought there'd be something I wanted more than the junk. The fix." His grip was iron on my hips.

But I said nothing.

Because the dull ache in my hips was nothing like the bare and pulsating agony in Gage's voice.

In my heart.

"And I've found it," he murmured, face close to mine. "You're the thing I want more than anything. It's not a healthy want, baby, what I feel for you. Because from the second I took my first hit, everything I loved was gonna be tainted by that monkey. My addiction. Everything will be warped." He pressed his lips to mine. "You're my cure, baby," he said against my mouth. "But I don't want to be your disease."

I smiled sadly. "That's what love is, Gage, a disease," I whispered.

He stared at me, then kissed me, hard, brutal, unyielding. I clutched the edges of his cut and kissed him back, sharing in the pain coating the room.

The kiss lasted a long time.

It didn't move on from that, to something else, because I knew there was more to Gage's story. It was unimaginable to think it, but there was.

And it needed to come out now.

So I pulled back from Gage. He let me.

"Is that what they're from?" I asked, running my fingers lightly over the skin. I knew I could only do it that way, for a short amount of time, especially now that all his pain was on the surface.

Even though I barely made contact, Gage still flinched.

I flinched inwardly too, at the thought of all that history mangled in scar tissue, still paining him.

He was a man without limit, without fears.

Until it came to his own skin. What lay beneath it.

"Did someone do it to you... after?" I choked, unable to say the words.

"After my wife killed my daughter and I murdered my wife?" Gage asked coldly, with such impact that it was my turn to flinch.

I nodded once.

"No. Well, fuck." He lifted his arm, gazing at it as if it were an unfamiliar map. "Some of them might've been from someone else. I was too high to notice pain for a good while. It all melded into one. Into nothing. Don't remember any wounds when I surfaced. Then again, I didn't notice anything but my need for junk. The horror in my reality." He shrugged. "But most of them come from that, from reality. The need." His eyes moved from mine, the first time he'd ever averted his glance. He seemed... ashamed?

"Gettin' clean is different for everyone," he said. "Some people do it 'cause they're locked up and got no other choice. Most of those people don't stay clean for long, because if someone needs junk, they'll find it, no matter where they are. The Devil always provides for sinners who ask. Rest of 'em take up somethin' else to distract from the need. Smokin'. Eatin'. Fuckin'. Some got support, but support means shit. You're born alone, you die alone, and you battle addiction alone. 'Cause addiction is birth and death all rolled into one—you can't separate the two. Methods to get clean, stay clean... not many of them are healthy, because addiction isn't healthy in the first place, so the cure sure as shit isn't gonna be. Obviously my version of a cure was a lot more fucked up than your garden-variety junkie, and that's saying something." He chuckled, the sound ugly and wrong. Full of the truth. He glanced down to his arms again, then gripped the knife that was always at his belt.

My stomach roiled at the meaning.

But it couldn't be that.

Even with Gage, it couldn't be *that*.

"Every time my skin cried out for nothingness, I gave it pain, blood," he said, confirming my worst fears. "'Cause that's exactly what junk is. Someone said it's like being taken to Hell and thinking you're going to Heaven. But it doesn't matter *where* the fuck you're goin'. You don't care. That's the whole point, not caring. The pursuit of nothing. Not Heaven, not Hell, nothing. So I had to give myself the opposite of nothing to get clean."

I couldn't speak for the longest of moments because my vocal cords were paralyzed in horror. In the time Gage and I had been together, the time I'd come to love him more than anything else in my world, I'd entertained all sorts of nightmares about his past.

And even my depraved imagination couldn't have come up with *that*.

I knew he'd lost someone, because when someone loses an important person to them—when that person is stolen, brutally early—it does something to the complexion. Shadows behind the eyes, like a superimposed image on top of the flesh. Like an invisible tattoo is only visible under ultraviolet light, this pain, this loss, is only visible by people who've known death.

So yeah, I'd known Gage's story would break my heart.

I didn't know it would shred it to pieces and then lay them at my feet.

He'd lost his *daughter*.

I found myself desperate for some kind of instrument to turn back time. To reach into the past and grab onto her when she'd been alive, pure, beautiful. Because she was a piece of Gage before he'd lost himself to the darkness. And he was beautiful in his darkness, but her, with his light?

I should've been more bothered about the admission of murdering his wife. That was kind of a big deal. When your boyfriend tells you he killed the mother of his child, it should rip apart any future you're entertaining with him.

For me, it only solidified it. Because I'd said goodbye to all of my black-and-white conventional beliefs when I'd climbed on Gage's motorcycle that night, when I'd sacrificed the last piece of myself and lost myself to the darkness.

And my darkness pulsated with the need for Gage's wife to be alive, only so I could kill her again. I didn't have violent, homicidal thoughts. I got dark, but never that dark. I didn't have the stomach for it. I didn't even wish the man who'd sold to David dead.

I wished him suffering. Pain.

But not an end to his life. Not an end to chances to make his life better.

But this woman had beauty in her life. This woman had a half of Gage, had a family with him, and she'd murdered it.

A little girl.

Bile rose in my throat.

I struggled to stop myself from throwing up at the thought. That's how violently ill it made me. Just hearing it. A decade on.

I couldn't imagine what it was living it.

How *Gage* lived it.

But I know killing that woman—that monster—was an unforgivable sin, at least in the eyes of whatever passed for God these days.

But not to me.

I didn't consider it a sin. I considered it a service.

Because after, Gage had literally *torn the skin from his body.* Cut at it. Hacked at it. Scarred it forever.

I swallowed razors. "Do you...?" I swallowed again, seriously worried about my ability to calm my stomach. "Do you still do it?" I asked, my voice a shadow.

His eyes were leveling. "No, babe, not since I patched into the club. Not since Ranger found me while in his own personal Hell and the club dragged us both out. Not gonna lie, there're times when the pursuit of the opposite of nothing seems impossible without a knife, blood and pain—I mean my own, since I do it to others often enough—but then I met you. And you're my new torture. Though I'm not sure which of us I'm torturing more."

I forced myself not to break his gaze. "You're not torturing me. You're loving me."

His eyes were cold. "My love is torture, Lauren."

"Without love, life is a tomb," I whispered.

"Robert Browning doesn't mean shit in my life," he growled back.

"The very fact that you know that's Robert Browning means *everything.*" I stepped forward, boxing him in, using my body to make sure he couldn't escape. Because he was used to battling, and he was used to winning. But I wasn't going to let him win if that meant he was going to leave. "You made your tomb because you think your past defines your future. That your darkness defines the amount of light you're going to be entitled to."

"I'm not entitled to shit, Lauren," he hissed. "You most of all. Your fucking light."

"Why?"

He glowered and the cords of his neck strained with his need to move. To fight. But that would mean he'd have to fight me to move. And he didn't seem like he was ready to do that yet.

"Why?" he repeated, voice low and dangerous. "Just fucking *look* at me, Lauren." He yanked up his sleeves, thrust his arms in my face. "This is fucking why!"

He was trying to push me away and hold me tight at the same time. Because there were two different versions of himself, like there were of me. My light and dark side. But he had only the blackest of midnights and the onyx of the grave inside him. Because he was blaming himself for too much. For his daughter dying. For not noticing an addiction that he himself had battled.

For killing the woman suffering from that addiction.

For killing countless people after that.

"You're carrying your guilt around like a pebble in the base of your shoe. You can still walk with it. Live with it. But it's uncomfortable. Painful. Unnecessary." I held up my hand when his eyes glittered with fury. "Don't misunderstand what I'm saying, Gage. I'm not talking about your suffering. Your grief. People who torture others—or worse, torture themselves, do not have monopoly over suffering, Gage. But hearing your story, the *nightmare* you've freaking lived, that you're always going to live, has showed me that if I want a life with you, then that suffering will always be between us." I took a breath as he tensed. "And I want life with you. Death. Suffering. Make no mistake about it, because I need you. More than I need the sun. More than the ocean. More than the order of my life. Because suffering in chaos is better than pretending I'm not suffering in logic. But you need to let go of that guilt for what you think you did to your daughter, because it won't serve you. It's going to destroy you."

"It already fucking has."

I shook my head. "You're here. In front of me. And you've

BATTLES OF THE BROKEN   345

changed my life. People who've been destroyed don't do that. But I know you need to destroy others to do that. To keep on. You need blood, pain, death. And you don't think I can handle or understand that that's going to be a constant need. That I don't realize that no matter how good things are with us, it won't change the bad you need. But I do. And I can handle it. Will continue to do so until we conclude."

He was gripping my neck by the time I finished. "There's no fucking conclusion to this story, Will. To this nightmare."

I smiled. "Good."

And then he kissed me.

Tore off our clothes.

And we tried to find sanctuary within one another.

Gage

He didn't know how to feel after spewing his past out at Lauren like that little bitch from *The Exorcist* and her not run screaming from the room, never to be seen again.

He should've known better. Known his woman was made of tougher shit than that. Tougher shit than him. Because she'd felt his pain. Every inch of it. She'd sucked it all up and taken it upon herself, attached it to her bones.

He fucking *hated* that.

Hated himself for giving her more ugliness.

But then he loved her for it. Loved her so fuckin' much he could barely breathe.

And that's why he didn't leave her after she'd made it clear that she wasn't going anywhere. That she wasn't being scared away.

He didn't leave her because he *couldn't*.

So he did the best thing he could. He fucked her hard. Brutal. Beyond anything they'd ever had. He hadn't tried to fuck the pain out of her—he'd fucked it into her. Unrestrained. All of his violence and darkness.

And she'd loved it.

He took her to the edge, then pushed her off it. Because she'd passed out with him still inside her. He'd literally fucked her unconscious.

He'd wanted to slip into oblivion with his dick still inside her, her hot and comforting weight on him. But he didn't find it. Couldn't.

So he'd slowly slipped out of her, taking more care with her sleeping body than he ever did with her waking one. He eased her glasses off her face, folding them and placing them on her bedside table, where she put them so she could shove them on upon waking.

She was really blind, his Will. He hated that in theory, but he fucking loved her in those glasses. Every time she absently pushed those things up the bridge of her nose, his cock ached.

He'd gone to the bathroom, warmed a washcloth and cleaned himself from her, the marks covering her milky skin hardening his cock once more.

He shouldn't have found satisfaction in the evidence of the pain he caused her. But he did.

Then he watched her. For hours, just watched her sleep, her silky hair splayed upon the pillow. Her eyelids fluttering in her dreams. Her scent pressing into him.

His arms itched, not just with the truth of what was on top of them being laid out. Underneath, he itched for a fix, because the past he'd been running from had finally caught him.

No, he'd finally stopped running. For Lauren.

And he'd known it was coming, this new and visceral craving. Maybe that's why he couldn't sleep, because he was waiting for it to hit. Bracing.

He was glad Lauren wasn't awake.

He could barely see through the need for the junk. Even with her right in front of him serving as an anchor, a reason—the only reason in the world—not to seek out nothing when he had everything in his grasp.

The craving still won.

So he stood. Dressed quietly. And skulked into the night. Where demons like him belonged.

When he got to the bar outside Hope where Lauren had unwittingly saved him and damned herself that night, he didn't sit on his bike like he had then. Didn't pause. The engine had barely stopped rumbling beneath him before he was halfway across the street.

In another heartbeat he was in the dingy alley where people paid for the drugs with scraps of cash and scraps of their souls.

He didn't have any of his soul left to barter, and whatever crumbs were left were lying in a bed in a loft by the ocean.

FOURTEEN

One Month Later

Lauren

What followed after Gage opened the doors of his hidden closet and let all those decomposing, mangled, and skeletal bodies out was not peaceful.

That's what books and movies told you, right? That after a couple's demons met, made nice, and exposed themselves, there's a peace?

Nothing left to hide?

There might have been nothing left to hide, but that didn't mean there was *peace*.

Especially not since I woke up the morning *after*.

And everything was split into *before* and *after*, the serrated knife of truth splitting the days between when he told me about his past and everything that had come before. It didn't stop the before from being important. If anything, it made it more so.

But it changed the after.

Gage was different when I awoke to him sitting in the chair across from my bed, the one positioned for the perfect and beautiful view of the ocean. I often got up and watched the sun rise from that chair. More recently, I'd been watching the sun rise with Gage bending me over that chair.

But he wasn't watching the sun rise—it had long entered the sky, since I'd obviously been dead to the world longer than usual— nor was he bending me over the chair. The tenderness between my thighs likely wouldn't have allowed for that, though I craved it the second my eyes met his clear and alert ones.

He was fully dressed, elbows on his knees.

"How long have you been watching me sleep?" I demanded, my voice still sleepy.

"A while," he said. That was all he said. He didn't move, didn't blink as his eyes kept hold of mine.

Ice grasped my soul. "You're not leaving me, are you?" I asked, my voice no longer snatched by dreams. No, it was grasped by a nightmare of him convincing himself to leave in the darkness.

His body jerked, and some of that horrible blankness left his expression. "Never." The word was a vow. A promise.

But uneasiness still clutched the bottom of my stomach.

I pulled back the comforter, my naked body exposed to him.

He let out a harsh hiss.

"Prove it," I demanded, the tenderness between my thighs forgotten, only because the tenderness of my heart drowned every- thing else out.

Gage was across the room before I could blink.

And he did prove it.

Twice.

I was still assaulted with goose bumps every now and then throughout the week following that, something feeling... off. And not Gage's usual off.

I didn't ask him what it was because I knew asking was no use. When Gage wanted to tell me something, he'd tell me. And he'd do it in his own time.

I also didn't because I was a coward.

I convinced myself it was a throwaway fear for my article, since everyone was so convinced it was going to get me kidnapped or killed. It garnered attention around the office, mostly because no one realized I had it in me.

Jen had taken me out for virgin cocktails to celebrate. I was going to invite Gage, so the two of them could finally meet, but she insisted it be just us two.

"He steals you away often enough," she'd said with a wink.

Gage had known I'd had in me. And though I'd expected him to be mad as hell about the whole thing, he hadn't exactly had the chance to yell at me, what with being arrested and all that.

Well, almost arrested. Troy had skillfully avoided me since then.

But since our conversation had veered off me doing a story of a well-known drug dealer, exposing him, and onto Gage's past, we hadn't exactly had a chance to discuss it. I'd expected Gage to *make* a chance, being alpha male and protective and all that.

Amy couldn't believe he hadn't already. She'd said, "Brock would've had me locked in some kind of cabin in the woods somewhere with nuclear weapons poised at every possible entrance and exit until he thought the threat was eliminated."

I'd laughed because I thought she was joking.

She wasn't.

It turned out every one of those men was protective as all hell.

Gage hadn't even put a 'guard' on me like the rest of the woman had during the early months of their relationships. Then again, the early stages of their relationships had been full of bombings and kidnappings, so I kind of understood why Gage hadn't put one on me.

And I knew he loved me.

He showed me every day.

Not in the same way the rest of the men did, but in his own dark, depraved and inventive ways.

But Amy was rubbing off on me, because I found a little piece of myself not wanting flowers or chocolates or nipple clamps—though Gage had come home with those and they were fabulous. I wanted a bodyguard to show he cared about me possibly getting kidnapped by a drug lord.

I obviously wasn't overly worried, mainly because I worked for a small-town newspaper, not the *New York Times*, and he was a small-time drug dealer who probably didn't even read the newspaper, let alone ours.

Also because I simply wasn't interesting enough to get kidnapped. Gage being my boyfriend was all my life could handle. Then again, Gage in anyone's life was going to be more than most people could handle.

Gage probably knew all those things, but still.

So I broached the subject. Not about the bodyguards, just about his lack of general fury on the matter.

"You think I'd be mad about you writing the story?" he asked, seeming genuinely surprised.

"Well, yeah," I said. "You're, um..."

"Insane?" he finished for me.

"You," I corrected.

He shrugged. *"Same difference."*

I rolled my eyes. "But you were pissed off about me being outside the bar that night."

Something worked in his eyes and I caught it, but then it was gone again and slipped through my fingers.

"Yeah, babe, I was pissed because I was pissed at myself for not

getting the fuck away from you. I was also pissed at you for doin' such a thing without so much as a fucking weapon."

I chewed my lip. "Well you were there, and you're a weapon."

His eyes flared, focusing on my lip. "Yeah, I fuckin' am," he agreed. "But you didn't know I was there, so that doesn't count."

I huffed out a breath. "So it wasn't the act itself? Of putting myself in danger?"

He yanked me to his chest. "In an ideal world, a woman like you would never be put in danger. She would have a man who wasn't at all like me to protect her from it. But it's not an ideal world, so you're gonna be in danger. I'll try to protect you from it— I'll die tryin'—but you need some danger to survive. In case you hadn't noticed, I'm not like the other men in this club in a number of ways. My thoughts on what our women should and shouldn't be allowed to do is one of those ways. Demons don't discriminate between gender. So women should be able to fight their battles. They bleed the same as men, so it stands to reason that they can cut just as well too."

I blinked. "So you're a feminist?" I joked.

He chuckled. "I'm a realist, babe. Don't believe in wrapping my woman in cotton wool for the world. Mostly because as soon as I close the doors, I'm gonna rip off that wool and put her in a fuck of a lot more danger than the world could." His eyes glowed and my stomach tightened.

"So, the article?" I probed after getting my fluttering stomach under control.

"Proud as fuck of that, Will," he murmured against my mouth. "My baby excels at everything you put your mind to. Not exactly a fan of you going behind my back to research the story, but I get it. This was your dragon to slay. Fuck if I want to spear every single one of them. I know better. You gotta fight your own battles. With words, that's okay. Gets any more real than that, I'll be fucking tanning your hide, you put that beautiful body in danger without

BATTLES OF THE BROKEN 353

me by your side. Because I'll let you battle, babe. I'm not built to crush you like that. My only condition is that I'm standin' beside you when you do."

And that was that.

Until I realized I hadn't asked him why he wasn't worried about retaliation—on the small chance that a drug dealer did read a small-town paper.

I found out soon enough.

Some couples did Sunday brunch.

Gage and I did Sunday bomb making.

No joke.

It wasn't every week, obviously. Gage would be on some kind of watch list if he was making and using bombs every week. I was surprised he wasn't already.

But we went out to his little abandoned warehouse almost every week, bomb or no bomb, because there was a kind of serenity in the absolute solitude of it all. And there was a sickening satisfaction at being able to scream in the wide-open country air as Gage fucked me on his motorcycle. Or chained up in the warehouse—yes, chained up—or any of the other places we were discovering.

So I always felt a sick kind of excitement riding out there, the bike vibrating beneath me, my arms around Gage. He almost always rested his hand atop mine, which of late was resting lower than his midsection.

Much lower.

He had seemed off that morning, and it only intensified when we dismounted. He took my helmet from me and laid it on the seat of the bike, then snatched my face in his hands.

"You know how I said I want to be able to stand beside you while you fight your battles?" he asked. "Because I know you've got the strength to fight them your way?"

I nodded the small amount I could.

He gestured to the warehouse with his chin. "What's in there is me asking you to stand beside me while I battle. For the both of us."

"Okay," I said immediately.

He jerked slightly, as if surprised. "You don't even know what's in there."

"I don't need to," I told him honestly, fear curling in my stomach like a snake. Fear that would've stopped me before but now only fueled me. "I know what's here." I tapped my finger above his chest. "That's all that matters."

"Fuck, I love you," he growled, then brought his mouth brutally down on mine, unyielding in his ferocity.

It was hard to breathe afterward, let alone walk unaided, so I let him drag me into the warehouse. It was only when I saw what —actually who was inside that I regained all of my faculties very quickly. And I tried to snatch my hand from Gage's.

He obviously didn't let me do it, his hand tightening around mine to the point that I thought it'd bruise if I continued my struggle.

So I stopped. ˎ

Took a deep breath.

Stared at the man in front of me.

The man tied to a chair in front of me,

The man who'd sold my brother the drugs that killed him.

"That's why you weren't worried about retaliation," I murmured, eyes on the man. "Because you had him here."

His clothes were filthy, ripped. I didn't know if that was a result of his kidnapping or part of the uniform drug dealers wore. Because he didn't look like he had been beaten at all.

There wasn't even a speck of blood on the man. Nor an injury.

It was strange.

And it was strange that that's what I considered out of place. Not the drug dealer my boyfriend had kidnapped and tied up in *the warehouse he reserved for making bombs. No, the fact that he hadn't killed him, or at least tortured him.*

How I could've changed so much in such a short amount of time should've scared me. But maybe I wasn't changing. Maybe I'd always been that way, stifled underneath everything I thought I should've been.

His eyes were alert, panicked, but he didn't struggle. He wasn't gagged, but he didn't speak. Sweat drenched his clothes, and the putrid scent of vomit and human filth assaulted me now that my initial shock was taken care of.

"He's going through withdrawal," Gage said, his voice blunt and flat.

I jerked my head to Gage, who wasn't looking at the man in front of us but at me.

"Smart dealers don't get addicted to their product. Eats into the profit." He nodded to the man. "Not a smart dealer."

I looked back at the man I'd built up in my mind as this villain. As a monster. But he was just a man. And not even much of one. Drugs had whittled the flesh from his bones, the soul from his eyes.

How had I not seen it with David? This hopeless, hollowed-out look?

Because David was the best at everything.

That included being a drug addict.

Or more accurately, hiding that he was a drug addict.

"You haven't touched him," I said, my statement somewhat of a question.

"Couldn't," Gage grunted. "Intended on taking care of him the second I realized your intentions that night. And I know what I said about fightin' battles, but you'll agree that I wasn't exactly seein' straight at the start of things."

I raised my brow in response.

He met my look. "Yeah, well I was gonna. But I couldn't.

Didn't trust myself to. I wasn't in Hope that night for club business."

All teasing expression left my face.

Gage's eyes roved over me. "Don't know what would've happened had you not been there. Could lie to the both of us and say nothin', but I don't lie to myself anymore. And I'm not gonna lie to you. So I didn't trust myself to do shit to him after that night. Then it didn't seem like you were pushin' it. And you distracted me, babe. You distracted me from both the desire for a kill and the desire for a fix." He paused. "No, you fuckin' saved me."

He glanced to the man, as if he were part of the chair rather than a living, breathing human being who was listening to us. Though his eyes were faraway and it didn't seem he was listening to anything but the screams inside his head.

My eyes went back to Gage because it was too hard to look at that man, to see what my brother might've been on the inside.

"And that night, the night after you saved me from one of many arrests on a long rap sheet, saved me from my own demons, I decided it was about time to save you. Or myself. Regardless, that's how he ended up here."

"Are you going to kill him?" I whispered.

His eyes were unyielding. "That's up to you."

"Me?"

He nodded once. "This isn't just my battle. Not just my decision. Not my fuckin' life anymore. And this is your dragon, though he doesn't look so big and mean up close. He's pathetic, in fact. You go either way. I'll let him go, or we bury him." He shrugged as if he were asking if I wanted Chinese or pizza for dinner. "I'm good with both."

I let out a hysterical giggle.

Gage didn't look at me strangely for such a weird reaction. There was no such thing as a weird reaction with Gage.

He just waited.

And then I stopped laughing.

Because it was real.

The man who'd killed my brother—or at the very least was some sort of accessory—was sitting there, immobile, at my mercy.

A very small and dark part of me itched to snatch Gage's knife and plunge it into the man's heart. But looking at him, at how utterly pathetic he seemed, I knew it wouldn't be doing much. Or anything at all. He didn't even much look like a human anymore.

I forced myself to pull out of Gage's arms, and he let me with a hard jaw because I knew that's what I needed. To confront my dragon.

My palms were damp as I came to a stop in front of him.

The stench was closer. There was vomit and human excrement surrounding him. I held my breath.

"Are you sorry?" I choked. "For what you do to people? Are you sorry?"

He blinked at me as I spoke, eyes clearing slightly, his face covered with a grimy layer of sweat.

He smacked his lips, a wet and grotesque sound. "Please."

At first I thought he was begging for his life, and a small flower of pity bloomed within me. Maybe I couldn't save David, but I could save the man who'd damned him. David would've liked that.

But then the man spoke again.

"Please, just a bump. Just a bit. I'll die without it."

I jerked back like he'd hit me. The flower of pity withered inside me.

Because this man was tied up, forced to be sober but he was begging for a fix instead. And sure, it was an illness, but the cure wasn't anywhere but inside. Gage had literally cut the flesh from his body to get clean. He battled every day. Every single day. I saw it now. I knew it.

And for the rest of his life, it would be a battle. He'd fought through the worst of it, but there was no end to the fight.

This creature in front of me wasn't ever going to win that battle, let alone fight it.

I angrily brushed a tear from my cheek and turned my back, walking toward Gage's steady gaze.

He didn't pull me into his arms. He knew better. He just watched me. Waited.

"Put him out of his misery," *I said, my voice clear.*

And then I turned and walked out, too much of a coward to watch it being done, or do it myself.

Gage met me outside a few moments later, pulling my back into his front.

He kissed my neck.

"That was quick," *I whispered.*

"Takes considerably less time to end a life than it does to bring one into the world," *he murmured.*

I choked out a dark laugh.

He squeezed me.

"I'm sorry for making you do it," *I whispered.* "For not being strong enough to do it myself."

He yanked me around so his hands were either side of my neck, eyes on mine. "You never fuckin' apologize for that shit," *he growled.* "Took great pleasure in endin' his life. You know that's part of my cure, baby. Death. You know it and don't judge it. You're still standin' right here." *He pressed his mouth to mine.* "Fact that you're standing makes you the strongest person walking this earth. Don't you ever let me hear you say different."

So there was that, among other things.

Like Gage convincing me to paint full-time.

Which happened to be what we were discussing, almost arguing about, as I hurriedly buttoned my blouse, late for meeting Amy. We were going to watch Mia and Gwen's boys play a soccer game. Something everyone from the club usually attended—the two big burly bikers named Bull and Cade usually front and center—but there was some kind of 'club business.' I was learning quickly that that served as a blanket explanation which most of the women didn't get much of an elaboration on. Not because the men didn't trust them, but because they were protective. And because it was the club's code.

But Gage and I were different. So he wasn't about trying to protect me from such things. "We're working on bringing down a human trafficker Rosie fucked with a few years back," he said. "And I hope to fuck it's me who gets to bring him down when we do."

I bit my lip. "Yes, me too. Only if you'll be safe."

He grinned. "Yes, baby, when I'm murdering one of the most dangerous men in the underworld, I'll do it *safely*."

I grinned back. "That's all I'm asking."

Obviously Gage was protective over me. That was apparent when Troy approached us in the grocery store, of all places.

Gage stood in front of me. "Unless you want a broken nose to mess up that pretty face, I'd keep walkin', Officer."

Troy folded his arms. "Your old lady won't be able to get you off twice," he hissed.

Gage grinned. "Oh, she gets me off a fuck of a lot more than twice."

"Gage," I hissed, heat creeping up my cheek.

He looked over his shoulder. "What? I'm just proud of your skills, baby."

I groaned.

"I'm not here to cause shit. Or to disrespect Lauren," Troy clipped.

Gage stepped forward. "I respect her plenty," he said evenly.

I gripped Gage's bicep, pulling him back. My bare palm flat-

tened over his scarred skin. I could do that now. He barely even flinched with the touch and let himself be pulled.

"Then what is it you're here for, Troy?" I asked coldly. I hadn't entirely forgiven him for the whole debacle, but I still liked him. He was a good man who didn't understand what was outside black and white. Hence me holding on to Gage to make sure he didn't hit him again.

"Dealer you did the story on seems to be missing. We had enough for an arrest, went to his place," he said. "No one there. No one's seen him."

My stomach dropped slightly, but my expression didn't change. "Even drug dealers are allowed vacations, Troy."

He squinted at me as if he were inspecting the words. "Yeah, they don't normally take them though. Unless their vacations take them south. Way south." He looked to his boots, meaning clear.

"And why are you informing us of this in the frozen pea section?" I asked as Gage stayed silent.

"Curious if you knew anything, since it's a big coincidence that not long after you do a story exposing him, he disappears."

"I disagree. It's actually extremely logical for a man to leave town after he's exposed in illegal activities."

"Drug dealers are rarely logical."

"And I'm rarely fuckin' patient," Gage interrupted. "So I'm done with this, unless you want to take it outside? Leaving your badge and your pussy in here, of course? Yeah, didn't think so. Next time you get curious, you take me down to the station. Not Lauren. And you better have a lot of shit to back up that curiosity. Police officers who fuck with me frequent the south on their vacations too."

And that was that.

We hadn't seen Troy since.

"I don't fuckin' get why you're not makin' a living out of it," Gage said, watching me rush around the house. "You're good at shit at the paper. Know that. I read everything you write. But this." He gestured to the easel in the living room, facing the ocean —a big development for me to take it out of the place where I'd shoved it away like a skeleton—a painting half-done.

Not of the ocean.

Of *Gage*.

"That's more than fucking good, Will," he continued. "That's fuckin' *magic*. That's shit the world needs to see to make them believe in someone who makes pain somethin' more than what it is. You need to share it because you need to see how fuckin' magnificent you are."

I folded my arms against the warmth of the beautiful words. "You're just saying that because it's you," I tried for sarcasm.

It didn't work.

He narrowed his eyes, not speaking, coaxing more out of me as he always did.

"I'm just not ready," I whispered. "You seeing those paintings, me telling you about that six months of my life that I've always been ashamed of."

He clutched my hips. "Insanity isn't something to be ashamed of, babe," he hissed. "It's a natural reaction to this fucked-up world. It's showin' there's no such thing as sane." He stroked my cheek. "It's beautiful."

I smiled, my eyes tracing his arms. "I agree," I murmured, then admitted "Maybe I just need a little more time to convince myself of that."

Gage's jaw was hard, but he nodded once. "We've got time, babe," he agreed. Then he threw me over his shoulder and I screamed. The swat on my ass silenced me. "But I need a little more time convincin' you of how beautiful I find you."

We were late to the soccer game.

Really freaking late.

I FINALLY ARRIVED at the front of the park, where Amy was waiting, still disheveled.

"You're late. But then again, so am I. Likely for the same reason." Amy smirked knowingly as she handed me a cup of iced tea, not looking at all disheveled.

It was getting hotter now, hot enough for less clothing. Hot enough for Gage to wear short sleeves. Now his scars were part of him, not something that stuck out like they did at the start. Their ugliness was a reason he was so beautiful. But not everyone was like that, so people stared when we went out.

Because people loved being spectators to pain. Especially when they could trick themselves into thinking they weren't participants. Even now, as he idled his bike at the entrance to the park, parents and their children focused on the skin of his arms, staring, whispering, averting their gaze.

It angered me at the start.

It didn't as much now.

Because they were the ones who were missing out, living that narrow life of thinking that ugliness was bad and uniformity was beautiful.

"Will!" Gage's voice carried over the stares and the whispers.

I turned from Amy.

"Love you."

I gaped at him. He was free with his feelings. As free as he could be, at least, but shouting, "I love you" in a park full of people wasn't exactly what I'd expected from Gage.

Which was why he did it.

And why it warmed me better than the April sun.

"I love you too," I shouted back.

He grinned and roared off.

Amy linked my arm in hers. "*That* just made coming to

watch such a stupid sport totally worth it," she said, sipping from her cup and deftly dodging children while in heels.

I merely smiled and sipped my tea.

"I can't believe you've exchanged 'I love yous' before either one of you has been rescued from a kidnapping attempt." She paused. "Though I guess we could factor in you storming into the station and blackmailing an officer as a kidnapping rescue."

I laughed. "Why is everyone waiting for a kidnapping?"

Her eyes emptied of their usual lightness. "Because we've got something special here with these men. And they've obviously got something special with us. And this is a kind of a special that comes with a price. You and Gage are the most special of them all, because you're two people the world almost stopped from getting such things."

I'd told her about David on one of our many walks, and about the six months after. She'd squeezed my arm, softened her green eyes and gazed at me without an ounce of judgment. Like right now.

"That's why everyone's waiting for that price. Terrified for it," she whispered.

I blinked at her. At the naked fear in her tone.

Before I could reassure her, an accented voice floated our way.

"Over here!"

Gwen was waving from a spot a few feet away and the moment was broken, Amy winking at me and continuing to drag me along.

"Gage yelled, 'I love you,' in the middle of the park and it was amazing and they should've sold snacks," she told the group at large.

The group being Mia, Gwen, Lily and Kingston's 'grandma', Evie. Though it had to be said the woman was the furthest from a grandmother one could get. And that was saying something, consider my own. Sure, she looked to be of the right age, kind of. The lines on her face were deep and betrayed a hard life, everything about her was hard.

But somehow, soft enough to make her ageless. But scary. She was wearing head-to-toe black, a sheer lace shirt with a black cami underneath, tight black jeans, and spike heeled ankle boots that were too edgy even for me.

I'd seen her at the club party, hovering around the older man I knew to be Steg, the former president. Former, not just because his salt and pepper hair was mostly salt now, because he'd been shot in the chest the same day Gwen had delivered her baby in their clubhouse.

Still, he was like his wife, somehow ageless, brutal, unwilling to bow down to the frailness of old age.

The corner of her mouth turned up with Amy's words, and I guessed from her, that worked as approval.

I felt warmth at that small smile, at that small gesture of acceptance from the notorious matriarch of the biker family.

"Holy fuck," Gwen breathed. "No way. Gage did that? Are you sure he wasn't admitting it was him on the grassy knoll?" She winked at me as she spoke.

But Amy didn't give me time to answer. "Oh my God, coffee!" she exclaimed, snatching a cup out of Gwen's hand.

Gwen scowled at Amy's other hand. "You already have coffee. Why are you stealing mine?" she hissed, her pretty face contorting into rage with a speed that was equal parts scary and impressive. "They cut your hands off for that in some countries, you know."

"This isn't coffee," Amy replied, shaking the other cup. "This is a mimosa. Parents get *judgy* when I bring a champagne flute." She rolled her eyes, sipping from Gwen's cup. "Apparently it's not *seemly* to drink at your son's baby dance class."

"It isn't seemly at all, Amy, just downright bad parenting. I'm shocked and appalled and frankly disappointed," Gwen said, folding her arms. "That you didn't bring me one too," she added with a wink, swiping Amy's cup.

I smiled as they bickered.

"Oh shit!" Mia exclaimed. "I forgot to check the boys for knives."

I started to laugh, because checking two boys under ten for knives at a soccer game was obviously a joke and Mia had a killer, albeit a little insane, sense of humor.

But she went running off in the direction of the team huddle.

Gwen didn't go running. She shrugged when Amy looked at her expectantly. "This is not my first rodeo, I already confiscated Kingston's weapons," she deadpanned, sipping from her cup.

I shook my head and chuckled, letting the warmth of the sun heat me.

Little did I know the sun was about to fall from the fricking sky.

FIFTEEN

"I swear, when our kid grows up, it's not playing soccer," I said, sinking down on the sofa. "Seriously, it's a brutal sport." I scrunched up my nose. "Or maybe it was Mia's boys who made it that much more brutal. I don't even know how they managed to tie up that one kid in the goal netting. I guess it was pretty impressive." I paused. "Though I'm sure Kingston helped, he's better at getting away with it than the others."

It took me a second to understand the silence that came after my words, realize it wasn't Gage's normal silence. No, this one was filled with something that raised the hair on my arms.

My eyes snapped up to meet Gage's.

He'd been staring at me since I'd gotten in, obviously, because that was Gage. But sometime between his harsh and beautiful kiss hello and me sinking onto the sofa and talking, his stare had changed. Emptied.

"What?" I asked, tensing, bracing.

"When *our* kid grows up," he repeated the words I hadn't even been fully aware that I'd said. That had tumbled right out of my fantasies and into the air because I'd been so comfortable. So happy.

That was a grave mistake.

I saw that now.

But it was too late.

With everything Gage and I had shared, all the wounds we'd exposed to each other, I'd settled comfortably into the fact that we were tattooed on each other's souls. Our demons were all but married, and I'd imagined that same permanence with a certainty that was obviously a mistake. Gage hadn't spoken about marriage or anything like that, but he'd made promises about life and death. About forevers. So I'd logically taken 'forever' as marriage and kids.

But there was no logic here.

Only pain.

"Well, I mean... I'm not talking *now* or anything," I said quickly, my voice shaking for reasons I didn't quite understand. But I also knew that I meant maybe not now, but soon. Because I was in my early thirties, though I wasn't worried about my biological clock. More about creating a family, something beautiful from the ugliness that brought us together. "I just mean—"

"I don't want kids, Lauren. Or marriage." The words were spoken flatly. Cruelly. But that was the point. Gage was using them as shields—no, as weapons to push me away, prod at me so I would retreat.

Sweat beaded on my temples as my heartbeat increased and panic started to set in. "Well I know obviously now isn't the most ideal time. We haven't even been together for—"

"No. Not now, not ever."

I flinched.

He had no reaction to it. Not even a Gage reaction to show what my pain was doing to him. There was nothing. It was like my offhand words had scooped out his soul and there was nothing of him left.

"What?" I asked, my voice bland and empty. I hated it.

"I don't know why you're acting so fucking surprised. You've heard about my past, know what I went through."

I stood, intending on going to him, on taking his hands, but his entire body repelled me, created a barrier that I didn't even dare cross. So I just froze in front of him, an awkward distance that didn't feel right between us.

But it somehow felt permanent.

"Gage," I whispered, pain etched into the single word.

"With all the ugliness you've seen of the world, why the fuck would you want to bring another person into it?" he clipped.

I flinched again, but I was determined to not back down, to try and fight. "With all the ugliness I've seen, why wouldn't I want to add some remarkable kind of beauty to it?"

He looked at me a long time with that brutal and empty gaze. The pain that gaze roused rivaled that of him telling me about his daughter. It was different though. Then, he was opening up to me, showing me everything bloody and broken inside him.

Now he was slamming everything closed, taking away everything with that gaze.

My hands shook at my sides.

He stepped forward, quickly, purposefully.

"You've known true sorrow and it's made you so fucking kind. So fucking remarkable." He brushed my cheek and I flinched. Not because his grip was so hard. No, because it was so soft that it was barely even there. "I've known true pain and it's made me cruel. Cold. I'm barely able to give you what you need, Lauren. What I can give you, it's not what you deserve, but I was makin' peace with that, 'cause I'm not the good guy. But no fuckin' way can I give you that." He shuddered. Actually shuddered. "No fucking way can I watch you grow with my child, see you glow with life and see that happiness again. Because it'll drive me over the edge. I fuckin' know that. I won't be able to handle feelin' all that happiness. I'll go in search of nothing."

His hand left and he stepped back, his boots an echo in the halls of Hell.

"I may deserve nothing, Will, but you sure as shit don't."

I waited for more.

Because an ending to what we had needed to be more than that. It needed to be a battle. It needed blood, suffering, pain. Me clutching on so tightly that my nails ripped off.

It couldn't be that simple and agonizing.

That anticlimactic.

But it was.

Gage turned around and left. I was still in a state of shock until the door slammed, and a short time after that, his bike roared away.

He hadn't even paused at the curb.

He just left.

I stood dry-eyed in the living room for a long time, gazing blankly at the shards of me that had been crushed under Gage's motorcycle boot as he walked away.

Then I sank to the ground.

And those broken pieces cut me to shreds.

Gage

He didn't know where to go after leaving Lauren's apartment. Hell would've been a nice respite from the utter emptiness he'd felt since walking out that door. And then he'd gotten his wish, since the itch, the *need* to fill that emptiness with junk thrust him into the pit again.

But he was glad for the distraction, focusing on fighting his need for a fix instead of fighting his need to turn his bike around and bowl through Lauren's door, take back every word he'd said, tell her he'd give her fucking everything. But he couldn't. Because he was a fucking coward. Because he was afraid she'd give him everything and then the ugly world would take it away.

And he couldn't fucking take that.

He wasn't as strong as Lauren was to forge through her fear, her ugliness, and create something beautiful. And that meant he didn't deserve her.

So he pulled his bike into his house, was inside the empty living room before he really knew how he got there. No fuckin' way he'd go to the club. Not like that. He was actually scared of what he'd do to one of his brothers if they looked at him the wrong way. He didn't trust himself not to kill a member of his family if that meant his need for blood might chase away some of his need for *her*.

So that's why he was at his empty house. Because there was no one to hurt there but himself. And he'd stopped himself from yanking his knife from his belt and dragging it down his arm.

Instead, he'd yanked something more dangerous from his pocket and laid it on the table in front of him.

He stared at the phone.

And it stared back.

With more force, more strength than anything else he'd gazed at. It was a fucking *phone*. He'd stared at some of the worst people to walk this earth—before he'd stained the soil with their lifeblood, that was.

He'd stared down the barrel of a gun many times. And once, it'd been his finger on the trigger of the gun he'd stared at.

And all those times, he'd felt nothing.

Maybe a tiny bit more than nothing, which was why he did the things he did. Why he chased death, to make sure he didn't spend too much time thinking about how it chased him. So he couldn't dwell on what it had already taken from him.

How it had already taken everything.

Those times, staring at things that could kill him, it was death that kept him alive. And it was the feeling that was a smidge more than the abyss of nothing that kept him chasing it.

Blood.

Violence.

Danger.

Pain.

But when he was staring into her hazel eyes, he saw a fuck of a lot more than nothing. Felt a fuck of a lot more than nothing.

It made him feel everything.

And that was worse than staring down the barrel of any gun.

Fuck, that *was* the barrel of a gun.

And it was those hazel eyes, her warm and soft touch amidst the hardness and coldness of his world that had him staring at that phone in the first place.

The phone that was a lot more dangerous than any murderer he'd sat across from, anyone he'd killed. More dangerous than the murderer he saw in the mirror.

But he found himself dialing.

Listening to the ring that felt like dirt on his fucking grave.

Hearing the faint and tired voice on the other end of the phone tore through him like a bullet. Paralyzed him like knife shredding through his spine.

His grip tightened on the phone as demons clutched at his throat, choked silence out of him.

Heavy breath covered his silence. A hitch in those breaths that sounded something like hope. But Gage wouldn't know what hope sounded like. What it fuckin' felt like. Hope abandoned the damned.

"Christian?" the soft voice asked.

Another bullet.

A muffled sob broke through his heavy silence. "Christian? Is that you?" That time it wasn't a question but a plea.

His insides shredded. He was sure she would've forgotten. That he would've been the black mark they'd painted over by now. That he was nothing more than a scar.

"It's okay. You don't have to talk," the voice hiccupped, full of fresh pain, not something that had even scabbed over, let alone scarred. There was a pause, a slight muffling of the phone. "Gary!" the broken voice called to the background.

And then he didn't hear any more because the phone smashed against the wall seconds after Gage had thrown it.

He barely noticed the carnage against the ringing in his ears.

The need for a fix.

For blood.

For her.

He stood, going to satisfy one of those needs.

Lauren

One Week Later

I didn't get out of bed for an entire day. That might've been nothing to people who partied till the sun came up, binged on Netflix, or were just plain lazy.

I was none of those people.

I was strict with my wake-up time, though being up and ready for the day wasn't the intention. People were *supposed* to be up, being productive; it was what the normal structure of the world demanded. So I did it, because it was what was *expected*. Even on the days that my mattress seemed to grow arms and my mind grew roots, urging me to clutch to the nothingness of sleep.

But I didn't cling to that nothingness for the same reason that I didn't drink coffee or alcohol. Because it was easy. Mind-altering. A coping mechanism.

Until Gage, of course.

Then there was no wake-up time.

There was only us.

And my mattress didn't need to grow arms when I had scarred ones around me. And my mind didn't need roots since it belonged to Gage.

And he was gone.

I'd expected him to come back. To realize that walking away wasn't an option when we were so tangled in each other.

But he didn't come back.

And I didn't get out of bed.

Then Monday came. And my alarm sounded.

I hadn't moved in twenty-four hours.

I didn't want to move for twenty-four years if that meant I wouldn't be moving toward Gage. Or that my body wouldn't be aching from his touch. Already that ache was disappearing. It was hard to tell though, through the repeated slicing of my heart with every breath I took.

It was tempting. But I didn't do it.

I went to work.

I smiled at people.

I did my job.

Then I went home.

And I saw the half-painted image of Gage at my window. It was easily my best yet.

"Paint me like one of your French girls," he purred with an accent.

I burst out laughing as he laid a gentle kiss on my nose, as if he sensed that I was nervous.

Beyond nervous.

I'd never painted someone living before.

Every single face in my studio—or broom closet—was painted by memory. Since a lot of them were David, there wasn't much choice but to paint them from memory.

And painting was so painful, so private to me, that doing it front of Gage—doing it of Gage—was being naked in a way I'd never been.

He gripped my face, searching my eyes. "Know you're scared of this. Just means you're doin' something right."

And then he kissed me again.

Not on my nose, or tender.

He snatched away all my uneasiness with the kiss, and when he was done, I was pretty sure I could conquer the world.

"Sit," I commanded, nodding to the chair by the window.

He grinned wickedly. "I like it when you're bossy, Will. Save some of that for later."

My stomach dipped at the prospect. Gage was in charge in the bedroom. And not in a way that took away my power. In a way that empowered me more than anything else ever had or ever would.

But the thought of having him at my mercy, at playing with that darkness he'd let out in me... I swallowed roughly.

"Paint first, fuck later," Gage said, voice thick, as if he'd read my mind.

And with what I thought would be great effort, I started. But once my paintbrush started moving, it became a blur. As simple as breathing.

I didn't notice the time go by.

Gage did.

"You have to sit still," I snapped, looking from my canvas to my subject as he shifted in the chair.

He gritted his teeth. "How the fuck am I meant to sit still with *you standin' there, looking like an angel ripe for the picking, screwing your nose up in concentration, begging to be fucked?" he growled.*

My brush paused and my breathing stuttered. I glanced back down at my canvas. "Well, considering you're a self-professed badass who can do anything and everything, I'm sure you'll figure it out."

There was a heavy silence after his surly grunt.

And then when I thought he was settled again, he moved. The brush was out of my hand and I was over his shoulder before I could properly understand what happened.

A sting erupted on my ass after a loud slap.

"Fuck now, paint later," he decided.

It was only when I felt a sharp pain in my palm that I realized I was on my knees, ripping at the canvas with my bare hands with such vigor that I'd stabbed myself with the wooden backing of the canvas.

I looked down at the blood, disinterested in it. The pain was little more than nothing. I pressed against the small shard of wood sticking out of my palm with detachment. The pain intensified as it ripped farther into my skin.

I toyed with the idea of pressing harder. Ripping, pulling, tearing at my skin as I did with the canvas. It was tempting.

But then I pulled it out, pushed to my feet, washed out the wound, poured disinfectant on it, and bandaged it correctly. It was funny how easily the shackles of my normal life fastened around my body now that my heart was dead.

I carried on like that for a week. A zombie of my former self. No, I was my former former self. Before Gage. It just felt like a zombie because I knew what it was like to be alive.

If Jen noticed the fact that I was precisely on time for work every single morning, she didn't say anything, just smiled and handed me a cup of tea, talking about stories, the weather, nothing. It was a kindness, not probing me or my broken heart. Especially since it was already being probed with knives from breathing.

Some women knew you needed to pretend that your world wasn't imploding just to get through the day, that to be a friend was to pretend right along with you.

Jen was one of those women.

Amy was not.

I had purposefully left earlier in the morning so as not to catch her wanting to walk with me—though she didn't do it as often, as she'd walked in one morning to Gage fucking me against the wall. She hadn't even blushed, just nodded once and said, "As you were."

I nearly vomited at the thought that it would never happen again.

Gage would never be inside me again.

I knew Amy would make me face reality, that she'd try to help me heal, help me fight. She was that kind of woman. All of them connected to the club were.

Hence me avoiding them.

Ignoring all the calls and texts.

Until Friday came and so did a knock at the door.

I was going to ignore it, but it was purposeful and obviously not to be ignored. And I didn't procrastinate. Because logical people didn't do that.

My legs were dead weights descending the stairs.

I had barely opened the door before a small and surprisingly strong figure pushed through it. She was a flash of blush pink and a floral perfume that definitely smelled expensive.

"Wh... Gwen?" I stammered, looking back up as she glided up my stairs effortlessly in shoes I would've tumbled from on a flat surface.

"I'm getting us wineglasses. We need wineglasses," she called over her shoulder, disappearing in the direction of the kitchen before I could tell her I didn't have wineglasses.

Or wine.

And I couldn't follow her and tell her that because a baby— yes, a live human *baby*—was thrust into my arms.

A beautiful and rather frustrated-looking—yet still crazily inhumanly put together—Amy stared at me. "Take him, would you please? He's being a total asshole."

I looked down at the baby in my arms, who was just as surprised as I was to be there. He was probably one of the most beautiful infants I'd ever seen, with striking large green eyes and a smattering of amber hair on his adorable little baby head.

Amy winked at me, and it was then I realized she'd been holding her baby in one hand and a bottle of wine in another. Like Gwen, she traipsed up my stairs in heels even higher than the woman before her, and a figure that was scientifically impossible given the age of the beautiful and placid baby who was happily toying with locks of my hair.

"You can't call your own baby an asshole, Amy," a soft voice called to her.

It belonged to Lily, who was holding an adorable baby and smiling at me in sympathy and apology before hustling in my door.

"Um, yes I can if he's being one," Amy said, stopping on the stairs and looking from the baby to Lily. "And he's his father's son. So he's being an asshole. And he'll grow up to be an asshole. But he'll get his mother's looks. And wits. So hopefully he'll pull off being an asshole, like his father seems to do." And then she disappeared at the top of the stairs.

"It's easier if you just go along with it," Lily said. "They mean well, really. Apart from when they call babies assholes." She gave me another shy smile that lit up her almost violet eyes. The same eyes the quiet baby in her arms had.

And then she followed Amy up the stairs.

Mia was next. "Don't worry, I didn't bring the hellions," she said, kissing me on the cheek. "I brought something better." She held up two bags. "Processed sugars and complex carbohydrates!" And then Mia went up my stairs too.

Bex wasn't smiling or holding anything like the rest of them. Her gaze was hard and a little intimidating.

"He's doing absolutely fucking horrible, if that helps," she said.

My stomach clenched and I squeezed the tiny human in my arms for some strength. "No, it doesn't," I whispered.

She nodded. "It never does." She nodded to the stairs. "At least these mad bitches might serve as a distraction. Or at the very least a reminder that you're not alone."

And she climbed the stairs too.

I waited just in case anyone else decided to show up.

In case one person in particular decided to show up,

But his bike wasn't sitting in the spot where no one was allowed to park. No, a cherry red BMW with a car seat was parked there, half on the curb and half off.

I stared at it for a long time. Then the small human in my arms started to fuss.

So I closed the door and climbed the stairs too.

"THAT'S *IT*?" Gwen nearly spluttered her glass of wine from her mouth. "He doesn't want marriage or kids?"

I chewed my lip, hoping for a small amount of pain to distract me from the massive hole in my heart.

It didn't work.

"Um, yeah. Is that not enough?"

She nodded, then shook her head. "For normal men, maybe. And for normal women. Gage sure as shit isn't a normal man. Like *way* off the spectrum." She leaned forward and patted my hand. "In a good way, of course."

"Or in a bad way," Bex interjected.

"Which is, of course, absolutely good," Amy put in.

"Great," Mia said with a grin.

Lily just shook her head and smiled, mouthing, "Go with it."

The hand patting my own moved to squeeze it. "And honey, you're nowhere near normal," Gwen continued, her voice warm. "That's a good thing. The best. Because normal is boring. A construct. And not something men like ours live within. They tend to smash down constructs."

"Or blow them up just because they're *bored*," Bex cut in.

Amy gave her a look. "But we got to toast marshmallows on the flaming remains. Plus Lucky bought you a kickass cherry-red Jeep to replace. Win-win."

Bex shrugged.

I gaped.

"So unnormal and fabulous people don't break up for normal reasons," Gwen clarified.

"Not that this is a real breakup, honey," Mia offered, her eyes soft.

My broken heart—which was a constant ache—sent a sharp burst of pain through my nerve endings. "Yes it is."

She smiled and it was sad. "I know two things, babe. You put Chris Hemsworth in a movie, any movie, I'm watching it. And I know these men. Well, I know my man. And he's beautiful and unique and a total fucking puzzle twenty-three hours and fifty seconds of the day." Her smile warmed. "But he's also of the same breed as all the men of that little club. The thing about these men? Once they find their unnormal and fabulous women, they aren't going to let them go. Like ever." Her eyes shimmered. "No matter what demons they've got clutching onto them."

"Or what demons are clutching onto you," Bex said, her voice scratchy.

My heart bled a lot for these kind women. I knew their histories, their tragedies. Bex's was worse than most, from what I'd heard. And I knew it wasn't the full story, but the bit I'd heard had tears stinging the backs of my eyes before I even knew her.

Now I *knew* her. Knew her connection to Gage that I hadn't had the chance to learn about.

I knew all these women.

What they'd been through should've been enough to take away their ability to smile for life, or at least darken whatever happiness they would ever have. But it didn't. My living room had never shone so bright, felt so warm, and it had nothing to do with the sun streaming in my windows.

"So," Gwen said, jerking me out of my pity for them. They didn't need pity. No way, no how. They'd made it through their darkness to find sunshine. "You and Gage can't possibly be breaking up because of *normal* reasons like marriage and children. That just does not jive."

"Plus," Amy said, draining her glass and leaning forward to pour another, "like Mia said, these fuckers are all of a same breed. And they're all about pounding their chests, pissing circles around us and telepathically tattooing their ownership on our foreheads." She grinned at me. "We mere mortals might not be able to see it, but it's like some kind of flashing sign to every alpha male in the vicinity."

"That or the fact that our men can be scary as all hell when anyone with a dick looks at us the wrong way," Mia interjected. "Zane damn near ripped the arms off a guy in the supermarket who was just asking me my opinion on what peppers he should buy. I mean seriously, *peppers.*"

Amy grinned at her. "Honey, he was *not* asking you about peppers."

Mia furrowed her brow. "How do you know? You weren't even there. I could have the look of a pepper connoisseur, if you will. The Jamie Oliver of pepper choice."

A chuckle almost escaped my mouth, taking me by surprise. I didn't think I'd feel like smiling, let along laughing, for the longest time.

"Have you looked in a mirror lately?" Amy asked. "Because I'm sure the thing you see is not a pepper connoisseur. It's a stone-cold MILF."

"I'm not stone cold," Mia argued. "I'm smokin' hot, thank you very much. I'm married to stone cold." Her face brightened. "Oh my God, that's a wonderful new nickname. I'm getting Zane and I T-shirts and we'll wear them to the supermarket."

Amy rolled her eyes.

"Seriously, that would make a great TV show," Mia continued, eyes dreamy. "Smokin' Hot and Stone Cold put away another ruthless killer, plus bust a cockfighting syndicate."

"I don't think it's called a cockfighting syndicate," Lily said, eyes light.

Mia waved in dismissal. "Details. I'll pay writers to do the boring research. I've got the million-dollar idea, plus the pretty face. I've got to give them *something* to do."

"Technically *I* gave you the million-dollar idea," Amy interjected.

Mia waved again. "More details. I'll mention you in my Emmy acceptance speech."

Amy narrowed her eyes. "I want 50 percent."

Mia narrowed hers back. "Thirty."

"Forty-five."

"Thirty-two."

And somehow, when I'd been so sure that heartbreak had

physically severed the muscles necessary for me to smile, the corner of my mouth turned up.

It wasn't much, but it was something.

And when you were dying from the inside out, not much was better than nothing. It was the only thing left to hold on to.

SIXTEEN

I woke up coughing.

Being strangled by the very air around me. The air inside my lungs. An invisible hand clutching at my throat.

At first, my sleep-addled mind thought it was a panic attack that had woken me up from a nightmare—something that happened rarely but enough for me to know that it would pass, as long as I realized it was my mind controlling my body's processes and not my body itself failing. It wasn't a surprise, since in the nights I had slept in the past week, I had woken up with that same strangling feeling.

But my eyes burned as I tried to blink away the last of my sleep, and a bitter and acrid smell filled my nostrils.

Smoke.

Smoke was filling my room, and I was coughing because it was entering my lungs and I couldn't breathe through it.

My body worked for me while my mind tried to grasp the reality that my apartment was on fire. Panic clutched at my chest with the same force as the smoke that had filled my bedroom.

The wood of the floor was still somehow cool on my bare feet.

Was that good?

No, nothing was good. My freaking house was on fire. I was going to be burned alive.

Calm down, Lauren. Panic will kill you surer and quicker than the fire. Especially since smoke inhalation is one of the main killers in house fires.

Right. The longer I stayed in one place freaking out, the longer I was letting smoke pollute my lungs and slowly rob me of the ability to breathe and live.

I was attached to the ability to breathe.

Gage's face entered my mind, and instead of the chaos he usually brought, he urged calm.

If I wanted to be around for his chaos, I needed the calm to keep me alive. I needed to believe what the women had told me that afternoon, that this wasn't the end of us.

If I was going to live for anything, I was going to live to make sure they were right.

I looked around my bedroom, which was hard to do with all the smoke, but there were no flames which meant the fire hadn't spread. There was a window directly off my bedroom, and an attached fire escape. It wasn't in the best condition, rusted and unused; it was more for the aesthetic of a New York-style building than anything else.

My hands fumbled on my nightstand, finding purchase on my phone as everything else tumbled to the floor, including my glasses. But I needed the phone more than I needed to waste time scrambling for them. So I tightened my grip around the device, then rushed over to the window, yanking up my nightshirt to cover my face from the worst of the smoke.

Tears poured down my face as the fumes burned my eyes, and I tried to blink them away furiously, not rub them—that would make it worse.

I fumbled against the window fastenings, yanking at the

wood to bring the crisp night air into the room. Saltiness from the ocean battled against the scent of the smoke rushing out to meet it. I sucked in desperate and hungry breaths, my body crying out for clean air. Of course, that made me splutter and cough, and my throat burned, but I could breathe. And that was the most important part.

My vision was still blurry from not picking up my glasses, but I didn't need to see in order to kick my leg out the window and lay my foot on the chilly iron of the fire escape.

It creaked slightly as I put pressure on it, and I really hoped it would hold my weight. I blinked away the worst of the grit in my eyes and glanced down at my phone, typing three numbers into the unlocked screen—maybe I was wasting time by calling 911 before I was safely out of my apartment, but if the fire escape failed me, I'd go tumbling to the ground, and even though the fall was only one story, I'd likely be injured. Maybe too injured to call anyone.

My area of town was all but deserted at that time of the night. Plus, fire was silent, tearing through the night with only heat and smoke and amber flames to alert anyone of its presence. I was lucky it didn't just kill me as I slept.

So unless someone was taking a moonlit stroll, I couldn't take my chances on someone else noticing it. It could be too late.

The phone was to my ear and the shrill dial tone never seemed louder, nor did a response from the other end of the phone seem to take longer.

"911, what's your emergency."

"My name is Lauren Garden and my apartment is on fire," I said, my voice raspy yet somehow even. "It's 35 Ocean Blvd. Hurry," I pleaded.

"Miss, I'm going to need you to—"

I cut the call off. I didn't need a trained professional, miles away and safe in their office, to try and calm me down. I needed to do that. Plus, they couldn't save me. Nor could the man whose image had been tattooed on my mind since I awoke with death in my throat minutes—or was it hours?—before.

I had to save myself.

And standing half in, half out of my apartment wasn't going to do that. I had to make a choice.

As I was about to take my chances with the integrity of the ladder, I paused. One side of my body was prickled with goose bumps as the air assaulted my bare skin, the other burning with the rapidly increasing temperature of my apartment.

The apartment that was *on fire.*

A fire that would likely rip through most of my possessions before the local fire brigade could put it out. We didn't have a round-the-clock crew in Amber. We were a small town, barely needing the few paid firefighters we even had. The rest were volunteers, which meant they would need to yank themselves from their beds, race over to the station, wait for their crew, and then come over.

My apartment would likely be cinders by then.

As well as everything inside it.

My paintings.

I had pulled my foot back in the room and was halfway to the door before I figured out what I was doing, I reached back and yanked at the throw I had on the end of my bed.

It was stupid. Reckless. Maybe suicidal to go back into the structure that was on fire when the fresh air and safety was only feet—and a short, treacherous climb—away. But it was also unthinkable to let years, decades of my work, those pieces of my soul, just melt away and become nothing but ash.

They were my *memories.*

All the beautiful ones, and more importantly, all the ugly ones. How was I supposed to even live with myself if I didn't at least try to save some of the only things I had left of him? Of myself before he was gone?

With one hand, I whipped off my nightshirt, thankful I was wearing a cropped Calvin Klein tank underneath. It wouldn't do much for the local firefighters to rescue my topless self from a burning building.

Or your shirtless corpse, a voice shot at me. The sensible voice that was also urging me back to the window as I sloppily tied my shirt around the bottom half of my face.

For the second time in recent months—the first being when I'd hopped onto the back of the motorcycle in the middle of the night—I ignored that voice.

And I used the throw still in my hand to turn the handle and wrench the door open. Heat assaulted me with such force that I was certain my skin had been flayed from my face.

It hadn't, but I likely would've needed to pencil in an eyebrow appointment—if I survived, that was.

Though smoke was thicker and my vision blurry, I still saw the flames. Caught them eating up sections of my sanctuary without mercy, without hesitation. The vision of my home being taken away from me, literally before my eyes, punched me in the chest harder than the wall of smoke and flames.

Move, a different voice than the one before ordered. *If you're going to do this, there's no time to stop and mourn, to be weak. You've got to be quick if you want to succeed. If you want to survive.*

Again, without thinking, I slammed the door to my bedroom shut, having realized I'd left my window open, and standing in the doorway was not only eating away at time, it was giving the flames what they needed to breathe, to quicken. The one thing *I* needed to breathe—oxygen.

My eyes focused on the room, the way the fire was thickest at the front of the apartment, eating away at the frame of the structure already. It was closing in on the door to my studio, but it had yet to fully engulf it.

Which meant this idiotic crusade could still work.

And I moved. Against the smoke that clutched my throat from the inside, that worked into my eyeballs like glass, and the heat of the flames that were fingernails ripping at my skin.

I wrapped the blanket around myself to try to protect my bare skin from the worst of it. But it wouldn't do much.

I'd forgotten about the need for the blanket to shield me from the worst of the heat from the door handle, scalding my palm on the burning iron.

The pain was immediate and intense. Enough to yank last night's pasta from my stomach and have it almost crawl up my throat.

Almost.

I made myself turn the knob, even as I felt my skin melting, charring against it. The pain took over everything—or *tried* to take over everything. But then I made myself think about how excruciating the small patch of burning on my palm was. Then considered what that would feel like covering my entire body.

And it got me moving. It was almost a blur, like someone else with more strength of will was manning the controls inside my brain. Then I yanked the small window in my studio open, with my uninjured hand.

The air kissed me, taunted me with its cooling and clean oxygen.

I coughed into it and tried to suck up as much unpolluted air as I could. But I didn't have time for that. I was scooping canvases and throwing them out the window before I could think about what would happen to them if they landed wrong on the concrete below. They could be ruined and smashed from the fall and I could've almost—maybe actually—killed myself trying to save them.

I couldn't think about that. So I didn't.

The air increased in heat and intensity. The window I was throwing my canvases out of was tiny, not designed for a person climbing in and out of. Nor did it have a ladder attached to get me safely to the ground.

A quick glance to the flames licking the door told me I only had seconds. I snatched at the prints that were closest to my heart, that wouldn't be able to be thrown out the window. The sketchbook full of memories too raw to be on display in the room. And then I ran. The wood was unsteady and hot against the balls of my feet, and I stumbled as something stabbed into my foot as I was halfway back to my bedroom door. The pain was intense, but nothing compared to my palm, which answered the call of the flames around it, itching to consume more of my skin.

I moved through the flames, stopping right in front of the door I'd closed for all of those sensible reasons, like not letting the flames spread. Now one of my hands was all but useless, the other clutching the images I'd risked my life for.

Smoke curled in my throat, seemed to fill it with ash. My body tried to repel it as I coughed uncontrollably, panicking as the fit didn't give me any space to suck in what little air was left in the room.

My body swayed.

My throat was closed.

Eyes filling with grit.

I'm going to die.

And then the door was wrenched open, a figure darker than smoke filling it. The figure that rushed at me and had me gathered in its arms before I realized I'd collapsed into them.

"Lauren," he growled against my neck as he buried me into it. I clutched my art to my chest as my coughing slowed and stopped, Gage striding across the room and through the open window.

The air was cool and beautiful and clean. But I already had beautiful and clear air the second my face pressed into the bare skin of Gage's neck.

I worried about how Gage was going to maneuver the fire escape while carrying me. I worried about the rust on the fire escape and the considerable amount of weight Gage's muscled form added to the load the aged iron would have to take on.

But I needn't have worried, because this was a man who I'd been sure would've been able to save me in the middle of a plane crashing. And I'd had that thought the second I met him, when I knew nothing about him.

And now I knew everything about him, and I knew I was in safe arms. No matter how sure he was that they were going to destroy me. They were the only thing that was going to save me.

Then those arms were shaking me. Or was the world shaking?

Of course the world was shaking. It always did with Gage.

"Lauren, baby. Please, I need you to breathe." His growl was thicker than the smoke taking up residence in my throat. It was full of more pain than the sharp and burning sensation in my palm.

My throat cleared and my chest burned as I sucked in the air that Gage was so desperate for me to welcome. And welcoming that banished the darkness creeping at the sides of my consciousness.

"Fuck. Okay, that's it. That's my girl," he murmured.

I was rocking. There were lips against my head. Sirens were either far away or really close; my ears couldn't hear anything but my strangled breathing and Gage's soft murmurs.

It was an effort to push past the grit and smoke in my eyes, but I did it. The world was too dark and too bright at the same time. Blurry.

My glasses were probably melting.

Like I would've been.

"You saved me from a burning building," I croaked.

The lips left my head, and Gage's sharp features cut through the soft and blurry edges of my vision.

"Saving someone from a burning building doesn't do much for the street cred of a self-professed villain," I teased, the words glass against my throat. "You're going to have to kick a puppy or something."

The arms around me tightened. "I didn't save *someone*," he growled. "I saved you. And you're not someone. You're the fuckin' only one. And you saved me by suckin' in that air. By openin' your beautiful eyes."

"Well how about we save each other?" I offered as the darkness danced in my vision again. "You know, it's only fair in a post-feminism society."

And that was how I passed out. Not saying soulful and romantic words to the man who had saved my life.

No, commenting on the state of affairs in regard to gender equality.

IT WAS the air that woke me up.

Much like the way the lack of it had jerked me awake when my apartment was on fire.

But it wasn't the lack of it. It was the *abundance* of it.

Not dirtied by smoke but stripped of all bacteria, full of disinfectant. A hospital. I knew before I opened my eyes because of the smell. Because of the scratchy sheets covering me. The gentle beep of what I guessed was the heart monitor.

I had almost died in a house fire.

It was the logical place to be taken, after all.

"Well, burning your own house down is a bold move to get his attention, and it worked. Color me impressed."

I craned my neck to see a black-haired, tattooed, and beautiful woman sitting beside me. Her arms were crossed, eyebrow raised as she regarded me. Everything about her should've made such a stare hard: the heavy liner around her eyes, the stark black of her clothing, the fact that her body was covered in tattoos.

But it wasn't. Because it wasn't the outside that governed how someone made you feel when they stared at you. It was what was inside their irises. Behind their words.

I knew that better than most people.

"I would say it's a totally crazy move, but my husband blew up my car because he was *bored*." She shrugged. "So I'm not one to judge."

I smiled. Tried to speak, but all that came out was a hacking cough.

Her teasing smile left.

"You're not supposed to talk for a hot minute," she said, eyes dark. "You know, considering the fact that you almost freaking died of smoke inhalation." She narrowed her eyes. "Don't do that again. You scared the shit out of everyone. Sure, they've been waiting for *something* to happen, but not this." She scanned my hospital bed. "I'll give you a rundown. Every single woman is in various states of motion. Amy has been on and off with Barney's all morning getting you a new wardrobe." She winked. "She's like, a fricking lifetime member there." She sat back, folding her arms. "Mia is on the phone with contractors, yelling at them and telling them to drop everything they're doing to work on the place the second the fire inspector's done. And he'll be done soon since Mia has already spoken to him too. Lily has checked you over, because she's totally more competent than any doctor, and you're only in here as a precaution. You burned your hand pretty good."

My eyes went down to the hand in question, the white-hot

memory of the pain overtaking me. The skin felt hot, scalding, the pain intense but not unmanageable. Likely because I was on some heavy painkillers.

"It's going to take a bit to heal, and there's going to be a scar," Bex continued. "But you've already got those. This is just one the world can see."

My eyes shimmered with her words, the knowledge in them.

"And the cause of the fire is now being determined," she said, moving on. "There's a guard posted outside the door, because well, it's *Gage*." She rolled her eyes. "And because I've never seen that man look wilder than when he told me to stand here and guard you with my life." She raised her brow. "And he didn't mean it metaphorically. The fucker would fully expect me to do it. So let's hope this prospect has his shit together if anyone decides to attack." She winked.

Attack?

"But I don't think they will, since everyone's so convinced that this is malice, but the early word is it's electrical. Sometimes there's nothing more malicious than plain old life."

I blinked at her.

"Oh, and speaking of malice. Gage is off planning to kill someone most likely, but I doubt he'll be gone for long, since a fire can't live without oxygen, and that fucker is an inferno and you're the air."

She winked again.

At her words, and the memory of Gage pulling me out of a burning building and knowing he was coming back, I relaxed into the bed. Something I never would've done under normal circumstances.

But normal was a construct.

Thankfully.

Gage

"Who could've done this?" Cade demanded the second he sat his ass at the gavel.

It didn't escape Gage that Cade was looking straight at him when he uttered the question. Now he was faced with his president's blame along with his own.

Not that it added to the weight he'd felt the second he'd pulled up to Lauren's house. Drove past as he had every single night for the past week, but didn't toy with going in like he had before. He'd climbed off his bike the second he pulled up to the curb. When he'd seen the fucking *flames*. Felt the smoke snatch away his oxygen, even though he wasn't near enough to breathe it in.

She had been near enough to breathe it in.

That was enough to suffocate *him*.

The mere fucking prospect of her not drawing air on this earth.

The reality of it was enough to kill him.

He didn't speak immediately, mostly because his fucking throat was paralyzed by the thought of losing her, so Cade continued.

"We aren't running shit that'll get us killed anymore," he said, voice hard, mimicking his face that was the default when sitting in that chair. Despite the relative peace they'd been enjoying, Cade was always bracing. As were the rest of his brothers at the table who had it.

Something Gage vowed he'd never have.

Something to lose.

Because living a hard, fast, and deadly life was fucking great if you were young and stupid or old and tortured. And only if you were willing to get right with the fact that death was something you dealt as well as dodged every day.

But the second you grasped on to something you never wanted death to fucking *breathe* on, let alone touch—that's when you were fucked.

And Gage had watched the men around him finding that shit, getting fucked, almost losing everything that mattered to them. He'd brushed away the demons that had clawed at his mind when he'd done so, and his resolve had strengthened to never be in their position again.

Sure, they had good women who they thought invented fucking Harleys, a family that brightened this shitshow called an existence, but all that could go. Instantly.

Gage's chest tightened as those demons gained hold.

The ones that were as old as he was, and the newer ones, ones that smelled like strawberries and had skin like peaches and cream.

He tightened the grip on the knife he'd been clutching, itching to sink it into flesh. To stain it with the blood of whoever was responsible for nearly taking his woman from him.

Because it had to be *someone*. There weren't just accidental fires that almost took away his entire world. No, that shit didn't happen.

It had to be a real, tangible enemy.

"So what you got going on the side to bring in circumstances that's getting a woman's house burned down, almost with her inside it?" Cade snapped Gage from his thoughts of sinking that knife into someone's flesh.

He met hard gray eyes that had lost a fuck of a lot of their menace thanks to a hot wife and two kids.

"I ain't runnin' nothing on the side," he bit out. "Well, nothing that would have people burning down *my woman's* house, *almost* with her inside it. If they wanted revenge, they'd go for me. And if they were gonna go for her, they wouldn't be going for almosts and burning down a house. They'd be putting a bullet in her brain."

The second the cold and seemingly empty words left Gage's mouth, he wanted to snatch them from the air, rip them into fucking pieces so they didn't exist in this world, so the prospect of his woman staring at him with lifeless eyes did not fucking exist.

He clenched the arms of his chair with enough force to splinter the wood.

"Any way this could've been what the fire inspector is thinkin'?" Cade asked. "Accidental?"

Gage thought on the possibility of a fucking *accident* almost taking Lauren away. A breach in some wire. A stove left on.

Accidents didn't exist in his world.

Not when it came to life and death.

"No," he growled, standing, unable to take the itch for nothingness a second longer. "Someone did this. We'll find them, and I'll flay the skin from their body." He thought of Lauren's blistered and charred palm and fought the urge to carve out his own hand just so she wasn't suffering alone.

But she wasn't.

No fucking way she would be again.

He'd already been trying to find the strength to walk through her door, swallow his words and his demons and give her something. He was never going to be able to exist much longer without everything, not without chasing the nothing of the needle. She was his cure, and he was her disease, but that wasn't stopping him anymore.

"For now, I'm going to my fucking woman."

Lucky exhaled a loud sigh. "You're back together now? I don't have to worry about me getting shot because I drank the last beer?"

Gage glared at him. "My woman was almost burned alive tonight. What the fuck do you think?"

Lucky's expression sobered. "I think maybe you'll shoot me anyway," he murmured.

"Might, if I didn't have somewhere better to be."

And he did.

Home.

SEVENTEEN

Lauren

Two Weeks Later

I couldn't go anywhere alone.

Anywhere.

Even to freaking *work*.

There was someone on a motorcycle sitting outside the offices all day.

All freaking day.

Like some gorilla group might come up and try to kidnap me in the middle of the office.

Jen had peered out the window on the second day I was cleared for work—which was only three days ago, and that had *not* been Gage's choice. In fact, there was talk of handcuffing me to furniture.

"Gage, I'm not going to stop living life because of pain. You taught me that," I whispered.

His eyes hardened. "This is not the kind of pain I was fuckin' talkin' about," he said, cradling my hand. "You should never fuckin' suffer this. You've had enough."

I didn't release his gaze. "No, I've never had enough. Not when it comes to pain."

And then the handcuffs were used. But for a much different reason.

So there I was, working. I couldn't do much, on account of Niles barely letting me do anything because "I'm not getting scalped by your boyfriend if you burst a blister." But I was there. And keeping busy.

"Wow, this man must be super serious about your safety," Jen continued, still peering out the window, cradling her coffee. "And these guys are also seriously *hot*. He's kind of doing us a favor, even if it's unnecessary." She glanced back to me. "The fireman said it was accidental, right?"

I screwed up my nose to fight the stab of pain at the thought of my charred home. It was going to take *months* to repair—fully rebuild in some parts. I obviously had full insurance coverage, because I was me, but insurance couldn't replace what had taken me years to put together.

"You've got your life, Will," Gage murmured. "And I've got you. The rest of it can be rebuilt. Together."

I blinked away the tears. The trauma of having my house almost burn down—with me inside—had kind of distracted me from having to face reality. The one where Gage was back and holding me and not letting me go, his entire form squeezed into my hospital bed, me lying pretty much on top of him. The nurses had tried to stop him, of course, but Gage had glared at them and they'd backed away. And he held me, gripped me like a life raft in the middle of stormy seas. After he'd seemed so adamant to never let me hold him again.

"Together?" I whispered, the one word a pathetic plead. I didn't even care at that point.

He tightened his hold around me. "Of fucking course, babe. You think I'm gonna be stupid enough to let you go when I literally pulled you out of the flames *and* you're somehow still here? Either the Devil or God has given me a miracle. Not stupid enough to let it go."

A tear ran down my face.

Gage wiped it away.

"But you said you couldn't... you didn't want—"

"I was a fuckin' coward. Not sayin' it's gonna be tomorrow. But I'm gonna be ready to give you everything one day. 'Cause you've done that for me. Made me stop cravin' nothing. That deserves everything."

Everything.

Marriage.

Kids.

The things he said he'd never have, the things I understood why he could never have. Because his soul was more scarred than his skin could ever be.

"Gage, you don't—" I started to say, realizing a dream of kids or marriage was nothing when my beautiful nightmare was right here.

And that beautiful nightmare interrupted me, as he was fond of doing.

"You never tried to change me," he muttered, not meeting my eyes.

That's when I knew how much this was hitting him, how much it was scarring him, because Gage never avoided my gaze. Not once. Not when I told him about David with a pain that I guessed was hard to witness. Or the first night we became us, when he told me he'd just killed a man. Not even when he recounted the story of his daughter's death.

"You should've, you know. But you didn't. I showed you how fucked up I was, how wrong, and you didn't try to do shit to make it right." His arms flexed around me. *"Didn't try to make me right."*

"Just because you're not right doesn't make us wrong," I said. "In fact, it's what makes us. You. Because I don't have to battle being broken anymore."

He stared at me for a long time.

"Neither do I," he said. "And that means I want to try with you. Give you things I thought I'd never have again. Because thinkin' even for a moment that I'd never have you here in my arms again, it almost killed me. And I need to give you life in order to make sure I don't die again."

"Well yeah, they said it was accidental," I replied to Jen, jerking out of those memories, the ones that should've been dark and painful since they took place in a hospital room after I'd almost died. But they were the complete opposite.

She turned to face me fully. "But you don't believe them?"

I chewed my lip. "Well, they're the professionals, so I should, and they're right, I *could've* forgotten about my hairdryer. But I just don't see how. I'm really particular about that kind of stuff. Like *really* particular. It just doesn't seem likely that I'd forget something so obvious."

Gage was of the same opinion. Because he knew me. And he didn't "give a fuck what assholes with clipboards said." Which was why, when he wasn't with me—which was pretty much all the fricking time—he was at the club, or out "following leads." Which he'd told me himself was literally beating up people who may have some kind of grudge with him. Enough to try to burn down my house.

But apparently that list was small.

"Anyone has a big enough grudge with me to try shit, I kill them before they get the chance to carry it out," he'd told me.

So there was that.

Which meant we had to start to believe the impossible, since we'd ruled everything else out. That it really was just a hairdryer I'd forgotten to unplug. No late arrival of some kind of courtship drama that was somewhat of a tradition in the Sons of Templar family.

I'd expected everyone to be disappointed with all the teasing Amy had been subjecting me to before. But there had been no teasing when she came to my hospital room and yanked me into her arms.

When she'd pulled me out of her embrace, she'd wiped her eye. "Now, I've told Barney's you're a six, but you feel like a four, so I've got some calls to make." She'd turned to walk out the door and paused, looking over her shoulder. "And if you ever almost die in a fire again, I'll kill you."

But I still had my guard while Gage was away doing Gage things. Most Gage things were him gently and maddeningly making love to me.

Not *fucking*.

Making love.

He had yet to handle me with that beautiful brutality that came before.

"Can't bring myself to bruise the skin that I've seen burned to a crisp in my fuckin' nightmares," he'd rasped, slowly moving inside of me. "Need you to heal first. Need you to heal me first."

As much as my softer and more vulnerable parts enjoyed the change of pace, the darker part of me was crying out for that roughness, relished the annoying itch in my palm.

Jen was regarding me with sympathy as I absently scratched the thin bandage. "Of course you don't want to believe it, babe. But you've been kind of... *distracted* with your new and fabulous relationship, right? When we're in love, all of our normal behaviors kind of fly out the window. We find ourselves stopping from

BATTLES OF THE BROKEN   403

doing the things we've always done and start doing things we thought we'd never do."

She obviously didn't know about the brief breakup. I thought I'd done a terrible job of hiding my sorrow. Amy certainly saw right through it, but maybe that was because Brock had likely told her something about Gage.

Jen hadn't even *met* Gage, and she was busy with her own stuff, in and out of the office all week, talking about organizing the "best story of her life" and not telling anyone.

I thought on her words. On the bruises covering my body. On the handcuffs still attached to Gage's headboard.

"Yeah, I guess you're right," I said finally.

ARMS WENT around my waist and I jolted, not even realizing I was no longer alone in the guest bedroom of Gage's house that he'd repurposed into my studio.

His house was furnished with everything from my own that we'd been able to salvage. It was more than I'd expected, since being inside the inferno had me certain it was going to engulf my entire home.

The fire crew had arrived only seconds after Gage made it to the ground with me in his arms.

Pretty much my entire living room was gone. As were all my books, carefully collated and collected over my whole life. That was what hit me. Not my expensive cushions or throws or sofas. No, the two-dollar copy of *The Road* that I'd bought with David when we'd skipped school and trolled the vintage shops. Or the well-weathered copy of *The Bronze Horseman* my grandmother had given me.

Every cover held not only the stories within the pages, but

the ones attached to the books themselves. It wasn't the things I cared about losing.

It was the memories.

I'd broken down. Once.

The first night after I'd been discharged from the hospital and Gage drove me to his place, without question. I had a hideously expensive designer suitcase full of equally hideous designer clothes that Amy had acquired for me.

I'd argued about paying her back, though it would likely cost more than my house repairs, but she'd said, "You bought a round of drinks one time. We're even."

And she was *serious*.

It was too much to take.

So I'd just smiled and nodded, Gage's hand on the small of my back, guiding me onto the curb where an SUV was waiting. Obviously I couldn't ride his bike, and that had me disappointed. We'd had a lifetime packaged into a week without each other. I ached to have my arms around him, to feel the vibration between my legs and the freedom in my soul.

I ached for something else.

Gage.

As if Gage sensed the way my body quivered, his hands bit into my hip. "Soon," he growled in my ear.

And then I paused, not because of the guttural growl. Well, a tiny bit because of it.

Gage was instantly alert, dropping the suitcase with a violence that likely would've made Amy faint and cupping my face. "What, Will?" he demanded, searching me as if I might've gotten shot without him noticing.

"I'm fine," I said quickly.

His eyes immediately went to my bandaged hand, and my foot, also bandaged underneath my flip-flop. Not injured enough to keep from walking, but I had to limp. "You're not fine," he clipped.

"Okay, whatever. But I was thinking about this." I nodded to the curb.

"Can't have you on the back of the bike," he said, misunderstanding my meaning. "No fuckin' way I'm riskin' that."

"No," I protested. "That was the very spot where you dropped me all those weeks ago, without a second glance."

He froze, then snatched me into his arms. "Oh, there was second glance,' he growled. "There were a thousand. All I thought of was you. More than the fuckin' junk. I only left 'cause I thought I was doing you a favor." There was a heavy pause and his eyes darkened. "Fuck, baby, I thought that's what I was doing before. But both times I was being a coward. Runnin' away from you is not something I'll ever do again."

My form stiffened. "You better not. Because I'll chase you, limp or no limp."

The side of his mouth turned up. "Lotta things chase me, Lauren. You're never gonna be one of them. Because you're always gonna be at my side, battling the things that chase the both of us."

And then we got in the car.

And drove to his house.

It was cute, well-maintained and not at all what I expected from Gage.

He carried me inside.

"Gage," I squealed. "It's a bride you're meant to carry over the threshold."

He stopped in the middle of the living room. "I'll just do it twice, then."

I froze and he gently put me on my feet, taking my hands. "I meant what I said, Will," he murmured. "I'm not runnin'. Not from you, or myself."

Then he laid a hot and heavy and desperate kiss on me before I could start crying everywhere.

The crying came later.

In the dead of night when I jerked awake, not because I couldn't breathe but because I could. Because I was terrified that none of it was real. That the fire wasn't. Because if the fire wasn't, then Gage wasn't either.

Then he didn't come back.

Arms tightened around me. "Lauren?" he demanded, voice clutched in worry.

My body shook. "I almost lost everything," I hiccupped.

"The fire didn't take it all, baby. We'll rebuild. I'll rebuild. I promise."

"No," I said against his mouth. "The fire brought you back."

He froze. "You can't say that shit," he growled. "Not when I can't fuck you."

I moved, careful of my hand, running the other down the bare skin of his abs. He hissed and caught my wrist before I could grasp his hard length.

"Lauren," he warned. "I don't wanna hurt you."

"Then don't leave me again," I demanded.

His hand flexed at my wrist. "Never," he promised.

I laid my lips to his once more, kissing him with violence and need. He met me, only just restraining the totality of his own brutal need.

"I need you inside me," I whispered, "so I know this isn't a dream."

There was a heavy pause, and then I was flat on my back, Gage's hands ripping at my panties, kiss ripping at my soul.

"This isn't a dream," he growled, exploring my wetness, preparing me. "This is a nightmare." He thrust into me with a desperation that mimicked mine.

"Then I hope I never wake up," I moaned as he moved slowly.

"Me too, Will."

And then there were no more words.

Only our bodies moving in a painful and beautiful rhythm, chasing away the demons.

Or welcoming them in.

"Will?" Gage said, gently taking the paintbrush from my uninjured hand and turning me to face him.

The vision rocked my world slightly, and not in a good way.

I'd been fighting dizzy spells for the past couple of days, putting it down to all the trauma of the past few weeks.

And smoke inhalation wasn't something easily recovered from. The effects could end up being more severe than actual burns. I kept that in mind while battling nausea and dizziness.

I didn't tell Gage because he was only just starting to treat me like the world wasn't going to break me.

Which meant *he* was starting to break me again.

My wrists were red from the handcuffs used last night.

And I loved it.

No way was I going to risk that beautiful pain for something that Gage couldn't control anyway.

"I'm good," I told him, finding concern in his blank stare.

He frowned at me, as if he could see something more. But then he yanked me in for a brutal kiss before tucking me into his side and looking at my latest project.

No one else was allowed to look at my works in progress. It was like gazing at my insides during open heart surgery, seeing all those ugly pieces before someone covered it with skin.

But Gage had seen all my ugly pieces.

And there was no hiding from him.

"Wow, baby," he murmured, eyes running over the canvas.

It was David's face. Which wasn't unusual, considering most of the paintings in the room—the ones we'd actually saved, that hadn't been damaged from the fall—were all the broken beautiful men I loved. Gage and David.

Most of the ones of David were memories I'd snatched from him laughing, smiling, living.

This one was different.

This was his face, curled into a feral grimace, much like the one I'd seen on the dealer who'd sold him his death when he was pleading for a fix that day in Gage's warehouse. One half of his face was painted in brutal detail, down to the tiny mole on the corner of his lip. The other half was melting, as if fire were making the paint drip and sizzle. Bones of his face were exposed, crumbling, decaying. The part of him no one had seen. Not even me.

I was seeing it now, ten years too late, and that was because of Gage. And that was the greatest gift he could give me, understanding what lived underneath David's skin so I didn't torture myself quite as much for not noticing it.

"Is it too ugly?" I asked, biting my lip. It was unlike anything I'd ever done. I'd painted my own ugliness, but also made it beautiful.

"Yes," Gage said immediately, and my stomach clenched, not just from the ever-present nausea. "And that's what makes it magnificent."

I smiled and glanced up at him. "I love you," I whispered.

He smiled. Actually smiled. "I love you too, Will."

The moment was utter sweet perfection, so it only made sense that bitter ugliness would soon tear through it.

Gage

He was comfortable.

That's what did it.

Because the fire had scared him more than anything in his entire life—he hadn't been scared when he'd found his daughter, because the worst had already happened; he hadn't had the luxury of fear, only the punishment of sorrow—but it had also relieved something in him. Relaxed it.

Because that was it. The thing everyone had been waiting for.

Bracing for.

But they were fucking *wrong*.

And being wrong in their world wasn't just dangerous. It was fatal.

They were in church.

The women were all outside, cackling, drinking, and playing with the kids. He'd caught Lauren nuzzling Brock and Amy's kid and it had hit him in the gut. With the thought of her holding their baby, treating it with every ounce of love and care it deserved. Showing him the beauty of hope. Of family.

It hurt because his little girl should've been in that family.

It killed because she wasn't.

And Gage wanted to burn the world to the ground for that fact alone.

But Lauren was showing him that destroying the world wasn't his only option.

It would hurt, but everything in his life did.

And it would be worth it.

"Lauren doing good?" Cade asked as he sat at the ahead of the table. "She looks a little pale."

Of course the fucker would notice that. He noticed everything.

Gage did too.

So he'd seen her gray pallor getting worse over the past week. Watched her curves lessen slightly as she only took small bites of the meals they'd shared, lying about having a big lunch.

It worried him. But he also did the math, and it got him doing something he never should've been doing.

Hoping.

Thinking about his woman growing with his baby.

Giving him another reason not to destroy the world.

"She's fine," he clipped, sitting down, not ready to voice his hope till Lauren told him.

"Good. No way could the world handle it being any other way," Cade said dryly.

They'd been there when Gage tortured every person who may have had something to do with the fire. Watched him refuse to give mercy.

And they just knew him.

"Still can't believe that's your girl," Asher said, looking to the sounds of the laughter.

Gage's entire body stiffened as the demons she tamed when she was in his presence reared up immediately.

His eyes narrowed on his brother. "That's my fuckin' *woman*," he hissed. "You got something more to say about her?" It was a challenge, a dare for him to keep talking about the perfect fucking being Gage had somehow managed to clutch in his scarred and bloodstained hands. He was willing to kill for her in a heartbeat.

His loyalty to his brothers wasn't even important if someone, even fucking Asher, tried to come for her.

Asher held up his hands in surrender. He'd seen that reaction before. All the brothers had. Just not usually directed at someone wearing a Sons of Templar patch.

"No, brother. Not anything bad, that's for sure... which is kind of the point. I don't think it would be humanly possible to say anything bad about her. Which is why I'm confused as all hell. She's not crazy. And she's yours, that's fuckin' easy to see." He paused, looking at the door. "And fuck, you're hers too. Blind man could see it. But fuck, I just imagined you with some crazy badass chick who blew up kittens or something."

Brock chuckled.

Even Cade smirked.

Gage did not. Because Asher had hit some form of truth without knowing it, and something tugged at the corner of Gage's mind.

"Get with the program," Lucky interrupted Gage's thoughts on stabbing Asher. "This fucker would *never* find a woman to out-crazy him. If he did, it would not end well. Only so much depravity can exist within an enclosed space, you know? And Gage has Amber and the greater Southern California area covered. Even fucked-up crazy motherfuckers like Gage need something to keep them a little sane. Like their constant, you know? Like a lighthouse. She's his lighthouse."

The entire room looked at Lucky. Gaped at him.

As did Gage. Because the motherfucker was right. Lauren was his fucking lighthouse.

"All right, I'm callin' Nicholas Sparks and tellin' him he's outta the job, because you're gonna be killing the romance world if you keep talkin' about fucking lighthouses," Brock said.

But he stopped talking about lighthouses.

Because Amy burst into the room, and the look on her face had every single man standing and drawing their pieces.

"You don't need them," she said, eyes on the guns, her voice quiet, shaking. "But Gage...."

She didn't finish speaking before Gage sprinted past her and into the silent living room.

As silent as a fucking tomb.

Which it was.

Since in the middle of it, Lily was doing CPR on Lauren's fucking prone body.

"I'M afraid I can't tell you anything, sir, since you're not family."

Gage's fists tightened beside him and his skin crawled with

the need for a fix. The need for blood. Violence. His mind craved something, anything to take the edge off.

"I'm afraid I'm gonna have to rip one of your fuckin' arms off if you don't tell me exactly what I need to know in the next thirty seconds," Gage bit out, voice even, words a promise.

He wouldn't fuckin' hesitate to put the doctor through the glass doors directly in front of them. The only thing giving him pause, keeping the little fuck alive, was the possible fact that Lauren might need the doctor.

The fuck in the white coat paled and tried to step back, eyes darting around for the security they'd taken care of on arrival. They'd done this shit before. Too many fucking times.

"Not so fast, Doc," Brock said, grinning as he stood behind the doctor, hindering his escape. His grin was more a baring of teeth, the rest of his brothers taut and wired, Gage expected out of concern for another woman wrapped up in this shit. A woman his wife had become close with, and the fucker would rip the stars from the sky if they were just a smidge too bright for Amy. So he was about to do anything he could to make sure she wouldn't be burying her new friend.

That they wouldn't be burying Gage's *woman*.

His insides coiled and shredded with the mere thought of that. The paralyzing terror that came with the thought of having to stand while another precious thing in his world—the last he'd ever had—was covered with dirt.

No, it was simple. He wouldn't be standing if that happened.

He'd be burying the person responsible.

He'd be covered in their blood and pain.

Then he'd plunge a needle into his vein, pump so much junk into his blood that it wrenched him down into the grave.

He wouldn't survive losing her.

That much was certain.

Which was the rest of the reason that Brock wasn't letting the doctor go anywhere. Why both Bull and Cade flanked Gage, Ranger and Lucky close by. Because every single brother knew what Gage was capable of. Knew how unhinged he was in the best of circumstances.

This was not the best of circumstances. This was the worst of them.

So they knew Gage might very well burn this fucking building to the ground if shit went any further south.

But was there any further south than Hell?

Gage didn't think so.

His brothers were there to make sure the doctor gave them answers.

But they were also there to lock Gage down if he uttered a death sentence.

"I'd start thinking of us as family right about now," Brock continued, clapping the doctor on the shoulder. "Since we *really* look out for our family. Personally, I make sure my slightly unhinged brother doesn't rip the arms off doctors I consider family. Doctors who tell me shit, that is."

The man's cheeks reddened with panic, his previously sterile and detached demeanor dissipating in the face of his possible demise. His throat trembled as he struggled to swallow.

"Ms. Garden is currently in a coma," he said, voice slow.

Gage's heartbeat slowed right along with it, his entire body beginning to shake.

"Easy, brother," Bull said from behind him, likely preparing to hold him back if he decided it was time the doctor retired.

Gage barely heard him, his effort going toward staying lucid, to holding on to the slim hope that the world wasn't going to take the last chance of his survival away from him. He was teetering on the edge of true insanity. The doctor didn't know it, but he held Gage's life—and his own—in his hands.

"Her liver and kidneys had begun shutting down," he continued. "At this stage, we're working toward stopping it. But we're not sure what's causing it, so we're tentative to use any drugs to counteract her organ shutdown..."

"How the fuck can you not know what's causing it?" Gage demanded. "You're fucking doctors. That's your job." His voice was low. Controlled. Calm.

On the outside, at least.

The closing of the ranks around him told him his brothers recognized the tone. The one Gage used when he was shutting down his humanity to prepare himself to paint the world with his pain.

With blood.

Death.

"I'm trying to do my job," the doctor said. "We're doing everything we can with the information at hand. At this stage, we need to run more tests. Need to see if her lifestyle—"

"She's thirty years old, healthy, doesn't drink. Doesn't smoke. Doesn't even fuckin' *drink soda*," Gage interrupted before the doctor could say something that might get him killed before he could save Lauren. And he fucking would save Lauren. There was no other choice. No other option.

Gage forced his hands to stay at his sides when they itched to grab the lapels of that coat, shake him until he got the answer he wanted. "There is no natural fucking reason for her to be lying in that bed. So you find the unnatural one. You save her, you might save yourself too."

And on that, he turned and walked out. Before he could do something he wouldn't regret, but that might get him killed.

And he still had a reason for inhaling and exhaling.

For now.

GAGE'S DEATH threats had been real enough to get him into the ICU, where Lauren was currently attached to numerous machines.

Keeping her alive.

His entire vibrant, beautiful and broken world was being kept alive by fucking *machines*.

His knees gave out beside her bed. He collapsed to his knees, his arms outstretched over the mattress, clutching her hand.

It was cold.

Like his blood.

Like his soul.

He stayed kneeling for a long time. Mostly because he couldn't physically make his body obey, his mind keeping him down with images of Lauren's body decaying underneath the dirt.

"Never in my life asked you for anything," he said to the room. "And you've only given me things in order to take them away. To punish me for every single one of my sins. Maybe I deserve it, but *she* doesn't. No way in fuck, if you exist—which I highly doubt—would you let her wither away like this. It's not fucking *worthy* of her. She deserves life. Maybe not one with me, but I don't care. With everything you've taken away from me, I deserve that much. Her. And you're *going* to give me her. Because if you do exist, and I lose her, I'll do what even the Devil didn't manage to do. I'll reach up there and fucking lay waste to the heavens."

That was where he was at that moment.

So fucking helpless he was taking to praying to and threatening an absent God.

Because that was all he could do.

Pray.

TWENTY-EIGHT THOUSAND, eight hundred seconds passed until someone answered that prayer.

Or the threat.

Gage was thinking it was the latter.

That was why no one's prayers got answered.

Because they weren't brazen enough to threaten God.

And threats—promises—were what got shit done.

"Gage?" a soft voice asked.

He jerked to look at the familiar blonde doctor who'd worked on a number of the Sons family. Saved most of them.

She was well regarded.

By Jagger most recently.

Gage stood immediately from where he'd been on his knees.

She didn't comment on that.

"Well?" he barked.

She didn't flinch at his violent tone.

She'd worked with them for years. She was used to it.

She didn't answer, merely moved around Gage, pulling a vial and syringe from her hand and checking Lauren's vitals before she injected the syringe into the IV.

It killed Gage to wait. Be silent.

He wanted to shake the fucking doctor, despite what she'd done for the club, despite the fact that she was a good woman. That didn't mean shit if she couldn't save Lauren.

The world didn't mean shit if they couldn't save Lauren.

She watched the screen where Lauren's vitals had been sitting dangerously low. Just above dead, actually. Gage knew the numbers by heart. They were etched into his insides. He'd been watching them for about twenty-seven thousand seconds, after all.

And then they moved. Which was what he'd been terrified of.

But they moved.

But not down, not pushing him into the ground where the Devil could fully embrace him instead of just sinking his claws into his soul.

They moved up.

He exhaled.

Fully and completely.

Sarah, the doctor, did too.

She faced Gage. "It wasn't making sense that Lauren's organs were shutting down without any obvious illness," she said, clutching his woman's hand with a kindness absent from most in the profession. Detachment was what most doctors worked with; it was needed because, like Gage, they saw too much death to get attached.

"My colleagues focused on finding the illness, because that's how they work, within the rules." She paused. "But I know the club, so I had an inkling that it wasn't an illness. And they don't work within the rules, so I took a chance that what was killing Lauren didn't either."

Gage flinched. The words were spoken with the upmost kindness, but they cut surer and truer than any knife Gage had sunk into his skin.

"Lauren has been poisoned with small doses of Taydoxilne," Sarah continued, eyes on the machines. "I couldn't say for how long, but enough time to slowly eat away at her immune system without her noticing."

"Taydoxilne?" he repeated.

She nodded, still holding Lauren's hand. "It's a new drug, originally created for weight loss, if you could believe it. It was heralded as a miracle because it was a powder that was completely tasteless when dissolved in water and melted off the pounds." She shook her head. "But trials showed that in patients who didn't lose weight, it began to literally eat away at their immune system and organs. So slowly it wouldn't have been noticeable had they not been monitored. Obviously the trial was stopped and the drug discontinued." She frowned. "So I'm not sure how someone got a hold of it to give it to Lauren." She looked to Gage. "I'm sure *you'll* be finding that out."

The words underneath the ones she spoke were very clear.

"I'm sure you'll be making them pay."

He nodded once, violently, unable to speak.

If his mind weren't paralyzed by the sight in front of him, he might've been impressed with the doctor, what hid underneath her professional exterior, something Jagger had obviously seen.

But Gage didn't care about shit right then.

Nothing except the woman in the hospital bed with the slowly climbing vitals.

"I can't say how long she's been exposed. At least a month, maybe more." She gave Gage a hard look. "But it's not something anyone could have caught, not something a big biker could've noticed, unless he had a PhD and was getting weekly blood tests," she said, as if she knew Gage was resting the blame firmly where it belonged, on his shoulders.

Because Lauren didn't live a life where she was slowly poisoned. Gage lived a life where the only thing he loved would be slowly taken away from him though.

"We're lucky Lily was there to administer CPR, that Lauren's strong." Sarah smiled.

"She's going to be okay," Gage managed to grind out. It wasn't a question. It couldn't be a question.

Sarah's eyes met his. "I've given her the same drug used to help the patients in the trials. They all made full recoveries, though they weren't exposed to as much as Lauren, so she might take a little longer, considering she experienced almost complete organ failure. But yes, she'll be okay."

Gage's heart started beating again. For the first time in ninety-nine thousand, one hundred and two seconds.

EIGHTEEN

"Poison?" Cade repeated, his voice holding only the slightest hint of surprise. And with Cade, the fact that there was even a slight ripple in his iron demeanor meant he was shocked.

Gage nodded once, sharply, pain coming with the movement. Because for as long as he didn't see Lauren's open, awake, and alert eyes, everything hurt. Every fucking heartbeat. Sarah said she was going to recover fully, but he didn't believe words. He couldn't, because they were too good to be true. Getting her back when he'd tasted the world without her.

So he would only believe this bitterness was temporary when he heard her voice, saw that light behind her eyes. Because anything less than that would be giving in to hope. And Gage knew hope was deadly.

It had taken everything in him to leave the hospital, despite the fact that her family—who had arrived moments after Sarah had left, Anna leading the fray and giving him a fierce hug—and the women were there, looking out for her. He wanted to be there so she could look out for him. So she could fucking save him by opening her eyes.

But someone had put her in that bed. Someone had thrust him into another level of Hell, one deeper than he ever knew existed.

And that someone had to die.

Which was why he was sitting in church, battling not to tear his fucking skin apart and hoping he'd get to be tearing someone else apart before Lauren put him back together by opening her eyes.

"Fuck," Cade said in response to Gage's nod.

They'd never dealt with this before. All the violence against them had been tangible, something horrible, brutal, but not something fucking invisible, something running through his woman's *veins*. They couldn't beat it out of anyone.

There was muttering around the table.

"Woman's weapon," Bull grunted.

Gage's eyes snapped to him. "What?"

"Poison. It's a woman's weapon. Mia would likely have somethin' to say about me bein' sexist sayin' that, but that doesn't mean it's not true. Men use their fists, use weapons where they can see the damage. The blood. Because men are animals. We're out for blood. Women, on the other hand, are out for *pain*. And they don't need blood, because that's too simple, too obvious, too easy to wipe away. Women like to destroy from the inside out, fight with something that men don't know what to do with."

Silence hung in the air.

Gage burst out of his chair.

Cade's eyes followed him. "You know who did this?"

"Oh I know who fucking did this," he seethed. "Me."

TAPPING on the keyboard was razors inside Gage's skull.

"Jade Masters dropped off the face of the earth approximately two and a half months ago," Wire said, crushing a can in his fist as he finished it. It joined the graveyard of energy drinks that the fucker lived on.

"Soon as I left LA," Gage clipped. "Soon as I scraped that bitch."

More tapping. "Looks like it," Wire agreed.

"Fuck!"

Wire didn't flinch, even though he was so full of caffeine every second that him not having a heart attack was a surprise.

"Should've fuckin' realized the bitch wasn't gonna let it be that," he said, consumed with fury at himself. "Didn't think she'd be that crazy."

"The thing with women, especially scorned women, is that they're always that crazy," Wire replied, not moving his eyes from the screens around him.

"You gonna tell me where I can find her?" Gage demanded, his palms burning with the need for blood. To fucking bleed the bitch dry. Didn't matter that she was a woman. She'd stopped being a fucking person the second she made the decision to even think about taking Lauren from him.

Wire frowned at the screen. "Normally I'd be able to do so in a matter of seconds, but this bitch is good at hiding her tracks. Crazy ones normally are." He glanced at Gage. "You should know that better than anyone."

The door to Wire's cave opened.

Cade locked eyes with Gage, and the look on his president's face made his heart stutter.

"She's awake."

And as much as his body cried out for blood, for death, something fought harder than his demons.

Lauren.

Life.

Lauren

Waking up in a hospital for the second time in a month was not great.

Especially since I woke up feeling like a bus had hit me and I had to comfort my hysterical mother into some semblance of calm, which my grandmother did by demanding she "get your shit together and try not to make your daughter want to lapse into a coma again just to escape your bullshit."

It was safe to say my mother and grandmother didn't exactly get along.

Because my father had chosen my mother carefully. So she was the exact opposite of my grandmother. Sensible. Ordered. Logical. Everything I pretended to be.

Hence me not calling her or my father when my house had burned down. Because it caused worry they didn't need. And I wasn't ready to show my mother who I really was.

We'd called my grandmother, and after making explicitly sure I was okay, she told me it was a good excuse to redecorate.

It took a lot to rattle her.

And after properly looking at her after she yelled at my mother, she looked rattled.

She was still expertly put together, down to her leopard-print heels, but she was coming apart at the seams behind her eyes.

My father stood at my grandmother's words, likely to start an argument, but someone entered the room and snatched away the oxygen.

My inferno.

He didn't even glance at my family who all gaped at him—well, apart from Grandma, who did a finger wave—in utter shock.

Sure, he was shocking at the best of times. With his sheer expanse, his cut, his scars, his muscles.

But this was something else. Where my grandmother was

coming apart at the seams, there was nothing holding him together. His chaos was etched into every inch of him. His hair was wild around his shoulders, tangled as if he'd been almost ripping it out. The veins atop his scarred arms pulsed. His face was painted in pure violence.

Until his eyes met mine.

He was across the room in two strides. My father actually scuttled from my bedside. He had no idea Gage was mine; all he saw was a biker with death in his eyes striding toward his daughter's hospital bed. But still he stepped aside. And I didn't blame my father for that.

The Devil himself would've stepped aside.

Gage reached my bed and my body responded to him violently.

But he didn't touch me.

He just stood there shaking, eyes running over me. No, eyes *clinging* to me, as if I was the only thing keeping him topside.

"Who is that man? Should we call security?" I heard my mother hiss.

"Probably," my grandmother said. "If only for the entertainment of seeing Gage snap him in two." She sighed. "But they need privacy, and as much as I want to ignore that need and watch the show, I'm feeling charitable."

"What?" my mother demanded. "I'm not leaving my daughter in a room with *him*."

Grandma laughed. "You'll have a hard time with her leaving a room without him. Let's talk about this over terrible hospital food. Come on now, shoo."

I didn't even look to the slight scuffle, imagining my grandmother shooing my parents from the room. There wasn't much fight. Battle. Not because they were bad parents but because they didn't fight. Or battle. They just accepted life.

Normal.

"Gage," I whispered, my voice throaty, echoing in the room my parents had long since left.

He'd spent the time just standing there, fists clenched at his sides, staring at me.

He flinched when I spoke.

Flinched.

"This is 'cause of me," he said, sounding more hopeless than I'd ever heard him.

"What are you talking about? Because unless you poisoned me, which you wouldn't because that's far too subtle for you, then this is *not* your fault."

The doctors who'd visited me the second I woke up told me I'd been poisoned. Obviously my mother lost it at that. I'd just nodded.

My grandmother had smiled, but there was a lot of pain in the faux show of happiness. "Only the most fabulous people get poisoned."

My parents had been demanding to know how I, their safe and logical child, could be poisoned.

Then Gage had come in, explaining everything and nothing.

Likely my grandmother was doing her best to tell them, hopefully the bare minimum.

Pain saturated Gage's eyes. And guilt. Similar to what laid behind them when he told me about his daughter, but different.

"It fuckin' is. I did fuckin' poison you. The second I put you on the back of my bike."

I narrowed my eyes. "I thought we'd gone over this. It was *my* choice to get on that bike, and I thank the powers that be every day for that. You're tarnishing me by loving me, Gage. And you're not pushing me away again." It took a lot for me to put strength into those words, considering I was barely recovered enough to stand on my own two feet, but I would've used the last of my life to make sure Gage went nowhere.

His fists tightened. "No, babe, I won't. No matter if it is the best thing for you."

"Gage, don't make me get out of this hospital bed and smack you," I said through my teeth.

He grinned. "Would like to see that, but I'll fuckin' smack you if you move while you're still healin'." His eyes held promise.

And though I'm sure it wasn't the intention, my core clenched at that promise.

"Lauren," Gage bit out. "You're not allowed to look at me like that not only when I can't fuck you, but when I'm trying to tell you somethin' serious."

I rolled my eyes.

"You were poisoned by a woman named Jade."

I froze. Because like when he'd told me about Missy, there was a lot more to the words.

"We used to date in LA," he continued. "No, we used to *fuck*."

I flinched at the words and the images that came with them. I already hated Jade, if not for poisoning me then for having me conjure that image.

Gage clenched his jaw at my flinch but continued. "Was a crazy time for me in general. Got caught up with her. 'Cause she was dangerous, and not in the good ways like you. She was gonna destroy me, one way or another, because she was part of a street gang that made me look well-adjusted. I realized that the second I laid eyes on the bitch. Guess she was a suicide wish wrapped in a woman's body." He shrugged. "Even though things were as good as they could be with the club, my brothers were still *bad*. Was a weak moment, a weak collection of moments adding up to ten years. I was tired. So fucking *tired* of it all. So I toyed with destruction, and I toyed with her. It was toxic. Nasty. She was the human version of heroin, and I got addicted for a while. Not because she made me feel anything, but because she made me feel *nothing*."

He was still as he spoke, didn't move, didn't touch me as I ached for him to do. He just kept talking.

"I realized I might've been tired of the shitshow that was my life, but I wasn't ready for it to be *over*. To stop battlin'." His eyes glittered. "So I scraped her off. She didn't take it well. Shit went down. People died. There was a small gang war." He shrugged. "Thought it was over. Had an inkling to watch out for her comin' back into my life, though I didn't think I'd need to watch carefully because if she did, I'd notice it. Bitch is too crazy to do anything but blow up a building to show me a new pair of shoes or some shit." He shook his head. "Near-fatal mistake babe. It almost cost me you."

Then he wasn't still anymore, moving to kneel beside the bed, clasping my hand in-between his as if he was in prayer. "Never would've been able to live with myself had you not woken up. Had—"

"I did wake up," I interrupted, unable to hear the utter agony, the pure blame in his voice. "So we're going to stop all the self-deprecating shit right now."

His eyes flared at my curse.

I smiled. "Yes, I'm cussing to get your attention."

"Will, 'shit' isn't cussing, and you've already got my attention. You've *always* got my attention," he growled, laying a kiss on the fingers he clutched in his hands.

I sucked in a breath at the small contact. "Okay, well then hopefully you'll hear me when I say this is not your fault. We are not beholden to the actions of others. And we definitely do not take on sins they commit in our name. This woman had you. She lost you. As someone who has you, and has lost you, I know how tenuous that grip on reality can get. I'm not making an excuse for this vile woman. But it's part of my point. There's a reason they call love a disease, Gage. Because it turns foul and fatal when it dies in one person while the other still suffers."

"I *never* fuckin' loved her," he interrupted. "Never loved anyone or anything but my baby girl and you. She never fucking had me, babe. Because there was nothing to have... until you."

"Have you found her?" I asked.

"We will."

"And what will you do when you find her?"

"Oh, I'm gonna kill her."

The words were ugly and hard and should've sickened me. But they didn't.

Because I was already sick.

With that disease they called love.

MY RECOVERY DIDN'T HAPPEN OVERNIGHT. I was close to complete organ failure. To death. I knew just how close because I saw the shadow of the grave in Gage's eyes. Felt it in how lightly he touched me, as if he were afraid a tight grip would be the nail in my coffin.

Someone might hold tighter when they thought someone was going to float away, to the point of pain. But Gage's way was pain. That was his normal.

My grandmother stayed for as long as it took me to get out of hospital—which was almost three weeks in all—by which time my room looked like her New York loft and her LA townhouse had had a baby. Pretty much the second I'd woken up—once Gage had let anyone near me—after she'd scolded me for "giving her the scare of her young life," she'd began decorating. She refused to let me "wither in this depressing room full of death and *polyester*—which are one and the same, if you ask me." And of course, she'd had me out of the hospital gown and into silk pajamas as soon as I was well enough to stand for long enough.

Well, it was *Gage* who'd put me in the pajamas, and though I was well enough to stand—for short periods of time, at least—he refused such a thing to happen, carrying me to the bathroom and changing me. His jaw had been hard during the process. And he'd been silent. His mouth, at least. His demons spoke louder than any words.

His eyes were hard and intense on my stomach, brushing it with his hands before he cradled the flat skin—I had lost a lot of weight, there being a reason they called it 'dead weight,' after all —with his palm. His eyes stayed there for the longest time. I was afraid to move, to breathe, because there was something in that gaze. Something precious and painful.

"Thought you were pregnant," he murmured, eyes meeting mine, hand still on my stomach. "I noticed it, you getting sick, because I notice everything when it comes to you." He paused. "You hadn't had your period, so I thought..."

My stomach clenched.

I had been skipping my period on my birth control because I'd been greedy and selfish and didn't want anything to interrupt what Gage and I had.

"I was terrified at the thought," he continued, voice a low rasp. "Terrified enough that I itched for a needle to take the fear away. But instead I gripped on to you swelling with my baby. Giving me a light I didn't know was left in the world for me."

Tears streamed down my face. Gage's hand left my stomach and brushed them with his thumb.

"That's why I didn't fuckin' do shit," he clipped. "I was too busy being fucking happy that I didn't know my world was eating away at you from the inside out."

I couldn't take anymore.

"Stop," I choked. "You are not allowed to do that, Gage.

Blame yourself, punish yourself for being happy about that. She's not taking that." My voice was feral, as was my soul at that point. I needed her dead at my feet, for making Gage hope for something that scared him more than anything.

And for taking that away.

"She's going to die," I promised, and his eyes flared. "But that hope won't. I won't let it."

I took his hand and placed it on my stomach again.

"One day," I promised.

"After we make her bleed."

I nodded. "After we bury her."

My grandmother was decorating because she couldn't do anything else to chase away the reality that she might've lost another grandchild, the last one she had.

Much like my parents were doing everything they could to chase away the fact that they'd almost lost their last remaining child. So where my grandmother was flitting in and out, trying to convince the doctors that "a coat of paint would be *me doing you a favor* instead of the other way around," my mother hovered. Like didn't leave my bedside. She fussed with my pillows, my water, my heart rate.

It got frustrating.

Especially the better I got.

But I knew I had to let her.

My father was different. Distant. Almost cold. But I knew he cared, considering he barely left either, sitting in the corner of the room, reading the paper, then a book, then another book.

I knew that meant it'd hit him, because my father was not a man to sit and read a book. To sit for long periods of time. My dad 'puttered.' There was always something to fix, a man to see, a job to be done. He was barely stationary. Increasingly so after David's death. Like if he made sure the taps were never dripping, the lawn was always mowed and the gutters were always clear, it might mean he didn't have to face the death of his only son.

But he didn't leave to fix a thing. Barely spoke to anyone, as was his way. He barely blinked at Gage—who was as constant as my mother, but he slept here too, with me tucked in his arms, though I wasn't sure how much he slept—which was not his way. My father was straitlaced. Sensible. Where my grandmother had abhorred all of my beige boyfriends, my father had adored them. Well, in the way he adored people, which was nodding and telling them their investments were "sound."

And it had been in the back of my mind—before I almost died, of course—what would happen when he met Gage. There would be no nods, or comments on investments. There would be drama. Or at least his version of drama, which would've been a furrowing of his brows and a request for a "private word" with me.

None of those things had happened.

But I was finally out of the hospital and would make a full recovery with the proviso that I took it easy for the next month.

My parents had left.

I was glad of it. I loved them both dearly, but it was suffocating, especially since my mother had decided to resurrect David's ghost. She never said his name, but he lingered in the hospital room with her sorrow. I needed to get better, and I couldn't get better around their pain.

We were in my living room. I didn't know how it was almost fully repaired; Gage had obviously stood over the contractors with a gun to get it done.

"Wanted you to come home to your sanctuary," he murmured in my ear as he carried me over the threshold. "And I needed mine back."

And he gave it to me.

For a time.

GAGE

Two Months Later

He was uneasy.

It had been almost three fucking months and they hadn't found Jade. She was smoke, had melted into the air as if she knew it was the one thing that would drive Gage to the edge of insanity.

Lauren was the only thing that held him back.

Barely.

And that was because she was breathing. Healed. Smiling.

Radiating fucking light.

And he had her in his arms.

They were going to find Jade eventually.

And they would kill her.

He needed to find solace in that.

For now, he found solace in the magical creature in front of him.

"Happy birthday," he murmured, hand outstretched

"It's not my birthday," she said, eyeing the envelope suspiciously. Gage was sure she would've treated it like a bomb had it been slightly larger. Though she was getting fuckin' better at handling them than he was. His glasses-wearing, logic-driven woman excelled at making bombs.

He grinned inwardly. "Well of course. It wouldn't have been a surprise otherwise."

She sighed and his dick hardened. With her just fucking *breathing* on him. He wondered if that would ever change, if he would one day stop being so affected by her to the point of madness.

He didn't think so.

She bit her lip. "Gage, my birthday isn't for eight months."

No, he *knew* he'd never stop being affected by her.

He clenched his fists to the sides, mainly to stop himself from forgetting the envelope altogether and fucking her on the kitchen island.

Her eyes flared as she sensed his need. She always did that. Saw right through him, even though he knew for sure there was no emotion on his face. Not an ounce. Didn't matter though, not with his Will.

"Open the fucking envelope," he demanded.

The sooner she did, the sooner he'd bend her over the counter and sink into her hot and greedy cunt. He was getting better. Once she was well enough to take him—really fucking take him—things were bad. And for him to say it, it was *bad*. He needed to be inside her constantly, with a need that surpassed his normal violence. Because fucking her was when he felt the grave the least. When the images of her fucking headstone sitting right beside his daughter's didn't yank fire from the pits of Hell and lay it on his soul.

She took it.

Every time.

Matched his hunger. His violence.

And just when he thought she couldn't take more, she took more.

Fucking *perfection*.

The longer she stayed flush, healthy, the more weight she put on, the more she was able to do without needing to rest, the more she painted, he was able to relax.

Slightly.

As much as was possible for him, at least.

It was hard. He itched for junk, for nothing if not a relief from feeling so fucking terrified all the time. But Bex had picked him up for meetings. Every single day. Only now they were back to once a week, because she seemed to sense that he wasn't as bad.

And it had been *bad*.

In an effort to stave off the bad, he tried something new. He tried doing something good. Something that lay inside that envelope.

Lauren gave him a gut-punching smile and then did as he asked. He didn't breathe as she read the envelope.

He knew it was a risk.

But his existence—including Lauren—was built on risks.

"Gage," she breathed, her eyes wide, still staring at the envelope. She stared for a long time.

Gage waited. The view was fuckin' worth it.

The wait was fuckin' worth it when she moved her eyes upward and locked her gaze with his. They shimmered with tears.

"You rented out the gallery?" she whispered.

Though she was a near expert in reading him like he was fucking Nietzsche, he was still useless as tits on a bull when it came to figuring her out. Gage was able to figure most people out. Because people were simple. Pathetically so.

Lauren was the exception to that rule.

The exception to *every* fucking rule.

So he had no idea what her reaction would be.

"You believe in me?" she asked, her voice low and sweet when he'd been prepared for her to yell about how this was her decision and she should be allowed to make it.

Though he was shocked, he didn't hesitate. He yanked her into his arms, relishing how her soft and warm body melted into his. "Yeah, baby, I believe in you. Only thing I believe in."

She blinked at him through wet lashes. "Okay."

He blinked back, lashes not wet. "Okay? It's that easy? You're just gonna do it?"

"Well, I don't think it's that *easy*, since everything we've dealt with to get us right here has been hard," she said dryly. "I'm ready for a bit of easy."

And Gage, who'd been prepared for his life to be hard until he took his last breath—didn't think there was another way for him to exist—agreed.

That's when the pounding came at the door.

He rested his head against hers, closing his eyes a moment. "I'll get rid of them, Will," he murmured, pressing his lips to her forehead and reluctantly stepping out of her arms. "And then I'm fuckin' you on the kitchen island."

Her cheeks flushed and her eyes flared at his words. Gage left her there before he had to fuck her without answering the door.

He got to the bottom of the stairs and wished he'd done that instead.

"You better have a fuckin' good reason for being here," Gage snarled, looking at Troy and the two uniforms beside him. "'Cause otherwise I'm going to be making my complaints. And trust me, you *don't* want me doing that."

"Going to be hard to do that from a jail cell," Troy said. "Christian Mathers, you're under arrest for murder."

Of course he and Lauren didn't get easy.

NINETEEN

Lauren

"This is a new low, Troy," I hissed across the table.

He looked at me with an expression resembling pity, but I wasn't buying it. Because he had arrested Gage. For *murder*.

And he had all but forced me into the interrogation room with the whole club standing tense sentries like a repeat of last time. Though, unlike last time, I had a sinking feeling that Gage and I wouldn't be walking out of there.

"I have evidence, Lauren," he said evenly. "DNA. Fingerprints."

My stomach dropped, but I didn't let that show. "Doesn't matter. He's innocent." Gage was far from innocent of murder, but of that crime, he was.

Troy stiffened. "You don't even know who it is."

I laid my palms flat on the table. "It doesn't matter, since he didn't do it," I said through clenched teeth.

"What makes you so sure?"

"Because if he did, he wouldn't be stupid enough to leave evidence."

Troy leaned back as if I'd struck him. "Jesus, Lauren," he muttered. "What has he *done* to you? This isn't who you are."

My back straightened. "You don't know a *thing* about who I am, Troy," I hissed. "You think you know everything because of what you see on the surface. Because that's all you see—surface. You have no idea what's underneath."

I stood, the scrape of my chair ringing against the room. "Am I free to go? Or are you going to try to charge me next?"

He sighed, running his hands through his hair. "Of course not, Lauren."

"Right." I turned on my heel, intending to stomp out so I could break down privately in the ladies' room.

I'd give myself two minutes to do that.

That was all.

Because then I needed to get my shit together.

Gage needed me.

And no way was I letting him down.

My mind wandered for a moment to opening that envelope and the feeling of warmth that had spread over me. I held on to that, because no way was I losing it.

"You want to know who it is, the man he killed?"

I stopped with my hand on the door, regarding Troy with carefully blank features. "Sure, tell me the name of the man who you're wrongfully convicting my boyfriend of killing."

"Harvey Hayes."

The name was worthless. I had no idea who he was, and I was about to tell Troy that.

"But I'm sure Gage didn't catch his name before stabbing him in the middle of a bar full of people," Troy continued.

I froze.

For about a second.

BATTLES OF THE BROKEN   437

Then I turned the knob. "You better get your keys ready, Troy, because you're going to be using them to unlock Gage's cell pretty soon."

Then I walked out the door, wishing I believed the words that had sounded so firm.

"ARE you sure you don't want a cocktail?" Amy asked, sloshing her glass at me. "Because if there's ever a time to take up drinking, it's the day your boyfriend gets arrested for murder."

"Don't tell her to drink," Mia scolded. "She needs a clear head for the interview."

"What interview?" Gwen demanded.

Mia rolled her eyes. "The one I'm going to get Lexie's publicist to set up. About wrongful prosecution."

"He hasn't been prosecuted yet," Amy said, sipping the drink she'd outstretched to me.

Mia waved her away. "Well wrongful imprisonment, then, planting evidence. Whatever. I watched *Making a Murderer*, and that's the main thing. We're going to make sure everyone knows Gage is innocent." She paused. "Well, not *innocent*. But of this crime, at least." She bit her lip, looking at me. "Right?" she clarified.

"Right," I said firmly. "No way he did this. Not because I don't think he would murder a guy for touching me in a bar—that's totally within the realm of possibility—but no way would he get caught."

"Okay, that's what we need to say in the interview," she decided. "But maybe not verbatim." She started tapping on her phone.

The women were providing a welcome distraction from the truth.

Which was Gage had been arrested for murder and they had fricking DNA evidence to prove it. I wasn't an expert by any means, but I knew that actually meant there was a chance that Gage could be prosecuted.

That there could be a trial.

No. This was *not* going that far.

The men already knew it was bullshit and they were shut away in 'church' while we sat in the women's version, the bar at the club. I had to put my faith in outlaws.

But for now, I needed some kind of quiet.

My hand itched for my paintbrush. For solace. But that was only found in Gage. And they wouldn't even let me *see* him. I hadn't fought Troy on that earlier because the frayed thread I was holding on by was in danger of snapping. But I would tomorrow.

I stood. "I'm going to go home."

All eyes went to me, and Mia, who was discussing the "best lighting for innocence," stopped talking.

"I'll come," Amy said immediately.

I shook my head. "I think I just need to go alone, you know?"

She frowned, looking like she was going to push the issue.

Lily, of all people, chimed in. "Yes, honey, we know," she said softly.

I smiled in thanks.

And I drove home.

But I didn't find any solace.

Only more chaos.

Gage

"You sure you don't have more to say?"

"Yeah, you need to invest in some new mattresses, and oh, you're a fucking piece of shit," Gage replied, cracking his knuckles as they uncuffed him.

They were in the interview room. The club lawyer would be walking in the door at any moment; hopefully Gage would be walking out with him a handful of minutes later. They had him on retainer and he was the best, though they hadn't needed to use him in years.

Gage wasn't surprised that it was him to make the man work for his money.

He at least thought he'd be *guilty*.

"You're gonna regret this fuckup," he promised.

Troy leaned forward. "This isn't a fuckup. The DNA evidence proves otherwise."

Gage sat back in his chair. "DNA evidence means shit. And despite you actin' like it most of the time, you're not an idiot. If, hypothetically, I were to murder someone, no way would I be leavin' DNA evidence."

"There's no hypothetical here. You *are* a murderer," Troy hissed.

"Prove it," Gage challenged, voice calm.

He was far from calm.

He hadn't slept a wink.

And it had nothing to do with the mattress.

It had everything to do with who wasn't lying next to him. Who wasn't staving off the itch that ramped up to almost unmanageable levels in an enclosed space.

The night had lasted for forty-eight thousand, one hundred and two seconds.

Some of the longest of his life.

He wasn't worried about the charges. They were bullshit. Though it would be one of life's great ironies for him to go to prison for a murder he *didn't* commit.

He was worried because something wasn't adding up about this shit. Jade entered his mind, and he held on to the thought, tasting it. Sure, it could've been her, since the fucking bitch had *poisoned* Lauren, but she'd been silent for months. He didn't think this would be her next move.

But you couldn't predict the next move of a crazy person. He knew that too well.

So he kept it in his mind. It was killing him that he couldn't fucking do shit about it. Couldn't hold his woman. But he had faith in his club. They would know it was bullshit. Would be going through every possible scenario.

The door burst open and shocked Gage from his mind.

He expected it to be a snake in a ten-thousand-dollar suit.

Instead it was a geek in a cut.

"You can't go in there!" someone yelled behind them as the sounds of a struggle echoed into the room.

Gage would've smiled if not for the look on Wire's face.

Troy was standing, hand on his gun. "You can't burst in here while I'm interviewing a suspect."

Wire's face was grim as he held up a tablet. "I do if I have evidence stopping him from being a suspect and showing him to be the fucking *victim*."

GAGE HADN'T THOUGHT Troy was going to look at what was on the tablet. Fucker had an axe to grind, and cops didn't usually give a shit about evidence when that was the case. Especially when it had to do with the Sons. Since Crawford had left, there was a new chief, one who was little more than a ghost and let his deputies work for him. He had the same agreement as they'd had with Bill not to fuck with the Sons, but he also wasn't gonna destroy evidence to save them.

Gage thought for a moment that Troy might bury it just to damn them.

But despite how much he hated the fucker, he respected him for letting Wire sit down, lay it out.

In that moment at least.

When Wire laid it all out—the falling-apart cabin by the sea that they'd finally traced Jade to, with all sorts of fucked-up shit, including his fucking DNA and meticulous notes and plans on how to use it—Troy dropped the charges. Well, pending his own deputy's inspection of the area. Which meant he wasn't gonna let Gage go.

Yet.

And then it was time for the snake in the suit to arrive.

Who managed to get Gage released.

Troy didn't fight that as much as Gage had expected him to. He could've, if he wanted. Theoretically could've held Gage. But he didn't.

He almost respected him for that.

Then he thought of the night spent in that cell, without Lauren, thought of that beautiful moment ripped apart by the knock at the door.

He eyed Troy. "If *anything* happens to Lauren 'cause of this shit, 'cause of you lockin' me up when I could've been protecting her, I'll burn this fucking precinct to the ground."

It was on that that his lawyer ushered him off.

And he went straight to Lauren.

HE KNEW it the second his foot hit the stairs.

It was *wrong*.

Because the entire place reeked of flowers and raspberries. Perfume that was meant to be alluring and classy, yet the second it touched his nose, it repulsed him.

Because it was Jade's.

He sprinted up the stairs, yanking out his piece. His mind assaulted him with everything he might find up there, the death he might be faced with.

That was forced away.

Because he wasn't faced with death.

Lauren sat in the middle of the room, tied to a chair, gagged. Her hair was mussed and matted with blood, an angry welt raised on her cheek.

Blood boiling, he didn't even think of anything but her as he rushed over. Her eyes bulged in a silent scream.

The prick of the needle surprised him. His body froze in ecstasy at the familiar pain, long enough to let whatever the fuck it was in the drug enter his system.

"Ah, you've made it too easy, baby," a voice purred. "Now I'm going to have to make it hard."

Lauren

Gage collapsed on the floor in mere seconds. His eyes didn't leave mine the entire time. Horror spread through my veins at the way his irises began to glaze over, at the way the drug reached in and yanked away the comprehension in his eyes.

I didn't try to scream from behind my gag. I knew it wouldn't work. I'd been doing it all night.

Since I got home.

Since I found Jen—no, *Jade* in my kitchen.

I'd been surprised when I got to the top of the stairs to see her sitting at my island, sipping from a glass of red wine.

She put it down when our eyes locked, smiling warmly at me. But there was something off about it, something that made me go back on my heel and tense up.

"Jen, how did you get in here?" I asked, trying to remember if I'd locked the door in all my haste that morning. Maybe I'd left it unlocked and she'd heard, come over to commiserate. Yeah, that was it. I totally hadn't locked my door, and of course she'd know. Niles knew of every arrest made in Amber. But then again, Niles had mentioned how she had some sort of family emergency when I'd finally been cleared to go back to work—with a leather clad shadow following me everywhere, of course—and she'd been in and out of the office. I hadn't even seen her, only spoken to her on the phone once when she'd called to tell me how horrified she'd been to hear about my 'virus'.

That was the cover story.

To stop Troy from sticking his nose in, as Gage had said. Well, Gage had said "so that cop fucker doesn't stick his snout in and I don't have to kill him."

My doctor had somehow been very cooperative with this story. I had a feeling she was somehow connected to the Sons of Templar.

Or maybe she just knew it was a bad idea to cross them.

Whatever it was, the official story was a 'virus'. My parents had somehow gone along with this too.

Gage had spoken to them, I had no idea what he said, but it worked.

So it was weird that Jen was here.

Something bitter touched my tongue, but I ignored it.

"It's sweet of you to come, but—"

She stopped in front of me. "Ugh, I'm not sweet, you stupid bitch," she snarled, silencing me. "Thankfully, I can show you that now."

Then she hit me over the head with something heavy and hard.

White-hot pain exploded in my eyes and then there was nothing.

Until I woke up tied to a chair in the middle of my living

room. She hadn't said a single thing since I'd opened my eyes. Not one.

It was deeply unnerving. Well, the whole experience was obviously deeply unnerving. The woman pretending to be my friend was actually Gage's ex who had tried to poison me, most likely framed him for murder, and now was in my living room holding a gun after she'd knocked me unconscious.

All that was unnerving.

But what was truly terrifying was her silent pacing. Back and forth.

There were no big villainous monologues of what she did and how she got away with it. No insults. No death threats. No more violence.

Just her pacing, swinging the gun in her hand as she did.

She did it for *hours*.

And I wondered how in the heck she'd ever passed for a sane person. How she'd tricked everyone. Because this kind of crazy should've been impossible to hide.

Gage had showed me all the wonderful things that weren't impossible.

And now I was seeing all the wretched, ugly, and maybe fatal things.

I thought of him a lot. With every heartbeat.

I spent the night hoping he'd stay locked up. That he wouldn't come looking for me and find the utterly insane woman who had a gun.

But I *knew* he would.

I wasn't surprised when he reached the top of the stairs. Because he'd told me he was the villain, but that he was always going to save me. Even if it was going to get him killed.

They say in times of great stress, people can lift things their body physically shouldn't be able to. There was no greater stress on a human psyche than insanity.

Jen—Jade should not have been able to drag Gage to the chair she'd positioned across from me. Should not have been able to lift him onto that chair and sit his terrifyingly limp body on it.

But she did.

And worse, his eyes were open the entire time.

They were glassy and uneasy until she propped him on the chair without binds.

She cupped his cheek. "Ah, you thought you'd seen the last of me, my love," she whispered. Then she leaned forward and pressed her lips to his.

After she straightened, the glassy look was gone. His eyes were ice, filled with panic and death and violence. It was a glare that promised revenge. Brutality. But it was encased within his still body.

Too still.

His limbs were slouched unnaturally on the chair, knees knocking into each other and splayed on the side. His arms were drooped over the arms of the chair, wrists dangling limply.

Jade looked to me, her almond eyes glowing. "Nimbex." She waved the syringe after picking it up off the floor. "It's a nerve agent that paralyzes you but keeps you conscious at the same time. Used primarily for preparing the body for general anesthesia and surgery, but I think it'll work just *fine* for what I've got in mind."

I blinked at her rapidly, but then my eyes went to Gage's.

"Anesthesia isn't part of the menu," she continued, pacing the room. "Because I want to make you *hurt*." She yanked at Gage's neck, jerking him to face her and then letting him go brutally so his neck lolled forward.

She propped it back up again, caressing his cheek before straightening and looking to me.

"I've got connections in the drug business," she said. "I'm sure by now, Gage has filled you in on our history. He's so terribly honest for a villain. Well, my family, the ones he blew up"—she narrowed her eyes at him—"their business was drugs. But not just the ones our Gage is a slave to. No, we dabbled in all sorts. That's how I found out about the one that almost killed you."

She scowled at me, walking forward to slap me.

It might've stung, but it was the utter fury and helplessness in Gage's eyes that hurt more.

"You were all so fucking blind, weren't you? I was right there in front of your faces the entire time. Women will always be the demise of men who think they're strong."

She smiled again.

"And you were the stupidest of them all. Because it was so easy."

Her smile was gone, as if I'd screamed at her out loud like I was in my head.

"Why the fuck didn't you die?" she hissed. "It would've been so much *easier* if you'd burned. But then I got to play with you after that. It was fun. Destroying you slower. But I was getting bored. That's why I upped the dose. But you weren't predictable, so I couldn't give you enough. And then you wouldn't fucking *die*. Then I wouldn't have had to get messy and kill that idiot, frame Gage for it." She smiled. "Though I will admit it was fun, playing with him, cutting him up just like a crazy man with a knife might."

She sauntered over to Gage, leaning over seductively and yanking his blade out of its sheath.

His eyes bulged.

I tasted bile at the thought of her using it on him. Of him having another scar when that knife had already inflicted enough.

When life had already inflicted enough.

I exhaled when she straightened and clutched the knife before pacing again.

"Women can be villains too," she said, her voice shrill. Unstable. "That's the kicker here. We're all in a post-feminist world, right?" She looked to Gage. "Even you bikers seem to understand the importance of equal rights. Maybe not in theory but especially in practice, considering every single one of those notorious 'old ladies' leads you men around by your dicks."

She gave Gage a look, one that told me her sanity was frayed, crushed, nothing but a memory, if it ever existed at all. I couldn't believe that she'd managed to hold it together, hide all that behind red lipstick and pencil skirts. It took a special and deadly type of insanity to hide it like that.

Gage was dangerous.

Deadly.

But he couldn't hide that.

This woman could. And fear circulated through every part of my body thinking that meant she'd be the one who ended him.

She scratched her head with the barrel of her gun. "You see, all I wanted was to be that for you, Gage. Why couldn't I be that?" Her voice was low. Pleading.

Gage didn't answer. His entire body was still, courtesy of the chemicals she'd injected into his system. But he wasn't still. No, his eyes showed the battle he was waging as his gaze zeroed in on Jen. It was in his utter stillness that I saw the ferocity of his fight.

He was powerless.

And that was one of the worst things she could've done.

That's why she was more dangerous than a man with a gun and a temper. Because women like that were smart. When they wanted to hurt someone, it wasn't with a bullet. It was with everything and anything they could.

She stopped, her eyes darting from me to Gage and then rushing to get into his face. "Why couldn't I be that?" she screamed, spittle flying from her mouth. She stayed there a moment longer, gun clutched in her manicured hand. Fear that she was going to use it sent lances of pain through every single one of my already screaming nerve endings.

But she didn't.

She jerked, as if she was being woken up abruptly by a deep slumber, her body snapping back straight. Her eyes fluttered rapidly as she blinked, as if trying to focus on reality. Her exaggerated inhales and exhales echoed through the silent room.

"What I was *saying*," she said, voice terse, as if one us of had interrupted her, "was that women are better villains because we *hurt*. We hurt more than you. And we feel pain deeper." She strode over to me. Cold steel kissed my temple, and Gage's eyes widened in a silent roar. "That means a special number of us can inflict pain deeper."

She was going to shoot me.

I was going to die.

My eyes hungrily took in every single inch of Gage. Trying to isolate him from the horror around me, hold on to him, imprint a goodbye on him.

Tears streamed down his face.

The pressure of the gun at my temple was nothing compared to that agony-filled stare, those tears on Gage's face.

I barely noticed the release of that pressure, my mind too focused on what would happen to Gage when I was gone. The fear for his life with my death dwarfed everything around me, even the reality of the absence of my death.

A shooting and white-hot agony in my thigh was enough to plunge me back into that reality.

Into the absence of death.

Pain was the ultimate absence of death. It was the only way we knew we were alive.

"See, you ripped out my heart and laid it bloody at my feet. And you didn't even *care!*" she screamed, yanking Gage's knife out of my thigh, the steel soaked with my blood.

I glanced down at the steady stream of crimson. It didn't hit an artery. It hurt—a lot—but it wasn't going to kill me.

Jade would.

Eventually.

If I didn't fight.

If I didn't *battle*.

She paced the room.

I fiddled with my binds.

"Now I'm going to do the same to you," she said, her voice suddenly low. "Just not metaphorically." She glanced at me, and I immediately stopped struggling. "And not *your* heart. Because I know the way to hurt you, really *hurt* you like you did me, is to take away the one person in your world who makes sense. And then you'll be thrust into chaos, into insanity like me. And then I'll make you live with it."

She ripped my gag off.

"Kill me," I said immediately. "That's what you want, right? Revenge for stealing your man? Well that's what I did. I *stole* him. He did everything to me that I'm sure he never did to you. He loved me," I taunted her, my death wish born from desperation.

I wasn't thinking logically at that point. No, there was no shape or form to my thoughts, a kind of crazy similar to Jade's. But mine was about saving the one I loved rather than punishing them for happiness.

I didn't look at Gage because I knew I'd see the accusation in his eyes. The fury. The pain. He didn't want this. I was being cruel, making him watch someone else he loved die in front of him.

Logically, it would've been kinder to take that pain on myself, go through the unfathomable horror of watching him die if only to spare him more pain.

But I was working on love. And it wasn't about being kind.

No, it was being cruel, even if that cruelty was him drawing breath when I couldn't.

Jade paused, smiling at me. "Oh, so nice. So *gallant* that you're willing to die for him," she said sweetly.

"I'll do *anything* for him," I said, working at my binds that were finally loosening.

She smiled again. "I know," she whispered. "Why do you think we're all here?" She waved the gun around. "I'll do *anything* for him too." She moved away from me and a sick bitterness erupted on my tongue. "Including putting him out of his misery." She pointed the gun at Gage's chest.

It was then that I looked at him, saw the panic turned to relief as he met the barrel.

"No!" I screamed at the same time the gun went off.

At the same time blood covered Gage's chest, a crimson rose blossoming before my very eyes. His heart bleeding from the inside out.

In all the movies, time slowed at those moments. Gave the doomed heroine and hero the chance to say their goodbyes in a lingering glance, where a lifetime was contained. Gave them a moment to communicate all the pain and love into it.

But this wasn't the movies.

And I wasn't a heroine.

Gage surely wasn't a hero.

So time didn't slow—it snapped into a cold, loud, agonizing blur, where the glance wasn't lingering, and a lifetime wasn't contained. It was snatched away in the most violent way possible.

The gun in Jade's hand was still smoking, and she was looking at it in vague wonder and surprise that only existed on the face of someone who'd broken from themselves and couldn't quite figure out anything from the pieces.

Then, as blood spurted hideously from Gage's mouth, she smiled in a cold and lucid realization.

"I exploded your heart," she said, voice brimming with glee.

My binds gave way.

Another thing that happened in movies: the struggling captive broke free of their shackles just in time to save themselves, save the world.

I didn't save myself.

Or the world.

Both were lost to me already.

But I launched myself at Jade anyway, my fingernails sinking into the flesh of her cheek, grotesquely tearing away at the skin.

She let out a shrill and garbled scream, but it was too late. I'd taken her down with the weight of my body, heavier now with the weight of my sorrow.

Dead weight.

I itched to tear her apart with my bare hands so her skin and blood and bone crusted under my fingernails, so her death sank into my skin.

But there wasn't time for that. Not when the whole world laid dying beside us.

So I reached for the gun in her flailing hand, even with my ruined shoulder that had popped when I wrenched myself free from my ropes. It was laughable how easy it was to get it off her. But she wasn't fighting now. What was the point? She'd gotten her wish.

This was the ending that no one told you about. The one where the villain won.

I held the gun level, hot from her grip, cold from the grave she'd called upon with it.

I didn't hesitate to jam it against her temple and squeeze. The resounding bang was loud, maybe. My ears were filled with a low and painful roar, so I didn't much notice. It did go off though, her body going limp as blood, brains, and pieces of her skull splattered over my face.

I didn't even pause, didn't let go of the gun, just scrambled over her body, crawling through the growing pool of Gage's blood to get to him. It was sticky and warm, but when I gathered him in my arms, he was so *cold*.

All of his warmth was seeping out onto the floor.

All of *his life.*

His eyes were staring at me, blank and glassy, and I was taken back ten years, assaulted with the very same stare I'd received from my brother. From the other half of me.

I shook uncontrollably, certain I was looking into the grave again. That another part of me was being torn, ripped, clawed out of me.

But he blinked, slowly, and purposefully, in such a way that it seemed like an effort to wrench his eyelids back up.

Tears ran through the flesh and bone on my face. "You're not dying," I told him. I *ordered* him.

His mouth quirked up. "You know I like it when you're bossy," he croaked, spluttering.

Warm blood sprayed on my face once more.

He wasn't paralyzed anymore, no longer in the clutches of whatever Jade had plunged into his body. It was draining out of him. Like his life.

"You're not leaving me," I hissed. "You *promised.*"

As if moving through sand, he slowly raised his arm into the air until he cupped my face. "I'll find you, Will," he coughed. "I promise I'll find you."

He made a horrible hacking sound in his throat, the rattling of his failing lungs cutting through my eardrums like blunt knives.

Then his eyes flickered, exploded with light.

Then they didn't.

Then everything left them.

And he just stared at me.

I blinked, hoping it was a trick of the light. The absence behind that stare. I pretended I hadn't noticed Gage's weight depress into me. That the blood on the floor was warmer than his body.

"You can't do this," I whispered to Gage's lifeless face, rocking him gently, as if such a tender motion might counteract the violence of before. "You can't do this!" I screamed. But not to Gage—to the air, to whoever was in charge of this torture chamber that was the world. "You can't take another thing away from me! *You fucking can't!* You cannot take him." I squeezed Gage harder, my arms protesting, the bones of my ruined shoulder grinding together in what I was sure should've been agony. "I won't let you take him!" I screamed with the last of my voice before that too gave up on me.

The silence that followed was heavy. Unnatural. Disgusting. It haunted me. The air was thick with death, and the loneliness hit me hard. I had Gage in my arms, but there was no one inside of him. He'd seeped into that air, and I couldn't hold him anymore.

I continued to rock him, my eyes unseeing like his.

I must've really unseen something, because I didn't see anything else for the longest of times.

TWENTY

"Come on, honey, why don't we go get you showered?" a soft and kind voice asked. "Get that blood off you."

I looked up robotically, my left arm hanging useless at my side. No one had noticed it yet. But I'd come in with a dead man, screaming and covered in blood, so it was kind of easy to miss.

I saw Lily, sure I did. She was right there, standing in reality. And I was living in reality. I didn't have the luxury of escaping it. The pain didn't let me. The demons didn't. They'd chained me to the horrible, stark, and ugly truth that I was living with.

She flinched when we made eye contact.

I was sure I looked bad.

Dead.

I sure felt it.

"Why should I shower? That's not getting the blood off me anyway," I said, my voice flat.

I slowly moved my gaze back to the man in the bed, my good hand clasped around his scarred wrist. I squeezed as tight as I could, digging my nails into his skin. I wasn't going to tenderly wake him up. That wouldn't wake him up.

"Pain is how we feel alive, Will."

The voice was so sure, so loud, I was convinced it was him speaking.

If he didn't have a tube down his throat and wasn't currently conversing with the gatekeeper of Hell.

My nails dug in harder.

It wouldn't be tenderness that brought him back.

It was going to be pain.

"LAUREN, IT'S BEEN *TWO DAYS*," a less gentle voice than the rest said. "You haven't eaten. Slept. You're still covered in freaking blood. That's just *gross*."

Amy was trying, and failing, to soften the sharp edges of the moment.

"This is *Gage's* blood," I replied. Then my brain showed me the explosion of Jade's skull as a bullet ripped through it. "Some of it," I corrected. "I'm not cleaning this blood off me until he wakes up and I'm certain he'll bleed again. Till I'm certain I'm not fucking wearing the last pieces of the man I love."

She sucked in a harsh and audible breath. "Wow. You're *so* fucked up. You guys are perfect for each other."

"No we *weren't*. And that's the point."

There was a long pause where Amy didn't try to offer me support, empty words of reassurance about Gage's strength. She didn't tell me to have faith or hope.

She knew such things didn't exist here.

And she knew that no matter how strong Gage was, there was nothing to guarantee he would get through this. That *I* would get through this. It didn't matter that every couple before us merely brushed by death, maybe got a deep graze that would never quite heal.

We were nothing like those other couples.

Death had already sunk its teeth into us; only time would tell whether it would completely and utterly tear us apart.

"GAGE IS gonna be pissed when he wakes up. That you've been sitting here, letting the life waste out of you," a husky and even voice said.

I didn't look up. "*If* he wakes up," I corrected.

Various nurses and doctors had been moving around, speaking to me, speaking at me, knowing it was futile to say such things as "visiting hours" or "proper procedure" near me anymore. I was a bloodied and unhinged part of the furniture.

They spoke about blood loss, about infection, about "low chance of survival." I didn't listen. There was no point in listening. Either he woke up or he didn't; listening to them wouldn't change that.

"*When* he wakes up," Bex repeated, moving into my eyeline, which was at Gage's side since he was always in my eyeline. I wanted to be the first to see those eyes when they opened. Or the last to witness his final heartbeat.

I didn't answer Bex.

She didn't talk. I saw her look at the fresh, ragged nail marks up Gage's scarred arms. Most normal people would have something to say about a person scratching the skin away from a person in a coma.

She said nothing.

"Gage saved my life, you know," she said finally.

I didn't reply. She knew I knew. Everyone knew about him and the rest of the men rescuing Bex from where she was being held captive. Where she was being brutalized in some of the worst ways imaginable. And even worse ways people couldn't even imagine.

"He was the one who took me to my first meeting."

That had my eyes jerking to her. For a fragment of a second, anyway. Then I remembered how important, how *vital* it was for me to keep my gaze on Gage. So I moved it back, loudly exhaling when I saw his heart was still beating.

It hurt doing that. Breathing. Of course it did—my ribs were shattered and broken from my heart exploding. But physically it did too. And it was getting worse. But it was easy to ignore when I focused on the pain in my chest.

"Not many people know Gage is an addict," Bex continued.

"Recovering," I snapped.

"Addict is always an addict, recovered or not."

I didn't reply because her voice mimicked Gage's.

"Gabriel physically saved me from my Hell. And I mean in the literal way of breaking in and unchaining me from the bed I was being raped in. Killing the man who'd been doing it."

I flinched.

She wasn't handling me with care like the rest did. Like they thought I was fragile and if they spoke in gentle words, I might not break. Bex knew I was already broken, so it didn't matter how she spoke to me.

"I also mean figuratively, that he reached into the flaming pit and wrenched me out. Sure, I did some of the work too. I'm an independent woman, after all."

I imagined she winked based on her tone.

"But there are different kinds of Hell for each of our demons. At any time, they're trying to drag us into a different one so we can experience a new type of suffering. That's what life is, after all. Various types of suffering." She paused, and I watched her trail a black-tipped fingernail down the scars on Gage's arms.

"Gage took me out of another one. Or at least he showed me I wasn't the only one in there. I owe him a debt for that. I can't do much about that." I saw her nod toward the bed in my periphery. "But I can do something about this."

She was standing right in front of me at that point, blocking my view of Gage.

I panicked, wanting to move, needing to move, but my muscles didn't obey me. They were locked, solid iron from being in the same position for so long.

"You need to get out of my way," I hissed between my teeth.

She gazed down at me, eyes hard and soft at the same time. "Nope," she said firmly. "I'm going to make it so when Gage wakes up, it isn't to the view of his old lady looking like a fucking corpse. He's coming out of Hell. You really want him to think he's still there?"

I let her words sink in, though they fought against every one of my instincts that told me I had to sit right there for as long as it took.

"I'm makin' sense," she said. "So how about you stand up. Then you can come back and not scare Gage back into the pit once he comes back."

She outstretched her tattooed arm.

I stared at it for a long time.

Then I grasped it.

And tried to stand up.

But of course by then, the stab wound I'd sustained and forgotten about—and no one had noticed because of the sheer volume of blood I'd been covered in, assuming it was all Gage's—had gotten infected and spread poison throughout my body. And the arm I outstretched was attached to the shoulder I'd dislocated ripping myself out of the binds far too late to stop Jade from shooting Gage.

So the second I took Bex's hand, I fell into a pit of my own.

MY MIND WAS COTTON WOOL.

That's exactly what it felt like. Too soft. Too grainy. Uncomfortable. Not the right shape. Moldable when it should've been solid.

Images moved behind my eyes. They were shut, but I wanted them to open.

It didn't work.

Only various shapes and lights moved.

"You didn't think to fucking *check* her," a familiar voice growled.

It was too familiar. My heart skipped with it. But it couldn't be real. It was too awake. Too alive. And the last time I'd seen him, there was no life left.

It was the cotton wool. *Tricking* me.

"Brother, she wouldn't let anyone near her. It was enough to get *us* near *you*," another voice replied.

Not as important as the other one, so I didn't bother tasting the sound of it to figure out who it was.

"She screamed at us, waved a gun every time we tried to get close to her. When she realized who we were, and that's only because I think she forgot who the fuck *she* was for a second, she finally let us touch you. She just sat there in the hospital waiting room, not looking at anyone, not talking—fuck, barely even *breathing*. Didn't let anyone near her, let alone examine her. Second you were out of surgery, she very calmly told the doctor she would scratch his eyes out if he didn't move and let her into your hospital room." There was a chuckle. "Didn't think she was much like you before, but fuck was she then. And she refused to move for three days. Three days without sleeping, eating, barely talking. And she was so fuckin' covered in blood that we didn't notice—"

"It should've been a first fuckin' priority to *notice*," the too-good-to-be-true voice growled.

"Brother, we didn't think you were gonna make it. Never had someone that close to death—"

"And I don't give a fuck if I was shaking hands with the reaper himself and getting my own personal tour of the pit. She comes first. Every. Fucking. Time."

My heart warmed.

It must've been a dream.

A nice one.

IT TOOK work to open my eyes. But I did.

It wasn't the snap moment that seemed to happen all the time in movies. It was a slow, lazy process, like waking from a sleep that wasn't ready to go.

Escaping from a death that was determined not to let go.

There was grit behind my eyes, making my vision grainy and blurry at first. And there was a not-at-all-gentle pressure on my left hand, the bones squeaking and protesting. My right shoulder ached dull and deep.

My thigh itched.

My entire body felt heavy yet drained, as if someone had sucked all my blood out and replaced it with cement. It wasn't pleasant.

Memories didn't rush in. They came sluggishly, on a slow-moving river, passing by my lazy gaze. I had to make the effort to grab the more important ones. I didn't need to remember Gage being shot. The shards of glass embedded in my chest did that for me.

The edges of them dulled slightly when I thought about moments that I wasn't sure were real, but the pressure at my hand and the dark shape beside me told me they might've been.

That voice wasn't coming from Heaven or Hell. It was coming from both, because that's what this place called reality was.

The grip on my hand tightened to the point of agony as my vision cleared and locked on icy eyes. Eyes that had been on me for much longer than mine had on him. I knew because his stare was iron, determined, much like I imagined mine might've been when our positions had been reversed.

He leaned forward as I blinked him into existence.

"Will," he rasped. "Thank fuck."

He closed his eyes for the longest moment, the grip on my hand loosening enough to stop the bones from breaking. With his eyes still closed, he lifted our intertwined hands and laid his mouth on my fingers. It was a soft and tender gesture, though his hands were still squeezing me in a grip bordering on brutal and his entire body was etched in barely restrained violence.

I devoured him, but I frowned as I lowered my eyes and saw he wasn't sitting in a chair, and there was a tube connected to the hand not holding mine, trailing to an IV.

"You're in a wheelchair," I said, my voice scratchy and raw, the words barely intelligible.

His lips left my hand, his head snapping up. His eyes feasted on mine as if he wasn't expecting me to speak now. Or ever again.

He was beautiful. The lines of his face slightly sharper around the edges because of his weight loss. His beard was longer than usual, somewhat wild but still groomed. Scarred arms were exposed in the black wifebeater he was wearing, the fabric clinging to the muscles that had yet to disappear despite being freaking *shot*. My heart stuttered at the sight of the white bandage peeking out from the top of the tank, wrapping around his back and shoulder.

My eyes snapped back up to his.

"You're in a wheelchair," I repeated. "And you would pretty much rather do anything in the world than so obviously expose your perceived weakness at not being able to walk after being *shot in the chest*, unless you're actually meant to be in bed and nowhere near upright, which I suspect is the case." I narrowed my eyes. "I wouldn't even be surprised if you got someone to steal that wheelchair, because no way would the doctors give it to you so you could get out of bed."

Gage's eyes didn't leave me the entire time my raspy voice forced out all of those words. He watched me, attention rapt, like I was telling him the secrets of the universe instead of scolding him. Then, after a long beat of silence, he laughed.

Like threw his head back and laughed. Well, as much as he could.

I wanted to keep glaring at him, but the sound—though rattly and slightly strained—was full, bursting with pure happiness mingled with bone-deep relief.

I knew it because that's what my smile was for too.

He stopped laughing, wincing and shifting slightly in the chair, but never letting go of my hand. "Only you, my rainbow, my Will, my Lauren, can make me fucking laugh when the last time I saw you, you were *tied to a fucking chair*. After thinking I was going to Hell and not knowing if I could be at peace there knowing that trip saved you." He squeezed my hand. "And baby, I would've been relieved in an eternity of torment had it saved you. All I fucking see is you tied to that chair..." He said it as if that was more traumatic than getting shot. "Rest is blurry," he grunted. "But I remember you killing her. Proud of you. Hate that that's on your soul. Should hate it more. A good guy would, but I'm not that. So I'm proud. But I'm also pissed as fuck with you, and as soon as I'm able, and you're well enough, I'm putting you over my knee and spanking the shit outta you for this." He nodded to me in my bed.

"I hardly *chose* to be held captive," I snapped.

His eyes darkened. "But you fuckin' *chose* to forget to take care of the one thing in life I give a shit about—you. You do know you almost fuckin' *died* from a blood infection, Lauren? That I woke up and you weren't there because they were treatin' you for septicemia. Had to get it outta Bex that it wasn't the result of your injuries, only 'cause I damn near ripped my hospital room apart with the knowledge that it was 'cause of me. And don't worry, I still shoulder most of that blame for what happened to you."

"Gage, this wasn't your fault."

"Shut the fuck up," he growled, the only man who could savagely say that while holding my hand as I lay in a hospital bed. "I've got the talking stick right now, and I've got a lot to say about you *refusing fucking treatment* for wounds that almost killed you." His voice was flat and cold. Gage's version of a roar. His ultimate level of mad.

But something lurked underneath.

"You scared the shit outta me, Lauren," he said, kissing my fingertips again. "You never, *never* play with your life like that 'cause of me. Fucking never. Promise me that."

"I won't," I said. "Because I had to see you *die in my arms*, Gage. I literally saw you die. I was covered in your blood, and I was too fucking scared to move, to wash it off in case that's all I had left of you. So you can curse, demand and try to muscle your way through this, but you're not getting your way because I'm not living through that again. I'm not *dying* through that again. So how about you make me a promise? Never get shot in the fucking chest again."

His face didn't change throughout everything I said. He flinched once, but his expression didn't shift. Well, not till the end, at least. And then he smiled, because of course Gage was about to find some sick amusement in this.

"Only we could fight moments after mutually waking up from life-threatening comas," he muttered.

I rolled my eyes and fought my mouth twitch. "You forgot to make your promise."

"Will, I promise to never let anyone shoot me in the chest again," he said solemnly.

I nodded. "Good. And I would like another one please."

He grinned. "What now?"

"I would like you to marry me."

The grin disappeared and he froze. "What did you just say?"

"I want you to marry me," I repeated. "And not here in a hospital bed, because I don't want *this* to be the photo sitting on our mantelpiece. But soon."

He didn't speak.

It should've made me nervous. Should've sent fears of rejection snaking into my mind. But this man would die for me. This man *did* freaking die for me. Then he came back from the dead and freaking lived for me. So I wasn't afraid of the silence.

Though it did bring a sick amount of satisfaction to shock Gage mute.

"You want to be my wife?" he rasped.

I smiled. "I want you to be my husband."

He continued to stare at me in wonder. "Yeah, I think I can make that happen."

THREE MONTHS Later

"The doctors said it was a miracle that it didn't hit your heart. They don't even really know how it didn't," I whispered, tangled in Gage's arms, as I was often in the past three months.

His hand squeezed mine. "I do. 'Cause my heart's not in my chest." He opened my empty palm slowly. "It's in here."

He laid his lips to that palm before setting it down on his bare chest again.

I traced the puckered scar with my finger, the pain radiating right to my own heart. The ink ended and began abruptly around the fresh pink skin. "Does this mean the gates to Hell are closed now?" I whispered.

His arms tightened. "No, baby. They're never closed. Just means I don't have a reason to care anymore. Since it's not my front door."

His eyes moved down to the black diamond resting on my fourth finger, the rock glittering in his gaze. He'd slipped the three-carat white gold ring on my finger the day he'd gotten out of the hospital. I'd been released before him because, although I'd had a life-threatening infection, an aggressive course of antibiotics worked quickly and efficiently. My only problem was a broken collarbone, which was not fun.

Like *at all.*

Though it was a pain in the ass and made it difficult to do anything, it wasn't a reason to stay in the hospital. Getting shot in the chest required a longer stay, so a very pissed-off Gage swore and threatened doctors every single day.

And somehow, between all that, he managed to find a ring.

"Wanted to carve out a piece of my heart so you could wear it, but doctors advise against that if I wanna keep it beatin', so this is the next best thing."

Obviously it was the single most beautiful piece of jewelry I'd ever worn.

Gage toyed with it. "You nervous?" he asked.

I quirked my brow. "I've been in a house fire, poisoned, held captive, and stabbed. You think I'm nervous about a *wedding* after all that?"

"You should be, since your choice of groom will promise a lot worse than that."

I laid my lips on his. "Here's hoping," I murmured. "Care to give me a preview?"

He flipped me so his body was covering mine, fingers biting into my hip. His teeth tore at my bottom lip. "Oh, baby, I'll give you the whole fuckin' show."

EPILOGUE

I glanced down at the phone buzzing on the wooden table beside me, a small smile reaching my face, and more importantly that little part inside me still cold with dread. With expectancy. Because I was *happy*.

So happy that I felt like there had never been a person on this earth to be so excited for their next breath, their next moment, than me.

And with that happiness came the fear that had been following me around since the start. Not the start of me and Gage —though it sure had intensified—but since the moment I lost David and figured out that happiness was as flimsy as tissue paper, easily torn by the brutal and merciless hands of fate.

I reasoned that fate didn't discriminate with those who deserved to have that paper otherwise known as their life torn—if *anyone* really deserved that. No, fate just did it at any point, at any time, and I was terrified that it didn't happen with those who'd caused the most suffering, but those living with the most happiness... like me.

And even though I felt safe, content, and utterly secure in my life with Gage, I was terrified that there might be something my big, strong, scary, and secretly soft biker wouldn't be able to protect himself from. I knew he'd protect me, but who was protecting *him*?

And it was the ringing of my phone and that particular scary and secretly soft biker's name—soon to be my husband—flashing on the screen that chased away most of the dread.

A sliver of that would always remain, I guessed. Because people who'd known loss and suffering didn't get the joyful ignorance of unbridled warm happiness. They'd always have that little cold spot inside them. But I decided that wasn't a bad thing; it just made the warmth that much more precious.

And we'd had a lot of warmth over the last few months, if only a little dulled by the cold grip of the grave Jade had introduced into our lives.

Obviously I wasn't charged with her murder.

Self-defense and all that.

I think Troy was too busy blaming himself for not seeing it, for being too busy trying to lock Gage up while she held me hostage to even think about punishing me more.

He hadn't even fought Gage when he'd circled his hands around the cop's throat when he'd knocked on my door two days after Gage was discharged.

Yes, Gage thought strangling a police officer days after he was discharged from the hospital was appropriate.

"Gage," I murmured as Troy began to turn red. "You don't need to be straining yourself like this." My voice was calm and even, because I had kind of expected a version of the scenario before me.

He glanced to me, then Troy, then sighed loudly. "Fine," he muttered, letting him go.

Troy rubbed his neck, resting the other hand on his thigh for a moment.

"I came to apologize," he said, voice raspy.

Gage inspected him much like he would an insect I wouldn't let him crush. "Didn't kill you, so apology accepted. I only accept apologies once."

And he turned on his heel and climbed the stairs.

Niles felt equally bad about employing a murderess. He was literally crying when I handed in my resignation.

"It's not because you hired Jade," I said. "Well, maybe it is. Because it took her almost killing me to realize that I should probably live my life. Really live it. And as much as I love you for everything you've done for me, I can't live it here. Not anymore."

He nodded through his tears. "Of course. You've never belonged here." He squeezed my hand. "And that's a good thing."

We had moved my gallery opening to start right after our honeymoon. I was terrified.

So that meant I was doing something good.

And Gage did something that terrified him. Something that was completely and utterly good, if only it hadn't been stained by the dirt and ugliness of the past.

He invited his parents to our wedding.

He was literally shaking when he made the call.

Gage.

Shaking.

So yeah, he'd been terrified.

And I'd been perched in his lap—because he wouldn't let me be anywhere else—his scarred arms flexing around me with every ring of the dial tone.

By the time I heard the whisper of a voice on the other side of the phone, I was struggling to breathe, my bones protesting at Gage's grip. But I didn't say a thing. Because this small discomfort was nothing compared to the agony Gage was feeling right now.

And I would never let him be alone in his pain. Because he never let me be alone in mine.

Gage's eyes were plastered to mine. His fingers were going white with the force in which he was clutching the phone. I was vaguely worried it might shatter in his hands. But I was more worried about the heart inside of the ribs of the man I loved shattering.

Because I heard the low murmur of someone on the other side of the phone, the light and soft tenor to it had me guessing it was his mom.

But Gage was silent.

He was too terrified to speak.

The man who made bombs on Sundays, who killed drug dealers without blinking, who punched police officers, who walked in the Valley of the Shadow of Death, and was afraid of none of that ugliness, was afraid of the utter goodness that was his mother.

Because nothing could hurt you more than beauty.

I leaned forward and pressed my lips to his, not letting his eyes go. I didn't speak, he didn't need words. He needed strength.

The strongest man I'd ever met needed strength. From me.

So I gave it to him.

And he spoke.

The conversation was clipped. On his side at least. I could hear a lot from the other side of the phone.

"So you'll come to the wedding?" Gage asked. "Meet my Lauren?"

His arms flexed around me.

My heart flexed in my chest.

So they were here, waiting to watch their son—who they thought they'd lost forever—get married.

We'd met them yesterday when they arrived.

They weren't what I was expecting.

I guessed I expected the mammoth presence that was Gage to be sprouted from two big and burly parents, with stern expressions and hard edges.

But everything about his parents was soft.

His mom was tiny. Shorter than me and in heeled wedges.

She had been pretty once.

Before the world had ripped through all her beauty and happiness and drained it from her. Deep lines were etched into her elven face, her hair graying and piled artfully atop her head.

But it all disappeared, and the beautiful woman she once was appeared the second she glimpsed Gage and I.

His hands tightened around mine.

She came running toward us.

I expected her to yank Gage into her embrace, and I guessed he expected it too, since his entire body was taut. But it was me she yanked into her arms. And for a small woman, she had strength. I shouldn't have been surprised. You needed strength to go through what she did and still stand. Still live.

She smelled of vanilla.

"Thank you," she sobbed, her arms iron around me. "Thank you for bringing him back to us."

I let her hold me for a long time, until the first wave of her tears had dried against my shirt.

Gage's father was dry eyed when she let me go. And he was just staring at Gage in utter wonder, still, as if he were afraid he'd disappear if he moved.

"Dad," Gage grunted, his voice throaty and uneven.

The older, smaller, graying man in front of the larger one with his eyes flinched with the single word.

And then he reached up, slow as anything and trailed his finger along Gage's temple.

"Christian," he murmured, cupping his face. "My boy." He paused, looking to me with kind eyes filled with agony. "My man," he corrected.

It wasn't easy and soft from there. There was still a long way to go. But we had time.

And Gage's parents were good people. They were going to wait for their son. They had waited decades already.

Gage's terror had given way to something that would turn into a good thing.

I was terrified of this day. But that was a good thing too.

I finally picked up the phone.

"Hey," I murmured. "I'm going to see you at the other end of an aisle in T minus ten." I glanced at my racy lingerie in the mirror.

"Are you in your dress?" he clipped, voice rough.

I smiled, my palms resting on the ivory lace of my corset, tight enough to push my modest bosom up and loose enough to make sure I could breathe. I had matching frilly boy-short white panties on with a matching garter belt, attached to sheer white stockings with lace trimming the top edge.

"No, I'm not in my dress," I whispered, my stomach already dipping at the thought of what he'd do to me once he saw this.

There was nothing but a low hiss of breath on the other end of the phone, then dead air.

I blinked.

Did he just hang up on me?

Minutes before our wedding?

Now, I knew my biker was brusque and all tough guy and had to hold on to his badass card and make sure he didn't have long and soulful conversations in public, but it was his wedding day.

Surely he could handle a "Love you, baby. See you soon, and I'll make my life by marrying you." Okay, he couldn't handle that, but a clipped "I love you, babe" would've sufficed.

As I was about to redial and say just that, the door to the small room flew open. I expected it to be my grandmother. Amy. Lucy. Or Bex. Or Gwen. Or perhaps Mia. Or any of the crazy women who had befriended me throughout the courtship, who had been my rocks throughout the whole thing. I'd gained not only a soul mate through this but a whole girl posse.

It wasn't my girl posse though.

It was the biker in question.

And fuck, did he look hot.

And deadly.

He was in black, head to toe. Suit—with his motorcycle boots on, obviously—tailored to perfection, black shirt underneath, open collar, his tattoos snaking up his chest, his hair fastened in a small but sleek ponytail and beard trimmed.

He paused for maybe a fraction of a second as he took me in much the same way I was him—with pure and unadulterated hunger.

Then, like always, he recovered and slammed the door shut, the brutal sound jarring me from my perusal.

"I can't believe you hung up on me!" I shouted, narrowing my eyes at him, then looking down and remembering what day it was and how he was supposed to see this after we exchanged our vows.

"Wait! You can't see me," I screeched, covering his eyes as he crossed the room in two strides to snatch me into his arms. "It's bad luck to see the bride on her wedding day," I groaned.

His fingers bit into my hips and immediately moved to delve into my panties—which, of course, had been soaking wet since the second he'd appeared in the doorway.

Well, the second he'd growled at me on the phone, actually.

He entered me without warning and I gasped, my hands falling from his face to reveal his carnal gaze.

"We've had our fair share of bad luck," he told me, right after he'd kissed me senseless and slammed me against the wardrobe, his fingers still coaxing me to climax. "We make our own, remember, baby?" he murmured against my mouth. "You're my luck, my fate, my destiny. And I'll be making sure my woman is walking down the aisle with my cum inside her and the memory of my cock in her pussy."

And forty-five minutes later—when the ceremony was supposed to start twenty minutes earlier—I did just that.

Gage

Five Months Later

Gage was on his way out for Ben & Jerry's.

For the second time that night.

That was because the first batch he'd bought "smelled weird." He hadn't even blinked, merely threw the full tub of ice cream in the trash—though it smelled just fine—kissed Lauren hard on the mouth, soft on the belly and then walked out the door for more ice cream.

He wasn't skulking into the darkness for a fix, or to kill someone. No, he was searching for *ice cream* that didn't *smell weird* for his pregnant wife.

His beautiful, magnificent, pregnant wife, who he'd thought already carried the whole world inside her before. Now she held the whole universe.

It wasn't easy. Descending the stairs was pure pain, fucking leaving her for a handful of minutes to get ice cream torture. A dark shadow of his mind told him to abandon the ice cream, the utter pain and terror mixed with the joy at watching Lauren grow with their child, to chase nothing.

That voice would always be there.

He'd always battle against it.

But Lauren was worth it. Every fucking second of that battle.

So he was battling when he found Anna on the doorstep. She had been in Amber for the last three months "to watch Lauren get fat," but Gage knew better. Because the woman was terrified just like him. Of how good things were.

And he fucking liked having the crazy woman around. You never knew what would come out of her mouth, what her day brought. She'd demanded Gage show her how to blow things up two days before. "I assume you know how," she'd said with an arched brow.

He grinned. "Oh, I fucking know how."

So he and his wife's eighty-year-old grandmother blew shit up while his wife lay on a sun lounger—a very comfortable distance away—reading a book and tanning.

Yeah, that was his life.

He was surprised to find her out in the shadows, as she wasn't a woman who was built for them. Not the physical ones, at least. She was chasing the spotlight because of the shadows chasing her. He was also surprised to see the ember flickering a few inches from her mouth, flaring with her inhale, dimming with the plume of smoke she blew into the night.

He was surprised, but of course he didn't show it. Emotion was cloaked out of habit, survival. It was a hard thing to shake. He could only manage to shift his mask with Lauren. And he suspected it would stay that way forever. Because people could change, if they met the right—or the wrong—person. If that person was the fucking stars in the sky and the oxygen in their lungs, the pain in their soul.

But even then people didn't change *much*.

Cade still never smiled at anyone but his girls.

Bull barely spoke more than five words to anyone but his wife, and she didn't let him get in the words he did speak.

Bex only let Lucky touch her for a prolonged amount of time.

In their lifestyle, as with most things, more was more.

But in those particular aspects, less was *everything*.

"Didn't know you smoked," he said, leaning against the cool

brick, inhaling the salt air that he associated with Lauren. Fuck, he associated everything with her.

Anna let out a choked cackle. "I don't."

Gage didn't say anything, didn't even look pointedly at the flaming stick proving her wrong. He just looked toward the ocean.

"Want one?" she offered after a companionable silence. She was a woman who knew how to talk. She also knew when to shut up.

"Gave up," he grunted in answer.

She gave him a sideways look. "Ah, Lauren?" she guessed.

He nodded once.

"With some women, it's not what you'd do for them. It's what you'd give up for them." She smiled. "My granddaughter can recite all the risks of dying, but she didn't seem to grasp the concept of living. Actively shied away from it, in fact. Until recently."

She let the silence hang.

"You know, happiness is a farce," she said, inhaling deeply. "Heartbreak isn't rare. Or special. It's wretchedly common, actually. I would hazard a guess that there're more broken humans wandering around this world with their shattered dreams encased in a blacked heart." She took an inhale. "Present company included. Love isn't rare. It's also wretchedly common. That's why heartbreak is, you see. It rarely ever works. We're flawed, mortal. We die easily. Lie even easier. Life happens, destroys beautiful things. Or then we destroy the same beautiful things because we're sure life's going to anyway and we want to be first in. But you know what's rare? Decidedly uncommon?" She nodded to the door. "What you have with her. I'm not going to call it beautiful, because I'm an old lady who's seen enough of the world to know that kind of love isn't beautiful. But it is the rarest thing on the planet. I think now, after everything, even the way life has showed you how it destroys beauty, you'll make sure it doesn't destroy that. And then make sure you don't destroy it either. Because then I'd have to kill you."

And then she walked back into the house.

Gage had had a lot of death threats in his life. A few had even tried to make good on those threats. He'd buried every one of those people.

Not once did he hear one as convincing as the one from his woman's eighty-year-old grandmother.

IT WAS ONLY two days later that Gage found out Anna was not just there to witness miracles and dole out death threats.

No, she was there to live out the last of her life.

He found out because he came home early to pick up the "normal-smelling ice cream" from the freezer while she was at a barbeque at the club.

Not one single man said a word at the fact that he jumped at her request.

They couldn't.

They'd all done the exact same thing.

They were all fucking whipped.

And fucking happy.

So that's when he found Anna laying a note on the kitchen island. To her credit, she didn't try to hide it, didn't try to cover up.

"Fuck," she sighed. "I always wanted to do the cool thing and disappear like they do in the movies, but I guess I'm sprung."

She handed the note to Gage.

He read it, then crumpled it in his hands.

"You can't just disappear," he growled, the first time he'd ever gotten like that with Anna. "It'd *kill* Lauren." He shook with the knowledge of just how much it would hurt her.

"Oh, but I can," Anna said. "Because I know it won't kill her. I'm looking at the man who'll make sure of that. Who, in fact, is proof that pain doesn't kill my beautiful and strong grand-daughter."

He clenched his fists. "You'd be that selfish?" he spat, not locking it down even if he was in front of a dying woman. The good guy might. Gage was not that. "Deny her a goodbye?"

Anna smiled with twinkling eyes. "Ah, but that's what you get to do when you're dying. Be selfish."

Gage narrowed his eyes. "We're all fucking *dying*," he hissed.

She nodded. "True. But I'm just unable to escape the fact. And I'm not denying her a goodbye. I'm denying myself the ugliness of my demise. I don't fear leaving this world. Just the people in it."

She walked forward to cup Gage's face. "But I know you'll keep her wild. And she'll keep you safe. And that beautiful great-grandchild of mine will bring all sorts of chaos and pain, but most of all, beauty."

And then she stepped away and walked out the door.

Gage didn't see her again.

Not alive, at least.

And he didn't utter a word of the conversation to Lauren. The only secret in the world he'd ever keep from her.

Lauren

Three Months Later

I stared at the slab of rock accusing me with its ugly truth.

A tear rolled down my cheek.

It was quickly brushed away by the man holding me in his arms.

One scarred arm was resting on the swell of my belly, as it was almost constantly, the other trying to wipe away my pain.

"She couldn't have held on long enough to meet her great-grandchild?" I choked. "We're supposed to hold on for that. Death is supposed to wait for that."

Gage kissed my temple. "She held on longer than she was supposed to, with all that pain she was carrying around, Will," he murmured. "And death doesn't wait for anyone."

His words weren't light, full of lies to try to cover up the ugliness of my grief. No, they were harsh but gentle.

Painful.

Exactly what I needed.

I gazed down at the stone.

Anna Garden.

She loved life.

It loved her back.

She was also a stone-cold fox.

And she was Mick's.

She'd added the fox part, obviously. It was written in her will. The one that left me half of everything. My father got the other half.

I'd added the part about Mick.

Gage let me stand there in silence for a long time.

I would've stood there for a lot longer.

Except the human inside me had other ideas.

We made it to the hospital, though I wouldn't have been surprised if I gave birth in a cemetery—it was Gage's baby, after all. But he didn't let that happen.

Because since the second I'd found out I was pregnant with our son, there was not a single risk taken with that.

So Gage made sure David Mick Mathers was born in a hospital.

And he made sure he was the one to cut the cord with the same knife that had caused him so much pain. The knife that had torn at his skin. That had saved him.

He cradled our son in those scarred arms, tears streaming down his face. His eyes locked with mine and I saw the pain in his. The memories of another child clawing at him, teasing him with how easily the world could be taken away.

But he didn't surrender.

He battled.

And he did that by laying his lips at the top of our son's head.

ACKNOWLEDGMENTS

This book was hard to write, for a number of reasons. And it was hard to let go of, if you've made it this far, you know just how long I held onto Gage and the entire Sons of Templar family.

They are where it all started and writing this book was like coming home in a number of ways.

But it was also hard. One of the hardest books I've ever written. Not just because of Gage and Lauren's demons, but because of my own.

I am so thankful for the people who helped me through all my struggles, to get me here, to the end of this book. I'll forever treasure the wonderful people I have in my life.

Mum. You're always going to be here. Right at the top of this list. Because without you, I wouldn't be here. I wouldn't have turned my love of reading into writing if you hadn't told me I could be anything I wanted to be. Thank you for your faith in me. Thank you for always being my best friend.

Dad. Another person that's forever going to be at the top of this list. A list you're never going to read, but I know you're around, somewhere. You taught me to be a bad ass little girl before the world stole you away. I carried those lessons with me and now I'm a bad ass woman. Because of you. I miss you every single day.

My girls, Polly, Harriet, and Emma. The truest of friendships take no notice of postcodes, of time spent without speaking, and that's what I've got with the three of you. I am so very lucky to have girlfriends who are always there for me as a shoulder to cry on, a partner in crime, or someone to drink wine with.

My #sisterqueen, Jessica Gadziala. What would I do without you? No, seriously, what in the heck would I do? You are always there with support, wisdom and a kick up the ass when I need it. I can't wait to take over the world together.

Amo Jones. You've been with me since the beginning and I'll be with you till the end. Ride or die.

Michelle, Annette, and Caro. You ladies are something special. I cannot tell you how much your support has meant to me this past year. I love you all, to the moon.

Ginny and Sarah. Thank you for putting so much work into this book, for helping me turn it into what it is now. You ladies are everything to me.

All the ladies at Hot Tree Editing. Thank you for your hard work on this book, and understanding the craziness of my life. You rock!

And you, the reader. Thank you for reading this book. You have made my dream come true just by taking a chance on me. I will be forever grateful.

ABOUT THE AUTHOR

ANNE MALCOM has been an avid reader since before she can remember, her mother responsible for her love of reading. It started with magical journeys into the world of Hogwarts and Middle Earth, then as she grew up her reading tastes grew with her. Her love of reading doesn't discriminate, she reads across many genres, although classics like Little Women and Gone with the Wind will hold special places in her heart. She also can't get enough romance, especially when some possessive alpha males throw their weight around.

One day, in a reading slump, Cade and Gwen's story came to her and started taking up space in her head until she put their story into words. Now that she has started, it doesn't look like she's going to stop anytime soon, with many more characters demanding their story be told as well.

Raised in small town New Zealand, Anne had a truly special childhood, growing up in one of the most beautiful countries in the world. She has backpacked across Europe, ridden camels in the Sahara and eaten her way through Italy, loving every moment. For now, she's back at home in New Zealand and quite happy. But who knows when the travel bug will bite her again.

Want to get in touch with Anne? She loves to hear from her readers.

You can email her: annemalcomauthor@hotmail.com
Or join her reader group on Facebook.

ALSO BY ANNE MALCOM

The Sons of Templar Series

Making the Cut

Firestorm

Outside the Lines

Out of the Ashes

Beyond the Horizon

Dauntless

The Unquiet Mind Series

Echoes of Silence

Skeletons of Us

Broken Shelves

Greenstone Security

Still Waters

Shield

The Vein Chronicles

Fatal Harmony

Deathless

Faults in Fate

Eternity's Awakening

.

A Dark Standalone

Birds of Paradise

73732865R00267

Made in the USA
Columbia, SC
06 September 2019

CAPRICORN
 (December 22 to January 19)

Capricorn is more determined and persistent than any other sign. Achievement means everything. But she can worry too much about what others think of her. Capricorns have a strong need for security and know that, unless controlled, their emotions can drown them.

Capricorn's hobbies are artistic ones like photography and painting – hobbies that can be enjoyed alone.

Cat is a worrier. Her parents have moved again, and her nightmares and fear of the dark have returned. But Cat's determination to make new friends leads her to return again and again to the house of her nightmares. And the horrible truth is revealed at last.

Whatever your sun sign, you'll want to read
Zodiac, the series written in the stars.

ARIES (Mar 21 to Apr 19)	SECRET IDENTITY
TAURUS (Apr 20 to May 21)	BLACK OUT
GEMINI (May 22 to June 21)	MIRROR IMAGE
CANCER (Jun 22 to Jul 22)	DARK SHADOWS
LEO (Jul 23 to Aug 23)	STAGE FRIGHT
VIRGO (Aug 24 to Sep 23)	DESPERATELY YOURS
LIBRA (Sep 24 to Oct 22)	FROZEN IN TIME
SCORPIO (Oct 23 to Nov 21)	DEATH GRIP
SAGITTARIUS (Nov 22 to Dec 21)	STRANGE DESTINY
CAPRICORN (Dec 22 to Jan 19)	DON'T LOOK BACK
AQUARIUS (Jan 20 to Feb 19)	SECOND SIGHT
PISCES (Feb 20 to Mar 20)	SIXTH SENSE

SERIES CREATED BY JAHNNA N. MALCOLM

ZODIAC

CAPRICORN

DON'T
LOOK BACK

JAHNNA N. MALCOLM

Lions
An Imprint of HarperCollinsPublishers

First published in Lions in 1995

Lions is an imprint of CollinsChildren'sBooks,
a Division of HarperCollins*Publishers* Ltd,
77-85 Fulham Palace Road, Hammersmith, London W6 8JB

1 3 5 7 9 8 6 4 2

Copyright © Jahnna N. Malcolm 1995

The author asserts the moral right to be
identified as the author of the work

ISBN: 0 00 675056 7

Printed and bound in Great Britain by
HarperCollins Manufacturing Ltd, Glasgow.

To Sherry Odom,
a favourite Capricorn

CHAPTER ONE

CAPRICORN (December 22-January 19)
Your sun in Capricorn's tenth house wants to
shine but struggles. It doesn't help that a full
moon is playing havoc in Pisces tonight. Don't
give in to your fears – conquer them.

Cat Milligan tried to scream, but the musty
scent of lavender choked her. She reached out
and her hands groped blindly in the darkness.
Her fingertips brushed thickly textured wallpaper
and she recoiled in horror.

"Oh, no," she gasped, stumbling back.

She was in the House.

"Not again."

Panic shook her and Cat glanced wildly
round, searching for a way out. To her right was
a dining room filled with an ornate wooden
table and eight straight-backed chairs. Dust
covered the table and sideboard laden with

tarnished silver and china.

Cat spun round. To her left lay an old-fashioned parlour, with a shabby red velvet love seat and matching couch resting on a frayed oriental rug. Potted ferns and palms drooped in the corners, parched for want of water.

"Kitty Cat?" Her name was whispered from the top of the massive wooden staircase.

"No!" Cat struggled to back away. She didn't want to go up those stairs. "I won't go."

"Hurry!" The whisper came again, low and urgent.

Cat tried to run. Her arms and legs pumped and there was a sensation of movement, but she went nowhere. Suddenly an icy breeze swept through the door behind her, leaving goose bumps underneath her nightgown.

The breeze propelled her forwards, up the huge staircase with its heavy walnut bannister. On the landing she heard a sound. Someone was laughing. Something else, perhaps a pet, was whining or mewing. *Maybe it's a kitten in trouble.*

Cat was drawn towards the sound. She floated past door after door, searching for the right one. Her feet touched down in front of a narrow door unlike the rest. She opened it, and found a rickety staircase that led to a small door encased in darkness.

"Go back *now*!" a voice shouted inside her. "The bad thing. The bad thing is up there, waiting for you."

Cat's mouth moved but she felt as if she were talking underwater. "Can't go back. Must go forwards."

With heart pounding like a jackhammer in her chest, Cat went up. Her hand slid along the thin metal railing. *It's so cold. Everything is cold here.*

First the right foot. Then the left. *Must go up. Through that door.*

Fear roared in her ears, clashing with the staccato thumping of her heart. There was no turning back.

Two more steps, and I'm at the door.

Cat stared at the strange pistol-grip handle gleaming in the sharp-edged shadows. The musty smell of lavender was stronger now. Behind the door, the frightened whimpering echoed from inside.

"Open it." The whisper was like a command.

Cat tried to resist but she had no control over her body. She watched helplessly as her arm bent and her fingers closed upon the handle.

The metal vibrated in her grip and turned.
Without warning the door burst open.
Cat screamed. And screamed.
And screamed.

CHAPTER TWO

*W*hen Cat Milligan awoke, someone was holding her down. Heart pounding, her body covered with perspiration, she struggled against her captor. The tangled sheets and blankets worked against her and she couldn't escape.

"Cat!" a woman's voice said with authority. "Catherine, stop!"

She lay still at once, but shivers ran the length of her arms and legs. She recognized her mother's voice. *I really am awake. Mom is never in my dreams.*

"Are you all right?" her mother asked. The weight on Cat's chest went away and the bedside lamp came on, bathing the bedroom in a rosy glow from the burgundy lampshade.

"I'm fine," Cat lied.

"You had that nightmare again."

Cat wanted to deny it but couldn't. The nightmare had haunted her since the age of five and the symptoms were always the same. Her own voice rasping, "The door, don't open the door!" And then the screams and convulsions.

"Oh, Cat." Her mother sat on the edge of the bed. "I thought we had put that behind us."

Cat sat up, pulled her nightgown down over her legs, and hugged her knees. "It is behind us, Mom," Cat murmured, weakly.

Mrs Milligan reached out and stroked Cat's brow. "Was it the same house?"

"Yes. The one with the—" Cat could barely utter the word. "—stairs."

Mrs Milligan sighed heavily. "Honey, we've never lived in a house with stairs. Your father and I made sure of that. We've carefully avoided apartments, or even houses with basements, because of your fear. This house is flat as a pancake. There isn't a stair on the whole property. Not even one step. Please." She folded her hands tightly in her lap. "Please try not to start this again."

Cat's eyes filled with tears as she looked at her mother. Mrs Milligan look tired and old beyond her years. Cat knew her nightmares had put those deep lines in her mother's brow and peppered her hair with grey.

"I'm sorry," Cat murmured for probably the billionth time in her life. "I can't help it."

Mrs Milligan forced a smile to her lips and hugged Cat. "I know that. It's probably the move, dear. It's been stressful on all of us."

"I think I'm having a little trouble adjusting to a new place," Cat said mechanically.

Her father's job as district attorney had taken them to several big cities. Each time they moved the nightmares would become more frequent. And each time they did, Cat would give the same excuse. "I'm just having a little trouble adjusting."

Mrs Milligan took her hand and pulled her to the bedroom window. "Come here. I want to show you something."

A purple and pink dawn was spreading out behind the green, rolling hills of the countryside. "It's beautiful," Cat murmured.

"Asheville is your home," Mrs Milligan said. "You were born here. So was I, and my mother before me. Your roots are here in North Carolina. And you should always feel safe and protected."

"Safe and protected," Cat repeated. But I don't.

"Atlanta was way too big for us," her mother went on. "So was Charleston. Practically from the moment we left eleven years ago, we've

13

been dreaming about returning home to Asheville."

"I know." Cat didn't want to spoil their dream with her nightmares.

"So," Mrs Milligan gave her another hug "we'll just go forwards. I'm already so proud of how you're doing at this school."

As opposed to all the others, where I did so terribly. Cat had been a loner in Atlanta and Charleston. But it had been difficult for her to make friends when she missed so many days of school.

"I'm trying my best to fit in," Cat told her mother. She was, too. Her normal routine at a new school was to hang back and wait for someone – anyone – to speak to her. But upon enrolling at Thomas Wolfe High, she had forced herself to be outgoing. On the first day of school, Cat took a front-row seat in her homeroom and made a special effort to introduce herself to everyone seated round her. It had paid off, too.

"I'd say you're doing better than just fitting in," her mother said, smiling a genuinely proud smile. "The Delta Phi sorority asked you to pledge, and they only choose...how many girls a year?"

"Six," Cat replied. "But I think Sara might have had something to do with that. She's so outgoing and pushy. She probably forced them to make me one of their pledges."

Mrs Milligan laughed. "Sara is pretty bold. You could use a little of that Sara Bright assertiveness."

Cat nodded. Sara had been sitting directly behind her in their homeroom that first day. She was thrilled that Cat had spoken first. "Usually that's my job," Sara had told her.

"That sorority is over a hundred years old," her mother continued. "I remember it from when I went to high school. Practically every girl at Thomas Wolfe wanted to be a Delta Phi."

"It's the same way now," Cat said, smoothing her thick auburn hair into a ponytail. She normally slept with it in a plait, but it had come undone during her nightmare. Cat grabbed a rubber band from her dresser top and looped it round her nearly waist-length hair. "You should have been in the halls when Marli made the announcement of this year's pledges. Practically everybody who wasn't chosen was upset. Some girls even cried." Cat shook her head. "Sometimes I wonder if having a sorority is worth making so many other people

15

miserable."

Her mother squeezed her hand. "All clubs exclude and include, that's the nature of the business. Don't worry about it." She walked Cat back to her bed. "Now get back in bed. There's still time for us to get a little more sleep."

"OK." Cat really didn't want to be left alone but the approaching dawn had leached most of the shadows from her room. She felt she could control the residual fear.

"I want you to remember something," Cat's mother murmured as she pulled the blankets over her. Cat looked up into her mother's eyes.

"Your father and I love you very much. No matter what happens, we're there for you. The last few months have been really good for all of us."

Cat knew she was referring to the fact that no one had been forced to stay in her bedroom and hold her hand throughout the night so she could sleep. Things had been better. "I know, Mom. Thanks." She watched her mother go, then got up out of bed. She wasn't about to chance the nightmare again.

Just to be on the safe side, Cat recited an exercise one of her therapists had taught her. It was called "This is my room." She'd learned it when she was in first grade and had used it all the way through school.

She stood in the centre of the room, her arms open wide. "This is my room," she began. "Where I am safe from harm." She moved to her wardrobe. "These are my clothes." They hung neatly in the wardrobe, blouses first, followed by skirts, dresses, and jeans and slacks.

"Grandma's oak dresser that she gave to me when I was twelve." Cat placed her hand on the wooden chest. An antique brush set, a small shell filled with hair ornaments, and a photo of her parents were the only things adorning the top.

Cat moved slowly along the wall. "My pictures." Two dozen of her favourite black-and-white photographs filled the wall across from her bed. They were hand-matted and framed. Even though she'd taken hundreds of pictures over the last couple of years, her favourite pictures hadn't changed. Cat liked stability.

"This is my desk." The small rolltop had been specially modified by her father to hold her PC, and several of the pigeon holes inside the desk held rolls of camera film. Cat was very organized – the rolls waiting to be processed had orange dots with dates and her own brand of shorthand on them detailing the contents.

"My camera." Her Nikon sat on its own special shelf.

"My view." She gazed out the window. A thin, ash-white fog had gathered and draped the tree-crowned hills. It looked cold, but touching her fingers against the glass told her it wasn't.

"My fears are gone." Cat flung her arms in the air to shake away her demons. This was the finish of the exercise. Usually it helped calm her. But today, she still felt uneasy.

"Outside," she murmured. "Get away from the walls." Quickly stripping off her nightgown, Cat dressed in jeans, thick cotton olive-green sweater and sneakers. She slipped on her Atlanta Braves baseball cap, then tucked her Nikon 35mm with short telescopic lens into her camera pack which she belted round her waist.

Cat listened to make sure her mother had gone back to bed, then eased up the window and let herself outside. *It's better being outside.*

Fall was coming to the mountainous countryside round Asheville. But the colourful foliage wasn't what she photographed. Instead, Cat focused her camera on the bare limbs thrusting up tall and stark against the rising dawn. She liked the contrast of black and white. Too much colour fed her overactive imagination.

Cat climbed a hill near her house and spent the next hour lost in the calming world of black and white. When finally she glanced at her watch, she realized she'd lost all track of time.

This is ridiculous. I've been up since four and now I'm going to be late for school. Cat snapped the lens cap back on her camera and tucked it back in her waist pack.

Before sprinting down the hill, she took one last look at the little town of Asheville nestled snugly in the Great Smoky Mountains. *I know I should feel safe. But I don't.*

Somewhere out there, the House was still waiting.

CHAPTER THREE

The full moon is waning. Your mental state should improve. Your self-esteem is coming back. Sometimes you feel like you're psychic – and maybe you are. Transiting Venus is trine your Sun, which is perfect for companionship.

Cat parked her yellow Tracker 4x4 in the student parking lot, then jumped out and pulled at the black convertible top. Less than a year old, the vehicle was a high point in Cat's life. Money had been tight when she was growing up, but lately her dad's career had taken off and her mother had been able to return to work as a nurse.

Mrs Milligan had always claimed household duties had been too pressing for her to work, but Cat knew better. It was because of Cat and the chronic nightmares that she had stayed home.

"Hey, girl!" a cheery voice called out. "Need some help?"

Cat looked up to see Sara Bright, wearing a floral print baby-doll dress, ruffled ankle socks and red high-top sneakers, coming across the parking lot. "Sure," she replied, tugging at the stubborn snaps on the car's canvas top.

Sara dropped her books on the car next to Cat's and dug in her purse. "But first, did you read Star Trax today?"

"No, I didn't see the paper this morning." Cat and Sara made a point of reading their horoscopes each day and comparing notes before school.

"Well, fasten your seatbelt," Sara said, waving a newspaper clipping in the air. "You're going to have a great day. Transiting Venus is affecting your Sun, and love is on the horizon."

"How about fame and fortune?" Cat asked, cocking her head to try to read the clipping. "Capricorns need money to enjoy their romance."

Sara shook her head. "Sorry, Cat, no money. Just love with a capital L-U-V." She reached over and pinched Sara's arm. "Lucky you."

Cat couldn't help giggling at her friend. Tiny Sara, with her cropped brunette hair looked like an elf. Her eyes were a delicious milk-chocolate brown that made boys' hearts melt when they stared into them. Cat had observed the effect first-hand. Even the sternest teachers lightened up when addressing Sara.

"What does the day look like for Scorpios?" Cat asked, finishing snapping her side into place.

"Don't ask." Sara made a face and shoved the clipping back in her bag. "I'm supposed to pay close attention to detail today."

"What does that mean?"

Sara rolled her eyes up and recited from memory. "Check for mistakes in your homework and pay close attention to any new rules. It's the little things that will trip you up if you're not careful." Sara threw her hands in the air. "I might as well go back to bed if all I'm supposed to do today is check my homework and follow rules."

"Ah, it's not that bad," Cat said, taking off her baseball cap and tossing it in the back seat of her car. "Remember what mine said last week? 'Tact is usually your strong suit, Capricorn, but not today. So don't open your mouth – you'll probably stick your foot in it.' Now that was bad."

The first bell rang, signalling that they had fifteen more minutes before the school day would begin.

Sara looped her bag over her shoulder. "Come on. I'd better do what my horoscope says. I have to go to my locker, fix my hair and retouch my lipstick before school starts."

"Hey!" Cat put her hands on her hips. "What about my car top? You said you were going to help."

"Ooops, sorry. I totally spaced out." Sara grabbed the opposite side of the black canopy and quickly snapped it into place. "Have I ever told you how much I like your car?" she asked.

"Many times," Cat replied, with a grin. She knew she was one of the few sophomores who had a licence and a car to go with it but that was because she was older than her classmates. She'd been held back a grade, due to her battle with chronic nightmares.

"Well, let me tell you again." Sara cupped her hands round her mouth and spoke more loudly. "I really like your car."

A trio of boys Cat recognized from the student council was strolling through the parking lot and turned to look.

They grinned and pointed at Sara. One of them shouted, "Look, it's Rainbow Bright!"

Sara kicked her leg up behind her and struck

a pose with one hand tucked behind her head.

Cat gave Sara a mock scolding glance as they gathered their books. "You're a flirt."

"I cannot tell a lie," Sara replied solemnly. "I am."

"And you take pride in that character defect."

"It's not a defect," Sara argued, "it's a skill." The girls walked by the Harkness Day Care Centre on the way to the high school cafeteria. A three metre chain-link fence made a steel border separating the day care centre from the school grounds. On the other side, swirling through merry-go-rounds, seesaws, swings, and a sandbox, dozens of pre-schoolers screamed in merriment and mock terror under a thick canopy of trees.

"I don't think Marli likes flirts," Cat said, referring to their sorority's president. "I think I heard her say something about it at our first pledge meeting."

"Marli's such a Libra," Sara said with a shrug. "All she cares about is how she looks and what people think of her."

Cat's eyes widened. "Don't let her hear you say that."

Sara wrinkled her nose at Cat. "You're taking this whole pledge thing way too seriously."

Cat shifted her books and watched a small boy in the day care centre chase a little girl in a Batman cape through the jungle gym. As she watched the children, Cat debated whether to tell Sara why receiving the invitation to pledge the Delta Phis had been one of the highlights of her life. Not because she was going to join a sorority but because, for once, she was an insider.

Sara waved her hand in front of Cat's face. "Am I right?"

Cat blinked, turning her gaze away from the playground. "Maybe a little bit. But Sara, those girls are the tops in our school. They're the smartest, prettiest—"

"And the biggest snobs," Sara finished for her. "You're new to this place, but in the past the Delta Phis have had a habit of making the rest of the girls at Thomas Wolfe feel like dirt."

Cat pursed her lips in thought. "Well, they can't be all bad. I mean, they asked you and me to join."

Sara stopped dead in her tracks. "Now, honestly, Cat, do you really think they'd be interested in someone like me if my mom and grandmother hadn't belonged to that sorority?"

Cat frowned. "What do you mean?"

Sara ticked off her problems on one hand. "I'm a so-so student, my mom has no money and socially I'm a wash-out. My dad blew that."

Cat didn't want to admit it to Sara, but she had heard about the scandal involving Sara's dad. Mr Bright had been a teacher at the high school. Two years before, he'd had an affair with the girl's softball coach, who was also married. They'd run off together, leaving Mrs Bright with Sara, her two brothers, and no income. Luckily, Sara's mother had been able to get a job in a small flower shop on Patton Avenue.

"Mom's broke all the time," Sara continued. "It's just because she was once a Delta Phi president that they invited me to pledge. It's their duty."

"But you're a good person," Cat protested. "That counts for a lot."

"Does it?" Sara looked doubtful. "Look, I'm raining all over your parade. You should be proud of being invited into the Delta Phis. You're this year's big surprise. They don't take many outsiders."

"But I'm not an outsider," Cat protested. Having been an outsider nearly all of her life, she hated the word. "I may be new now, but I

26

went to pre-school with a lot of you. I think I even have a class photo with most of the Delta Phis in it."

"Twenty three-, four- and five-year-olds," Sara chuckled, "all with crooked fringes. I think my mom cut mine the night before that photo was taken. It started at one eyebrow and sloped straight up to my parting. Very attractive."

Cat was opening her mouth to laugh, when a flash of movement caught her eye. A brown-haired girl at the day care centre, no older than three or four, threw an empty pail into the sky, then streaked for the nearest seesaw.

She had been standing by the sandbox where another little girl sat staring at Cat with dark hollow eyes. She was pale and thin and wore a pink and white checked sundress. Her hair, which was pulled into two bunches was very blonde, which made the dark circles under her eyes stand out even more.

The little girl started to move.

"No, don't!" Cat shouted. She was instantly filled with panic and tears blurred her vision. When it cleared, she saw only the laughing brown-haired girl on the seesaw.

The other little girl had vanished.

"Are you OK?" Sara asked, staring at Cat.

Cat blinked several times. "Yes. I think so."

"You sure?"

Cat clutched the fence, wrapping her fingers through the links. "Did you see her?" She searched the platoons of children racing inside the play yard but saw no sign of the little girl.

"Who?" Sara stepped beside her and peered through the fence.

"The little girl. The thin one with dark circles under her eyes."

Sara scanned the group. "I don't see a little girl with dark circles." She paused. "Are you sure you saw one?"

"I'm positive." Without knowing why, Cat continued searching frantically for the girl, moving along the line of fence to peer under the play equipment and round the side of the building. "She was in the sandbox staring at me. She seemed so lost and lonely. And then she was gone."

Sara stared at Cat. "Maybe she ran inside to get some cover-up for those dark circles."

Cat looked at Sara in confusion.

Sara shrugged. "It was joke. But she probably did go inside. To use the bathroom, or something like that." She looped her arm through Cat's. "Come on. We need to get to class before we have to go to the office for admit slips."

Cat turned slowly away from the day care centre. Goose bumps still prickled her forearms and the back of her neck.

"You look like you've seen a ghost," Sara said, studying her face as they walked.

"I've spent my life seeing ghosts," Cat murmured. She closed her eyes, trying to clear her head and picture something simple and unthreatening like the big red metal school doors. Instead, the image of the little hollow-eyed girl seemed painted on the insides of her eyelids. She felt dizzy.

"Hunk alert!" Sara suddenly hissed, locking her knees. "Over there. By the hickory tree." Sara squinted (her vanity kept her from wearing glasses) at the dark figure leaning against the lightning-blasted hickory tree towering over the school yard. "Oh, shoot. It's your guy."

Cat blushed immediately when she recognized Taylor Dunne standing in the shadows of the scarred tree. He was dressed in jeans, boots, and a Confederate Army-styled blue denim shirt that had faded over years of washings. "I wish you would quit calling Taylor my guy," Cat whispered.

29

"You're dating him, aren't you?" Sara asked, putting one hand on her hip.

"Dating sounds so formal," Cat replied. A few weeks ago he'd bumped into her at the theatre downtown. Both of them had been alone and he'd quietly asked if she wanted company. At first she'd been nervous and didn't know what to say. While going to school in Atlanta, with her classmates knowing as much as they did about her, she'd never dated. Finally she said, "Sure." They'd gone out twice since and were going out again on Saturday. "We're seeing each other," Cat corrected Sara. "That's all."

Sara shrugged nonchalantly. "Then he's your guy." She squinted at him once more. Taylor held an artist's sketchpad in front of him in one hand. His other hand moved fluidly across the blank surface although he didn't appear to be looking at it. "What's he doing?"

"Sketching. He wants to be a professional artist."

Sara blinked in surprise. "Really? That's cool."

Cat was amazed that Sara didn't know that about him. Taylor had gone to school in Asheville all his life, just like Sara. His hobby should have been common knowledge. "He's very good."

Sara pointed. "Do you see *who* he's sketching?"

Cat looked. Seated in profile at one of the picnic tables in the school yard was Fiora Madden. Already exotic because of her dark skin and the cascade of ebony curls that ran down her slender back to her trim waist, Fiora had the added luxury of being half-Italian.

"Wait a minute. Look who Fiora is sitting with." Cat pointed to the four beefy guys surrounding her. "The entire front line of the football team."

"So what else is new," Sara said with a scowl. "Fiora has every guy at Thomas Wolfe wrapped round her finger."

"Taylor might be sketching them," Cat suggested. "He loves to do character studies. You know, quick sketches. He showed me some he's done of people at the bus stop downtown. Old guys, fat women with too many shopping bags. Little kids, tired and cranky. They're wonderful."

Sara held up one hand. "OK, I was wrong. Taylor isn't drawing the prettiest girl at our high school. He's just doing a character study of the

31

bonehead football team."

"Right." Cat pressed on, trying to get a grip on the emotions sailing through her like leaves caught in a whirlwind.

"Cat!"

Sara looked back over her shoulder. "Well, here he comes now," she murmured. "Maybe he can show us the picture and end our dispute."

Taylor's dark locks were tousled and wild, trickling down into the collar of his shirt as he jogged up. "Didn't you see me?" He focused his cobalt-blue eyes on Cat and suddenly she felt weak in the knees.

"Yes, she did," Sara answered for Cat. "But she thought you were busy."

Cat gave Sara her best "I'm going to strangle you!" look, then turned to Taylor. "She's right. I didn't want to disturb you."

A stray lock fell forwards over Taylor's brow and he tossed his head. "It was no bother. I've just been waiting to catch you before class."

Cat's throat went dry instantly. *He's going to cancel our date on Saturday. Right here in front of Sara and the entire student body.*

"I was wondering if you had any plans for after school," Taylor said.

"No." Cat relaxed a little. Maybe he's going

to wait to cancel. At least I won't be humiliated in front of so many people.

He shoved one hand in the pocket of his jeans and tossed the lock of hair out of his face once more. "I'd like to take you somewhere. Just a drive. Maybe we can make a little picnic of it."

Cat was smiling so hard her cheeks hurt. "Sure," she giggled. "I'd love to."

Her bubble of happiness burst almost instantly as Bryce Holtz, the varsity star linebacker, stuck his ugly face between them. "Let me see what's on that pad," he demanded, reaching for Taylor's sketchpad.

"No." Taylor yanked it out of his reach. "It's none of your business."

Darryl Frederick, one of the other beefy players, joined Bryce. Standing side by side, they formed a human wall, blocking Taylor and Cat's way. "You hear Bryce. Show him what you've been drawing. The girls don't like you sneaking round drawing dirty pictures of them."

Taylor took a couple steps back. "That's ridiculous. I draw caricatures, and that's it."

"Prove it," Darryl said, folding his arms across his chest.

Cat stepped in between the two football players. Looking Darryl square in the eye, she hissed, "He doesn't have to prove anything to you."

Bryce made a swipe at Taylor's book while Darryl tried to shove Cat out of his way.

"Leave her alone," Taylor shouted, which distracted him just enough for Bryce to knock the pad out of his arms. The sketchpad hit the ground and flopped open.

The revealed drawing caught everyone by surprise. The girl in the picture was obviously Fiora, dressed in a flowing garment that pooled at her feet. A high cowl framed her face, off-setting the sardonic smile that gave her features an evil glint. Four ugly trolls sat on the table and benches round her, fawning and attentive as she poured them drinks in cups made of hollow-eyed skulls. The Bryce-troll was easily recognizable because of the No Fear sports gear shirt he wore. Concealed in Fiora's hand was a small bottle bearing a skull and crossbones. The school yard had been turned into an eerie landscape filled with creeping vines and upthrust thorns of broken rock.

Bryce glared down at Taylor. "What's that mean?"

"It looks pretty self-explanatory to me," Taylor replied, as he bent to pick up the pad.

Darryl got to it first and quickly flicked through the rest of the pages. The collection of drawings was mesmerizing. Fantastic monsters with gaping, fanged jaws, collections of human skulls and assorted bones on castle ramparts and high cliffs. They were all drawn in charcoal and pencils, skilfully rendered blacks and greys on the bright white paper.

Skilfully drawn, but almost horrifying to look at. Cat squeezed her eyes shut to block out the monstrous images.

"You're a freak!" Bryce shoved Taylor's shoulder, knocking him backwards. "Just like your brother! Total losers."

"Mr Holtz!"

Cat turned and saw Mr Seavers, the football coach, standing in the nearby doorway.

"Front and centre, Holtz," Mr Seavers barked. "You, too, Frederick. I think we'll start the day with a visit to the principal's office.

"Come on, Coach, he asked for it," Darryl grumbled as he followed Bryce and Mr Seavers towards the school building.

"Mr Dunne?" the coach called. "Do you want to talk about this?"

Taylor looked up at the coach, who was obviously waiting for him to accuse Bryce of starting the fight. "No. It wouldn't do any good anyway." Taylor stood up, brushed off the back of his jeans and retrieved his sketchpad. His cheeks were flushed pink with embarrassment. "I'll catch you later."

He turned and ducked into the swarm of students heading for the main hall.

Sara, who had witnessed the entire exchange, touched Cat's arm. "Well, that wasn't exactly a promising way to start the day."

"Oh, that makes me mad," Cat fumed. "Why did they have to pick on Taylor? He didn't do anything." She ran one hand through her hair in frustration. "Why do people have to be so cruel?"

"Taylor brought a lot of it on himself years ago," Sara replied. "He carried a major chip on his shoulder because of his brother."

"What about his brother?" Cat asked.

"Travis is five years older than Taylor, but he's a major criminal. He used to steal cars, then he got into dealing drugs. They finally sent him to prison about four years ago."

"I see," Cat nodded. *We all have secrets.*

"When we were in junior high, the least little mention of his brother and Taylor would start a fight. Now I guess he deals with it by drawing."

She shot Cat a nervous glance. "Extremely weird pictures."

Cat didn't reply, even when Sara said goodbye and reminded her of the Delta Phi meeting at lunch. She was too upset. First the nightmare that had disrupted her sleep. Then the strange little girl in the sandbox. And now Taylor and his sketchpad full of monsters. It was too much to handle all at once.

Cat took a deep, calming breath and tried to focus on her first class. "Don't dwell on the past," she repeated her therapist's words to herself. "Keep moving forwards, one step at a time."

CHAPTER FOUR

"This meeting of the Delta Phis is officially called to order," Marli Kendrick announced as the bell rang, signalling that the lunch period had begun. The president of the Delta Phis stood under the big elm tree at the edge of the school grounds, looking like a page out of a preppy fashion magazine in her navy-blue pleated skirt and plaid waistcoat. The collar and cuffs of her white blouse were trimmed in plaid piping that matched her vest, and a navy-blue bow held her hair in place. "We've got a lot of business to cover this afternoon, so you pledges listen up."

Cat and Sara sat cross-legged at the back of the circle of girls surrounding Marli. Cat opened her bag and took out the bean sprout, tomato and avocado on toast sandwich she'd made herself for lunch. After draping a paper towel over her ankles, she opened a Thermos containing cottage cheese and started to eat.

Marli never ate at meetings. She was rail-thin. In fact Cat couldn't remember ever seeing her eat. Marli held a small cloth-covered notebook that she referred to only occasionally. "First Vicki will do the roll call and then we'll get started."

Vicki Hamilton, a thin girl with thick glasses, stood up and read the roll. As each girl's name was called, she would raise one hand and answer "Here."

Cat couldn't get over how formal this meeting was. All of them seemed to be acting like miniature versions of their mothers. *No, worse, like old ladies at a garden club tea.*

After Vicki sat down, Marli once again took her place at the centre of the circle. "Fall is our busiest time of the year because of the Homecoming Parade and Dance, the haunted house for Hallowe'en, and the Thanksgiving charity fund-raiser," Marli began. "Practically every year we win the prize for best float in the homecoming parade. That's why it's so important for us to come up with a winning idea before we leave today."

"*This* is serious business?" Sara whispered to Cat, rolling her eyes. "You won't catch me stuffing paper napkins in chicken wire for a stupid old float."

"Sara?" Marli trained her steel-grey eyes on Cat and Sara. "Did you have something you wanted to share with the group?"

Sara paled for the briefest of moments. Then she raised her lunch box. "My bologna, cheese and peanut butter sandwich? I made it myself. You're welcome to it."

Some of the new pledges giggled and Marli shot Sara a tight smile. "Very cute. But in the future, try not to talk during the meetings. It's distracting and, well, a little rude."

That shut up the rest of the pledges and sent a pink blush up Sara's cheeks. She winced, murmuring, "Excuse me, everyone."

Marli flashed a triumphant smile. She'd put a pledge in her place, maintaining her position as president. "Brenda and Vicki were up late last night brainstorming. Some of their ideas are very cool. Brenda?"

"Thanks, Marli." Brenda Hubbard, in white shorts, citron polo shirt and Delta Phi visor that snapped under her brown ponytail, hopped on to the stone wall circling the elm. Brenda was Marli's right-hand girl and keeper of the sorority flame. She knew the rule book by heart and was the first to let anyone know if they'd crossed over the line. Sara called her Sarge behind her back. "This year's homecoming theme is Reach for the Stars," Brenda said. "So Vicki and I made a list of star-type titles, like Wishing on a Star."

She looked to the group for their reaction. Several of the seniors nodded approval. Marli, clutching her notebook off to the side, made no response. Brenda took that as a rejection, and went on to the next title.

"Be a Star. We thought we could all do a Hollywood take-off. You know, wear sunglasses and wave, since we are the stars of the school."

"Gag me with a pitchfork," Sara whispered to Cat, who nearly choked on a beansprout, trying not to laugh out loud.

Marli, who was carefully watching the other girls, had noticed the cool response to Brenda's idea. "I thought that was cute last night, but I guess it does sound a little conceited," she said tactfully. "We may be stars at Thomas Wolfe High, but we don't need to brag about it. What else have you got, Brenda?"

Brenda stared down at her list and read off the titles. "Twinkle, Twinkle, Little Star." She looked up quickly at the girls. "Just kidding. Let's see, we have Stars of Tomorrow, Stars and

Stripes, and Stars in Your Eyes."

"Major groaner," Cat whispered under her breath to Sara, who giggled right out loud. Brenda heard and shot them both dirty looks.

"OK, OK." Brenda crumpled up the sheet on her pad. "Those were just a few suggestions. If any of you can do better, go for it." She dropped back down on the grass in a sulk.

Sara offered Cat a bite off the wedge of pecan pie she had taken out of a plastic bag. "Come on. Pecans are good for you."

"Too sweet," Cat said, wrinkling her nose.

"Like those titles," Sara replied, with a shudder. "They spent a whole evening, and came up with that?"

"That's what they told Marli," Cat chuckled. "I bet they thought them up ten minutes before the meeting started."

Marli had once again taken the floor and called to the back, "Cat, did you have some idea you'd like to offer?"

"Me?" Cat pointed to herself with her sandwich. She could feel her cheeks instantly blaze red. "Well, um, yes. Since the, um, theme is Reach for the Stars, how about—" She said the first thing that came into her head. "Star Power?"

"Star Power," Marli repeated. "Hmmm. How do you see the float decorations?"

"Well, uh," Cat stalled. The newspaper's horoscope sticking out of Sara's notebook caught her eye. "It could have an astrological theme. The float would look like a Zodiac wheel, indicating that a Spartans' win is written in the stars. We could all dress like signs of the Zodiac. You know, Leo is the lion and Gemini, the twins."

Sara picked up on Cat's idea and jumped in enthusiastically. "And Marli, since you are a Libra, you could be dressed like that Greek goddess holding the scales of justice."

"Oooh, we could all dress like goddesses," added Michelle Morgan, the sorority's fashion plate. "And be holding something that indicates our sign. I'm Aquarius, the water bearer."

"Brenda, since you are a Taurus, you could wear a pair of bull horns," Sara said with a devilish grin.

Brenda rolled her eyes. "That's glamorous. What's your sign?"

"Scorpio," Sara replied.

Brenda gave her an icy stare. "It figures."

"This could be very cool," Marli said, tapping her pencil against her chin. "If all of us were in white, the items we held could be white, too. Brenda, you could hold a white papier-mache bull's head and maybe decorate it with glitter."

Sara nudged Cat with her elbow. "Marli likes it. It's a winner."

"We could wear white face make-up," Kim Corbett chimed in. "And make ourselves look like statues."

"Then we could have a horoscope written on to the Zodiac wheel showing that the Spartans will win the game and trample the Red Devils into the ground," Cat added.

"Spoken like a true Capricorn," Sara whispered.

One of the pledges, Angie Perkins, raised her hand. "If we used New Age music, I could choreograph a short dance that would have us circle the float and end up in just the right configuration."

Marli grinned. "That sounds like fun. But..." She gestured to Brenda. "You're in charge of the float, Brenda. If you don't like Star Power for our theme, then we shouldn't do it—"

"No, no!" Brenda shook her head so hard her ponytail slapped her face. "If everyone else likes it, I'll go along."

Marli turned to the others, who were chattering excitedly about which character they wanted to be. "All in favour?"

"Aye!" The vote was unanimous.

Several of the pledges patted Cat on the back. "Great idea." "Way to go." "Wish I'd thought of it."

Sara squeezed her hand. "Major score."

Cat's heart was beating like a tambourine. *I did it. I spoke up in a group and they didn't think I was an idiot.* Maybe things really would be better in Asheville.

The lunch bell rang loudly, issuing a ten-minute warning, and Marli quickly brought the Delta Phi meeting to a close.

As she gathered her things, Cat looked round the schoolyard. A small cluster of girls by the water fountain were watching her with respect and envy. *That's usually me. On the outside but, like a true Capricorn, desperately wanting to fit in.*

Sara, who had managed to finish off her sandwich, pecan pie and the rest of Cat's sandwich, dug in her purse for an apple. She took a crunchy bite. "Boy, you really did it back there. Anybody who had any doubts about your joining the Delta Phis was certainly put in their place."

Some of the glow faded from Cat's triumph.

"I didn't know there was anyone who wasn't sure of my membership."

"Brenda."

"Oh."

Sara waved her apple in the air. "Don't be so glum. Brenda didn't want me as a Delta Phi either. So you're in good company."

Cat wondered about that. Membership in the sorority didn't mean much to Sara, but it meant a lot to her. After all those years of being an outcast, it meant she could take her place among her peers. Not just any place, either, but as one of the elite.

"Cat? Can I talk to you a minute?" Marli, now sporting a pair of Ray-Ban sunglasses, stood by the entrance to the main building.

Sara squeezed Cat's elbow. "I'll see you after school."

Cat nodded and turned to Marli.

"Good suggestion today," Marli said. "As sorority president, I want this to be the Delta Phis' most successful year. With ideas like that, we should have no problem."

Not used to praise from anyone other than her parents or counsellor, Cat blushed and didn't know what to say.

"There is one thing I'd like to mention about

this morning's incident."

Cat cocked her head in confusion. "Incident? What incident?"

"With Taylor Dunne. I understand you were with him when he was doing those weird drawings of Fiora."

"I wasn't exactly with him," Cat started to explain.

"Whatever." Marli lowered her glasses to the tip of her nose. "You're new here and I just thought you should know – Taylor Dunne is not the kind of boy a Delta Phi should be spending time with. Especially not a pledge."

Cat was stunned and couldn't speak.

"Are you doing anything after school tomorrow?" Marli went on, as if there was no chance of rebuttal. "I've invited some of the Delta Phis to my house for tea. I thought we might go over some of the details about the Homecoming Dance. If you and Sara want to write down your Star Power idea, with maybe even a sketch of how you see the float, we could talk about that, too."

Cat was still thinking about Marli's warning about Taylor. All she could mutter was, "OK."

"Great." Marli slipped her Ray-Bans into place and strode confidently into the building where Brenda and Michelle, looking like bodyguards, were waiting for her.

Cat spent the remainder of the school day brooding about Marli's warning. She needed to see Taylor again, just to confirm her feelings about him, but he wasn't in the halls. He wasn't in sixth period Biology either, which meant she had to be lab partners with Vivian Kleist. Vivian refused to touch the flatworm they were to dissect. Cat had to do the whole thing herself, pinning it back on the specimen board and then answering questions from Mr York. Afterwords Cat hadn't been able to completely wash the formaldehyde smell from her hands.

When the day finally ended, she hadn't seen Taylor once. Cat looped her purse over her shoulder, heaved her books on to one hip, and trudged to the parking lot.

Halfway there, Sara caught up with her. "Why the glum face?"

Cat quickly relayed the entire conversation with Marli.

"So Marli doesn't want you dating Taylor?" Sara asked when she finished.

"She didn't come out and say that," Cat replied. "But she strongly discouraged me from talking to him."

"What a crock," Sara said.

Cat agreed. "I don't mind following their rules at the meetings but when they interfere with my private life, that's another matter."

The parking lot was chaos, as usual. Engines rumbled and boys' voices drifted in shouts across the asphalt. Heavy metal music blasted from car stereo speakers and all of the noise was punctuated by the chirping of car alarms.

"So what are you going to do?" Sara shouted over the noise.

"About Taylor?" Cat asked, digging in her purse for her keys.

Sara dropped her arms to her side. "Duh."

Cat shrugged. "I don't know. After today, I might not have to worry about it. I haven't seen Taylor at all. He wasn't in Biology or the halls. We were supposed to get together after school but that's probably off."

"Maybe we should send out a search party," Sara joked.

"After what happened with those jerks," Cat continued, "I wouldn't blame him for leaving."

"Those jerks," Sara pointed out, "are going to be playing their hearts out for our team on Homecoming. And our Star Power float will be predicting their win."

Cat winced. "Now I'm sorry I suggested the idea. Is it too late to take it back?"

"Yep. You're just going to have to accept the winning float medal for the Delta Phis and get all the glory, while I—" Sara pressed her hand to her chest. "While I, your poor, idea-less friend, will stand meekly on the sidelines, cheering for you."

"You have never done anything meekly in your life," Cat retorted with a grin.

"But what's that I see?" Sara leaped on to the bumper of the nearest pick-up truck and, shielding her eyes with one hand, looked into the distance. "Taylor Dunne – the terror of the Delta Phis, in our very own parking lot?"

"Where?" Cat felt her pulse quicken.

Sara pointed dramatically to Cat's Tracker. Taylor, wearing a black canvas dustercoat, stood leaning against the hood of her car. A posy of daisies and lavender was clenched in his fist, wrapped in dark green tissue paper.

Sara hopped back to the ground, blocking Cat's way.

"Hold it." She pointed to Cat's mouth. "You've got a goofy grin on your face."

"Oh god, do you think he'll notice?" Cat said, trying to suppress her smile.

"Probably not. Didn't you see the dark glasses and white cane?"

Cat smoothed out her features as best she could and started walking towards her car. "Is my hair wind-blown?" she whispered out of the corner of her mouth.

"No more than usual."

"Thanks a lot." Cat screeched to a halt and frantically tried to smooth her hair.

"It's because I care." Sara slapped at her shoulder. "If you'll look closely, you'll see that Taylor is in no shape to notice anything. He's got the same goofy grin on his face."

Cat saw it. Taylor took a step towards her.

"He *is* cute," Sara said.

"Sara!" Cat hissed.

"Just thought I'd mention it."

"Hi," Taylor said. He fumbled as he extended the posy, as if he'd only just remembered he was holding them. "I'd like to apologize for this morning."

"That wasn't your fault," Cat assured him.

"Maybe. But if I hadn't let them catch me sketching, you wouldn't have been caught in the middle."

Cat sniffed the blooms and was reminded instantly of her dream and the sickening smell of lavender. Without thinking she thrust her arm away from her.

"Is something the matter?" Taylor asked.

Cat instantly put a lid on that memory. "No," she said. "It's just that the scent of the flowers is, um, overwhelming. Thank you. It's a beautiful posy."

"Where are you headed?" Taylor asked.

"She's taking me to my mom's shop," Sara volunteered. It was their standard routine. Sara's mother would drive her to school and Cat would give her a lift to the flower shop after school. At that moment, Cat wished it wasn't always the habit.

Taylor shuffled his feet, shoving his hands in the pockets of his duster. "I was hoping you'd still be interested in a picnic," he said. "We could talk about things."

"Drop me at the shop first?" Sara asked, sticking her head between them.

"Sure," Cat answered, then looked at Taylor to make sure that was acceptable.

"No prob," Taylor said with a smile. "I'll follow you over there, then you can follow me." He turned and walked away. In his long canvas duster, faded jeans, and boots, he looked like an advertisement for the Old West.

"Wow," Sara said, throwing her head back against the seat, after they'd climbed into Cat's car. "Did you smell his cologne?"

"No." Cat started the car and pulled out into the traffic. She glanced in the rear-view mirror and watched Taylor fall into place behind her in his primer-spotted green Mustang.

"You will," Sara said confidently. "And when you do, watch out! Didn't you say he was a Capricorn, too?"

Cat nodded.

"That explains the mysterious air about him and the fact that he's a loner," Sara said.

"Do I have a mysterious air?" Cat asked, shifting into third.

Sara nodded, firmly. "Oh my, yes. You just seem loaded with secrets."

Cat smiled. *If you only knew.* "I think I'm just naturally reserved. At least that's what my mother says."

Sara shrugged one shoulder. "That's very Capricorn. You are also cautious. It takes Caps a while to warm up, but when you do – look out!" Sara leaned across the seat and teased, "You may not be able to control those animal passions."

"Sara!"

53

CHAPTER FIVE

If she hadn't seen Taylor take the sharp left turn off the highway, Cat would never have known the little dirt road existed. She wondered why Taylor had chosen so lonely a destination. Suddenly all the suspicions and warnings Sara and Marli had given her concerning Taylor clouded her brain. Her stomach tightened.

A cloud of dust whirled after the Mustang, and almost covered the ruby glare of the taillights as the brakes came on.

Cat pulled over behind him but didn't turn off her engine. She glanced at the posy lying on the passenger seat and felt guilty. But it didn't make the strong sense of caution go away.

Taylor got out of his car, reached into the back seat, and brought out a wicker picnic basket complete with red and white tablecloth. His sketchpad went under his other arm. He approached her car with an easy smile.

"Hey, you're wasting time," he called.

"What's out here, Taylor?" Cat asked, still not moving.

From the look on Taylor's face, Cat could tell he was aware of her reticence.

"Cat," he said in a soft voice, "this is just a place I like to come. The river's only a short distance away." He pointed with his free arm. "And I made a snack for our picnic." Opening the wicker cover of the basket, he revealed the contents. "Fried chicken, potato salad, baked beans, and some rolls. I fixed it this afternoon."

"That's not what I'd call a snack." Cat stalled.

"Look, if the location's bothering you, we can go to one of the parks back in town."

Despite the words and the offer, Cat knew Taylor would be hurt if that was what she chose. She switched off the ignition and got out. "No, it'll be OK here."

He looked at her for a long moment, searching her face, obviously not happy with her lack of enthusiasm. Cat wanted to kick herself for making things so awkward. It was just another instance of her fears reaching out to destroy any chance she had of having a normal life.

"Come on." Taylor took off down a narrow trail.

Cat followed him, glad she had worn tennis shoes that day. She had to brush branches out of her face and step over creeping bushes. Robins, bluejays, and cardinals flashed in front of her. Cat was amazed they didn't smash into the thick walls of trees.

She heard the river before she saw it, a happy trickling of noise that deepened as they neared. She watched Taylor closely, and the goose bumps and warm feeling in her stomach started again. He was so handsome, so sure-footed in the woods.

Taylor came to a halt at the edge of the riverbank. Cat tried to stop, too, but the loamy ground was soft under her feet. The incline of the riverbank was steep and she stumbled forward.

Taylor caught her almost effortlessly, wrapping his free arm round her waist. "Easy. I've got you."

She enjoyed the sensation of the strong arm round her waist as he helped her right herself. She rested her weight on his shoulder. For a moment she let the need for help become a brief hug.

"Are you all right?" Taylor asked.

"Oh yes." Cat ran her hands through her hair

just so she could take them off him.

"Gets a little tricky getting round down here." Taylor started off again. The trail narrowed and they came upon a water-filled inlet spanned by a fallen tree. He walked on to it with no problem.

Gamely, Cat tried to follow, but the footing wasn't as sure as he made it look. She slipped twice. "I guess I'll have to give up that dream of being a tightrope walker," she joked in a shaky voice.

"Don't worry," Taylor said, taking her hand. His fingers were warm as they entwined in hers. "A couple more times across this log and we'll have you headlining the circus." They inched across the fallen tree as bullfrogs dived into hiding. The tree canopy overhead was thick and blocked out all the sun, leaving only shadows.

Taylor started to release her hand when they gained firm ground again but Cat protested, tightening her grip. "It's kind of creepy here. Please don't let go."

"It's my pleasure." Taylor's smile was electric as he took a fresh hold on her hand.

A few minutes later they were in a small clearing that had evidently been Taylor's destination from the beginning.

"Do you like it?" he asked.

Cat studied the landscape. Less than ten metres away, the Swannanoa River glittered and slipped in the afternoon sun. Autumn-coloured mountains rose in the distance, cradling low-hanging thin clouds.

"It's beautiful," Cat said.

Taylor unfurled the red and white checked tablecloth and quickly set up for the picnic. Fried chicken filled a small plastic bucket, and the potato salad and baked beans were already portioned out in individual containers. "It's my favourite place to think."

"I can see why."

He handed her a plastic fork and kept one for himself. "Not exactly the Plum Tree," he said, referring to one of Asheville's poshest restaurants.

"I think it's—" Cat caught herself before she said romantic "—fine." No way was she going to spoil this moment by saying something so incredibly obvious.

"I've spent a lot of hours out here since I found this place." Taylor reached into a small cool box and pulled out a diet soda. "I've got some bottled water if you'd rather."

Cat shook her head. "Soda's fine."

Taylor ate haphazardly, his attention divided between Cat and his sketchpad.

She watched him for a while, enjoying the way he looked against the rustic background. His chin was square and firm, and his hands deft and sure as he worked the charcoal stick across the sheet of paper. In minutes he had rendered the basic outlines of the river and the mountains. His fingertips gleamed from rubbing the charcoal into grey tones.

"You draw beautifully," she said, after she'd eaten her fill.

"Thank you. But I've drawn this part of the river so many times I could probably do it in my sleep."

"Then why—?" Cat bit off the question before she could finish it.

He raised an eyebrow. "Why was I painting Fiora and her personal goon squad?"

Seeing no way clear of the question, Cat nodded.

Taylor put the charcoal away and flipped the sketchpad pages back to the drawing that had caused so much trouble that morning. He'd obviously put in some more time on it since cutting classes that day. Fiora and Bryce and the others were in much greater detail, the latter now possessing long and hairless rats' tails.

He tapped one of the trolls. "Because this is what sells. Not river landscapes. Those I could sell at a craft show in the mall. On a good day. But I want to do more."

"Like what?"

He hesitated. "You'll laugh." He studied the picture of Fiora and the trolls.

"No, I won't."

"Promise?" Taylor was deadly earnest.

"Promise." Cat crossed her heart with a forefinger.

"Disney," he said simply. "I want to draw Walt Disney cartoons."

Cat looked back at the drawing. "If that's what you really want to do, I think you will. These are really good."

"Thanks. It means a lot for someone to believe in you." Taylor glanced at his collection of trolls again, then touched the paper to trace the outlines.

"I didn't know Disney did that much with monsters," Cat said. Her video diet had been restricted to the classics like *Old Yeller* and *Herbie the Love Bug*. Fantasy pieces like *Snow White* and *Sleeping Beauty* had been off-limits because of the nightmares.

"Are you kidding?" Taylor asked. "Everybody loves monsters. People love being scared."

"Not everyone." Cat looked at the river in the distance and tried to control the sudden rush of emotions. *Not me.*

"Something bothering you?"

Cat studied him, looked deep into his eyes, and wondered how much she could reveal. "I don't like being scared."

Taylor chuckled. "Nobody likes being scared in real life. I was getting into my car this morning and Checkers, our cat, jumped on to the hood. I nearly had a heart attack."

Cat managed a weak smile. "That's not exactly what I'm talking about." Taylor seemed so nice, so understanding. It couldn't be wrong to tell him. *If we're going to spend time together, he'll know sooner or later.*

"I have had nightmares most of my life," Cat said bluntly.

Taylor picked up a chicken wing and took a thoughtful bite. "Everyone's had nightmares."

"These were chronic. My parents had to take me to a therapist because they were so bad."

"How old were you?" Taylor asked.

Cat hesitated. "Younger." Last year *was*

younger.

"Did the therapist help?"

"Some, but most of the kids at school found out about the therapy." She looked away from him because her eyes were filling with tears. "I had appointments regularly that took me out of school. When I got back later that afternoon or the next day, I would be teased about it. They called me Fraidy Cat."

"Kids can be cruel," Taylor murmured.

Cat nodded. "One of the boys in my class even took a picture out of the yearbook and glued a picture of a straitjacket on it, then circulated copies all over the school."

"That must have been hard on you," Taylor said sympathetically.

Cat bit her lip and plucked at the blades of grass next to the tablecloth. "It was very hard."

"Do you still have nightmares?"

"I haven't had one in months," Cat lied. *I can't tell him about last night. Not yet.* What if it got back to Marli and the other Deltas that she was still disturbed? They might reconsider their position and warn Taylor away from her.

"When the dreams finally stopped," Cat continued, "I didn't have to go to therapy any more, but it was too late."

"Everyone had you pegged."

Cat nodded.

"I know the feeling." Taylor dropped the stripped chicken bone into the plastic trash bag he'd brought along. "Baggage like that stays with you for a long time, and nobody can be more unforgiving than other kids."

The hurt in his voice made Cat wonder if he was thinking about his brother.

"But things are better now?" Taylor asked.

She nodded. "The nightmares stopped and my dad got transferred back to Asheville. He and my mom are happy."

"Are you?"

She was surprised by the question. "I think so."

Taking up his sketchpad, Taylor started drawing. He was turned so she couldn't see what he was doing. "What were the nightmares about?"

"A house. With something frightening inside. I've never seen what it was." *But I know it's there. Waiting for me.*

"When I was little, I had nightmares, too." Taylor gave her a lopsided grin. "I used to dream about this slimy, tentacled thing from Mars that was always hiding under my bed or in the wardrobe. I don't know where the idea came from, probably some old issues of *Eerie* magazine I found in garage sales when I was a kid. My mom and dad got real tired of hearing about Martians." He looked at her. "What were you afraid of?"

Cat groped to find the words to explain. In all the years of therapy, she could never find the exact ones she needed. "There was this...bad thing."

"A bad thing?"

"Yes. There was a door in the house, and the bad thing was waiting for me behind it." Cat felt extremely vulnerable. *Please look at me and say I'm not weird.*

Abruptly Taylor turned his sketchpad round so she could see it. Charcoal lines formed a tentacled beast struggling to knock down a wardrobe door and get out. It had a bulbous head that looked like a turnip, sparse, stalky hair, and five eyes. The slash of a mouth held uneven fangs.

"There it is. The stuff nightmares are made of," Taylor said with a grin. "Doesn't look so grim in the light of day, does it?"

Cat stared at the picture and the chorus of voices from school years past came back to haunt her. *He's making fun of me. I don't need this.*

Cat leaped to her feet and ran back into the woods.

"Hey, Cat!" Taylor sounded alarmed.

But she didn't care. She sprinted for all she was worth, not even hesitating when she came to the fallen tree. She was almost across it when her foot slipped off the worn bark. Unceremoniously, she tumbled head over heels.

Strong hands lifted her to her feet. "Are you OK?" Taylor's face was filled with concern.

Cat pulled away from him and brushed leaves and grass from her clothes. "I'm fine."

"Why did you run?"

"You were making fun of me." She started to walk away.

His hand on her shoulder stopped her. "Cat, no. I wasn't making fun of you. I'd never do that. I was making fun of being afraid of things that aren't real. There's no sense in that."

She whirled on him, suddenly angry. "I've been told that all my life! By my parents. My teachers. My friends. But my dreams are real to me. Very real."

"I'm sorry, Cat." Taylor held up his hands and stepped backwards, away from her. "I didn't mean to upset you."

"You don't understand what it's like to live with fear. Spending your days dreading to go to sleep. Knowing when you do finally collapse exhausted, the bad thing will be there. Waiting behind that door. Wanting you to open it. One night I will."

"But you said you weren't having the nightmares any more," Taylor said.

"I'm not." Cat spun away from him, afraid that he would see the lie in her eyes.

"Look at me." Taylor took her by the shoulders and gently turned her round. "Cat, I like you very much. I'd never hurt you. Can't you see that?"

Cat took a deep, shuddering breath and confessed, "I've had the same dream every night since I was five. It has warped my life, and my family's. I couldn't go to sleep unless all the doors were open and every light was on in the house. It used to drive my parents crazy. Darkness, any darkness, would set off an anxiety attack. I couldn't even stand to be in a classroom watching a film without freaking. And no one understood."

Taylor's brow was creased in a deep frown and he said nothing.

That's it. You blew it. "I've got to go," Cat said in a small voice. "I'm sorry I ruined your picnic."

Taylor caught her hand before she could walk away. His eyes were dark and intense. "You didn't ruin our picnic. I had a good time. I'm just sorry you didn't have a good time."

"I did, though."

Taylor's face brightened. "Does that mean we're still on for a movie Saturday night?" He crossed his heart. "No monsters of any kind. I promise."

Cat smiled in spite of herself. "OK."

Without warning, he leaned in close. She felt his breath on her cheek, then his soft lips were hard against hers. Just as suddenly it was over, but the warm, fuzzy feeling in the centre of her stomach went on.

Cat had just had her first kiss and she hadn't even been able to prepare for it. Hurriedly she tried to brand all the sensations in her mind, not wanting any of the memory to fade away.

"How do you feel now?" Taylor asked.

"Much better." Cat's cheeks flushed pink. "You surprised me."

"Good." His grin was infectious. "I like to surprise people. Give me a minute to gather up the picnic stuff and I'll walk you back to your car."

"I'll help." When they had everything together, Taylor took her hand and they walked back through the trees. Cat felt safe. There wasn't a monster in the forest that would dare touch her with Taylor at her side.

Chapter Six

You're still a bit skittish, Capricorn, but that's just Mercury trying to outrun the Sun. Don't be nervous – it'll pass. If you have faith in yourself, you'll leap over all adversaries and obstacles just like your symbol, the Goat.

"So he kissed you?" Sara was ecstatic.

Sitting behind the wheel of the Tracker the next afternoon, Cat felt embarrassed. They were on their way to Marli's house to have tea with the other Delta Phis.

"Yes, he kissed me."

"You kissed him back?"

Cat put mock exasperation in her voice. "What was I supposed to do? Leave him there with his lips hanging out?"

"You could have."

"I didn't."

"You kissed him!"

"Yes." Cat was afraid the car next to them

could overhear the conversation. She turned up the radio to cover their words. Marli's address was Cottonwood Circle. Neatly typed and photocopied directions were taped to the dash.

"Now don't feel like you're gossiping out of turn," Sara said. "I promise to ask Taylor the same questions."

"You'd better not."

"Bribe me."

Cat looked at her. "Candy bar."

"Won't settle for anything less than a chocolate sundae. With nuts." She held up fingers. "Two scoops."

"OK."

"I'll watch you eat your frozen yogurt." Sara rubbed her stomach and gave a false smile of contentment. "Yummy." Immediately afterwards, she stuck a finger in her mouth and made gagging noises.

Cat shook her head. "You're merciless."

"Can't help it. It's my natural Scorpian way."

Cat checked the directions and took the next right turn.

"There's Audubon," Sara said, pointing. "It leads to Cottonwood Circle."

Even after taking off her sunglasses and squinting, Cat couldn't read the street signs.

"How do you know?"

"The top of that house. The pink one. It's on Audubon."

Cat stopped at the red light and stared at the tall house. It was a three-story Victorian building painted an elegant pastel pink. An uneasy feeling began in her stomach, then churned round inside her.

A car horn squawked behind her, breaking the spell. Cat glanced in the rear view mirror and saw a blue-haired lady in a white Cadillac getting ready to give her another blast.

"Any particular shade of green you want that light?" Sara asked.

Chagrined, Cat pulled across the intersection and took the following right on to Audubon. The pink Victorian was four houses down on the left. She slowed to a stop across the street in front of it.

The house sat back away from the street. Three gorgeous flowerbeds with rock trimming formed a triangle in the front. Vari-coloured petunias flowered brightly in the one closest to the street, while zinnias filled the two in front of the house.

Sara snapped her fingers. "Earth to Cat. Earth to Cat. Come in, Cat. Over."

Taking a deep breath, Cat let it out slowly, just the way Mr Hopkins, her therapist, had taught her. With severe effort, she broke the spell the house had put on her. No matter what, it wasn't the house of her nightmares.

"I'm OK," she said, and it sounded shaky even to her ears.

"Are you sure you want to do this?" Sara asked, continuing to stare at her.

"Yes." Cat glanced back at the pink house. Movement caught her eye. The drapes were drawn back in the right bedroom window on the second floor, revealing the small form of a child. A breath later, and Cat recognized who it was. *The little girl from the playground!* As she watched, the little girl waved but Cat wasn't sure it was in welcome – or warning. Just as she was about to call out to Sara, Cat blinked – and the little girl was gone.

"Cat?"

"Just a minute." Frantically, Cat scanned the house. "There she is!" Now the little girl was standing at the mesh fence enclosing the back yard to one side of the house. Her tiny hands were knotted in the steel wire. She looked like a prisoner. "Do you see her?"

"Who?" Sara leaned across the seat.

A brown station wagon with at least half a dozen small boys in baseball uniforms rolled by, obscuring their view. When it was gone, so was the little girl. "She was just there."

"Who?"

"The little girl from the day care centre," Cat murmured, running one hand through her hair. "The one with the hollow eyes."

"Kids move fast," Sara said. "You've seen how my little brother is. Here one minute, then up the neighbour's apple tree, shaking the squirrels from the branches, the next."

"I guess so." Reluctantly, Cat drove forwards. She found Cottonwood Circle easily enough, but when she turned on to it, real panic settled in. Her arms shook and her palms were wet with perspiration.

"Here we are," Sara announced.

The circle ended abruptly. Four houses lined the cul-de-sac like the points of a compass. A small parking area was filled to overflowing with cars Cat recognized as belonging to other members of the sorority.

"Park over there," Sara directed. "Marli's mom had extra space put in once they returned from New York."

Cat's reflexes were off, and she narrowly

avoided locking bumpers with a white Lexus. She switched off the engine and noticed her hands were shaking terribly. *Calm down. You're just nervous about the party. Relax. You'll be all right.* Cat took a few more deep breaths in an effort to subdue the panic that was dangerously close to taking over.

Cat and Sara hopped out of the car, looking like clones in their jeans and blue-and-gold Delta Phi sweatshirts. But Marli had said that dress was casual and they had taken her at her word.

The four houses on the cul-de-sac were all Victorians. Tall and stately, with plenty of landscaping, they made Cat feel like she was at the bottom of a canyon. She glanced up at the pale blue sky for relief. Instead, her balance whirled, setting off a bout of vertigo.

Sara caught her by the arm. "What did you have for lunch? You look a little green round the gills."

Cat took a deep breath. "I'm not sure. But I am feeling a little shaky. The fresh air will probably help."

She followed Sara mechanically. They threaded their way through the parked cars, and Cat had to lean on some of them to keep going.

"The pool's at the back," Sara explained. "It's covered, of course, but it's got a killer deck area, and there's a putting green. Mrs Kendrick played golf in college. She was hoping Marli would develop an interest but she never did. Her dreams of the next Nancy Lopez went down the drain, but the putting green stayed."

The Kendrick house faced slightly away from the circular drive and was partially hidden by tall, sculpted conifers. Cat got the impression of an immense, screened veranda, but not much else. It was two stories high and had a tall attic roof. The exterior was painted a soft ash-blue, with white trim, that looked new.

Cat was reeling by the time they neared the high privacy fence surrounding the back yard. The back gate swung open. It was Brenda. "Come on in. You're the last to arrive."

"Are we?" Sara asked pleasantly. "I hope we haven't held up the tea."

Brenda shook her head. "Hardly. We are just about to start, though."

"Oh, good," Sara said in a overly friendly tone. Then she murmured to Cat, "I don't think Brenda likes us. Do you get that feeling?"

Cat couldn't respond. The closer she got to the main house, the shakier she felt. The pool was surrounded by a gigantic deck area built on three levels. There was also a white gazebo, a separate conservatory, and a shed that probably contained equipment for both the pool and the lawn. Flowering shrubs still denied the approach of the coming winter, and the air was sweet with their scents.

"Welcome to my house," Marli greeted them as Cat forced her way up the deck steps on quivering legs. The sorority president was dressed in neatly pressed jeans and a black sweatshirt with a simple strand of pearls. Her blonde locks fell in amber waves to her shoulders.

A man in a white chef's hat laboured over a charcoal grill at the other end of the deck. A nearby table built into the flooring of the deck held a large punch bowl and several glasses. There was also a selection of small sugar cookies, and Sara was already helping herself.

"It's beautiful," Cat said.

"Thank you," Marli said graciously.

"You should see the house from out here to get more of the full effect," Michelle Morgan said, taking Cat by the arm and pulling her in another direction along the deck. "And before you go, you should really take a look at the front. It's amazing what they've done with this place."

Cat stumbled along after Michelle, then stopped and turned to look where the girl indicated. The house rose majestically above the deck, and the lines were as recognizable to Cat as her own features.

It's the House!

No question remained in her mind. All the terror that had built up over the last eleven years smashed into her. Without warning, her legs buckled and she collapsed to the ground.

She was dimly aware of the confusion that swirled round her. More of the Delta Phis rushed to her side. Sara took her hand and began massaging it, calling out her name. After a moment Sara checked her pulse. "Her heart's beating," Cat heard Sara tell the others.

"Let me through," a woman's voice commanded. The girls, frightened looks on all their faces, parted before the newcomer. Cat blinked up at the tall woman above her. She was probably in her early fifties, her dark hair shot through with streaks of grey. Her thin, angular face was pressed in firm lines which gave her a serious look. She wore a neat black dress with a silver stickpin in the shape of a cherub. "Are you OK, child?" she asked.

Cat tried to answer but couldn't.

"What's the matter with her, Aunt Clara?" Marli asked.

"I'm not sure," Aunt Clara replied. "It looks like she's had a seizure. Does anyone know if she's on any kind of medication?"

All heads turned to Sara, who shrugged.

"She looks so blue," Brenda said. "Do you think we should call 911?"

"Wait just a minute," Aunt Clara said. "She seems to be breathing better. What's her name?"

"Cat Milligan," Marli answered.

"Get me her purse."

Sara picked it up from the ground and passed it over.

Still hovering over Cat, Aunt Clara quickly opened the purse and took out Cat's driver's licence. "She's not diabetic or epileptic. That information would be suggested by restrictions on the licence." She dropped the laminated card back into Cat's purse. She squinted at Cat, obviously studying her intently, trying to see something in her eyes.

The anxiety attack diminished as rapidly as it had come, leaving Cat sick and weak.

"It's OK," she croaked. "I'm fine." Cat

stared up at the doubtful faces, grateful to look anywhere but at the House.

"You don't look fine," Aunt Clara admonished with quiet authority. "You just lie there a moment and let's see."

Mustering all her strength, Cat raised herself up, knowing if the anxiety attack didn't kill her, the embarrassment would. Hot tears burned at her eyes. *You've only been kidding yourself. No way the Delta Phis are going to let a geek like you into their sorority.*

"Maybe I'd better go," Cat said, brushing off her jeans and holding on to Sara's arm. "I still don't feel very well."

"One of us can take you home," Marli said.

"No!" The word came out more harshly than Cat intended. Marli's eyes widened slightly but she said nothing. "I can make it," Cat insisted. "I just shouldn't stay."

"I'll go with her," Sara declared.

Despite protests from the others, Cat grimly made her way out of the back yard and to her car, declining Aunt Clara's offer to come inside.

Cat was certain if she went into the House, she'd never come out again. Sara stayed with her but let her make her own way.

It took Cat three attempts to get the key in the

ignition. Driving was a barely coordinated effort.

When they arrived at the Bright residence, Sara said, "Is your mom going to be home? If not, I can come sit with you."

"No," Cat lied. "She'll be there." She didn't want anyone around.

Sara ducked out of the Tracker and closed the door, pausing just a moment to lean in through the open window. "Look, Cat, if you want to talk, or if you need anything, call me."

Cat nodded agreement, then got underway. She surprised herself. She actually made it almost four blocks, out of Sara's sight, before she had to pull over. Then she lost it completely, crying deep, racking sobs that shook her all over.

The House is real. It exists.

Cat knew that now, as surely as she had ever known anything in her life. And if the house was real – what about the rest of the nightmare? Was that real, too?

CHAPTER SEVEN

*T*he red glow in the small developing room bathed Cat as she worked. She used plastic forceps to extract the latest picture from the chemical tray. It wasn't quite ready, so she slid it back into the shallow depths.

Her father had built the darkroom in a corner of the two-car garage. It was her refuge from the nightmares and the House.

Therapy had helped when she was younger. Mr Hopkins had helped the most. But it wasn't until junior high, when she discovered photography, that she found a way to push the fears out of her mind completely – if only for a few hours at a time.

For someone so afraid of the dark, Cat found it ironic that the one place she could find peace was a photographic darkroom. Of course, it was never really dark inside. She made sure she always kept the red light glowing.

A knock sounded on the door, startling her

into tipping a tray full of chemicals on to the floor.

"Cat?" her father called. "Are you in there?"

"Yes, Dad." Taking a couple of towels from the stack beside the small sink, Cat started to mop up the spill. It soaked into the knees of the stained jeans she'd put on to work in.

"Do you know what time it is?"

Cat dumped the sopping towels into the sink and glanced at her watch. It was after six-thirty. "Sorry. I lost track of time."

"Your mother said you were supposed to cook dinner."

Cat felt defeated. She had forgotten. "I'm sorry, Dad."

"It's OK," her father said. "We talked it over and decided it was a good night for pizza anyway. Why don't you close up in there and get changed?"

Panic filled Cat at the thought of going out into the night. Even if there was still light when they left, it would be dark by the time they got back home. "Couldn't we just have it delivered?"

"I suppose."

"Better yet," Cat offered, "why don't you and Mom go out to eat and I'll raid the refrigerator.

You guys could use some time alone."

"It's the first opportunity we've had in six days to be a family."

"I haven't been feeling too well today," Cat said weakly.

"Cat, come on out of there, or I'm coming in."

Wiping her eyes and cheeks with the tails of her sleeveless flannel shirt, Cat steeled herself, flipped off the lights, and opened the door.

"What's going on?" Mr Milligan, tall and dignified in his three-piece suit, his grey hair neatly styled, stared down at her. Behind his glasses, his hazel eyes were bold and penetrating. Cat sensed how a witness must feel while being questioned by her father in court.

"Do you want to tell us what's the matter?" Mrs Milligan asked as she stepped from the doorway leading to the laundry room. She was still wearing her nurse's uniform, including her name-tag, which she generally removed as soon as possible. A portable phone was in one hand.

"That's what I was just trying to find out," Mr Milligan said. "Cat wants to give us a raincheck on dinner."

"Why?" Mrs Milligan stopped beside her husband.

"I just don't feel like going out tonight."

"Are you sick?" Her mother stepped forwards and pressed a hand to Cat's forehead. "You don't feel like you have a fever." Abruptly, the phone in her hand rang. She stepped away and answered it, then turned back to Cat. "It's Marli Kendrick. She wants to know how you're feeling after the fainting spell you had at her house this afternoon." Her gaze hardened. "There were two other messages from her on the answering machine. And several from Sara. Do you want to tell us what's going on?"

"Could I take the call first?" Cat was counting on it to buy her some more time until she figured out what she could say. Her mother handed her the phone. She pressed it to her ear and quickly retreated through the doorway, passing through the laundry room and kitchen. She walked down the hallway to her room and closed the door after her. "Hello?"

"I called earlier," Marli said.

"My mom told me just now. Sorry."

"We were all wondering how you were doing."

"I'm fine. Whatever it was passed shortly after I dropped Sara off at her house." Cat walked across the room and looked at her collection of eight-by-tens in simple frames on the wall, using the familiar, happier times to help manage her thin veneer of self-control. She made herself sound cheery even though she was sure Marli was calling to inform her she was no longer a Delta Phi pledge.

"Have you been to the doctor?"

"No. It went away so quickly I didn't think any more about it."

"Well, you certainly scared all of us. Aunt Clara is still very shaken up."

Cat was contrite. "I'm sorry, Marli. I hope I didn't spoil the party."

"It's not your fault, Cat. These things happen. When I talked to Sara earlier, she said you weren't sick until you came to my house."

Great. I'm going to murder Sara. "I – I was nervous," Cat explained.

"What were you nervous about? There wasn't anyone at the party that you didn't already know."

Cat took a deep breath and confessed, "It was your house."

"The house? What about it?"

"I used to have nightmares about that house when I was a little kid." She put strong emphasis on the word little.

There was a long pause. Then Marli asked, "Are you sure it was this house?"

Cat looked outside her window and saw night draping black silk over the mountains. "Even now I can picture the rooms in my mind." An involuntary shiver coursed through her. "The entryway has gold-and-green flocked wallpaper, a marble-topped table with a big wooden mirror, and brass wall sconces on either side of the door leading into the living room. The room on the right is the dining room, with double sliding doors, a huge oval table surrounded by eight straight-backed chairs. A chandelier hangs from the ceiling. The room on the left is the parlour with red velvet couches, an oriental rug, and lots of plants. Oh, and a stained-glass window facing the garden."

"That sounds sort of like our house," Marli admitted. "But the entryway is done in rose and alabaster, and the room on the right doesn't have a chandelier. It's all glassed in, and there aren't any sliding doors. The parlour is there, but no stained-glass window. And no oriental rug. There are several skylights, which brighten the whole place up."

Cat tried to picture the House as Marli described it but couldn't.

"You must have the wrong house," Marli said. "These old places are all alike on the outside."

"Maybe that's it," Cat grudgingly conceded. But the fear remained firmly rooted in her mind.

"That's what it has to be." Marli sounded convinced. "Why don't you come over tomorrow and see for yourself? It'll just be you and me. We can have a chat and spend some time really getting to know each other."

Even with the possibility that Marli's home wasn't the House after all, Cat still didn't like the idea of going. But refusing the offer could damage her remaining chances with the Delta Phis. "All right. What time?"

"Right after school."

Cat swallowed hard. "OK."

"Cat, I think you've got a lot of potential for the Delta Phis, and we have a lot to offer you. Take care of yourself and I'll see you tomorrow."

Cat switched off the phone and gazed at the door. Knowing she couldn't put it off any longer, she walked to the kitchen and found her parents seated in the breakfast nook. Both of them looked tense.

"You want to tell us about it?" her father asked.

Choosing her words carefully, she played down the anxiety attack she'd experienced at Marli's house. She also included a description of the pink house, but avoided mention of the disappearing little girl.

"The pink house belonged to the Parsons family years ago," her father said. "We used to live near there." His eyes were frank and probing. "Maybe we should consider setting you up an appointment with a therapist here in Asheville." He shrugged to soften his words. "As a purely precautionary measure."

Cat took a deep breath and forced herself not to overreact. There was no way she was going back into therapy and risk losing the respect of her peers the way she had in Atlanta.

"Dad, really, I can handle this. It's probably just the move and the school pressure. Even Mr Hopkins said I was going to decompress occasionally."

Her father looked at her mother. Despite their upbeat approach to the problem, both of them had resignation shadowing their eyes. They reached a silent agreement. Cat felt like she was plea bargaining for a lighter sentence against the world's toughest DA.

"OK, kitten," Mr Milligan said. "We'll see

how that works out. Meanwhile, pizza should be here in about twenty minutes. I ordered a large garden salad to go with it."

Dinner that night was stiff and formal. As soon as she could Cat beat a hasty retreat to her bedroom, pleading exhaustion. But she couldn't sleep. The cycle was starting all over again and she didn't know how to break it.

At fifteen minutes past one, she heard a soft knock on her door.

Cat blinked her eyes blearily and stared at the screen of her computer, where she'd typed gibberish.

"What are you still doing up?" her mother asked, coming into the room.

"It's a history paper I forgot about that's due in the morning." Cat knew she'd never been any good at lying to her mother, but it had been so long since she'd tried that she hoped she could pull it off. Actually the history paper had been written last week and turned in ahead of time.

"Are you going to be much longer?" Mrs Milligan sat on the bed.

"Not much." Panic filled Cat when she saw the cup of instant coffee she'd filched from downstairs to help keep herself awake. She was doing anything to avoid having the nightmare again. She faked a stretch, and moved her chair over till she blocked sight of the cup.

Her mother took a deep, shuddering breath. "I don't know what your father would say if he knew I came here to tell you this. The last few months have been wonderful for us, Catherine. I'm finally getting to work in the field I trained in, and your father has been able to step down from the frenetic pace of the Atlanta court system. It's like a dream come true."

The threat of tears in her mother's eyes hurt Cat immensely when she realized she was the cause of them.

"We've shielded you from so much over the years," her mother went on. "We knew you had problems of your own. So you didn't hear about how we wanted to have more children but were afraid they would upset you. We never let you see how we worried over the therapy bills that nearly ruined us. But now it's our time, Cat. Don't start having those nightmares again."

Cat was stunned. Her mother was acting as if she'd had some choice in whether she had the nightmares.

"Please, honey," her mother begged. "Please, if you can, don't start. People here like you. The Delta Phi girls have invited you to be part of their sorority. You don't need to do anything to get more attention. Don't let it begin all over again. I don't know how much more your father or I can take."

Cat sat in shocked silence as her mother left the room. Unable to hold back the hurt any more, Cat retreated to her bathroom, racked by sobs.

"You're nothing but a fraidy cat," she told her reflection in the mirror. She looked through the bathroom door and saw that she had on all three lights in her bedroom. The cupboard door was also open and the light inside was on. She couldn't remember switching them on, but she knew her mother must have noticed.

"I can do this," she said out loud, just to hear her voice. Steeling herself, she reached for the switch and turned out the light. Darkness cloaked her, partially blunted by the illumination streaming in from the bedroom.

Even at that, she could hear the insect-like whispers that sometimes echoed inside the House. They called out to her, the words indistinct but filled with hate and the promise of violence.

"Oh no." It was hard to control her rolling stomach as she started shaking. Having no other choice, Cat reached out and flicked the light back on.

The House was after her. The bad thing lurking behind that door wanted her. She only hoped she was strong enough to survive when it came for her.

Feeling more alone than ever before, Cat went to bed. She left the lights blazing, and stared numbly at the curtained window keeping the ravenous dark outside her room.

CHAPTER EIGHT

Transiting Moon is now void of course, which should allow your emotions to stop flip-flopping. But the planets can't help you if you don't help yourself. Face up to your fears.

Cat checked her make-up in her rear-view mirror. "You don't look much like a Delta Phi pledge today," she told her reflection.

Her pallor and bloodshot eyes were going to be a turn-off for most people. *Thank God it's a sunny day.* She covered most of the wreckage with a pair of sunglasses, grabbed her book bag, and got out of the Tracker.

She took the long way round, avoiding the gathering place at the school entrance so no one would try to talk to her. Just as she was about to enter one of the side breezeways, she saw Taylor. He was dressed in a dark blue and black plaid flannel shirt and black jeans, and stood with his back to a thick, gnarled oak tree with dead branches jutting out sporadically. He laboured over his sketchpad.

Cat remembered the kiss they'd shared just yesterday afternoon and shivered with excitement. Goose bumps crept up the back of her neck and covered her upper arms.

She took a step towards Taylor, then paused. *I can't talk to him. I look like a total wreck.* She started to turn away but caught herself. Cat desperately needed someone to talk to. When she swung back round, Taylor was staring at her.

"Cat?" he said, dropping the sketchpad to his side. "Are you trying to avoid me?"

Cat cradled her books to her chest and took a deep breath. "No. My mom and I had a fight last night. I was afraid I wouldn't be good company."

"I'm sorry." Taylor slipped his hand in hers. "Is there anything I can do?"

Cat's heart thudded painfully as she felt the warmth of his skin against hers. "No. We'll work it out. It's just that we never fight."

"That's not how it is round my house," Taylor said, with a chuckle. "With six kids and two working parents, if you can't pick a new argument, you can always continue an old one."

"Why won't you look at me?" a child's voice suddenly demanded from behind Taylor.

Startled, Cat saw the little blonde girl peeking out from behind the tree.

"Nanny, nanny, boo-boo, you can't catch me," the little girl chanted.

"I can too catch you." Cat leaped forwards. Her hand flashed out and for a brief instant she had her hand on the girl's shoulder. The flesh was too cool and the contact shocked her. "Oh!"

An arm slid round her waist and kept her from hitting the ground. "Are you all right?" Taylor asked.

Cat leaned against the tree, trying to regain her balance. "Yes, I was just trying to catch that little girl."

"What little girl?"

"That little..." Cat pointed behind the tree to a broad expanse of empty yard. The nearest hiding place was far away.

"Are you sure you're OK?" Taylor asked, ducking his head down to peer into her face.

Cat rubbed her eyes and turned to look every direction. The little girl had vanished. "I-I thought I saw someone there, but I guess I'm just overtired. When that happens my imagination gets away from me."

"When your imagination gets away from you," Taylor said, "it gets away good. You were talking to somebody I couldn't see and I thought maybe I was the one who was losing it."

"But now you know that I'm the one with the problem," Cat said in a quiet voice.

"That's not what I said, Cat."

"No, you didn't say it. Exactly." Feeling ashamed, Cat turned to walk away.

"Cat." Taylor caught hold of her arm. "I'm sorry. I really am. I don't know any other way to say it. It was just a bad choice of words."

"You're hurting my wrist."

He released her immediately and apologized. "Cat, I don't think there's anything strange about seeing someone there for just a moment. Sometimes I get so lost in my drawings, creating the lines and shadows and emotions, that I forget where I am."

Cat couldn't tell him how desperately she wanted to believe him.

He tried a friendly smile. "I remember even when you were a little kid you always had a vivid imagination. I did, too, but I never talked about the things I imagined the way you did."

Cat's eyes widened. "You never said you knew me from when I lived here before."

He shrugged. "We only played together a few times, but I saw you a lot. We didn't live far from each other."

Cat felt a swirl of emotions inside her. She had no memory of her time in Asheville, except from photographs in her parent's album. It was embarrassing to think that Taylor would know something about her that she didn't. "What do you remember about me?" she asked, cautiously.

"You were really outgoing as a kid," Taylor answered. "Always had to be doing something. Always talking. Everyone liked you."

Cat tried to imagine being popular, but couldn't. The long, hard years of junior high while searching for acceptance had washed all that away. "I don't remember you," she murmured. "In fact, I don't remember anything about Asheville."

"You were only five. I was seven. I was always surrounded by my mob of a family. But surely you remember your friend."

"What friend?"

Taylor's brow wrinkled. "I can't remember her name. But you guys were inseparable. If one of you was round, you didn't have to look far to find the other one. I think she left town before you did."

"I can't remember." Cat felt hollow inside. Her mind was a complete blank slate.

"I figured if you remembered anyone from Asheville, you'd remember her."

Sessions with Mr Hopkins came back to Cat, reminding her how they'd talked about her early years. "Memories are funny things," Cat said. "Some children can remember being rocked in the cradle, but other people's memories don't start until they're much older. I can tell you the names of every kid in my second grade class. And third grade. Probably fourth grade, too. I have a terrific facility for memorization. I won spelling bees in sixth grade. And geography bees. In fact, I was the youngest entrant in the state geography bee. But ask me to remember things before the age of five and it's like someone has drawn a thick black curtain."

"But you don't remember Asheville at all?" He gestured to the surrounding hills which were lit up with reds and golds and, for most people, would fall into the unforgettable category.

"No. I remember how Asheville felt," Cat said, squeezing her eyes shut. "But nothing about the town itself."

"How did Asheville feel?" Taylor asked.

"Like it was supposed to be safe and protected, with neat little houses tucked into cosy little hills. But something was not quite right."

Taylor studied her face. "You were so bubbly. I guess that's what surprised me the most when I met you again. You're a whole lot more reserved than I would have expected."

"Capricorns are reserved," Cat said, parroting Sara's words.

He shook his head. "You sure weren't when you were little."

"People change," Cat said, staring down at her feet. "Sometimes they can't help it." She wanted to tell him that the main thing she remembered from Asheville was the House and the bad thing behind the door. But she couldn't. Already this morning she'd been caught talking to people who weren't there.

"Cat!"

It was Brenda Hubbard, signalling to her from a few metres away. Taylor saw Brenda and took a step back, thrusting his hands deep in the back pockets of his jeans. The look on his face was definitely not inviting.

"We're having a meeting in a few minutes to discuss the Homecoming Dance," Brenda called. "Marli and I are rounding up everyone we can find."

"OK." Cat turned to Taylor. "Will you excuse me?"

"Sure." He cocked his head to look at her and a lock of his thick dark hair fell over one eye. "I didn't know you were a Delta Phi pledge."

The tone in his voice let her know that he didn't think it was a good thing.

"Yes, I am." Cat didn't know what to say. She felt caught in the middle, with Brenda only a few metres away, sneering at Taylor. "Well, I guess I'll see you later," was all Cat could come up with. She moved to join Brenda, feeling his eyes on her back the whole time.

"I didn't know you knew Taylor Dunne," Brenda said, coolly. Today she wore blue jeans and an olive-green cotton sweater that showed off her newly acquired tan from a recent session at Sun In.

"He didn't know I knew you," Cat replied.

Brenda gave Cat a smug smile. "Taylor doesn't much care for me or the other sorority sisters."

Cat had distinctly gotten that impression.

"But trust me when I say this," Brenda advised. "As a Delta Phi, you can do much better than someone like Taylor Dunne. And you *should*."

Glancing back at Taylor, Cat saw that he had gathered his sketchpad and was walking towards the other end of the building. The set of his shoulders told her he was deliberately not looking at her.

"Marli likes you," Brenda continued. "That's why she asked you to her house today."

"House?" A jolt of electricity shot through Cat, just at the mention of the word.

Brenda knitted her brow. "Yes, Marli's house. You couldn't have forgotten, could you?"

Forget that house? Never. It was permanently engraved on her memory.

"Cat?" Brenda poked her shoulder. "Did you hear what I said?"

Cat shook her head to clear the frightening images gathering there. "Yes, I heard," Cat mumbled. "And no, I didn't forget. I'm really looking forward to it." Cat flashed what she hoped would read as a genuine smile.

Brenda studied her. "Good."

Cat attended the impromptu meeting with the Delta Phis and sleepwalked through the rest of the day. The last period flew by, even though it was Geometry. Proofs and statements were still an enigma to Cat, and she was beginning to wonder if she'd ever catch on. Usually the class seemed to take for ever, but today was different.

Today, the House was waiting for her.

After dropping Sara at the flower shop, she drove mechanically to Marli's, deliberately taking her time. She parked in the spacious area before the house and screwed up her courage. Looking down, Cat noticed her camera pack resting on the floor by her feet. Just knowing the sleek black Nikon was inside calmed her. She strapped the pack round her waist and got out of the car.

Cat's heart thundered in her chest as she stepped up on to the porch. She took a deep breath and pressed the doorbell.

"It won't let you out," a small voice whispered from behind her.

Cat spun round, her nerves jangling. The little blonde girl stood about three metres away near a squared-off hedge.

"It's been waiting for a very long time."

Without thinking Cat pulled her Nikon out of the waist pack and raised it to her eye. Her finger unerringly found the button. The film advance motor whined as it shot the entire roll of film in less than a minute.

"Hey, what are you taking pictures of?"

Cat gasped and spun back to the face the house. Marli was standing in the open doorway. "The landscape." Cat gestured lamely at Marli's front yard. As she did, she shot a nervous glance back at the hedge.

The little blonde girl was gone. Just as Cat knew she would be.

"Terrific," Marli said with an uncertain smile. "Maybe you can let me see them when you get them developed."

Cat nodded. "Um, sure."

Marli stepped back, gesturing to the hall. "Well, come on in."

Cat slipped the camera back into the waist pack and stepped into the house.

CHAPTER NINE

"What do you think?" Marli asked, gesturing round the house. "Is it anything like you thought it would be?"

"The layout is familiar," Cat said hesitantly. The longer she looked at the house, the more secure she felt.

"Like I said, a lot of these places look the same on a superficial level. But Mom and Aunt Clara spent a lot of time fixing this place up after we moved in a few years ago."

The room off to the right wasn't a dining room. It was a solarium, all glass and bright sunshine and green-leafed tropical plants.

"Wow," Cat said as she studied it further.

"Like to see it?" Marli asked.

"Sure."

A skylight in the centre of the ceiling let in more light, while glass walls on three sides did the same. The aroma was heady, nearly intoxicating. Orchids appeared to be the flower

"You could get lost in a room like this," Cat commented, reaching out to touch the delicate blossom of a star lily.

"This room picks me up when I'm having a totally gross day," Marli agreed. "Come on. I'll introduce you to my mom. It's one of those rare afternoons that she's home from the hospital." She led the way down the hall, past the stairway leading up to the first floor, and into the kitchen.

Cat paid special attention to the stairway bannister. Instead of the engraved leaves from her nightmares, the bannister was covered with polished brass. Even before she entered the kitchen, she could smell the sweet odour of fresh-baked bread.

Aunt Clara, wearing a large white chef's apron with a wild spray of painted mushrooms forming the bottom border, was taking bread pans out of the oven with a thick mitt. Another woman stood behind a wooden baker's table, a mound of dough piled high before her. She was an older version of Marli, only a little heavier and with shorter hair. Her smiling face was dotted with splotches of flour.

"Cat," Marli said, "this is my mom, Dr Phyllis Kendrick."

Dr Kendrick extended her hand and shook Cat's. "It's nice to meet you. Marli has talked about you."

Cat took the hand and felt at ease immediately. "My mother's talked about you. She says you're one of the best surgeons she's ever worked with."

"Do I know her?"

"She's a nurse at the clinic. Laurie Milligan."

"Oh yes. I know Laurie. I also know she's one of the most competent nurses the hospital has ever had on its staff, so I'll treasure that compliment."

"Mom's making her stab at being domestic," Marli explained.

"When I work in the kitchen like this," Dr Kendrick said, "it takes away some of the guilt for being gone so much."

"Nonsense," Aunt Clara said as she emptied the two bread pans she'd retrieved, then put the loaves on wire racks to cool. "Phyllis happens to be a very good mother. It's just that she also happens to be a gifted surgeon. She divides her time quite nicely between the home and the hospital."

"My number one fan," Dr Kendrick said. "Without my big sister, there never would have

106

been a doctor in this family. She practically raised me and worked extra jobs to help put me through college and medical school."

Cat was surprised to find that the two women were sisters. Aunt Clara actually looked old enough to be Dr Kendrick's mother.

Marli told her mother and aunt that they'd be upstairs once Cat finished looking at the rest of the house.

Fifteen minutes later, Cat had seen most of the home, which looked like a page out of *Better Homes and Gardens* magazine. Each room had been decorated with superb taste and style.

Marli ended the tour with her bedroom, which was next to Aunt Clara's. Done in pink and white, Marli's room had a delightful fairytale feel to it. Marli took her place on the edge of the bed.

Cat made herself comfortable in a plush, straight-backed chair that looked like an antique.

"What do you think of the house?" Marli asked.

"It's beautiful."

"It is now," Marli agreed. "Mom and Aunt Clara put a lot of work into it when we moved here. It was quite a change for me. I'd been living in New York City until then. From apartment life to suburban life by way of divorce."

"I'm sorry," Cat said. "That must have been rough."

"It took some getting used to. Aunt Clara was living in this house all by herself when we got here."

"This house is really big for one person," Cat said. "It must have been really hard keeping everything clean."

"Everything was sort of in a shambles when we got here," Marli said. "Mom and Aunt Clara had grown up in Asheville. Aunt Clara was married once but her husband left her after their baby girl died."

"That's awful," Cat said.

"Mom says Aunt Clara was just devastated, and that was why her husband left her."

"I can imagine that would be a very hard thing to recover from."

Marli nodded. "Anyway, Aunt Clara gave the house to Mom when she decided to get out of New York and come back to Asheville. At first Aunt Clara was going to move to one of the small cottages outside of town because there were too many memories that haunted her in this house. Mom talked her out of it. I was still small and needed someone to look after me while Mom worked at the hospital. Then her practice really took off, they put most of the money into this place – and *voila*!" She opened her hands to encompass the home. "A brand new house."

Someone knocked on the door.

"Come in," Marli said, getting up.

Aunt Clara entered the room, carrying a folding tray that held plates with thick slices of freshly baked bread and tall glasses of milk. A small dish of butter and three different pots of jam were beside them. "I thought you girls might like something warm to eat," she said as she unfolded the legs and stood the table on the floor near the wall. "Bread is never better than when it's just come out of the oven."

"Thanks," Marli said.

Cat echoed her.

"So, how do you like our house?" Aunt Clara asked.

"It's magnificent," Cat replied.

"Thank you." Aunt Clara beamed as she helped herself to a slice of bread and a little blackberry jam.

"Actually," Marli said, "Cat thought she'd been in the house before. When she was small, she had nightmares about a house very much like this one. That's what helped trigger the attack yesterday."

Cat felt like such a fool. There was no way this was the house she'd dreamed about.

"Really?" Aunt Clara asked. "Where did you live?"

"I don't remember for sure," Cat said. "But the pink house further down the street must have been close by. My father was a lawyer here for a while. Before we moved to Atlanta."

"Tell me your last name again?"

"Milligan."

"My mind isn't what it used to be," Aunt Clara said with a dismissive wave. "Time was I could remember everything. Now I have to make lists just to go to the grocery store." She moved to the door. "You girls enjoy your snack and your talk."

The girls thanked her again as she left.

"Brenda tells me she found you with Taylor Dunne this morning," Marli said almost as soon as the door closed.

Cat nearly choked on the bread she was chewing. She quickly washed it down with a drink of milk. "Yes."

"I can see what the attraction would be," Marli said, calmly spreading peach jam on a slice of bread. "He's tall and good-looking, maybe the best-looking boy in the whole senior high."

"He's also a good friend," Cat said. "I've never met anyone else who listens so well when you talk."

"Still," Marli said, "Taylor's not someone you want to get involved with as a Delta Phi pledge. You need someone who's interested in doing something in the community. Someone who obviously has a future ahead of him."

Cat put her bread on her plate. Marli's words cut deeply. Until this year, anyone who had known Cat would have said she had no future.

"As a Delta Phi," Marli continued, "you're expected to be a leader of the student body. Whether you choose that role or not, people are going to be looking at you to see how you handle yourself. The behaviour you showed yesterday, not to mention your involvement with Taylor Dunne, could jeopardize your chances. Although our sorority is usually close-mouthed about things that happen between us, events do occasionally get out and become common knowledge."

"Yesterday won't happen again," Cat promised. "Part of my reaction might have been to the house, but most of it was probably this diet I've been on." It was only a partial lie. She was on a diet, but she hadn't been cutting back all that much.

"Believe me," Marli said with real feeling, "I understand about diets. It's a struggle to keep myself down to a size five. But I have an image to maintain."

All of the talk about image was really starting to make Cat uncomfortable.

"I know it can be intimidating at first, and there's no escaping the pressure of being a Delta Phi pledge." Marli smiled warmly. "But you've made a good start with the float idea. Just work on those things that are your strengths and stay away from the trouble areas."

The conversation slowly broke down into general talk about past events the Delta Phis had taken part in. Marli seemed very excited about the Homecoming Dance. After a while, Cat excused herself and asked for directions to the bathroom.

The bathroom had two doors. Cat must have taken the wrong one because when she came out, she found herself in an unfamiliar hallway. Trying to find her way back, she opened a linen wardrobe by mistake. She tried another door, but when her hand touched the metal, the contact became electric. Sparks zinged and raced up her arm as the door opened.

There, in shadows draped with cobwebs, a narrow wooden staircase led up into what had to be the attic.

Panic slammed into Cat. Her heart froze in her chest and she was afraid it would never beat again.

Somehow she managed to pull the door shut and stagger back into the main hall.

Marli was still in her room, sorting through some photo albums she'd promised to show Cat regarding Delta Phi activities.

"I have to go," Cat said from the door in a strained voice. "I didn't know it was this late."

"Cat," Marli called.

Pretending not to hear, Cat stumbled down the front stairs. She clapped a hand over her mouth and struggled not to throw up. The panic attack she had had the previous day was nothing compared to this one. She had trouble with the front door. When she finally got it open, she glanced back, afraid she'd see Marli.

Instead, Aunt Clara stood in the great room, framed by the hall doors. The tall woman looked at her curiously, wiping her hands on a dishtowel, but said nothing.

Cat pulled the front door shut behind her and ran for her car. Shaking and crying, she was barely able to go more than a block before she accidently killed the engine while trying to shift gear at a stop sign.

It's behind me. "Run!" a voice inside her ordered. "Run and hide!"

Cat leaped out of her car and fled. She ran a full block and then ducked into a familiar alley. Some inner direction guided her. When she reached an ice-blue garden shed behind one of the Victorian houses, she dived for it.

Flinging open the rusty door, Cat stepped into the darkness. She crossed immediately to the far corner and huddled on the dirt floor, her knees pressed against her chest. *I'm safe. It can't find me here.*

CHAPTER TEN

Your ruler, Saturn, is finishing up a two-and-a-half year transit of Cancer, which is making you melancholy and discontented. Don't allow it. The fear of dark places in the mind can only be lessened by the light of your own determination.

*T*hat night the dream – the same dream she'd had for ten years – came back with a vengeance.

Cat had no idea how long she sat huddled in the rusty old garden shed. But when the light peeking in beneath the metal door finally disappeared, Cat crept out of her hiding place. She was mentally and emotionally exhausted. It took every ounce of energy she could muster to find her car and drive home.

She skipped dinner and went directly to her room, throwing herself on her bed. Sleep quickly overcame her. And then the dream returned.

The scent of lavender still hung heavily in the air. But this time, it was mingled with the smell of freshly baked bread. Cat followed the smell to the kitchen where a shadow opened the oven door and removed a tray that glowed like an ember.

Tiny voices screamed shrilly but Cat couldn't tell where they were coming from. The small blonde girl sat at a table in the corner.

"You're late," the little girl said. "I told them you'd be late."

"Shush!" the shadow said, taking her place at the end of the table. She opened a small coffin at her elbow that contained pale yellow margarine and scooped some out with a knife.

The screaming voices were louder now. Hypnotized by the events unfolding round her, Cat stared at the cookies cooling on the baking sheet. There in miniature were the girls of the Delta Phi sorority, their faces rendered in peach icing. The little blonde girl lifted a screaming Sara-cookie that kicked and fought desperately, and calmly bit off its peach-frosted head.

"It's time," the shadow figure said. "Time to show her."

Before Cat could even attempt a scream, her shoes, which looked like little pink bunny slippers, took her into the hall stairway. Without hesitation, they pounded up the stairs, took her down gloomy halls, past closed doors, and up a narrow flight of stairs until they reached *the* door. The pistol-grip knob gleamed like silver in the dim light.

"Open it!" one of the shoes commanded.

Against her will Cat watched her hand seize the knob and turn it. The door swung open. She tried to hang on to the door frame, but her slippers took her into the room. For the first time in eleven years Cat glimpsed the interior. The wallpaper was torn and peeling, and bare wood thrust out above her. The rose scent was stronger than ever.

Two human shapes were at the other end of the room, locked in an embrace. One loomed large; the other much smaller. Cat feared for them both, although she didn't know who they were.

She screamed but no sound came out of her mouth.

"*Cat!*" The whisper was hoarse but managed to penetrate the thick veil of sleep. "*Cat, I see you.*"

Cat bolted up from the bedspread. She was still in her clothes and her heart was pounding.

"Mom?"

The room was fully lit but still it took all of her courage to leave the bed and creep towards the bedroom door. "Mom? Was that you?"

There was no answer.

The sensation of being watched oozed down Cat's spine. She stiffened, afraid to turn round. She steeled herself and spun, bracing herself against the door.

The windows were like sheets of black ice. Nothing moved on the other side of them, but her vision was restricted because the lights were on in her room.

"Nothing's there," she told herself forcefully. "Stop scaring yourself, Fraidy Cat. Just go back to bed." She glared at the window in frustration and fear.

Still, the feeling that someone was watching wouldn't leave her. She wished she could see better. The lights were working against her. If someone was outside, they'd be able to see her easily.

Cat acted before she had time to reconsider her actions. With a quick flick of her arm, she switched the lights off. Then Cat leaped towards the window and peered into the night.

Someone was there! A gaunt figure dressed

in a dark coat and broad-brimmed hat stood outlined behind the curtains to the left.

Before Cat's eyes could fully adjust, the figure fled, moving away from the window frame. Footsteps thudded, echoing in the bedroom even as they faded.

Her knees buckled and she slid down the wall by the window. Cracked sobs tore loose from deep inside her chest as she hugged herself.

"Cat?"

She was afraid to move.

This time the voice was her mother's. Mrs Milligan switched on the light and came into the room. Mr Milligan was with her. Both of them were dressed in bath robes.

"What is it?" her father asked, reaching down to help her off the floor.

Cat pointed to the window.

Her father moved cautiously to look outside. A moment later he said, "Nothing's there."

Cat couldn't speak. Her body was racked with hiccuping sobs. But she knew she couldn't tell them about the strange stick person. They would only think she was making it up to get attention.

"Shhh, baby," her mother said, leading her to

the bed and holding her. "It's all right." Cat let herself gradually relax in her mother's arms, but she still didn't feel safe.

The House was waiting. It wanted her and she knew it wouldn't give up.

"I think it's time we found someone for Cat to talk to," her father said, slumping on the bed next to her mother.

Mrs Milligan nodded. "Tomorrow."

Cat knew they were referring to yet another psychologist. She wanted to scream no, but she knew they wouldn't listen.

Instead she murmured, "All right."

I'll go. But no matter what anyone thinks, I'm not going crazy!

CHAPTER ELEVEN

Neptune retrograde has had you in a fog. You want to daydream but all you have are daymares. By the weekend, you'll feel the pressure roll off like the mist, so lighten up, little Capricorn. You don't have to be giddy but turn the frown upside-down.

"Your eyes," Taylor Dunne said the next morning in the halls, "look like something you'd see on a Hallowe'en jack-o'-lantern."

Cat was appalled. She'd done everything she could think of to mask the fact that she hadn't got any more sleep.

"I stayed up late reading," she lied. "And the book was so good that, before I knew it, the sun had come up."

"What was the name of the book?" Taylor asked, genuinely interested.

"The name of the book," Cat repeated, stalling for time. She tried to think of every

121

novel she'd read lately and absolutely nothing sprang to mind. "Um, isn't that silly?" she giggled a little too loudly. "I can't think of the title."

Taylor raised one eyebrow. "That good, huh?"

Change the subject. Cat pointed to Taylor's sketchpad, which she was learning never left his side. "So how are the monsters coming?"

"Fine. I've done a few more since we talked. Would you like to see them?"

"No!" Cat visibly winced. "I mean...not this morning. Staying up late like that has made my nerves a little, um—"

"Fragile?" Taylor finished for her.

Cat nodded. "Yes, that's it. I don't think I could handle anything more than a cute little bunny, or a flower or two."

There was a long pause. Then Taylor asked, "Are you OK?"

"Why, sure," Cat stammered, nervously trying to smooth out her hair. "I know I look like hell, but I'm doing just fine."

The bell sounded, but Taylor didn't move. "Listen. If things aren't OK, I would hope you'd tell me."

Cat forced herself to smile. "Thanks, Taylor,

I really appreciate that." She gestured vaguely towards her English classroom down the hall. "Well, I better get to class. Mr Odom doesn't like it when we're late."

She could feel Taylor watch her walk the full length of the hall. As she entered the classroom, she saw that he was still standing where she'd left him, as if frozen in place.

At lunch, Cat skipped the regular gathering of the Delta Phis because she had to go and get the medical insurance paperwork her mother had filled out for the psychologist's office.

When she got back to school, she found an envelope taped on her locker.

Cat, we've got to talk. Meet me in the
toilets between 6th and 7th period.
Sara.

PE and World History seemed to last for ever. When the class bell rang, Cat was out of her seat like a shot, not even bothering to change books at her locker. Sara was waiting for her in one corner of the toilets, a worried look on her face. When she saw Cat, Sara whispered, "What's going on with you?"

"I-I don't understand," Cat stammered.

"What are you talking about?"

"I'm talking about the scene at Marli's house yesterday," Sara said. "When you didn't make it to lunch with us today, that's all Brenda wanted to talk about."

Some girls came through the door, laughing and chattering excitedly. Sara grabbed Cat by the arm and pulled her into the far stall so they could have a little privacy. "Brenda was telling everybody how you bolted out of Marli's house like some scared rabbit."

"How did Brenda know?" Cat asked.

"C'mon," Sara said. "You were there, and Marli was there. You want to take a guess?"

"Did Marli say anything?"

"No. She didn't have to. Brenda said plenty. I tried to explain that because you are a Capricorn you can sometimes respond a little too dramatically to a situation, but they didn't buy it."

"They?" Cat's forehead creased.

"Brenda made a motion today to have you ejected."

"No!" Cat's cheeks burned with embarrassment. Soon everyone at school would know what a misfit she was. Everything she had worked so hard for over the last two months was destroyed in just a few days.

"You're hanging on by a thread," Sara continued. "Marli's having a slumber party at her house on Friday night to test you."

Cold chills prickled over Cat. "Test me?"

"Marli said that any decision like that was really heavy, and that more time should be given to make it," Sara went on. "So she set up the slumber party to see if you could handle yourself. Brenda's expecting you to chicken out and not come. And even if you do, she's told everyone you won't make it past midnight."

Cat knew she didn't have a choice – not if she wanted to be accepted by the sorority. "I'll be there," she said in a choked voice.

Sara nodded. "I told them you would. You're an earth sign – which means that inside you are really strong and can overcome fears if you put your mind to it. I just wish you would tell me what's bothering you. Frankly, I couldn't care less if I get accepted by the Delta Phis." She looked squarely at Cat. "But I know this means everything to you."

Cat nodded, her throat so tight she couldn't speak. She wished she'd told Sara about her nightmares earlier but she had wanted to start off with a clean slate.

"I'll buy you a soda after school," Sara offered, checking her watch. They had two minutes to get to class. "You can tell me what's going on then."

"I can't," Cat said. "I've got an appointment."

"What kind of appointment?"

Cat looked at her friend, hating to lie, but not able to admit the truth. "A doctor's appointment. Just a check-up." *From the neck up,* Cat thought, remembering her Atlanta classmates' cruel sense of humour. "But I can still give you a ride home."

"That's fine," Sara said as they hurried along the hall to seventh period. "But if you feel like talking tonight, give me a call."

"Sure," Cat said, although she knew she wouldn't. By the time she finished with the psychologist, she knew she wouldn't feel like talking to anyone.

Cat checked the location on the psychologist's card again as she drove downtown. The address belonged to a small cottage sandwiched between two three-story buildings in an older section of the city. A cedar planter fronted the long, covered wooden porch at the front of the house, and it was filled with winter flowers and ivy.

A metal sign advertising "Jane Aspin, Ph.D., Family Counselling" in flowing yellow script hung from an L-shaped pole in the neatly kept lawn. Three of the four parking spaces in front of the gentle hill leading up to the cottage were empty.

Cat ignored them and parked two blocks away, round the corner beside a hardware store. There was no way she would chance anyone from school seeing her car in front of the psychologist's office.

She got out of the car and froze. The sensation that she was being watched made her shoulders tighten. Cat looked over her shoulder, but no one was there. Then she saw the little blonde girl peeking out from the corner of the hardware store.

Trembling, Cat ignored the vision. *She isn't real.* As she passed a line of red and green mowers that were marked down for clearance and placed on the sidewalk in front of the hardware store, she caught sight of her reflection in the store windows. The little blonde girl walked next to her reflection in the window. Smiling, the little girl reached up and took her reflection's hand. As soon as she did, Cat's own hand felt cold. She gave a choked cry of surprise and pain.

"Are you all right?"

Cat spun round.

Marli's Aunt Clara, in a tan raincoat, stood near the hardware store entrance, holding a small paper bag in her hand. A large-brimmed canvas rain hat shadowed her features. "I said, are you all right, child?"

"Yes, ma'am," Cat answered automatically.

"You look pale."

"It's chills," Cat said. "I think I may be coming down with the flu."

"That can be very exhausting," Aunt Clara said. "If that's what you're getting. You should take care of yourself. Drink plenty of juices and get some rest."

"I will. Thanks." Cat hurried on, not daring to look in the window again. Her hand was no longer cold. She risked a glance over her shoulder to make sure Aunt Clara had driven away before going up to the cottage. There was no doubt that Aunt Clara would tell Marli if she saw Cat going into a psychologist's office.

Cat pressed the door buzzer and listened to

the sonorous bongs inside the cottage. As she waited, she turned to look at the street, unable to shake the feeling that someone was watching her.

Half expecting to see the little girl again, she was startled to see Taylor duck into an alley across the street. She only caught a glimpse of his dark hair beneath his cowboy hat and his black duster coat, but it was enough to convince her of his identity.

Anger and fear battled within her. Taylor must have followed her after school. *But* why? If he'd wanted to talk to her, he could have caught her in the school parking lot.

Before she could make a move, the cottage door opened and a plump woman in a burgundy dress with silver-blue hair, looked at her through thick lensed glasses. "Catherine Milligan?"

Cat nodded.

"Please come in," the woman said. "Dr Aspin is waiting for you."

Wishing she had more time to track Taylor down and question him, Cat reluctantly stepped inside the cottage.

CHAPTER TWELVE

*I*nstead of the usual Norman Rockwell prints of ideal, small-town family life that Cat had seen in most clinics, the walls of Dr Aspin's cottage were filled with LeRoi Neiman sports prints. Their brilliant splashes of colour were a very definite break and intrigued Cat.

At the back of the hallway, a paned door slid sideways and a woman dressed in jeans, cowboy boots, and a beautiful Western blouse embroidered in black and teal stepped out. Her long chestnut hair was pulled back in a ponytail. She was trim and athletic, and looked much too young and outdoorsy to be a psychologist.

"Dr Aspin?" Cat asked timidly.

"Call me Jane," the psychologist said, offering her hand. Her grip was warm and confident. "Come on in and we'll talk."

The office was done predominantly in woods and dark colours. A desk with a PC sat against one wall under a watercolour painting of a lake that was almost too blue to be real. The prerequisite couch jutted out from another wall with two bay windows. Across from it was a comfortable easy chair covered by an afghan rug in Southwest colours.

"Have a seat," Jane said as she took a folder from her desk. "I've looked over your paperwork, just to familiarize myself with what we're going to be working on. Your mother has already talked to me this morning."

Cat scowled. "I don't like sitting on a couch."

"No prob." Jane pointed to the easy chair with the afghan. "Do you want my chair?"

"No. The one at the desk will do fine."

Without pause, Jane rolled the office chair round to Cat. "Would you like something to drink? I'm having a Diet Coke. My throat sometimes gets dry."

"OK." Cat positioned the office chair against the wall and sat down. Over the years, Cat had discovered changing chairs as one of the few ways she could assert herself in a doctor's office. It gave her a little bit more confidence.

When Jane returned, she handed Cat one of the cans of Diet Coke. It felt cold and refreshing in Cat's hands and gave her something to grip besides the sides of the chair.

"Your mom said you have a problem with recurring nightmares," Jane said as she made herself comfortable in the easy chair.

"Yes. It's about this house—"

"That's OK, Catherine—"

"Cat."

Jane nodded. "Cat. I don't need to hear about the nightmares yet. I really feel that if anything was there, your other counsellors would have got to it."

Cat felt better immediately. She wouldn't have to talk about the House. At least, not for awhile. "Aren't you going to tape this or write this down?"

Jane smiled. "I've got a good memory. And I want to get to know you without stumbling over paperwork. OK?"

"OK."

"What can you tell me about your life before the age of five? That seems to be when the nightmares started."

Cat shook her head. "Nothing. I've tried and tried, especially since returning to Asheville, to remember something. But it's like a blank sheet of paper."

"Didn't it strike you as odd that the

nightmares began when you left Asheville, and appeared to end when you moved back?"

"I've lived with those nightmares all my life," Cat said. "The only thing I thought was how glad I was they were gone."

"How have things worked out for you since your return to Asheville?" Jane asked.

"My grades are good. I've got more friends than I could have ever imagined having before. And a best friend – Sara Bright, who says she's born under the sign of glue, which means she'll stick by me till the end."

Jane chuckled and Cat continued. "Sara says that because I am a Capricorn some people think I'm aloof. She says that normally that can be a bit of a drawback, but it's been a real plus at Thomas Wolfe High School. She said the Delta Phis like girls with a little air of mystery, which is why they pledged me."

"Sara sounds like quite the talker."

Cat nodded. "She is. I like her a lot, in spite of that. I like the sorority and I really like my teachers at school."

"That's great," Jane said. "Is there anything you don't like?"

Cat leaned back in her chair. "Look, I know where you're headed with all these questions.

You're trying to figure out what I think is lacking in my life. A motive for why I'd need to get attention by bringing back the nightmares. But that isn't the case. Something really wrong is happening here." In clear, concise terms she told the psychologist about the feeling of being watched, and then seeing the gaunt figure outside her window during the night.

"You didn't tell your parents about this person?"

"No." Cat shook her head. "They don't seem to have a lot of faith in me these days."

"Oh, I think they do," Jane replied. "They're just scared and confused. They want more than anything to help you through this crisis. Did you check to see if this person was real?"

"How?"

"Looking on the ground under the window would have been a start." The psychologist set her soda to one side. "If you want to prove that this person is real, you're going to have to be your own detective. Let's hope this won't happen again, but if it does, look for clues you can give to your father. He's a district attorney, he can be swayed by evidence."

Hope dawned inside Cat. Jane was taking her seriously, and was even helping her form a game plan to meet the fears head-on, instead of simply waiting for them to disappear. "There's something else that's been happening to me," Cat confessed.

"Want to talk about it with me?"

Cat explained about the little blonde girl that no one else could see.

"Look out the window," Jane directed.

Cat did.

"Do you see her now?"

Nothing but the empty street met her stare. "No."

"Have you ever known anyone like her?"

"I don't think so, but she seems very familiar. Like someone I should know."

"Maybe you do know her," Jane suggested. "Or did. Have you ever been hypnotized?"

"Mr Hopkins put me in light trances and attempted to make adjustments to the nightmare."

"Did it help?"

"No."

"Did he ever take you back to your past before the nightmares?"

"No."

"Would you like to try today? I think it could do some good. Maybe we can find this little girl in the past."

"Yes, I'd like to try."

"Lean back in that chair," Jane instructed. She took a copper-coloured pen from the file folder as she got up and crossed the room. She held the pen a foot in front of Cat's face. "Follow the pen with your eyes. Don't move your head. And try to relax. Is there anything else you can tell me about this little girl?"

"I think she lives in this old pink house."

"OK." Jane's voice was soothing. "Let's go back, then. Let's find out if she's home."

The clock ticked. A light breeze flowed through the room. And Cat went back. Back in time. Back to a warm summer day in August, eleven years before.

Slam!

Cat heard the door close behind her as she dashed out into the morning sunlight. She felt good and full, the taste of blueberry waffles and buttery syrup still in her mouth.

"Mommy," she trilled in a voice she almost didn't recognize, "I'm going out to play."

"OK, dear," her mother called. She came to the door as Cat looked back. Mrs Milligan looked incredibly tall at first, then Cat realized it was because she was seeing her through the eyes of a five-year-old. Her mother was also slimmer, and seemed happier than Cat had seen her in years. "You kids need to stay in their back yard. I don't want to chase all over the neighbourhood looking for you."

"Yes, ma'am." Cat streaked as fast as her little legs could carry her. Her red hair, plaited in two pigtails, bounced on her shoulders as she ran through a dozen back yards, knowing her destination by heart. Inside her five-year-old mind, Cat was excited. The yards were filled with other kids playing on swings and slides, and wading in shallow plastic pools.

Near her friend's house, Cat saw an older boy sitting at the top of a slide, his legs wrapped through the bars as he read a book. He looked familiar and nice. Cat realized it was a much younger version of Taylor Dunne. She wanted to cry out to him, but five-year-old Cat kept running.

"Hey, where are you going?" two girls on swings yelled out. They were wearing identical sundresses, but Cat knew they weren't sisters.

"To see my friend," Cat responded.

"Cat, Cat, I see a rat, tell me what you think of that!" the girls chanted, then laughed uproariously.

Cat ignored them and ducked under a flapping wave of clothes suspended from a line. The pink house was just ahead of her.

The young blonde girl was waiting beside the house, her hair pinned back in pigtails. She waved. "Nanny, nanny, boo-boo, you can't catch me." Then she pulled back and started running.

"Wait!" Cat screamed. "Mommy said we have to stay in your back yard. We aren't supposed to go anywhere." She ran harder, as they fled from the pink house and ran farther down Cottonwood Street. "Amy! Amy, wait!"

The images blurred and Cat was suddenly aware of someone gently shaking her shoulder. Cat opened her eyes and gasped, "She's real! Her name is Amy. She was my friend."

"Amy what?" Jane asked.

"I don't know. Maybe I never knew." Cat felt like jumping out of the chair. The little girl *was* real.

"Hold it right there," Jane admonished. "I don't want you hurting yourself now that we've had a little success here. Let me get your parents."

"My parents are here?"

"Yes. You've been under for over half an

hour. It took a while to get back that far." Jane looked a little strained. "I'll be right back."

Cat leaned back in the chair, trying to remain calm.

Her mother and father appeared uncertain as they entered the room. Jane took a couple of folding chairs from a cupboard for them to sit on while she perched on a corner of the desk.

"We've turned up something in today's session," the psychologist said. She explained how Cat had been seeing the little blonde girl in her waking hours as well as her sleep. "Did Cat ever know anyone named Amy when she was little?"

Mr and Mrs Milligan glanced at each other for a moment in confusion. Then her mother frowned. "Oh, you mean from Asheville. Amy Parsons. She was one of Cat's little friends. They used to play together all the time." She paused. "But it's really quite a sad story."

"Tell me," Jane said. "It might help."

"I don't want Cat upset any more than she has to be," Mrs Milligan said.

"She's already been pretty upset these past few days," Jane said gently. "The truth is what she needs now."

"There was a rash of kidnappings in the

state," Mr Milligan explained. "Most of the kids were successfully ransomed back to their parents. But four of them disappeared for ever. Amy Parsons was one of them. The kidnappers were never caught."

"It was perfectly ghastly," Mrs Milligan added. "Amy's picture was everywhere. You couldn't go to the post office, the laundromat, or pass a telegraph pole without seeing this little blonde waif. One morning her picture was on a carton of milk I bought for breakfast. I didn't even notice it until Cat started crying. A few years after we moved, I heard the Parsons had moved away as well. Her mother never got over the loss.

"Where did Amy live?" Jane asked.

"I'm not certain of the address," Mrs Milligan answered. "I think it was on Cottonwood or Maple. But you couldn't miss it. It was a huge, pink house."

"Pink house?" Cat echoed, feeling the nausea return.

Her mother nodded.

"Cat," Jane said softly, turning to face her, "do you want to try to go back again? Maybe there was something you saw the day Amy was lost."

Cat started to say Yes. But the old fear clamped down on her. "Kitty Cat," an insect's whisper bubbled up in her mind. She felt chilled to the bone.

"No," she said in a strained voice. "I'm not ready to go back. Not yet."

CHAPTER THIRTEEN

*A subtle aspect in the cosmos is going to make
it rain on your parade today, Capricorn. A
transiting flick of the wrist from Mars makes it
a perfect day to shut the doors, pull the
shades, and curl up with a good book. In
short, stay home.*

"*I*'d give anything to stay home tonight," Cat
murmured after reading her horoscope.
"Anything."

She glanced at the clock on her bedside table.
It was five-thirty. Marli's slumber party – her
big test – would begin in one hour.

Cat walked to the window where she'd seen
the gaunt figure the previous night. When she
peered down at the ground, she could still see
the footprints she'd found. Her father, the
district attorney, hadn't been impressed. He'd
said the prints could have belonged to any
number of people – the paper boy, the

electrician, not to mention the gardener.

Cat glanced at the clock. 5.33. She was three minutes closer to the party. Her moment of truth. Just thinking about going into that house made her chest constrict.

"Think about something else," Cat murmured. She looked at the black-and-white photos lining her wall. Usually they brought her some comfort. Not today.

Cat moved to the cupboard where she'd set her overnight bag. She opened it and examined the contents. Nightgown, bathrobe, toiletries, clothes for tomorrow, and three flashlights (two back-ups, in case the batteries ran down).

She took her Nikon out of the waist pack to reload it. Taking candid pictures of the other Delta Phis at the slumber party would not only be a good ice-breaker, it might keep her mind off her fear of the House. She noticed the pack was smeared with dried mud. Mud from the garden shed where she had huddled three days before. Cat opened the back and saw the exposed roll of film inside. For a minute her brain was stuck, then she remembered taking pictures of the little blonde girl – Amy – just before going into Marli's house.

Cat held the film tightly. *Maybe I have proof*

that Amy, or the ghost of Amy, truly does exist after all.

She made a mad dash for the darkroom in the garage. Her hands shook as she prepped the roll of film.

If I can just look at Amy, see her face, then maybe something will come back. Some memory of before.

Cat developed the film as quickly as she could. There wasn't time to make prints of each negative so she decided to make a contact sheet of the entire roll. When the negatives were dry she laid them out on a clean sheet of photo paper and covered them with eight-by-ten of clear glass. Flicking on the enlarger's lamp she burned the images on to the paper.

Amy must have been the girl Taylor was talking about. He said we were inseparable. Cat dipped the contact sheet in the developer and waited breathlessly as the images appeared.

How could I totally forget a best friend?

Cat picked up the contact sheet gingerly with a pair of tongs and looked at the rows of pictures. There, captured in black and white, was Amy, standing in front of Marli's house, her face filled with fear.

"Yes!" Cat cried in triumph. She dipped the

contact sheet in the stop bath and fixer, then started the cold water rinse. Using a magnifying glass she peered at the other frames. Frightened little Amy could be clearly seen in all of them.

Cat trembled with excitement. *Now I have proof that I'm not just imagining this.* Outside the darkroom, the garage door creaked open, signalling the return of one of her parents. Cat checked her watch. 6.22 p.m. Eight minutes till Marli's party. But first she would show her parents Amy's picture.

Just as the car door shut and footsteps echoed on the garage floor, the images of Amy began to fade from the contact sheet.

"No!"

Cat slipped the negatives through the lens of the enlarger, thinking maybe something had gone wrong with the development process. But every frame was fine. Only Amy was disappearing. Even as Cat pulled at the darkroom door, Amy vanished from view, her haunting eyes the last image to fade away. By the time she got the door open, Cat held a useless sheet of pictures of the landscape in front of Marli's house.

"Cat?" Mrs Milligan stood in front of the darkroom. "Are you all right?"

"I'm fine," Cat managed to choke out. She knew her mother believed Dr Aspin had made progress with her problem yesterday. She wasn't about to disillusion her. "It's just that I ruined a roll of film by being careless."

Her mother gave her a reassuring hug. "Mistakes happen." She checked her watch. "Aren't you going to be late for your slumber party?"

"Only a few minutes. Marli said it started round six-thirty, which allows room for fudging."

Relief filled Mrs Milligan's features. "I'm glad you're going, honey. I think you'll have a great time over there."

Cat nodded, and reached back inside the darkroom to throw away the contact sheet and shut off the light.

"Your father and I are really proud of you," her mother said. "You made great strides yesterday with Jane. It never occurred to your father or me that you would be so upset about Amy's kidnapping. I didn't even realize you were aware of it. You never asked about Amy, about where she went, or anything. We just thought it was like all kids your age – out of sight, out of mind." Mrs Milligan studied Cat's

146

face. "Did you sleep last night?"

"My allergies were acting up." Cat said, rubbing at her eyes that were puffy and red from yet another night of tossing and turning. She leaned forward and kissed her mother on the cheek. "I've really got to go."

Mrs Milligan hugged her, hard. "You realize this is a very big step for you."

Cat nodded. Her mother was right. Because of her "problem", she had never spent the night at someone else's house. This would be Cat's very first night away from home.

"I'll be home all night if you need to call," her mother said. "But otherwise, I'll see you tomorrow."

Cat, who could barely control the fear and self-doubt churning inside her, murmured, "I hope so."

"Just think of yourself as a normal high school girl out to have a wonderful time," Mrs Milligan chirped.

Cat retrieved her sleeping bag and overnight bag from her room and hurried out to her car. *Normal high school girl? No!* She got in the Tracker and switched on the engine. "What normal high school girl sees ghosts peeking out behind curtains and trees?" Cat muttered as she drove towards Marli's. "What normal high school girl thinks she can photograph a ghost? What normal high school girl is so afraid of a house that she can barely walk in the front door without throwing up?"

The parking lot at Marli's house was full again, so she had to park across the circle. Night had fallen. Cat got out and started towards the house, carrying her sleeping bag and overnight bag. She was halfway round the circle, following the sidewalk, when someone stepped out from behind a tree.

Cat cried out in horror. The figure was tall and thin, with a brimmed hat. The same as the person outside her window. She dropped her bag and turned to run.

"Cat, wait." It was Taylor.

"Taylor?" Cat took a step forward, her heart still thudding in her chest. Her knees wobbled as she gasped, "You frightened me half to death."

Taylor's eyes were dark and serious. "What are you doing here?"

Cat blinked in surprise. His voice was harsh and a little frightening. "I'm going to Marli's. What did you think I was doing?"

He stared at her intently, the muscle in his

right jaw twitching. "I don't understand why you're doing this."

"What are you talking about?" Cat asked, retrieving her bag from the ground.

He stood in front of her, making no effort to get out of her way. "You were so open when you first moved to Asheville. So different from the other girls that live here. Now you're turning into one of those sorority snobs."

Cat had never seen Taylor's dark side. The one Sara had warned her about. But he was certainly showing it tonight. She tried to stay calm. "You know that's not true, Taylor. I would never deliberately be mean or cruel to anyone. I've spent too many years on the outside. I know how it feels."

"You say that now," Taylor said, bitterly. "But give you a few months and you'll be dressing and talking just like them."

Cat reached out to him. "Look, Taylor, these girls have invited me to be their friend. That's all. I want and need friends. You can't hold that against me."

"With friends like them," Taylor muttered darkly, "who needs enemies?" Without another word, he turned and vanished into the darkness.

"Taylor?" Cat took a few tentative steps that

pushed her deeper into the night. Her arms prickled as the old fear reached bedrock in her soul. "Taylor!"

There was no answer.

Cat spun round quickly. Someone was watching her. At that very moment. She could feel it. Could it be Taylor, hiding out there somewhere? In the darkness, he'd looked a lot like the person who'd been at her window. Maybe it had been him. After all, he had followed her to the doctor's office.

Cat spun slowly in a circle, afraid to leave her back vulnerable to any direction for too long. Finally, when she could no longer stand the fear, she shifted her bags and bolted for Marli's house. For a moment Cat thought she heard footsteps coming up behind her, but she didn't look. She focused entirely on the door to Marli's home and took the steps two at a time.

Don't look back. She pressed the doorbell hard with the palm of her hand and heard chimes within. *It's only your imagination.* She hit the doorbell again. *What's taking so long?*

Cat moved to the right of the door to peer in the windows. Only dark, black glass stared back out at her. She stepped back and looked up at the massive house. All the lights were off!

A scream coiled in Cat's throat.

Before she could voice it, the door was flung open and a girl jumped out. The girl tapped Cat on the arm, giggled, and shouted, "Tag! You're It!"

CHAPTER FOURTEEN

Without another word, the girl turned and vanished into the dark house.

Cat couldn't make herself move. She knew her heart would explode into a million pieces.

"Hello, Cat." It was Brenda Hubbard's voice coming from the darkness within. "We were beginning to think you weren't going to show up."

Cat squinted into the blackness. "I don't understand. Where are you?"

Brenda emerged into the doorway. "I'm in the living room, watching for late arrivals. Come on in."

Cat took a shuddering breath and followed Brenda into the house. Once inside, she could see that the house wasn't totally dark. Candles and hurricane lanterns were scattered about in a haphazard fashion, providing eerie pools of twilight at irregular intervals.

"Where is everyone?" Cat asked, clutching

her sleeping bag to her chest.

"They're playing hide-and-seek" Brenda said as she walked to a small desk that had been set up in the centre of the room. Two candle sconces burned at either end, highlighting the piles of sleeping bags and overnight bags heaped round the desk. "Just drop your things here."

Cat dropped her bags on the pile. Brenda sat down in the straight-backed chair behind the desk and stared coldly at Cat. "Well, go."

Cat cocked her head. "Go?"

Brenda rolled her eyes and spoke in an over-exaggerated way, as if Cat was a two-year-old. "Now that you've been tagged, you have to find someone else in the house and make them It."

The prospect of walking through the darkened house by herself chilled Cat to the marrow. "Where's Marli's mom and aunt?" she asked, stalling for time.

"Out. We have free run of the house until about eleven."

Cat nodded. "You've been here all evening?"

"Yes." Brenda continued to stare at her.

"Why don't I take your place?" Cat said, working extra hard to keep her voice steady. "You probably want to go play."

"Marli asked me to stay here until she came to relieve me. Then I'll get to play."

Cat looked into the darkness in the dining room and swallowed hard. "I just have to tag one person, right? I don't have to find everyone?"

Brenda sighed heavily. "Right. Whoever you touch is It, and they can't touch you back. They have to find someone else."

Knowing she could make or break her acceptance in the Delta Phis by her next move, Cat stepped away from the desk into the shadows. The island of illumination round the desk and Brenda seeped away from her as she went on with outstretched arms. In a matter of seconds, she was in total darkness.

"Yikes!" Cat squeaked, bumping into the long dining room table and bruising her hip. Giggles sounded all round her. *They can see me!* Because their eyes had become accustomed to the dark. Cat was working at a definite disadvantage.

Frustrated, fighting fear every step of the way, Cat chased the other sorority members through the house. She came upon the big stairway before she knew it.

Gripping the bannister, reassuring herself

that it was only wood and not anything else she'd imagined over the years, she went up the stairs. At the top, she trailed a barely-seen shadow down a hallway.

Clunk!

The sound came from her right. Cat turned and pushed open a door. The darkness in the room was complete but she was certain the girl was inside.

She stretched her arms out, seeking the wall. There was only one way in and one way out. Through the door immediately behind her. *Whoever's in here is trapped.*

Cat's fingers touched the wall and she jerked back. "Oh!"

The wallpaper texture was flocked. The same way it had felt in her nightmares. Cat sniffed. *That smell! Like lavender.* It permeated the room.

Click.

The door shut ever so quietly behind her.

Cat whirled at once and searched for the knob, unable to find it in her panic. "Come on, you guys, this isn't funny," she cried out. "I don't know this house. I don't even know what room I'm in. Guys?"

"Cat!" The whisper was low and raspy and

made her skin crawl.

She knew it was coming from somewhere in the darkness behind her. Panicked, she felt her knees start to give way underneath her.

Suddenly another voice filled the room. A little girl, speaking in a skipping-rope chant. Cat knew it was Amy. "Kitty Cat, Kitty Cat, turn round. Kitty Cat, Kitty Cat, the knob is round."

Flailing, Cat did as she was told and found the doorknob. As she started turning it, a strong hand clutched her wrist.

"Let go!" Cat screamed, yanking back. She managed to wrench herself away as she got the door open, and stumbled out into the hall. Still trying to regain her balance, she ran into someone. An arm reached across her shoulders. "No!"

"Hey, take it easy, Cat," a familiar voice drawled. "You're supposed to tag someone, not knock them out."

"Sara?" Cat cried. "Sara? Is that really you?"

"Yes."

Cat seized her friend's arm. She wanted to tell Sara about the person in the room who'd grabbed her. She could still feel the cold, hard fingers locked round her wrist.

"Cat," Sara whispered.

"What?"

"You can let go of my arm now."

"Sorry." Cat released her hold. She decided to keep quiet about the incident. What if there was no one there? What if they had disappeared into thin air like Amy in the photographs? Sara would think she was crazy.

"Are you OK?" Sara asked.

"I don't like the dark," Cat confessed, reaching for Sara's arm once more. She bent her head to whisper, in case another Delta Phi was listening. "I'm actually very frightened by it."

"I understand," Sara said sympathetically. "My little brother has trouble with it, too." She took Cat by the hand. "Come on. We'll go together and sneak up on the others. Most of them are hiding on the ground floor."

Relieved at the prospect of going back downstairs, Cat followed Sara's lead. They passed through the kitchen where the smell of baked bread still lingered. They found most of the other sorority members hiding in the breakfast corner, where Sara easily made a tag.

"OK, girls," Marli announced. "The game's over. Someone get the lights."

The girls quickly spread out and flipped on

all the lights on the ground floor. The candles were blown out and the hurricane lamps extinguished.

Cat blinked against the harsh illumination, but breathed a sigh of relief. *Passed one test.*

The group gathered back in the living room, slouching easily across the couches, two easy chairs, and the floor in front of the large television. They were chatting and laughing uproariously.

Cat sat stiffly at the end of one couch and watched as Vicki Hamilton surfed through the channels with the remote control. No one seemed to mind, or even notice, that Cat was being quiet.

"TV is boring," Vicki announced after covering all of the channels twice. "What should we do now?"

"How about Nintendo?" Angie Perkins ventured.

Sara smiled wickedly from her place on the floor. "How about a game of truth or dare?"

"Let's call our boyfriends," Michelle Morgan suggested. "Jason was really upset that I was coming to a slumber party instead of going out with him."

"He may not be home," Sara teased. "He

might be out on a hot date."

A chorus of boos and hisses followed Sara's words.

"Let's call them," Marli said. "If they're home, we can make them miserable because they're missing us.

"If they're not home," Kim Corbett added, "we can think of ways to make them miserable later for not staying in and pining away for us."

Everyone laughed, and Cat forced herself to join in.

"All right," Marli declared, "but we all have to keep it short so everyone gets a chance." She reached over the arm of the couch and lifted the phone. Just as she began to dial, the lights went out.

Cries of protest rang through the living room. Cat clutched the arm of the couch as tightly as possible.

"Come on," she heard Marli call out. "The game is over. Turn the lights back on."

Brenda's voice came out of the darkness. "I'm working the light switch, Marli, but nothing's happening. The power must be out."

CHAPTER FIFTEEN

"Someone's in here with us!" Vicki Hamilton cried out. "I heard something moving in the hallway!"

Cat was certain whatever was in the house wasn't human. She stifled sobs, trying to distinguish the line between nightmares and reality.

"Chill out," Brenda said in exasperation. A lighter snikked, spitting out a blue and yellow flame. Brenda looked totally composed as she applied the lighter's flame to a candle. "It's just a power failure."

"Someone's in the house," Vicki insisted.

Brenda thrust the lighted candle at her. "Take this and go and look. If you find someone, let out a scream. Until then, calm down. You're scaring some of the others."

"We need to get out of the house," Samantha Barnes, one of the new pledges whimpered. "Killers always go after the girls who stay inside the house. We're sitting ducks in here."

"It's raining outside, you'll wreck your hair," Sara teased. "There's nothing worse than a corpse who's had a bad hair day."

"Sara!" Marli's voice was harsh. "That's not funny."

"Sorry," Sara replied without remorse.

Brenda continued lighting candles, placing the newest one in Cat's hands. "Marli, we could go to your room and wait until your mom and aunt come home."

"Upstairs?" Cat whispered, staring at her candle's flame. If the group voted to move, she didn't think she could.

Marli shook her head. "Moving everyone in the dark would be a pain. We'll just sit it out here. I'm sure it's some sort of power failure. The lights will come back on soon."

"It isn't a power failure," Vicki Hamilton said. "I can see the lights of other houses through your front window."

"I bet it's our boyfriends," Michelle suggested. "They're probably mad at not being invited and have decided to scare us out of our wits as revenge."

"Yes," Kim Corbett agreed. "They're probably outside laughing themselves silly right now."

Brenda cocked her head. "I don't know. It could be the fuse box. Marli, do you know where it is?"

"There used to be one outside," Marli replied, "but the house was rewired with circuit breakers. They're in the basement."

"No way I'm going in the basement," Samantha cried. She was holding the hand of another pledge, Laura Crowe. "In the movies, anyone who goes down in the basement never comes back up. The rest of the group just finds little pieces of them throughout the rest of the movie."

"That's because everyone splits up," Vicki Hamilton murmured, raising her candle in the direction of the hall where she'd heard the noise.

"Right," Brenda said. "So we'll stay together."

"Besides," Samantha added, "who knows what could be waiting down in the basement?"

"Zombies," Laura whispered.

"Vampires," Kim said.

"A deranged serial killer escaped from the sanitarium," Samantha continued. She held up her hands in imitation claws to illustrate what a deranged serial killer probably would look like.

"We don't have a sanitarium nearby," Brenda pointed out.

"Oh, yeah." Samantha dropped her hands. "I guess that's a relief."

"I personally don't believe in zombies or vampires." Brenda said. "How about...we simply have a tripped circuit breaker or two waiting in the basement? Does anybody buy that?"

"But what would have tripped the breakers?" Cat asked in a small voice.

"Most of the house has been rewired," Marli answered, getting up. "But Aunt Clara's room sometimes throws the breakers when she plugs in too many appliances."

The feel of the flocked wallpaper she'd found in the upstairs room came back to Cat. She shuddered from head to toe, shaking so hard her candle's flame nearly blew out.

"Marli?" Cat asked. "When you redecorated, did you do the entire house?"

"No, there's about half the upper floor to go," Marli replied, as she picked up one of the lighted hurricane lanterns. "Look, I'm going down into the basement to check the breakers. Who's coming with me?"

163

All of the girls immediately jumped up to join her. Except Cat, who didn't move at all.

"Cat," Sara said, nudging her. "Are you coming?"

Most of the girls had got into the humour of the adventure now, and were giggling and pushing each other as they fell into a loose line. The fear had left them as abruptly as it had descended.

"No," Cat replied in a tight voice. She grabbed Sara's wrist and whispered. "Sara, please stay with me. I can't go down there, and I don't want to stay here by myself."

Sara hesitated only a moment, then sat down beside Cat. She glanced wistfully at the group of laughing girls as they trooped after Marli. Brenda looked back at them and raised an inquisitive eyebrow.

"The telephone may ring," Sara explained. "Somebody needs to be here to answer it."

Brenda didn't seem to buy her explanation. Cat knew she was dangerously close to flunking Brenda's test. But she didn't care.

"I'm not staying in this house one minute longer than I have to," Cat said, when the girls had disappeared. "As soon as the lights come on, I'm getting in my car and leaving."

"They'll kick you out as a pledge," Sara warned.

"Sara, there is something here," Cat insisted. "I ran into it during hide-and-seek. It's in that darkness, waiting."

Sara was stunned by Cat's words. "C'mon," she said, studying Cat's face. "You don't really believe that."

Cat met her friend's gaze evenly. "With all of my heart."

The doorbell rang.

"Yikes!" Sara shrieked, clutching her chest. "Geez, Cat, you're making me jumpy. I'm going to answer the door and I'll be right back."

"Don't answer it." Cat grabbed Sara's arm.

"Cut it out," Sara replied. "You're giving me the creeps."

"But who could it be?" Cat rasped. "We're all here. Oh, Sara, please don't answer it."

"Cat, stop." Sara hurried towards the front door. "I'll bet it's just one of the guys."

Cat leaped off the couch and hurried to follow Sara. She paused at the pile of overnight bags and quickly dug in hers for a flashlight. "Wait for me, Sara. Please."

Sara flung open the front door. No one was there. "Very funny," Sara said, putting her hands on her hips and calling into the darkness. "You really scared us. We're all shaking."

Still no reply.

Sara ducked her head outside. "Hellooo? Come on. I know you're out there."

Suddenly a figure in a dark hat and coat leaped on to the porch.

"Oh, my God," Cat screamed. "It's him!"

The figure outside her window. The person who had followed her here tonight. The one who had been watching her.

Adrenalin hit her nervous system in a white hot wave. She ran blindly for the stairs, seeking the high ground. Stumbling, she reached the landing. The yellow light spilling from the flashlight flicked out over the house, giving her a very disjointed view of her surroundings.

She could barely remember in which direction Marli's room lay, but she knew it had a phone. She could call 911.

Straight ahead. Now turn right. In her panic, she opened the wrong door. The flashlight's beam hit another stairway. *The stairway.* The one that led up to the door with the pistol-grip handle.

Cat spun, ready to seek out Marli's room again. That's when she heard it. Someone was sobbing. The sound was coming from the top of the stairs.

The nightmare, the one she'd had night after night for eleven years, descended over Cat like a dark blanket. She put her foot on the first step of the narrow stairway. *Right. Then left. Right. Then left.*

Everything was the same, just as she'd lived it thousands of times. Somewhere in the distance behind her, Cat was dimly aware of footsteps pounding in the front hall.

Cat reached the door and stared at the pistol-grip door handle. The metal felt cool when she closed her hand round it. She struggled to pull her hand back, but the whimpering had changed.

"Help me. Somebody help me."

Instantly forgetting her own fears, Cat turned the handle and opened the door. "Amy? Is that you?"

The sobbing stopped. There was no sound.

Cat shone the light round the room. *It's an attic.* Layered with the heavy musk of years of stale dust.

Bare beams framed the ceiling. Wreaths hung on the clapboard walls beside framed photographs, an old rolled-up carpet, a torn lampshade, and a faded red velvet sofa. A little further away was a tiny wooden rocking horse that looked familiar. A stack of cardboard boxes was to her left, labelled XMAS ORNAMENTS and MARLI'S SUMMER CLOTHES.

This is the House. Cat was sure of it. *But where is the bad thing behind the door?* Where was the cause of eleven years of nightmares? There was nothing threatening at all in the room.

Clunk!

The sudden noise startled Cat. She swung the flashlight towards the source and dropped the oval beam over the rocking horse. It was rocking slightly now.

Without warning, the memories jarred back into place, bringing all of the terror with them.

"Oh, my god – the horse!" Cat cried out, as the horror filled her brain. She put one hand to her head, gasping, "I remember. I remember everything."

The memory was overpowering, the weight of it almost too heavy to bear. "Got to get out," she mumbled. "Got to run."

She turned back to the door, but a figure in a dark coat and hat stepped in front of her, blocking the way.

A silver wire caught the light and flashed in the gloved hands.

"Kitty Cat, Kitty Cat," the figure whispered. "Where have you been?"

CHAPTER SIXTEEN

"Amy? Amy, where are you?"

Cat was a five-year-old again, her two thick plaits bouncing against her neck as she raced down the sidewalk on Cottonwood Street.

Amy, her pink-and-white checked sundress smudged with dirt, stood on the steps of the Martin house. The front door was ajar. Amy cupped her hands round her mouth and hissed, "Let's go see where the baby died."

Cat locked her knees. "No. Mommy said we have to stay in your yard."

Amy put her hands on her waist and swung her hips. "Nanny, nanny, boo boo, you can't catch me!"

"Amy, wait!" Cat stuck out her hand, but Amy was gone like a streak of lightning across the porch into the Martin house. Cat stamped her foot, impatiently. "Now we're going to get in trouble for sure."

Cat made her way on to the porch. The

wooden boards were old and creaky and gave her the shivers. Ever since Mrs Martin's baby had died, the curtains on the windows were always drawn and nobody went in or out. Some of the older kids in the neighbourhood had recently declared the place haunted.

Cat moved quietly to the front door and carefully pushed it open. She was immediately hit by the musty smell of an old house that had been closed up all summer – like dust and mildew and old lavender, all mixed together. Cat wrinkled her nose in disgust.

"Amy?" she whispered. The house was dark. She tiptoed into the entryway, which was covered in peeling gold-and-green flocked wallpaper. To the left was a parlour with a faded oriental rug and two shabby red velvet couches. The room was cluttered with plants and ferns that needed watering. To the right was a dining room with big oak table and straight-backed chairs. A chandelier hung from the ceiling on a thick black chain. Ahead of her lay the stairs. Cat started to turn but something caught her attention. A sound, almost like a kitten mewing.

She put her hand on the bannister and climbed the stairs to the hallway at the top. When she reached the landing the sound was louder. She cocked her head. *Not a kitten. A person. Crying.*

"Amy?" The sound was coming from behind a door to her right. She opened it and found another set of stairs, steeper and narrower than the first.

"Amy, are you up there?" Cat was so frightened, she could barely choke out the words.

"Help me. Somebody help me."

Cat crept up the rickety stairs to a big door with a strange handle. It looked like the grip of a pistol. She put her hand on the lever and the door clicked open. She was in the attic, which was jammed with boxes, old leather trunks and several stained lampshades. Closest to Cat was the newest addition to the pile, a baby crib, mattress and baby buggy.

"Mmmph."

Cat spun at the muffled sound. In the far corner a bare bulb hanging from the ceiling illuminated several play toys, including a wooden rocking horse. Seated on the horse was Amy, her hands tied, a gag round her mouth. Her eyes were huge and terrified. She gave Cat a pleading look.

From out of the shadows, a hand reached

towards Amy.

"Look out!" Cat screamed.

The grasping figure, caught off guard, spun and stared in Cat's direction. The rheumy eyes danced with madness. With a sudden movement the person flung out an arm and jerked the cord attached to the bare bulb out of the ceiling. Darkness swallowed the room.

Cat fled the attic, unable to scream for help, driven only by the need to hide. She ran out of the house, down the nearby alley, and ducked into a metal gardening shed. She hid there for almost the entire day, too scared to move. She heard her mother and Amy's mother calling for them for hours, but still she didn't move.

Shortly before dark, a neighbour found her and brought her to her mother, who'd scolded her terribly for hiding and frightening everyone. She was sent to her room as punishment. Cat wasn't able to utter a word about what had happened to Amy. She fell asleep, praying that it had all been a bad dream.

And for the next eleven years, it was.

Now Cat was in the attic again, face to face with her nightmare. She slowly raised the flashlight, shining the beam in the approaching figure's face. The person was older now, and much scarier because the passing years had taken the extra flesh from the features. But Cat could never forget those malevolent eyes.

"Aunt Clara," Cat said in a flat voice.

The woman's gaunt face was contorted with hate. "You came back. I thought you were a goner, but the Cat came back."

Cat backed slowly away.

"I knew sooner or later you'd remember," Aunt Clara said. "Then you'd tell. Couldn't have that."

Cat reached behind her feeling for something, anything, to use as a weapon. Her fingers touched a lampshade. *Where's the lamp?*

"Sorry," Aunt Clara said, watching Cat's movements. "We threw the lamp out years ago. It was my sister's idea. Everything must go. Out with the bad memories. So away went the cot, the buggy, the changing table and that lamp. All of Emily's things, gone."

"Emily was your daughter," Cat said, stalling for time. "She got sick and died."

"Emily was so small and fragile. She needed protection from the outside world. But you and your little friend wouldn't leave us alone. Every day you'd cry, 'Let me see the baby'."

A new memory filled Cat's brain – that of a pink baby, giggling and batting at a mobile over her crib. "She laughed a lot," Cat said suddenly. "And had a dimple in her cheek. Here." Cat touched her own cheek.

"After she died, you continued to come round. Tormenting me night and day with your silly little chants and songs. Constantly reminding me of my own little girl." Her voice thickened in her throat. "All those years of trying to have a baby, and failing. Then there was Emily, my last chance – and she was stolen from me. You children made me out of mind with grief."

"Is that why you killed Amy?" Cat asked, backing slowly to another pile of boxes. She used her right hand to feel inside them. *Clothes. Nothing but clothes.*

"She killed my Emily. Amy was sick and her mother never told me. She had a virus. Coming to my house, coughing her terrible germs all over my baby. Emily caught pneumonia. She was too tiny. Her little body couldn't fight it." Aunt Clara pulled the silver wire taut between her gloved hands. "Amy deserved to die for what she did."

"Amy was just a little girl," Cat said,

manoevring round the attic, avoiding stored furniture. "How could you?"

"I did it for my Emily." Aunt Clara lunged for Cat and tried to wrap the wire round her neck. Cat darted back out of the way and stumbled against a stack of cardboard boxes that burst open, spilling dozens of books on to the floor.

"Come here," Aunt Clara said. "Let's bell the Cat, and put an end to it."

Cat kept moving, evading each lunge with a counter movement of her own. Her fear was gone. At the moment when she should have been the most frightened, she didn't feel afraid. Instead she felt more confident and powerful than ever before, almost light with a new clarity. Finally she knew what was real.

"Cat!" a male voice bellowed up the attic stairs.

"Taylor!" Cat yelled. "I'm up here. With Marli's aunt. She's crazy!"

Clara lunged again as Taylor pounded up the stairs and hammered on the door. "Open up!" he shouted.

"She's locked it!" Cat called, never taking her eyes off Aunt Clara.

"Hang on." A massive thud sounded against

the door.

Clara flashed a cold smile. "Your boyfriend won't get here in time. Just like you were too late to save your little friend."

Cat found herself backed into the corner. She scooped up the wooden rocking horse, and heaved it as hard as she could at Aunt Clara. It knocked the woman backwards but didn't stop her.

"There's no way out," Aunt Clara hissed. "You're finished."

Cat realized her only hope was the attic window to her right. Picking up a pair of ice skates, she swung them with all her might at the window. Glass burst outward, glinting in the lightning flash that raked across the dark sky. Cat pushed the splintered latticework out of her way. Rain spattered her face as she pulled herself through the opening on to the roof.

The steep slope was tricky to navigate. Cat decided to head for the rear of the house, thinking she'd be able to jump down on to the patio roof and perhaps make her way to the ground.

Before she could take two steps, Aunt Clara burst through the window behind her and caught her by the ankle. Cat came crashing down, skinning her palms on the rough shingles. She screamed as another lightning bolt forked across the sky.

Clara's nails dug into her ankle.

"You got away once, Kitty Cat," the woman hissed, "you won't get away again."

"No one killed your baby," Cat shouted, kicking to free herself from Clara's grip. Reaching out with both arms, she caught hold of the chimney at the roof's peak. "It just happened. It was nobody's fault."

"Liar!" Aunt Clara had reached her waist now, and pinned her so she couldn't crawl any further.

Cat tried to fend off Aunt Clara's attempts to loop the wire round her neck but was hampered by having to keep her hands clamped on to the chimney. The glittering wire slid round her throat and began to tighten. As they struggled, Cat felt the camera pack round her waist dig into her side.

Risking everything, Cat released the chimney and pushed Aunt Clara back with a shove. The woman fell back, giving Cat enough time to pull out her Nikon. Switching the flash on, she waited only a second until the orange ready light glowed.

Aunt Clara came at her again.

"Stay away!" Cat thrust the camera up to the woman's face and the flash went off in her eyes.

Blinded, Clara lost her balance, then slid down the rain-soaked roof. In the space of a heartbeat, Clara disappeared over the edge, followed by the camera.

"AAAIIIEE!" The shrill scream of fury and surprise was cut short by an audible thud.

Cat slid out of control after Clara. She clawed at the roof, trying to get a grip, but her body went over the edge. At the last second, Cat managed to hook her fingers into the gutter. She hit the end of her arms with such force that she thought her arms would be pulled from their sockets.

Miraculously, the gutter held. Slick with rain, Cat didn't know how long her hands could hold on. "Help!" she screamed as she kicked out with her feet, trying to pull herself back on to the roof.

Cat glanced down and moaned. Aunt Clara lay spread-eagled on the ground below. One of her legs was bent up behind her in an impossible position.

Cat was going to fall and she knew it. Already her arms were growing too weak to sustain her weight. She would join Clara's crumpled body on the ground and her nightmare would be complete.

"Cat! I've got you." Taylor's face suddenly appeared at the edge of the roof. He was lying flat on his stomach across the roof. Reaching out, he gripped her wrist with one hand. "I'm going to pull you up."

"Oh, please, Taylor!" Cat could barely move her lips for fear she'd fall. "Hurry."

He pulled, and slowly she began to slide back up on to the roof.

"Grab my belt," Taylor instructed as she bent forwards across the gutter.

When she did, Cat saw that he was holding on to a garden hose with his other hand. It was tied to something inside the attic. Moving carefully, they pulled their way to safety. By the time she clambered back inside the attic, Cat was drenched. She was shaking with the cold and the close call.

Taylor reached for her and she fell gratefully into his arms.

"It was Aunt Clara," she gasped, clinging to Taylor. "She was the awful thing behind the door. All these years..."

Taylor pressed his lips close to her ear and

murmured gently, "It's going to be all right. She can't hurt you now."

Cat's whole body trembled. "But how did you know to come here?"

"I was worried," he replied, still holding Cat tight. "I saw someone following you from school a couple times, but I never got close enough to see who it was. That's why I came here tonight, to make sure you were safe." Taylor pulled back from Cat to look her in the eyes. "I didn't mean to yell at you. I'm so sorry."

"It's all right." Cat tried to smile through chattering teeth.

Taylor hugged her again. "Then when I saw the power go out in the house, I knew something bad was going to happen." He glanced at the broken window. "But I didn't expect anything like this."

"Amy was my friend." Cat squeezed her eyes shut and moaned. "My best friend when I was five. Clara killed her. I saw her do it, and I wasn't able to help."

Taylor folded his arms tighter round her. "You were only five years old. There was nothing you could do." His breath was warm in her ear as she wrapped her arms round him and hugged him back. "You're going to be all right now. It's over."

For the first time in her life, Cat believed it.

CHAPTER SEVENTEEN

The Sun is in Libra. You are feeling active, alert – and maybe even a little optimistic for a change. Try to behave yourself, Capricorn. There's a dark night ahead with a new moon just itching to send some romance your way. The stars never lie, and they say you are going to be kissed.

"**B**ig date tonight, honey?" Mrs Milligan teased. She peeked into Cat's room and glanced pointedly at the ironing board in the centre of the bedroom.

"The biggest," Cat replied happily as she put the finishing touches to the black knit dress she intended to wear. "Taylor's taking me to the Homecoming Dance at school."

"Congratulations on the float." Mrs Milligan said. "You girls looked wonderful as the goddesses of the Zodiac."

Cat struck her goddess pose with one fist

183

raised, indicating Capricorn's strength. "First place. Not bad for a new kid, huh?"

Her mother crossed the room and gave her a hug. "I'm proud of you for so many reasons." Mrs Milligan's eyes welled with tears. "To think you carried that terrible secret for all those years. It just breaks my heart."

Cat patted her mother's cheek. "It's over, Mom. Totally over. And like Dr Jane says – we go on. To a better and brighter future."

Jane Aspin was helping her deal with Amy's death and the ugly memory of how it happened. It had helped that Clara had survived the fall, with a broken leg and hip. She had confessed and told the police where they could find Amy's body. The little girl's funeral, eleven years after her death, had been held a week later. That event laid many ghosts to rest. Finally, Aunt Clara had been committed to a clinic for the mentally ill to be evaluated for trial.

The doorbell rang and Cat shrieked, "Yikes! My date's here and I'm not even dressed."

"I'll get the door," Mrs Milligan said, "and you take your time."

Cat slipped on the black sheath, which hugged her figure like a glove. The neckline was low and scooped all the way across her shoulders. Cat stepped in front of the mirror to apply one last coat of lipstick. Tonight her hazel eyes were bright and clear. No more hollow cheeks and dark circles from too many nights without sleep. Her complexion was positively peaches and cream. Cat shook her head and her shiny auburn hair bounced thick on her shoulders and down her back. She lowered her chin and murmured in her huskiest voice, "You looked positively ravishing."

"Cat, your gentleman caller is here," her father called down the hall.

Cat's cheeks flushed pink with embarrassment. "Dad," she groaned. "Don't call him that."

Quickly Cat grabbed the small black beaded bag her mother had lent her, stuffed the tube of lipstick in it, and crossed to the door. With an easy flick of the wrist, Cat turned off the light. A smile flickered across her lips. Less than a month ago, that would have been impossible for her to do. Things were definitely looking up.

Taylor was standing in the living room, chatting easily with her parents. He wore a loose fitting, double-breasted suit of charcoal grey, with a black cotton shirt buttoned at the neck, and no tie. And, of course, his cowboy boots. He was eye-poppingly handsome. Taylor was describing an art project he was working on and Cat could tell her parents were impressed.

Cat allowed herself a moment to appreciate him before saying hello. He was kind, funny and talented. With such wonderful qualities. how could she ever have doubted him? True, he was a loner. But that was OK. Taylor had even come out of his Capricorn solitude long enough to draw the Zodiac wheel for the Delta Phis' float.

Taylor turned to look at her, and whistled softly. "Wow!"

"I couldn't have said it better myself," her father added.

Taylor stepped towards Cat and thrust a bouquet of vari-coloured zinnias in her direction. During their long talks since the incident at Marli's house, he'd discovered her distaste for lavender.

"Oh, Taylor," Cat said, hugging the blooms to her chest. "They're beautiful."

"I'll put them in a vase in your room," her mother said, taking the flowers from Cat. "Now you two have a wonderful evening."

Taylor helped Cat drape an antique shawl round her shoulders, brushing her cheek with a light kiss. Then they went out to his car.

"How is Marli?" Taylor asked once he was behind the wheel. "Did she hear about your first place today?"

"I talked to her after we won and she was thrilled. She said she's seeing a counselor, and will soon be able to come back to school."

"What about the Delta Phis? Will they have her back?"

"Of course. Everyone loves Marli. She just needs to understand that what her aunt did is no reflection on her."

Taylor nodded. "That's something I'm still working through with my brother. But it takes a long time to put it behind you – the humiliation, the pain, all of it."

Even Cat and Taylor had moved to a new level of understanding. Ever since that night on Marli's roof, he'd really started to open up, talking about his family and their troubles with his brother.

Taylor drove smoothly, winding through the streets on the way to the dance, taking the route past Cottonwood Street. "I've been thinking. Maybe I was wrong about the sorority thing."

Cat folded her arms across her chest. "You were."

He glanced at her with a lop-sided smile. "But not about Brenda Hubbard. I still think she's a snob who lives to put everybody else down."

"You may be right there. Brenda was the only Delta Phi who was reluctant to stand by Marli. And they were supposed to be best friends."

The pink house came into view on the left side of the car. Cat glanced at it, noticing the two lighted windows. It had been Amy's house. But she knew she'd never see Amy there again. Her unhappy spirit had finally found peace.

Cat rested her head on Taylor's shoulder and sighed. Through the Mustang's windshield, she could see stars whirling in their orbits millions of miles away.

"The stars never lie," she murmured softly.

"What?" Taylor stopped at a red light and looked at her.

"My horoscope. That's what it said."

He laughed. "Can this be coming from Cat Milligan, the girl who has both Capricorn feet planted firmly on solid ground?"

"Yes."

"I thought you were into heavy reality these days."

188

"I am."

"Aren't horoscopes supposed to predict the future?"

"I like to think they suggest the possibilities that lie ahead."

"So what did your horoscope say?"

"That the stars never lie." Cat hesitated, then added shyly, "And that tonight I am going to be kissed."

Looking deep into her eyes, Taylor said, "That's one prediction I can guarantee."

Cat turned her lips to meet his, and lost herself in the thrill of his kiss. She was no longer running from the past. Now she welcomed the future with open arms and the highest expectations.

ZODIAC

*ARIES*TAURUS*GEMINI*CANCER*LEO*VIRGO*LIBRA*
*SCORPIO*SAGITTARIUS*CAPRICORN*AQUARIUS*PISCES*

Twelve signs of the Zodiac. Twelve novels, each one embracing the characteristics of a zodiac sign. Pushed to the extreme, these characteristics lead down twisting paths into tales of mystery, horror, romance and fantasy.

Whatever your sun sign, you will want to read Zodiac, the series written in the stars.

SERIES CREATED BY JAHNNA N. MALCOLM

TAURUS:
PATIENT, PRACTICAL
BLACK OUT

*T*ess can't remember much. Except that the Halloween party went wrong. There was a fire and people were trapped. But it wasn't an accident. Tess knows who the murderer is – if only she could remember... Her patience is put to the test in a deadly waiting game.

VIRGO:
PERFECTIONIST, ORDERLY
DESPERATELY YOURS

*V*irginia is always in control, so when disturbing letters arrive at her school newspaper office from someone signed Desperate, it is Virginia who deals with them. But when a friend dies, a photograph is maliciously destroyed and the letters from Desperate become more threatening... Virginia's orderly world is tested to the limit.

ARIES:
FIERY, DETERMINED
SECRET IDENTITY

*A*lex is a great musician. She's also a girl. Frustrated at not being taken seriously, Alex disguises herself as a boy, and it works - too well. Her band is a hit but if it becomes even more successful, will she be stuck as a boy forever?

LIBRA:
FAIR-MINDED, ROMANTIC
FROZEN IN TIME

*L*ily lives for her painting. With her boyfriend, she creates a mural that grows ever more beautiful as her own life becomes harsher. Then her boyfriend is killed by a gang. Has Lily lost him forever? If only she could be with him still in the beautiful world of the painting...